I0582361

She enjoyed learning more about American history and developing her writing skills through fun and engaging sessions. She also loved interacting with other campers who shared her love of writing.

—Payton's Parents

I have learned so much through EPC2022. I realize that I can now write historical fiction without fearing the research!

–Grace Patterson, *19, Ankeny, IA*

The camp was totally EPIC. I learned so much about France's involvement in the American Revolutionary War. I can't wait till next year to do it again! It was EPIC! It was for the children!! HUZZAH!!

–Carmene Miller, *13, Concord, NC*

We loved the camp for Carmene. She loved meeting the new campers and Ms. Jenny and Ms. Libby. Also, we got to see the improvement of her writing skills, for storytelling, which is a great interest that she has. We and her look forward to next year!!

–Carmene's Parents

Epic Patriot Camp has been a wonderful experience! Having published authors help me improve my writing skills has been almost as great as the camaraderie among my fellow Epic Patriot Campers! I loved it! I hope to do it again next year!

–Madeleine Wenzel, *16, Irmo, SC*

What a fun, rewarding experience for these Epic Patriot Campers! It has been a blessing to watch my daughter grow in her writing while making like-minded friends all over the country (world!) with a similar love for history and writing! Thank you, Jenny and Libby, for taking time to critique and encourage my budding author! We hated to see EPC end but know that the friendships made will continue to grow. We can't wait for next year's EPC!

—Madeleine's Parents

Epic Patriot Camp was such a blessing to me! To be given several creative workshops by my favorite author, make new friends, and learn how to publish a book was truly special and life-changing!

—Ella Quill, *17, Washington, D.C.*

Revolutionary and unrivaled! Parents of young writers will be hard pressed to find a better summer experience with a more lasting and positive outcome. It was a dream come true for my daughter to write alongside her favorite author and meet new friends along the way. She will lovingly hold this book for years to come and look back at the journey as one in which she was encouraged to follow her heart in sharing stories with the world. Jenny and Libby are larger than life heroes for their investment in our next generation. Huzzah for heroes! **–Ella's Parents**

The LEARNING, the FUN and the FRIENDS made EPIC 2022 the most amazing camp I've ever been a part of... EVER!

–Joy Elizabeth Tardy, *13, Keller, TX*

Jenny and Libby opened their hearts, homes, and God-given talents to mentor our students. The creativity and energy each teacher poured into their writing and life lessons was something you want for your aspiring youth! **–Joy Elizabeth's Parents**

Definitely learned a lot from this camp and its amazing directors. History isn't just stories about old people; it's stories about people who made choices that influenced our country today and this summer I realized just that. **—Abigail Gregorin,** *15, Evington, VA*

The end of camp is always difficult. The things you've learned, the people you have met, and the historical characters that have died along the way! This camp was a great opportunity to stretch my daughter's writing into a different genre and get great feedback from accomplished authors. Spado would approve. **—Abigail's Parents**

Epic Patriot Camp was such an amazing (or should I say EPIC) experience! Each week couldn't come sooner! I loved getting to (virtually) meet Jenny and Libby, two of my favorite authors! Every week, I took so many notes that I will use throughout my whole writing career! Jenny and Libby were so inspiring and instilled in me an even deeper love for writing. I learned so much valuable information, and I grew so much in my writing skills! I met amazing friends, and this is a summer I will never forget! Thank you, Jenny and Libby!!

–Bella Waugh, *15, Franklin, TN*

Epic Patriot Camp was just that—EPIC! Each week of camp our daughter was filled with such anticipation and excitement! Thank you, Jenny and Libby, for creating a safe space where our children can be vulnerable, dream up stories, and write! THEN to also have the privilege of sharing their stories with TWO published authors AND get personal feedback, wow! What a gift! Bella has become even more confident in her writing and is filled with fresh hope to continue and write in the future. Thank you! **–Bella's Parents**

Epic Patriot Camp 2022 has been AMAZING!! I absolutely loved it! I have made new friends for life, and I have learnt so much about American history!! I've always known that America has been vital in the world's development, but I've never realized how influential it really was! I've learnt about so many things—from the Declaration of Independence to the inventor of bifocal glasses, to the signing of the Declaration and why July 4 is so important to Americans today! HUZZAH for Epic Patriot Camp!

–Christopher Watt, *14, Canberra, Australia*

Best experience ever! I could never have imagined what God would do in my son through this camp, but it has brought me so much joy to see his passion for writing explode! I have appreciated the helpful critique and knowledgeable mentoring given by Jenny and Libby as he researched his nominated character, as well as the fun-loving nature of every session. This gave fuel to an unbridled enthusiasm in his writing, seeing him focus for hours on each chapter. THANK YOU both so much! See you in 2023!

–Christopher's Parents

THIS CAMP WAS ONE OF THE BEST EXPERIENCES OF THE SUMMER!!! TRULY INCREDIBLE!!!

—Emma Urrutia, *14, Mechanicsburg, PA*

My daughter Emma aspires to become an author and has been inspired by Jenny L. Cote. Joining the EPC 2022 was an answer to prayer. Not only did she grow as a writer, but she expanded her faith and friendship with others who have the same dream. Truly, Jenny and Libby have a gift to capture the attention of young minds and hearts, gently helping them to become better writers, love history and impact the life of others. May I mention my girl was never interested in history UNTIL NOW? Yes, indeed. Thanks for this valuable and inspiring event. **–Emma's Parents**

THE EPIC STORY OF 1776

25 PEOPLE, 13 COLONIES, AND 1 WAR

EPIC PATRIOT CAMP 2022   JENNY L. COTE

LIBBY CARTY MCNAMEE   MIKAYLA BADENHURST

ELYCE CORSETTI   PAYTON GRACE   CAMERON GRAHAM

ABIGAIL GREGORIN   OLIVIA HANKS   PERI JORDAN

ELLIOTT LAY   EDAN MACNAUGIITON

ABIGAIL MCGINNIS   CARMENE MILLER

EMMANUEL MORISSET   KIT P.   R.G. PATTERSON

KAYLEE PEARSONS   ELLIE POWERS   ELLA QUILL

MOLLY ROSER   ALEX ROBERSON   JESSAH SEMONS

JOY ELIZABETH TARDY   EMMA URRUTIA

CHRISTOPHER J. WATT   BELLA WAUGH

MADELEINE WENZEL

EPIC PATRIOT PRESS

CONTENTS

VIRTUAL EPIC PATRIOT CAMP

The book in your hands is the work of the twenty-five campers from the virtual Epic Patriot Camp 2022. They not only wrote the chapters, but they came up with the book title as well. We worked with each camper as they researched and wrote three chapters to answer the following questions for their character:

1) How did the American Revolution come to my doorstep?

2) How did I get involved in the American Revolution?

3) What's my story in 1776?

The point of camp was to encourage the next generation to learn America's epic history and to tell the story for generations to come. We taught them how crucial it is to get the research right, and to thoroughly study the good, the bad, and the ugly of history. Some campers were more thorough than others, and of course some are more mature than others, with more research and writing experience. You'll see their bibliographies, biographies, and acknowledgments in the back of the book. While we attempted to fact check their work, the scope of the project necessitated that we rely on their research to get the history right. We hope there are no historical errors, but we appreciate your understanding if any slipped into these pages.

One way to get young people excited about history is to weave in fun storytelling with historical fiction. Some people will never pick up historical books like we history geeks, so stories are a way to teach while engaging the non-history loving (is there such a thing?) reader. We encouraged campers to flex their creative writing muscles to write historical fiction, and some even chose to incorporate fantasy as well with talking animals. The point is to make history FUN while learning. Some of these young writers had so much fun that they are continuing to write their own books with their assigned characters. That's a good sign that we accomplished our mission with Epic Patriot Camp.

You will read many humorous scenes, and many tender, emotional scenes as well. The creativity of the campers blew us away! We're so very proud of each one of them, and we hope that history will come alive for you as you read this book. Please encourage our campers by leaving a positive review on Amazon, and by buying copies of this book for your local school, history group, library, and friends. We appreciate you helping to fuel the pens of the next generation, and we thank you in advance for your support. If you would like to learn more about Epic Patriot Camp, please visit www.epicorderoftheseven.com. For interviews or more information, please contact Jenny at jenny@epicorderoftheseven.com.

May the lifeblood of patriotism continue to flow from our pens into the hearts of Americans through the relentless pursuit of our EPIC history. HUZZAH!

Jenny L. Cote and Libby Carty McNamee

THE ORIGINAL EPIC PATRIOT CAMP

It all started with my villain, Banastre Tarleton.

I am currently writing a series of books on the American Revolution and have traveled to most sites where the war unfolded, both politically and militarily. My focal protagonist characters for the series are Patrick Henry and the Marquis de Lafayette, but Banastre Tarleton is my antagonist. My endless research includes reading books and documents, making site visits to museums and battlefields, and talking to historical experts. One of those experts is military historian and re-enactor Mark Schneider who happens to portray two of my three characters: Lafayette and Tarleton. (He also portrays Napoleon all over the world, so to say he knows history well is a bit of an understatement.) I'm forever indebted to Mark for his tireless assistance with my research over the years, as well as his insightful critiques of my work.

In January 2015, Mark was scheduled to portray Banastre Tarleton for the 234th Anniversary of the Battle of Cowpens. I decided to make the trek from Atlanta for the event as I had not yet visited the NPS Cowpens National Battlefield. Reenactments bring history to life! While at Cowpens, Mark introduced me to John Slaughter who was the NPS Superintendent of the Revolutionary Parks of the Southern

Campaign of the American Revolution. I asked John if he would be interested in having me do an event for kids at one of these NPS events, and he replied, "Could you do a whole week?" They had just received grant money to create a summer writing camp at Kings Mountain, and John immediately saw the opportunity to do something unique for June 2015 using my books and brand.

Our team met in March 2015 and developed Epic Patriot Camp, a creative writing day camp for kids 9-13 provided by the National Park Service. The goal of the camp was for participants to learn about the Overmountain Victory Trail leading to the Battle of Kings Mountain by researching a soldier and crafting a story about the soldier's battle experience. Kids spent time each day with me to learn new research and writing skills. They also put themselves in the shoes of those who fought in the battle through hands-on activities: colonial clothes, weapons demonstrations, militia drills, colonial trades and crafts, spending time on the battlefield, etc. The culminating experience was an overnight colonial style camp: canvas tents, open-fire cooking, lantern hikes, etc. On the final day the kids presented their stories from their soldier's point of view for family and friends. Epic Patriot Camp 2015 was an immediate success and led to subsequent years and other locations including Cowpens and the Muster Grounds in Abingdon, Virginia.

Then came Covid. The world shut down, and Epic Patriot Camp was discontinued. Frustrated, in 2022 I decided to create a Virtual Epic Patriot Camp experience and asked my dear friend, Libby Carty McNamee, and historical fiction author of <u>Susanna's Midnight Ride: The Girl Who Won the Revolutionary War</u> and <u>Dolley Madison and the War of 1812: America's First Lady</u> if she would partner with me. This online camp would be the same in terms of campers assuming the identity of a Patriot, Loyalist or French ally to research and write a character story, but we decided to focus on one year: 1776. No, we couldn't provide an in-person experience of hands-on colonial activities, but we could provide an opportunity for budding writers to become published authors. At first, we retained the same age range of 9-13, but because we received numerous requests from older teens, we opened camp to all ages. Campers chose either or a Tuesday or Wednesday group that met online for three hours each week for a month.

The result? We had twenty-five campers aged 10-19 from fourteen states, Washington, D.C., and even one from Australia. Not only did they bond with their assignments, but they also bonded with each other. It was our hope that Epic Patriot Camp 2022 would foster friendships with kids who shared a mutual interest for history and writing. Our hopes were not only realized, but they were surpassed! These campers set up their own out-of-camp meeting times just to hang out, and these "Huzzah Hang-Outs" have continued. They can't wait to return next year for Epic Patriot Camp 2023: Writing the Story of 1777.

Of course, Banastre Tarleton *had* to make an appearance before and during camp, giving us his lofty opinions while trying to make it all about him. He even suggested that *everyone* write his story to produce a multi-volume set. (Ah-hem. This is why he's my antagonist.) Thankfully, only one of our campers took on the identity of Tarleton, and you're going to love what she wrote with the help of his talking horse.

So, thank you, "Bloody Banastre Tarleton," for making Epic Patriot Camp possible. I hate to admit it, but it truly *is* all about you in a way, because it all started with you. Ah, but I know how the story *ends* in 1781, and I can't wait to chat with you then.

See you in our pages,

Jenny L. Cote

AMERICAN PATRIOTS

ABIGAIL ADAMS

by Peri Jordan

ABIGAIL ADAMS: HOW DID THE AMERICAN REVOLUTION COME TO MY DOORSTEP?

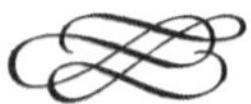

*R*evolution! That is what everyone is always talking about. Freedom. Independence. Change. It is a rather new idea in the minds of my neighbors and friends, but not to me. I have always dreamed of a fresh start and reshaping certain fundamental principles in our society. Most people are thinking about government and ridding ourselves of tyranny. However, I am not.

No, I think it fine to leave the changing of government to people like Thomas Jefferson, George Washington, Patrick Henry, and those intelligent gentlemen down in Philadelphia. What I want is much simpler and supposedly much easier to attain. I want freedom for women. I want my daughter to get an education. To have safety in her future marriage. So, I wrote a letter to the brightest man I know. He also happens to be my husband, and dearest friend, John Adams.

But first let me step back for a moment and start at the beginning. I was born on November 11, 1744, in Weymouth, Massachusetts. As a girl, I was not permitted to go to school. For years I was taught to do "ladylike" things such as cooking, cleaning, sewing, but never to read or write.

Finally, I decided to take it upon myself to learn things. Though my siblings never quite understood me, I first began to teach myself to read. Once I knew what each word meant, I could copy them. Then I wrote stories, letters, and pure gibberish, sometimes, until I knew every single letter by heart and knew how to string them together in an orderly fashion. At last, I began to read and read and read—history books, science books, religious books, anything I could get my hands on. But I never went to school to learn what to *do* with my newfound learning.

When I was fifteen, I met a bright young lawyer fresh from Harvard College. As I overheard his conversations with my father and brother, I learned so many things! They asked questions and speculated until they finally answered them. Then I began to ask the young lawyer my own questions about the law, politics, and government. Things that I never read about in any one of Father's books. He seemed impressed that I, a girl, would take interest in things like this. As we talked, we learned things from each other, and about each other. We grew to be friends. Then, more than friends. Four years later, we were married.

I loved John, and still do. And I knew that no matter what, I would be happy to be Mrs. John Adams forevermore. However, just a tiny bit of me knew that there was more to my delight. Because just a tiny bit of me could never forget how smart and influential he was. I always knew that he was bound to make changes in the world, and that he could make changes that benefited me, for our possible daughters, for women everywhere. So, naturally, I was delighted when our first child was a girl. Little Abigail, I was sure, would grow up differently than I did.

Now my little Nabby is ten years old, and she has three younger brothers. John Quincy is nine, Charles is six, and Thomas is three. They would have another sister, but poor Grace Susanna died shortly after birth. Now I give everything I have to Nabby and grieve for the fact that I have not much to give. However, that brings me to the present.

Currently, John is in Philadelphia assisting in the writing of a great document. They call it the "Declaration of Independence." I pray they will use it to bring freedom for the ladies as well as the men. Indeed, I have written a letter begging that of my husband. I pray he will listen for Nabby's sake—dare I say it, for my sake as well.

"Mother," John Quincy rushed through the front door, pulling me from my thoughts.

"What is it, John?"

He held up some papers with a wide smile. "Letters! I have one and Nabby has one, but the biggest one is for you." He handed it over. "It's from Father."

"Thank you very much, Dear." I tried to mask my excitement, but it was difficult. This letter might change everything. It might say my husband will vow to fight for the ladies. Be kinder to us than our ancestors were. Would he not take my side on this? Yes, absolutely—of course he would.

I sat down at my writing desk and opened the letter. With eager eyes, I began to read. The second phrase caught my eye, and I could not look away. *I cannot but laugh.* The words circled through my mind in a chorus of jeers and chants. *I cannot but laugh. As to your extraordinary Code of Laws, I cannot but laugh. I cannot but laugh. I cannot but laugh.* I put the letter down, resenting the prickling tears pooling in my eyes, threatening to overflow.

"Mother, is everything alright?" Nabby was at my elbow.

I did my best to smile at her. "Yes, Nabby. Everything will be alright."

She brightened up and asked hopefully, "May we hear Father's letter?"

I shook my head. "Not this time. It has nothing of any interest to you. More of an answer to one of my—" I glanced down at the page, and something at the bottom of the paragraph caught my eye, "saucy questions."

Nabby looked confused, but she smiled and turned away. I watched her as she sat at the table and began writing something on a piece of paper.

All I wanted to do was play my part and fight for what I believed in, including my sweet daughter. The revolution had been thrust upon me. It has barged into my home, tearing my husband from me and our four young children. Now it has taken my one hope, what I envisioned as Nabby's only lifeline. Could I fight back? Could I push past the ridicule and reach my goal?

Why not? If the men were fighting their war with swords and pens, could I not fight my own with knowledge and inspiration? I would teach my sons as well as my daughter to read and write—to love learning and to understand America's struggle for liberty.

And all the while, I will love my husband, as I encourage him to understand his hypocrisy. How can the men complain about having no representation in Parliament, while we women have no hope for a voice in either system? My husband fears that we will "completely subject them to the Despotism of the Petticoat" but this is not what I ask. I simply desire for men and women to be partners in liberty, just as I am his loyal partner for life.

ABIGAIL ADAMS: HOW DID I GET INVOLVED IN THE AMERICAN REVOLUTION?

I sat there for a long while, watching John Quincy and Nabby read their letters, and then play with Thomas and Charles. Even though they were still young children, I knew that soon I would wake up one morning to find three young gentlemen and one little lady in my parlor needing to be taught how to live in the big world outside of Braintree, Massachusetts. They must learn simple things like reading, writing, and arithmetic first, then move on to more complex things—concepts such as our struggle for independence and freedom. I thank Providence that my children are growing up while our country is being born, for they are the generation that will be the first leaders of America. I know that they will be capable of doing things that people will read about in history books a hundred years from now—but only if they are taught.

Again, I glanced over at the children. I decided that there was no better way to teach them about things going on in our world, than to go out into it.

"Nabby, please fetch my basket from the table. John Quincy, help Charles and Thomas find their shoes, if you would. I am afraid they have lost them again." All four of them scattered to all corners of the house. Once they were back, Nabby with the large woven basket, and the boys with shoes in hand, I continued. "All right. Now that everyone is here, it is time to go into town." Everyone cheered at this, for they loved to look at the shops and houses all along the streets.

We set out on our adventure, walking along the streets and alleyways until, finally, we reached main street where most of the shops were. First, we went to the baker for some fresh bread, then to the weaver for fabric. I planned to sew a new pair of breeches for Charles, who had finally torn his beyond repair. Once I picked out the cloth that I liked, we started home. Everything had been pleasant and enjoyable until we passed a tall, thin gentleman and a boy around Nabby's age. The man was the teacher at the school in town, and the boy was his son, Archie.

"Good afternoon, Mrs. Adams," the man said politely.

I did not fall for his act, for I knew he was one of the most rude and arrogant persons I had ever met.

"Good afternoon, Mr. Wadland."

He nodded and began talking. I barely paid attention—he was boasting of the many wonderful things he had been doing recently, and I had not much tolerance for it. I noticed out of the corner of my eye that his son stepped forward and began speaking to my boys.

"Hello. How are you all getting on? Charles?" Charles nodded shyly. "Thomas?" Thomas shrugged and stuck a thumb in his mouth. The boy scowled. "And how are you, Johnny?"

John Quincy's eyes flashed, and I barely had time enough to realize what was about to happen before he stepped forward, causing Archie to stumble back. "My name is John—like my father."

"Excuse me, Mr. Wadland—" I began, but the man cut me off, so I had to stand there helplessly as John Quincy and Archie began to quarrel.

"Oh, yes. Your father, John Adams the rebel," Archie said with a sneer.

"He's a patriot!" John Quincy fired back.

"No! Those who stand with our king are the *true* patriots. And we'll win the war, too."

"No, you won't! America is a free country, and there isn't any room for Tories here!"

"Mr. Wadland," I interrupted him in the middle of some story about meeting the one and only King George III. "I apologize, but I fear it is high time we get home. I beg you excuse us."

Mr. Wadland tipped his hat. "Oh, yes, of course. Good day, Madam."

I grabbed John by the arm and hustled all four of them away. "John, really?" I scolded.

"What, Mama?" he asked.

I sighed. "You know what I mean. You should not have been quarreling with Archie."

"Why not? He was insulting Father!" John protested.

"Just because someone else says unkind things, does not mean you may say mean things back."

John looked away guiltily. "I'm sorry, Mama."

"That's alright, John Quincy," I answered with an affirming smile.

"I wish *I* could have stood up for Father," said a small voice behind me. I turned to see Nabby trailing along forlornly. "I could have said all sorts of things about how kind and helpful Father is, even to the British sometimes, like after the massacre."

It was then that I realized Archie had not said anything to Nabby at all, not even looked in her direction. Neither had the shopkeepers or Mr. Wadland. They had said hello to me, then spoken to the boys. Now that I thought about it, I remembered that every time—except with Archie—they had addressed John Quincy first, as the oldest. This, of course, would be proper, except that he was not the oldest. The oldest was Nabby.

ABIGAIL ADAMS: WHAT'S MY STORY IN 1776?

Though Nabby perked up considerably on the way home, I remained thoughtful and silent. That boy had neither acknowledged my daughter as the oldest, nor had he even spoken to her at all! Was this how things were to be for her always? Getting pushed away and ignored by all? Suddenly I recalled my own childhood, and how my parents often told my sister and me to "Behave! Your brother's friends will be over soon!" even though we were the oldest. My parents never told William to behave because *our* friends would be over soon.

I sighed. I did not hold a grudge against my brother, but I also did not want my Nabby to endure the same things that I did. If she did, it would be harder for her than me, since I at least had a sister to share in my sufferings.

I looked over at Nabby, who was picking flowers in a nearby meadow. I smiled for a moment, until John Quincy, Thomas, and Charles went galloping through the field, heedlessly trampling everything in their way. Nabby simply sniffed and turned her head away disapprovingly, then gathered up her flowers and returned to the path.

"Mother, why *do* they have to be so rude? I suppose it is because they are boys, and they are allowed to do such things." Nabby said, slipping her little hand in mine.

"Nabby, I hope you know that isn't true," I replied softly. "The fact that they are gentlemen should mean they are polite and respectful to ladies such as yourself." Then, turning to the boys, I called, "Little men who trample flowers do not get pie after supper!" They all came to an abrupt halt, then turned and ran back through the field toward us. "Careful!" I shouted. "You are trampling more flowers, boys!"

Once they were safely back on the path, we started off again toward home. When we reached the house, Nabby hurried to put her flowers in water while the boys ran right back out again. Sitting down at my writing desk, I finished a letter, then sealed it up and set it aside. I looked around, searching for something to do, but there was nothing. I had washed the windows yesterday, the floors hardly needed sweeping, and supper needed no preparation for a long while yet.

As I was looking around, I saw Nabby sitting at the table with a piece of paper and an old pencil of my husband's. She seemed to be writing or drawing something, but I wasn't quite sure what. Her face changed as she became frustrated with it. Then she would get an idea and go back to happily scribbling. As I watched, I almost felt as though I saw her grow up right before me. Perhaps I was imagining things, perhaps I had dozed off in my chair and was dreaming, but I saw a young woman sitting at the table, writing. I suppose she was writing a letter, because she signed it with a flourish, folded it, sealed it, and set it aside, just as I had moments before.

The girl sat there, holding the letter for a while, until three rowdy boys burst through the front door, startling her so much that she dropped her letter on the floor, where the boys then trod upon it with their muddy boots. With a cry, she ran to it and picked up gingerly. She held it close and tried to wipe off the mud, but I could see it was ruined. She was quite upset, and she was about to go over to the boys, when the biggest one turned to her and demanded she sweep the mud off the floor, and then make them something to eat.

I wanted to run to the girl and help her, console her, do *something* for her—but all at once, she changed. Instead of a young teen-aged girl standing before me, there was a woman, fully grown. I could tell by her face she was the same girl, only older. I soon noticed that this woman had a ring on her finger. Because of this, I assumed that the man who entered the room a moment later was her husband. He said something to her, though I could not hear it, and she replied. They had a brief—yet slightly animated—conversation, ending in the woman retreating to another room in the house just as another man entered the house. They spoke for a while, but very soon, the woman returned. Instead of joining the men, she sat in a dark corner all alone, reading a letter.

I blinked, and everything was back to normal. The boys were still outside, and Nabby was still sitting at the table, but I could not forget my vision. Were men always to have such dominion over women in life and in marriage? My own husband feared the rights of women, and I think men everywhere do, but it is foolish. Men should not fear women but respect them as individuals.

How I wished I could change things. I had written to John, hoping that he could make the changes that I cannot, but now I realize that it does not take giant leaps to change the world, but small steps to make a change in one life. Then that life could change another, and that could change another, and another, and another, until the world is just a little bit better. So, what can I do? I can take small steps to change the course of my daughter's future, and perhaps the future of our nation. That is my role in this war for freedom. And I will do my best to make each step count.

JOHN ADAMS

by Molly Roser

JOHN ADAMS: HOW DID THE AMERICAN REVOLUTION COME TO MY DOORSTEP?

On June 29, 1767, John Adams picked up the latest newspaper at the local store and read the headline, "Townshend Acts Passed." He kept reading and the paper said that they would pay the war debts following the French and Indian War, including The Stamp, Sugar, and Quartering Acts. John Adams knew that there would be more acts in the future. This made him and a lot of other people very mad. All the taxing was causing widespread anger directed at the Mother Country. Townshend Acts were acts that would tax lead, tea, paint, glass, and paper. *These are awful!* he thought. Great Britain was unfairly taxing the colonies.

As John shared this news with others, they had similar reactions. "The Townshend Acts were passed, and Britain is taxing our lead…"

But before John could finish telling his neighbor what else they were taxing, his neighbor threw up his hands and yelled, "I make my living making leaded glass for church windows, and I can't afford this! Somebody in England is ruining me and I can't even ask him to stop!"

"I am so sorry," John told the man. "I need to get home." John walked a little further and eventually got home to his wife Abigail, his daughter, and his newborn son.

Months passed and peoples' anger rose like lava slowly building up in a volcano, waiting for a time to blow. So, on the evening of March 5, 1770, a few colonists were arguing with Private Hugh White. "Why do we have high, unreasonable, taxes on items we use every day but people in Britain don't!" one yelled. "No taxation without representation!" yelled another. After only a few minutes of arguing, the fight went to a whole new level. About fifty colonists were now in the mob, and they were throwing snowballs and sticks at the soldiers. The volcano had finally exploded.

Captain Thomas Preston, the officer on duty, sent soldiers over to control the people. His plan did not work though, and only angered the colonists when they saw the British soldiers with the bayonets. The colonists threw the sticks and snowballs harder and shouted louder than ever before.

"I can't afford to pay for stamps to send letters!" shouted a person in the front of the mob. "How am I supposed to paint pictures for people when I can't buy paint!" piped in someone in the back. Suddenly, a large stick hit Private Montgomery square in the chest. After that he aimed his musket into the crowd and fired. There were a few moments of silence, but the quietness said a million words. A few other soldiers followed the Private's lead and shot into the crowd. "You killed them!" screamed a person who was right next to one of the fallen colonists. The crowd of colonists soon left King Street.

John Adams was back in the local store to get the latest newspaper and this time the headline stated, "A Massacre in Boston." *Oh, no!* he thought to himself, quickly reading about the five dead colonists from the massacre on King Street. He started to wonder who the lawyer for the soldiers responsible would be. Would the lawyer try to convince the judge they were guilty so they would become popular for putting the British on the gallows? Would they list things that were untrue so they could get payback? He had to make sure that those soldiers got a fair trial, even though he did not approve of the laws they were sent here to enforce. Right was right. So, he formed a plan in his mind. John would be the lawyer for the British Soldiers who participated in the Boston Massacre. He did worry that people might be upset with him for trying to give the soldiers a fair trial.

The next day John was at the stables and was brushing his horse, Humphrey Ploughjogger. He remembered the time when he had to come up with a pen name for his writings for the *Boston Evening Post* so he would not be arrested. He eventually chose Humphrey Ploughjogger, the name of his horse. John gently combed his horse's hair until it met his satisfaction and then got fresh water and more hay for Humphrey. He brushed Humphrey's mane and tail one more time so it would be extra clean as he thought about what he was getting ready to do. This time he couldn't hide behind a pen name. Attorney John Adams would be featured in the headlines as the lawyer representing the lobsterbacks who had fired on the innocent people of Boston. What in the world would happen to his reputation, to his livelihood, and to his family? As he tidied up, John realized that come what may, he was on the side of justice and the law, and to that cause he must ever be true.

John left the stable and remembered to lock up so his horse would not be stolen. He walked home quickly so he could relax for a little while before his next big event.

JOHN ADAMS: HOW DID I GET INVOLVED IN THE AMERICAN REVOLUTION?

On December 16, 1773, at midnight, 166 people boarded the three ships called the *Dartmouth*, the *Eleanor*, and the *Beaver*. Some were disguised as Mohawk Indians but not very convincingly. They all grabbed boxes of tea and threw them down into the harbor. One person on the Dartmouth took out a knife and carved "no taxation without representation" along the wooden rail that went around the ship. They continued to drop the tea until all 342 crates were thrown into the harbor. Then, quickly, and quietly, everyone slipped away, avoiding arrest.

John Adams was excited and surprised that the people would do such a dangerous protest. The news was all over the harbor. He wondered how Britain would respond to this. Most likely, they would punish the colonists as they had done so many times before.

Time passed. One day, John Adams heard a knock at his door and when he opened it, a messenger delivered a coded message announcing the congress was having a meeting. Strangely, after packing his bags he had gone to the stable to saddle Humphrey Ploughjogger, yet his horse was already waiting for him outside the stable, saddled, and ready. John didn't stop to think about it, as his mind was already racing ahead to the Continental Congress in Philadelphia.

John had stopped halfway to Pennsylvania for a little while to eat and rest. He had learned from years of riding out to represent people as a lawyer, that he had to give Humphrey a carrot or two at the halfway point, or his otherwise fast horse would start walking deliberately slow. As John ate and fed carrots to Humphrey, he wondered what this meeting was about. Would it be like the one meeting where they talked about the response of the biting restraints that Britain put on the colonies because of the Boston Tea Party? He thought about it a little more and then mounted back up on his horse and continued the long ride to Philadelphia.

Once John arrived in the large city of Philadelphia, he started to search the town for the Pennsylvania State House. He wasn't sure where exactly it was, but Humphrey led him straight there. John dismounted and walked quickly up to the large, white, doors. He opened the doors and walked into the Assembly Room, and noticed he was early, benefits of a fast horse he supposed. He sat down in one of the seats and by the end of the morning, all 56 delegates had arrived. The meeting started when Richard Henry Lee, a delegate from Virginia said, "We need to break away from Great Britain and start our own country." He then showed the congress a text that he had written, "Resolved, that these United Colonies are, and of right to be, free and independent States, that they are absolved from all allegiance to the British Crown, and that all political connection between them and the State of Great Britain is, and ought to be, totally dissolved. That it is expedient forthwith to take the most effectual measures for forming foreign Alliances. That a plan of confederation be prepared and transmitted to the respective Colonies for their consideration and approbation." Another delegate chimed in, "I think we should send a declaration to Britain listing several grievances, and saying we are breaking away from them to start a new country."

One of the delegates said, "We don't all have permission from the states allowing us to vote for independence." "Let's write this Declaration of Independence and then show it to the states to see what they think to make it more convincing," suggested another. A delegate from New York asked, "Who will write this Declaration? I think that Richard Henry Lee from Virginia should write it." At that, just about everyone else agreed.

However, Richard Henry Lee answered, "I don't think I should. I am on the Committee of Confederation for writing the Articles of Confederation and that would be difficult to do both. Also, my wife, Anne has become very sick, and I need to take care of her. Since I will not be available, Thomas Jefferson from Virginia should write the Declaration; he is probably the best writer in here."

Thomas Jefferson stated, "I want to go back to Virginia and write their constitution, though. John Adams should consider writing it, we have all read his *Thoughts on Government*. I don't want to write the Declaration." In spite of his protests, the Congress was not swayed and insisted on Thomas Jefferson writing the Declaration. "Okay, fine, I will but I want Benjamin Franklin, Robert Livingston, Roger Sherman, and John Adams to help me write the Declaration. "Meet me here in four days and we will start to draft this thing," said Thomas. They all agreed and left the building, to prepare to draft the Declaration of Independence.

JOHN ADAMS: WHAT'S MY STORY
IN 1776?

There was one more day until it was time to write the Declaration of Independence and John Adams and everyone else was preparing to draft it. The Congress was still surprised that Richard Henry Lee did not want to write since he came up with the idea but understood that he was busy.

John stayed at an inn while waiting for the four-day wait to finish, giving him plenty of time to think about how they should write the Declaration of Independence. They would need to write all the ways they were being treated unfairly, and to explain the reasons why they were breaking away from Britain. The Continental Congress had to make their case for independence known to the British, or they would be seen as acting unjustly. They should also make sure that they showed that this was what they really want, otherwise they might think they are not being serious. The Declaration of Independence had to have the power to hold their cause together, so all that they had worked for would not collapse. Lastly, he wanted the Declaration to be honest and fair so people will help America when they need it, and that her cause would be seen as just and righteous.

John took out an old letter from Abigail. He missed his family and wanted to see them again but knew he must wait to see them until his work was done so America will be a better place to live. He wondered if change would happen immediately, or more gradually. For him, change couldn't happen soon enough.

The next day he rode his horse back to the Pennsylvania State House and put his horse in a nearby stable. His horse, Humphrey Ploughjogger, had never galloped so fast as he did that day. The people of Philadelphia quickly dodged into alleys and shops, afraid that John Adams had lost control of his horse. He hadn't, not really; Humphrey was just extra excited this morning for some unknown reason.

John Adams walked through the large white door and into the Assembly Room. A few people were already there including Roger Sherman and Benjamin Franklin. John Adams and the others shared their opinions about how the declaration should be written while they waited for Robert Livingston and Thomas Jefferson to arrive. "I feel that we should make our point clear, we wouldn't want any misunderstandings," suggested Roger Sherman. Then, as soon as he said that Robert Livingston walked in and said hello. John said, "Now we only have to wait for Thomas Jefferson to arrive."

They continued to talk for a few minutes and then Thomas Jefferson walked in. He looked around the room and said, "Good we're all here so let's get started." The group all sat down around a table and put a large sheet of paper in the middle. They all grabbed a quill and ink jar to prepare to write.

John thought back to the time he was a lawyer for the British soldiers who were at the Boston Massacre. He had made his best case for justice and given the soldiers a fair trial then, and now, John Adams would have to make his best case for America in the Declaration of Independence, and hope America would be treated fairly.

The delegates talked for a bit, all catching up on what they were discussing earlier. While they talked, John wondered if the people even wanted to start their own country, and like one person had said, they didn't even have the state's permission yet. Would they agree to this? Then his mind went to the Continental Congress. They would have to sign the Declaration of Independence. *Yes, we have to try,* he thought.

So, once they were all caught up, they began to edit until it mentioned everything the Declaration of Independence was meant to.

After seventeen long days of writing and editing the Declaration was finished. Thomas Jefferson, Benjamin Franklin, Roger Sherman, Robert Livingston, and John Adams all stayed to have a short meeting with the Congress to see if they wanted to add or take away anything. Everything went fine though. It stated:

In Congress, 4 July 1776

The unanimous Declaration of the thirteen United States of America. When in the Course of Human events, it becomes necessary for one people to dissolve the political bands which have connected them with another, and to assume among the powers of the earth, the separate and equal station to which the Laws of Nature and Nature's God entitle them, a decent respect to the opinions of mankind requires that they should declare the causes which impel them to separation.

It went on to spell out the rights of the States to separate from Britain and list the injustices inflicted on the States.

It was August 2, 1776, and John Adams was at the Pennsylvania State House where the Declaration was kept. He had gotten Massachusetts' permission to sign and that was what he was going to do. He went through the door and up to the Declaration. He picked up the quill and began to sign his name. John Adams knew that by doing so, he was officially declaring himself a traitor to the British Crown, but he did not pause, he signed his name as a free American!

SILAS DEANE

by Elyce Corsetti

SILAS DEANE: HOW DID THE AMERICAN REVOLUTION COME TO MY DOORSTEP?

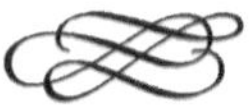

2 March 1776

Silas Deane watched as the frost on his window glinted in the early morning light. Puffy clouds sprinkled the sky, briefly providing shade to the snow melting on the cobbled streets of Philadelphia. Water trickled through the grooves, dampening the mud between the cracks.

He turned from the glass, leaving his quaintly furnished bedroom. The space was only filled by a bed and a few wooden chests for storage. The wallpaper was dull in color and lacked many patterns. It was hardly as lavish as his home in Wethersfield, Connecticut. He shut the door to his room and headed downstairs for breakfast.

Entering the dining room, a female slave he brought along from his home served breakfast. She laid his silverware down on the tablecloth, carefully placing a butter tray above the plate of fresh bread and the bowl of cornmeal. The female slave nodded to him, stepping back from the prepared meal.

"Thank you." He smiled, taking a seat at the head of the small wooden table. "You may go now." The scent of warm cornmeal and bread was especially delicious when he was hungry, and he promptly tore the warm bread and slathered butter on it. He sat back in his chair and ate in contentment, thinking over his plans for the day. He didn't recall any more work given by the Naval Committee; he had already completed his previous assignments with his usual diligence.

Silas paused, mind drifting back to home so far away in Connecticut. It had been too long since he returned to see his wife and children. He'd write a letter to them this afternoon, sending them his love and updating them on recent happenings.

While enjoying a last spoonful of his meal, a metallic creak and brush against the wooden floorboards by the front door caught his attention. Silas set his fork down on the plate, and called for the servant to clear the table, pushing back his seat to stand.

Approaching the front door, the metal mail plate swung on its hinges as someone pushed through an envelope. Crouching down, he picked up a neatly pressed letter with his address written on the back. Mail in hand, he went back upstairs, passing the door to his bedroom, going instead to his study. Taking a seat at his desk, Silas observed the letter, turning it over to examine the branded seal on the back. He did not recognize the design imprinted into the hardened wax and became curious. Since mailing was rather expensive, the sender must have had good reason to contact him.

He fingered the letter, reaching for the paper knife resting on his desk. Slicing through the rose-colored wax, he unfolded the paper.

In cursive ink, it read, *"We the underwritten, being the Committee of Congress for secret Correspondence, do hereby certify whom it may concern, that the bearer, the Honorable Silas Deane Esquire, one of the Delegates from the Colony of Connecticut, is appointed by us to go into France, there is to transact such Business, commercial and political, as we have committed to his Care, in Behalf and by Authority of the Congress of the thirteen united Colonies. In Testimony whereof we have hereunto set our Hands and Seals at Philadelphia, the second Day of March 1776."*

Silas' brow furrowed. Congress? He had been decommissioned from his service as a delegate in Congress only the preceding year. Why would they call on him now, in a letter no less, for a new and undoubtedly secret assignment to France? He well knew their struggle for both arms and soldiers, having been assigned to scrounge up ships and ammunitions for the Naval Committee. The purpose of this business transaction with the French would likely be for their invaluable aid in their war.

Adjusting his hold on the paper, five lavish signatures decorated under the bulk of the paragraph. He immediately singled out the signature of his old diplomatic colleague, Benjamin Franklin. Apparently he was now involved in this 'secret committee of Congress.'

He laid the paper on the surface of his desk, resting back in his chair and staring up at the ceiling.

"A mission to France," he murmured, baffled. He didn't speak a word of French, and his expertise was hardly in diplomacy. Other than that, sailing for France would take several weeks, if he even survived the voyage. He'd only be farther away from his family. Leaving them behind in Connecticut for months on end was already difficult; Silas didn't know if he'd be able to leave them behind in a whole other country for a number of years. He'd never travelled beyond Philadelphia. Letters would take months to arrive, only furthering the rift between them. He'd be the last to know if…if something terrible happened. The stinging pain of losing his first wife only made him more reluctant to travel abroad.

He glanced down at the letter, lying so innocently on the table. If he did accept the mission, when would Congress expect him to leave? What was involved in this business endeavor exactly? And how did they even expect him to communicate with the French?

He tapped his fingers on his desk. Of course, those questions were important, but nothing more than to feed curiosity if he himself did not answer the most important question. Did he have any desire to accept this assignment?

He long believed that the Colonies needed to obtain their independence from Great Britain. Taxing goods from stamps to tea was unfair and costly, putting more money in the King's golden pockets. Adding to that, they couldn't do anything to change the laws because they were denied equal representation in Parliament. Their only option is separation. Creating a new government with equal rights for every man.

Well, what could happen if he decided not to go to France? Surely, they must have selected him specifically for a reason, despite his seeming lack of skills in the area.

Silas stood, walking once again to the window illuminating his study. He pressed his forehead against the cool glass, staring up to the clouds as he weighed his options.

If he denied their offer…the Patriots would lack vital resources to fight the British. Their, *his*, goal of freedom would be merely a child's fantasy if the British bested them on every battlefield. They would lose without aid from France. Lose to Britain and be subjected to the King's tyranny forevermore. Perhaps the circumstances would be even worse as punishment for their rebellion. He couldn't let that happen. They needed him to win this fight, and he wouldn't be the one to turn his back on them now, despite the great cost to his family and himself. With God's help, hopefully the French would show mercy and decide to help them win their freedom.

Silas left the window, sat back down, and reached for a fresh piece of paper. Sliding the original letter to the side, he dipped the tip of his quill into an inkwell and began to write.

'My esteemed colleagues of Congress, I, Silas Deane Esquire, accept your assignment. I eagerly await further instruction.'

SILAS DEANE: HOW DID I GET INVOLVED IN THE AMERICAN REVOLUTION?

4 March 1776

Silas took in a deep breath of fresh ocean air. The smell of salt reminded him of his former business as a merchant. He spent a lot of time at the docks, arranging shipments and inspecting his ships to ensure his buyers received the highest quality goods. In whatever work he found himself, he would give himself fully to the assignment.

The day following the arrival of the first recruitment letter, from the Committee of Secret Correspondence, he was sent another, longer message containing specific instructions about his mission to France. Silas acted swiftly, writing to the owner of his small apartment to end the rental agreement, and sending his slave with a fare back to Connecticut. He had found a ship, the *Betsy*, leaving for France on the fourth of March and immediately arranged for his passage. It was a bittersweet time, having to uproot himself from the comforts he was used to and place himself in a new and foreign environment. But he knew without a doubt that this was what he wanted. It was a chance to do more for the Colonies and to deal a greater blow to the British.

He took one long, last look upon the town of Philadelphia where he had lived for a year as miles of ocean continued to separate him from his past. Exhaling, he turned his back towards the fading sight, and retreated down into the lower decks of the ship. It would be a long voyage, plagued with both dreams of fear, excitement, and a longing for home.

6 July 1776

Arriving in the bustling heart of France was overwhelming. The people of Paris moved in a whirlwind of activity, their foreign tongue disorienting him at every turn. Silas was easily flustered by his language barrier. Not only was he lost in this unfamiliar environment but having to rely on his own funds to pay for the journey from the Bordeaux coast to Paris was quite irritating. All the Colonial money he was paid by Congress had completely lost its worth as soon as the boat's underbelly touched French waters.

Nevertheless, it was important for him to find lodgings as soon as possible, or his true mission would be stalled. Not any residence would do; it had to be fitting for a "Bermuda merchant," his cover persona. *Hôtel Villars*, a French hotel in Paris, seemed to fit the match.

As soon as he arrived in France, he sent for an old acquaintance, Dr. Edward Bancroft, to join him. Once Bancroft came knocking on Silas's door, it was a joyful reunion. He learned much about his former student's dealings, the most shocking of which was how Benjamin Franklin employed him as his own private secret agent to work the inner circles of the British government. Silas did not hesitate in referring to Bancroft as his chief source information about the British.

After reuniting with his friend, Silas alerted Monsieur Dubourg of his arrival, the contact provided by Congress, and arranged to meet with him at the Frenchman's personal residence.

"As the first order of business, I require a meeting with your Foreign Minister, Vergennes," Silas stressed as he sat before Dubourg.

Dubourg faltered in his reply. "I am afraid, *Monsieur* Deane, that a meeting with the Minister at this time is not wise."

Silas paused to stare at the man, who appeared uncomfortable. "Pray tell, why? Such a meeting is of high importance. It cannot wait!"

"The British Ambassador, Lord Stormont, is already aware of your arrival in Bordeaux," he explained, heavily accented. "If you go to meet with Vergennes, he will undoubtably find out."

Silas stood, pacing the room in serious contemplation. "He may be aware of my presence, but there is little he can do to prove why I have come. By subjecting coward to him, the Colonies will have to wait longer for aid." Silas turned to face Dubourg. "The American Colonies do not have time to wait, and I have no time to waste. Schedule the meeting please."

"Stormont has spies everywhere," Dubourg insisted gravely. "Any bit of evidence, a discarded letter, a seal, a trace of funds, anything! Anything could be held against you, the Colonies, and France. The British must not know of our involvement. Not yet."

Silas locked eyes with Dubourg. "Do you not trust me to conceal whatever I can?"

"Of course, I-" Dubourg started to say.

"*Monsieur* Dubourg," Silas began tactfully, sensing his area of weakness. "I have been personally assigned by Congress, and a friend whom you are very acquainted, *Dr. Benjamin Franklin*, to fulfill these important negotiations. He trusts me to send the aid we need in our fight against the British. I would hate to disappoint him. Please, schedule the meeting."

Dubourg was quiet in thought. After a brief moment of silence and anxious dread, his decision was made. Standing from his chair, he clasped his hands behind his back.

"I will speak to Vergennes today," he conceded. "I will inform you when arrangements have been made."

Silas smiled. "Thank you, *Monsieur* Dubourg. I will patiently await your letter of success."

Written jointly by Joy Elizabeth Tardy (Marquis de Lafayette) and Elyce Corsetti (Silas Deane)

8 July 1776

Silas straightened his waistcoat. Dubourg was a man of his word, and the following day, a letter was sent to Silas's hotel, informing him of the arrangements. Silas was to meet with Vergennes in Versailles on the eighth of July. Bancroft had not come with Silas, choosing alternately to remain in Paris and be informed of the events upon his return.

Silas entered the large meeting room, Dubourg in tow, gaze locked onto the elder gentleman. Vergennes dressed in clothes of the French aristocracy, a pleated coat embroidered with intricately swirled golden threads and multiple silver buttons.

"Ah, vous dois être Silas Deane," Vergennes greeted the American with a smile. *"Un plaisir de vous rencontrer."* Dubourg quickly translated the Minister's greeting into English.

Silas smiled back and bowed in respect. "The pleasure is all mine, Minister."

Vergennes gestured to the table lined with ornate chairs, moving towards the head. Silas sat a respectful distance away towards the right side of the table, but close enough so he could hear Vergennes. Dubourg sat at Silas' left, prepared to translate.

"I understand that you have urgent business to discuss," Vergennes began.

"As urgent as it is important," Silas answered with a nod. "Shall we begin?"

5 November 1776

Silas was extremely busy throughout the months he lived in Paris. Busy almost as much as he was stressed. He wrote letters to Congress regarding the willingness of French soldiers to sail for America and fight for the Continental Army, all of which went unanswered. He strongly suspected that they simply chose to ignore his pleas for guidance. With the responsibility placed upon his shoulders, as often it was, he had chosen to accept the volunteers, and give them an appointed rank. America needed soldiers, and these Frenchmen knew how to use the arms they supplied to the Colonies. Should any dispute arise, Silas would be quick to point out the lack of information regarding recruitment.

Further causes of headaches included the poor reliability of correspondence across the ocean. If Congress decided to bother themselves with assisting him, their instructions were not guaranteed to ever reach him. He had heard news the tenth of August about a "Declaration of Independence" arriving in London. *London*, but not France? He was frustrated, and rightfully so in his opinion, that Congress had given no thought to send an official document of Independence to the country who had been aiding them to *gain* independence. Months passed, and still no word arrived. Silas began to question his assignment. Shouldn't he have been the one to announce the Declaration to the King of France? Was another envoy on his way to replace him?

Vergennes was feeling equally suspicious, if not more so. He suspected Congress had decided to cut off France's aid and seek peace with England. Silas was quick to dissuade the idea or negotiations could be lost, though he was just as ill-informed as Vergennes. The fact that European newspapers contained the full text of the document only made the situation worse.

But now was not the time to make his visitor aware of his grievances. Baron De Kalb, a willing fighter who thankfully spoke English, was signing a contract Silas had written for service in America. With the last swirls of ink, the deed was done.

"Welcome to the Revolution," Silas quipped, grinning to hide the weariness in his eyes, shaking the Baron's hand and retrieving the letter.

"I am honored and willing to be a part of it," the Baron replied with a smile.

Silas went to sit at his desk, beginning to fold the letter. "When you travel to the Colonies, this letter will be the most important thing you have. Show it to Congress so they may assign you wherever there is need."

De Kalb nodded. "Is there an abundance of need?"

"Oh yes," Silas confirmed, eyes not leaving the paper. It had to be perfectly folded… "America is a foot away from losing the battle. Experienced soldiers are desperately needed." He finished, holding the pressed and sealed letter out for the Baron to take. The German baron accepted it, glancing down at it for a moment before continuing.

"I know a *man,*" he paused to chuckle, "who holds valuable connections and longs to serve in your army."

"Go on," Silas prompted.

"He has been desiring to meet you for some time. If you would be willing to speak with him, I am certain he will accept your offer to acquaint."

"Of course," Silas stood from his chair. "What is his name, so I may have small knowledge for greeting?"

De Kalb smiled. *"Lafayette."*

6 November 1776

Baron De Kalb, a Quartermaster General also intent on fighting the British, told me Silas Deane from America had come to France to get aid. This was extremely exciting that an American was here in France. Oh, *comme c'est merveilleux!* I thought. Here was my chance to show I was ready to give my heart and sword to America! I wondered to myself if Baron De Kalb would like to act as interpreter so that *Monsieur* Deane and I could understand each other. When I mentioned to him, I would like to meet with *Monsieur* Deane, he surprisingly said, "I would like to introduce you to *Monsieur* Deane, and I will act as your Interpreter." I thanked Baron De Kalb and told him that would be *merveilleux*! I could not believe I was going to meet *Monsieur* Deane!

"It is a pleasure to meet you, *Monsieur*. My name is Silas Deane, envoy on behalf of the American Colonies." He smiled politely once the young man entered his office, waiting for the Baron to translate his greeting into French.

Baron De Kalb translated, and the conversation followed.

"*Enchante*, my name is Marie-Joseph-Paul-Yves-Roch-Gilbert du Motier, le Marquis de Lafayette, but you may refer to me as Lafayette."

Silas held back a disbelieving stare as De Kalb introduced the young boy. He would be lying if he said Lafayette's full name was not anything but impressive. Even with his decent memory, he only caught the tail end of the sequence of names. Swallowing a laugh, he extended a hand in introduction, of which Lafayette did not shake. *Monsieur* Lafayette bowed to him, oblivious to his mirth.

When *Monsieur* Deane extended his hand, I bowed to him. I was eager to talk about the war. Even though I was much younger than *Monsieur* Deane, hopefully this would not affect his decision. I then said, "*Monsieur* Deane, please let me be in the Continental Army, and help America win her Independence from England." Then to my surprise *Monsieur* Deane said:

"Regretfully, *Monsieur* Lafayette, I have to decline your request as a matter of age..." He stopped short of the most important parameter.

I stubbornly told *Monsieur* Deane, "My heart and sword belong to America. You may think I am too young to fight, but I carry experience beyond my youth."

Silas faced away from the two as he contemplated, hands clasped behind his back. Even though he had sent other willing volunteers to America, Lafayette was only a boy. He claimed to hold experience, but he could just as easily be another toll on the death count. He was reminded of his son, Jesse. He could never live with himself if he sent his own son to die on the battlefield. Would he be able to send Lafayette across the seas, only six years older than his son, and be able to live with the consequences?

Monsieur Deane did not wish to send me to America, nor was he convinced by my defense. After much consideration, I decided to inform him I was from the court of King Louis XVI and a Marquis. Maybe that would convince him to let me go to America. So, I said, "I can help you win the war, and get your men needed food, clothes, boots, and weapons. I have money to provide all of that. If you would only let me, go to America and fight in the war, I would use my fortune to aid your soldiers!"

Silas faltered. Lafayette had powerful connections. If he sided with the Colonies against Britain, perhaps the French court and the King would follow suit. He, along with his associates, would be of enormous value to their cause. And with almost limitless wealth and a desire to use it for America, Lafayette could provide necessary funds for arms and munitions.

However, Silas was still aware of the ban placed by the French King that no officer of noble birth could serve in America's war. He could not openly assist the determined young man in his voyage. He still desperately needed Vergennes's trust and aid to continue the negotiations between France and the Colonies. Silas knew by the fire in the young man's eyes that with or without his help, he would find a way to aid America. For the sake of secrecy, Silas had better be the one to offer his help.

He angled his gaze slightly towards the young man. "I am unable to grant your request." Lafayette was visibly disappointed. But he was not finished.

"*Publicly*," he added with a small grin. He strode towards Lafayette, halting right before him. "Privately, I know a man who can help you. His name is Carmichael. Speak only to him about your plans, and he will assist you in working out the details." Lafayette nodded seriously.

"To any who ask, I denied your request and you are remaining in France," Silas instructed. "I will not help you on the sole reason that I will not defy your King's command."

"I will need to write an official contract signing you into service," Silas further instructed. "Until I finish, there can be no evidence of us ever meeting again." Lafayette could barely hold onto his excitement, agreeing that it would be better if he kept his distance until he received word from Silas.

"Secrecy is of utmost importance. Nevertheless, I look forward to receiving word of your victories," Silas said, smiling at the eager Frenchman. "Farewell, brave soldier. It has been a pleasure to meet you *Monsieur* Lafayette."

SILAS DEANE: WHAT'S MY STORY IN 1776?

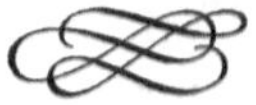

10 DECEMBER 1776

My assignment in France has lasted nearly a year. The days stretch on as more work fills my desk, and my quill blunts from penning a stream of endless letters.

I was relieved, though quite perturbed, at finally receiving an official copy of the Declaration of Independence on the seventeenth of November. Meeting with Minister Vergennes to formally apologize and present the document was humiliating, to say the least, not to mention irritating. Upon my return from the meeting, my quill was once again employed in the use of inking scathing remarks aimed at Congress. I nearly shredded the paper by hotly grinding the tip of the quill onto the sheet. It was dreadfully unprofessional, but the heavy responsibilities of my work have vexed me beyond what I could have ever imagined. I grow extremely weary, but do not worry over me, for I am determined to complete the mission.

There was a, how shall I say, *complication* made by a certain 'James Atkins' parading by the name of 'John the painter.' He made a name for himself by burning down British facilities. Famed by destruction, he forced a meeting with me some months ago with the fool's crusade of assassinating King George III. Such a cowardly move; thankfully, however, I convinced him to abandon that goal, and he left Paris.

Unfortunately, my troubles with him were not over. He succeeded in burning down a British naval yard, adding to his list of criminal activity, leading to accusations that Bancroft aided in the plot. I tried my best to ensure nothing evil would befall my old student, writing exaggerated letters to portray myself as the culprit with the intention of interception by British authorities. I have yet to see what will await me, as they have imprisoned Atkins for some time now.

I recently received word from Dubourg that Benjamin Franklin arrived in France. He was quite enthusiastic about sharing the news and providing the doctor's letters of instruction. Minister Vergennes did not share his open excitement, demanding why I had not informed him. I then had to explain the secrecy of the matter, for if the British knew that Franklin is here, they would no doubt accuse the French of aiding the Colonies and seek to attack them. For all the French have done for us, even despite the small annoyances, I am determined not to let that happen under my care.

The seventh of December, I met with the Marquis de Lafayette, to appoint him into service. I signed the letter of approval, and he now possesses it as his token of entry into our army. The devoted young man agreed to serve without pay, and I admire the spirit in him, though I doubt he will successfully arrive in the Colonies. King Louis XVI's strict order that no officers are allowed to leave France to fight in America may prevent his escape.

Now that the two delegates, Franklin, and that atrocious Arthur Lee, have arrived to share the load of my duties, I hope to complete my service soon.

I pen these words with confidence, that despite unforeseen complications I cannot mention in this letter, I shall return soon to the Colonies, welcomed back with fame as a true American. But above the glory, I will be content knowing the difficulties I faced led to America's freedom.

I pray that you and the children are well. All this I write with the hope I may see you and Jesse again soon, my love and heart, Elizabeth.

Yours affectionately,

Silas Deane

BENJAMIN FRANKLIN

by Christopher J. Watt

BENJAMIN FRANKLIN: HOW DID THE AMERICAN REVOLUTION COME TO MY DOORSTEP?

PENNSYLVANIA STATE HOUSE, PHILADELPHIA, 5 MAY 1775

"*I* was sailing here to Philadelphia when it happened." Benjamin Franklin spoke up from his seat. An inventor, councilman and now a member of the Second Continental Congress, he had just arrived in Philadelphia from London. He sat with the delegates of the Congress in the Pennsylvania State House discussing the latest disputes between the radical American colonists (now called "Patriots") and the British Crown. Since the colonisation of America, Great Britain had caused a few issues in the colonies, such as high taxes. Many people were upset with this and decided to meet here in Philadelphia last autumn for the First Continental Congress to discuss what they should do about it. Much had happened in the past few intervening months leading up to this meeting of the Second Continental Congress. There were about sixty people seated around tables discussing current events, with Franklin sitting at one of the tables in the middle.

"A unit of British redcoats sailed past me. Their intentions were to travel to Lexington with all guns blazing—literally, too. Arriving the next day on April 19, they showed off their muskets and cannons to display their dominance over the colonists. Thank the Lord that our friend Paul Revere was able to warn the colonists." He told his comrades. They were all listening intently, so he continued. "When the British arrived, they were met with an unwelcome surprise. A mob of about seventy colonists were waiting for them and attacked.

"'Disperse ye rebels!' A British major yelled, brandishing a well-used musket. Then a shot was fired. We still don't know who fired it, but it was perhaps one of the patriots. This resulted in mayhem. The fight got ugly—eight of our Americans were killed."

"Why were the British so agitated?" one of the members attending the meeting inquired.

"We have been informed that it could have been in the bid to capture the planners of the Boston Tea Party, Samuel Adams and John Hancock," he answered. In late 1773, a band of patriotic Americans dumped into Boston Harbour three hundred and forty-two chests full of British tea that had arrived in a shipment from Britain, due to high taxation on tea. This was known as the Boston Tea Party and sparked even more conflicts between the Americans and the British. "That was one tea party I'm glad I wasn't invited to. But in Lexington, the redcoats' main intention was to suppress the idea of a rebellion by marching to confiscate a secret stockpile of military weapons the colonists had gathered in Concord. Ironically, this sparked the first battle of the war to come. The victorious British continued to Concord afterwards and were victorious there too. On their journey back to Boston, however, two hundred and fifty of their men were killed by American patriots."

George Washington, a good friend of Ben Franklin, cleared his throat for attention. He sat at the table at the front of the hall where all those attending could see him. When all eyes were on him, he continued. "The Boston Massacre, the Boston Tea Party, and now the Battle of Lexington and Concord. This is no simple skirmish about some unjust laws; we've entered war. It's up to us to decide: is this war for reclaiming our rights, or is it for our independence from Great Britain?"

There were a few murmurs among the people with no response. George raised his voice for emphasis. "I asked you, *is this war for reclaiming our rights, or is it for our independence from Britain?*"

"Independence!" the patriots roared.

Samuel Adams stood up and came to stand next to Washington. "Well then, I say that we should fight for what we deserve! Our rights have been violated, and the Crown has let us down! I say we give the British the what-for! Let us raid their military encampments and show them what we're made of!" He yelled victoriously with his fist in the air as if they'd just won the war.

"HUZZAH!" the patriots shouted and threw their three-cornered hats up in celebration before erupting in elated conversation and laughter.

In the midst of the celebrations, Benjamin waddled up to George. "Well, you and Samuel have certainly got them riled up. Now it's time to see if you can lead them to victory." George looked around the room and nodded. Encouraging the Congress was one thing, but winning a war was something completely different. "Yes, it won't be the same from now on," he murmured without averting his gaze from the crowd. "I have absolutely no idea whether we'll be victorious or not. None of us do. We just have to hope and pray that we will turn out victorious."

He nodded. "Agreed."

After the meeting ended, Benjamin Franklin walked back to his home on Market Street. The sun was setting, and the streets were darkening. When he arrived home, he took out his keys and unlocked the door. It was a pretty house; a white picket fence on the left and around his back garden, red bricks and white shutters on the house, and a beautiful American Oak tree that stood tall and proud on the right. The tree was home to a very plucky squirrel, whom Benjamin named Beebee. Beebee was ratcheting and chattering at him as he came home.

"What are you going on about now, fine Mr. Beebee?" he asked the crazy squirrel. He listened more closely and heard a strange sound coming from behind him. It was like a snort or a whine, but almost like someone saying the letter *N* with their nose blocked. Looking closer, he noticed that Beebee wasn't barking *at* him, but barking at something *behind* him. Turning around, he saw a gorgeous black St. John's Water Dog puppy staring at him longingly. Her tail was wagging in a rapid arc and swept the pavement. She had pricked ears and the most adorable brown eyes he had ever seen. Unlike most Saint John's Water Dogs, she was completely black.

"Hello, there!" Benjamin smiled as he petted the dog. "You're rather friendly, now, aren't you?" She rolled over onto her back and let him scratch her belly. He chuckled as he stroked her. For the first time, he noticed a merlot-coloured neckerchief around her neck. It was ornately decorated with white Celtic patterns that had been professionally stitched. It was as if the neckerchief was made for royalty. Untying it from her neck, he noticed the symbol of Saint Edward's Crown. Next to it, he saw the word, *Shadow*.

This dog must be British! he realised. *And her name is Shadow. Hmmm...I don't know any British people whose dog's name is Shadow. She must belong to a lord or member of the royal family!* He immediately started looking around for a possible owner to hand her to but saw none. Then, remembering the Congress meeting earlier, he changed his mind.

"Not anymore you're not," Benjamin whispered. "You're one of us now. Come inside."

"Psst!" a voice whispered. "Psst! Shadow! Wake up!" Shadow stirred and looked around. She was in the drawing room of a house. A large fire crackled in the fireplace and Benjamin Franklin slept soundly in his armchair. His arm was draped over the side of the chair and in his hand, he held the document that he had been working on.

Looking around, she saw a Black-Billed Magpie sitting on the open windowsill.

"Nimbus!" Shadow exclaimed as she ran up to him. "What brings you here?" A good friend of Shadow's, Nimbus was a magpie who often helped her on her allocated royal missions.

"Splendid to see you again, good friend," Nimbus chirped. "His Majesty King George hasn't heard from you yet. He asked me to pay you a visit to see how well things are coming along. What intelligence have you gathered so far?"

"I've been secretly trailing behind a rather peculiar man for the last few weeks. His name is Benjamin Franklin," Shadow replied. "He attended a meeting this morning in the Pennsylvania State House."

Nimbus leaned in closer. "Yes?"

"It was all about a war between the Americans and the British Crown. The people there were all supporting events like the Boston Tea Party! They're all Patriots—all of them! And Nimbus, the Americans want Independence from Britain!"

The magpie fell back off the windowsill and into the peony bush behind him. "What? Independence? From *Great Britain*? How utterly preposterous!"

"Agreed. The Americans are clearly out of their minds. But don't worry," Shadow snickered. "I have a plan."

BENJAMIN FRANKLIN: HOW DID I GET INVOLVED IN THE AMERICAN REVOLUTION?

PHILADELPHIA, PENNSYLVANIA, 1776

"*R*ule, Britannia!" Nimbus the magpie cawed. "Britannia, rule the waves! Britons nev—"

"My goodness, is that bird singing *Rule Britannia?*" Thomas Jefferson gaped in awe. He, with John Adams, Roger Sherman, Robert Livingston, and Benjamin Franklin, all sat together in Franklin's office room discussing what to include in a Declaration for Independence. They had all been selected by the Congress, and decided to gather here, since Benjamin only lived a few blocks away from the statehouse.

"Of course, it is! What else do you think it's singing?" Adams answered, frankly.

Franklin lifted his head. "He's been hanging around lately and seems to love the open windowsills. Magpies are extremely intelligent birds, you know. Apparently, King George keeps one as a pet because of their high intelligence!"

"Don't be ridiculous, Franklin!" Adams scowled. "Birds can't talk! There's nothing more absurd than saying a bird can talk!"

"You'd be surprised," Franklin leaned back in his chair with his eyes closed, listening to the birdsong. Despite the derogatory phrases such as 'Britain ruling the waves,' *Rule Britannia!* was quite a lovely song - even if they could only hear the tune and not the lyrics, given that the current singer was a bird after all.

"Rule, Britannia! Britannia, rule the waves!" Nimbus glanced over to Shadow. "Do you think it's working?"

Shadow nodded. "Definitely - they're *all* getting distracted. At this rate, we'll be able to undermine the document before it's even written!"

"Jefferson!" came John Adams' rough, no-nonsense voice. "Can you stop contemplating whether or not birds can talk? We need to be focusing on the task at hand - the document!"

They all sat at Franklin's dining table, enjoying a well-earned lunch of beef and bread. "Mr. Adams, I do believe that we should take this rest to refresh ourselves. Dr Franklin has had his family prepare this meal for us to enjoy, and it would be an insult to carry on with business. Besides," Thomas Jefferson smiled. "I rather enjoy this discussion."

Nimbus sat by the window next to the dining room. It amused them that the bird followed them to every room, and it kept their minds off the Declaration. "Rule, Britannia! Britannia, rule the waves! Britons never, never shall be-" Nimbus was cut off as John Adams got out of his seat and shooed the bird away.

"Crazy bird!" he grumbled before seating himself back at the table. Still, Nimbus continued, this time from his perch on the oak tree outside.

"Rule, Britannia! Britannia, rule the waves! Britons never, never shall-" Nimbus was once again cut off by Adams, who this time slammed the window closed with a resounding *bang!*

"For goodness' sake, can I *never* finish that second line?" the magpie cawed in discontentment.

Shadow took that as her cue. In a black flash and a blur, she raced forward and leapt up onto the table to snatch the food. Everything came crashing down—the crockery smashing, the food flying across the floor, the tablecloth ripping. All that was left were five men sitting at their chairs with looks of utter disbelief and speechlessness on their faces.

When it was time for them to leave, Benjamin walked them out. "Many thanks to you, Jefferson. I believe that you will be able to come up with something that will change the colonies for the better!"

Thomas smiled. "I shall try, but I cannot guarantee anything!"

Philadelphia, Pennsylvania, 21 June 1776

It was a fine Friday morning when a courier strode up to Benjamin's front door. He carefully placed the document down in front of the door and knocked on the knocker before leaving to go deliver the next package. When Franklin answered the door, he picked it up and noticed a note attached to the document, which read:

Will Doctor Franklin be so kind as to peruse this and suggest such alterations as his more enlarged view of the subject will dictate?

Many thanks unto you,

Thomas Jefferson

"Ah, this must be the draft that he sent to me," he smiled and walked back inside.

When he got to his desk in the office, he began work. After their meeting, Jefferson had written a 'rough draft' of the Independence Declaration and sent it to Franklin, who was ill with gout and couldn't attend most of the Congress meetings anymore.

"Hmm...I don't think we need that." He crossed out the last three words in Jefferson's line, *We hold these truths to be sacred and undeniable,* with heavy black strokes. He changed the wording to 'self-evident' so that the line now read: *We hold these truths to be self-evident.*

"By writing 'sacred,' you imply religious value, and with an all-inclusive document, it should assert reason instead of religion," he commented before continuing. When he saw another line, he followed the same protocol, changing *invade and divulge us in blood* to a much less violent *invade and destroy us.*

Suddenly, there was a loud *thunk!* Benjamin looked up to see that Nimbus had crashed into the closed window next to him.

Suddenly, Shadow started barking at the magpie. "Nimbus, you stupid bird! This window is closed! Use the Drawing Room window! That one is open!" Unfortunately for Franklin, all he could hear was Shadow barking like the average dog.

Before long, the magpie had found his way in. Chaos erupted from every corner of the room. Shadow was barking, Nimbus was squawking, and Benjamin was in a flurry to figure out what was going on. There were feathers in his face as Nimbus fluttered around, and Shadow sent things crashing down as she chased the bird around the room.

When Franklin was fully distracted, Shadow took her chance. She swiftly ran up to the desk and scribbled out a few words on the draft in Franklin's editing style. Then, she called Nimbus and told him to fly out back the way he came, amongst other barks of complete nonsense to add to the distracting noise. As rapidly as the chaos had begun, there was peace.

"That was rather odd, wasn't it?" Benjamin Franklin laughed as he sat back down at his desk after closing all the windows to make sure that any 'stray' birds couldn't enter again. He frowned as he saw that some of the sentences had been crossed out in his signature editing style. *I don't remember this,* he thought, frowning harder. Shadow smiled in seeing that her devious plan had worked. *Oh well, it must be my ageing brain on the loose again. Now, what did this say?* He rewrote the line above the scribble mark as *reduce them under absolute despotism,* which was originally written as, *reduce them to arbitrary power.*

"I'm convinced that it is not the same as what Jefferson wrote, but he can read it as one of my 'editorial changes,'" he mumbled before moving on. The next line used to read as *Amount of their salaries* but, because he couldn't remember it perfectly, Franklin rewrote it as *Amount and payment of salaries.* He continued doing this throughout the document until he had finished editing.

"When in the course of human events," Benjamin Franklin began reading the final edited draft aloud. Shadow sauntered out of the office and into the Drawing Room, where she snatched a piece of fresh paper and a quill, and began writing at the side table, which was much easier to reach than Franklin's desk.

When she was complete, she called for Nimbus, who nearly thunked into the window again. Shadow sighed and opened the window for him to sit on the sill.

"Blast these stupid eyes—I can't see the glass pane in front of me!" he lamented. "Now, how can I help?"

"I have a new plan. I want you to send this to His Majesty King George III and let me know what he thinks of it."

Nimbus chuckled. "And may I ask what this plan entails?"

"This plan is different from all my others. And I do believe that it will prove to be rather successful." Shadow snickered. "Let us just say that it involves…," she paused for effect. "A powerful military weapon —cannons!"

BENJAMIN FRANKLIN: WHAT'S MY STORY IN 1776?

STATEN ISLAND, NEW YORK, 11 SEPTEMBER 1776

"*A* little over-the-top with the soldiers, don't you think?" Benjamin Franklin murmured as he, John Adams, and Edward Rutledge were escorted past a double line of Hessian soldiers —German mercenaries who had been hired by the British to aid in the current American Revolutionary War.

They were meeting with Admiral Richard Howe, or Lord Howe as he preferred to be called, to discuss the idea of a peace treaty between America and Great Britain. Arriving on a ferry from Perth Amboy, they were surprisingly welcomed by the British.

"It's an army camp, Franklin, what do you expect?" Adams grumbled in his infamous no-nonsense tone. The only reason the Congress had made him go along was to prevent Franklin from seeking peace behind every corner—as he had a habit of doing.

As they were escorted past the line of soldiers, one of the Hessians sneezed. "*Gesundheit,*" Franklin muttered to himself but received glowering looks from everyone.

"You didn't come here to show off your talent of speaking German!" Adams whispered sharply. "Just act *normal* for once!"

Behind the nearby trees, two animals observed the encampment very closely. One was a magpie, the other a dog. "Wonderful. Everything is coming along perfectly," Shadow looked over her shoulder at the magpie. "Are you all set?"

Nimbus chuckled evilly. "Yes, I'm ready. The Americans don't stand a chance!"

"This is my promise to you—if this peace treaty is successful, the American colonies will be allowed to have control over their own legislation and taxes," Lord Howe proposed. They all sat together in the hall, feasting on a meal that Lord Howe had prepared for them. It included wine, ham, mutton, and many other delicious foods that were often exclusively aristocratic.

"And if America were to fall? Would Great Britain support us?" John Adams raised an eyebrow without making eye contact.

Lord Howe avoided the direct question. "When America falls like a lost child, England feels it like a burdened father," he reported, heightening the drama. "Oh, if America were to fall, I would feel most inconsolable. I would lament as if it were the loss of a brother!"

"My Lord, we shall do our utmost endeavours to save your Lordship from such mortification," Benjamin Franklin retorted.

"Why then," Howe began. Adams furtively rolled his eyes. "Are such actions not possible to put an end to these extortionate extremities?"

"Because," Franklin replied, "it is much too late for any peace between the colonies and Great Britain that may require *any* allegiance to the reigning monarch, such as the king. Forces have been sent out and many towns have been burnt. We cannot expect liberty and joy under the domination of Great Britain *or* the British Crown. All former alliances with the two have been obliterated."

Adams shifted in his seat. "I am personally determined to maintain my loyalty to the idea of independence. I shall not depart from such thoughts, be it my own or not."

"We have one last suggestion," Edward Rutledge spoke up. "America becomes an independent nation and peace between the two can be assured."

Benjamin nodded his head in agreement. "Perhaps your Lordship could request the authority to negotiate with us to be such an independent nation? By doing so, your Lordship shall get your peace, and we shall be returned our liberty."

Admiral Richard Howe shook his head dramatically in disagreement. "Of such things, there is vain hope."

"Well, my Lord," Franklin reasoned, "as America is to expect nothing but liberty and independence, this could be complicated. The British dominion over America will have to change, otherwise this meeting is futile. I wish this not for myself, but for the benefit of this new nation—"

Howe interrupted. "Personally, I do not demand submission. But in hearing your arguments, I acknowledge that no accommodation for peace would be possible." He got up from his seat and showed them to the door. "I deeply apologize that you gentlemen had the trouble of journeying so far with such little purpose."

Before Franklin, Rutledge, or Adams could acknowledge the apology, a nearby cannon exploded, the sound deafening to those who were too close.

"Cannons?" the admiral yelped in surprise. "Why are my soldiers firing cannons? Is this an ambush?" He glared at Franklin, who shrugged in innocence.

Adams grabbed one of the Hessians by the collar and demanded, "What is going on?"

The German soldier winced. "*Ich weiß es nicht*! I does not know! I vaz just at mein post and den suddenly, boom! Von of ze cannons exploded!"

Adams let go of the pathetic soldier, who stumbled around in alarm, and fell with an "*Autsch!*" There was confusion everywhere, but all the soldiers stood their ground.

Suddenly, another cannon went off. This time, everyone saw where it came from—within the encampment itself. Relieved but confused, Rutledge leaned closer to Franklin. "What is going on?" he whispered.

"I have no idea. Seems like these British cannons aren't as mighty as they seem!" Franklin jested. Adams soon came up to them and was also baffled.

"These cannons are utterly useless! They fire themselves at random!" Adams scowled. "And those Hessian soldiers are *pathetic!*" He looked on as a Hessian soldier ran past, mumbling, *"Ich möchte zurück nach Deutschland!"*

Lord Howe looked around as everything settled down. Only two cannons had fired, but it was enough to startle the entire army.

"I am deeply sorry. Please accept my utmost apologies," Lord Howe told the three men. "I am certainly not deliberately responsible for this event!"

Franklin nodded his head. "I do not have faith that Great Britain will succeed in making peace with America now," he sighed. "But I shall do my best."

Adams didn't catch Franklin's sarcasm. "Seriously? I was tasked with making sure you *don't* seek peace behind every corner! And what do you do? You tell the Admiral that you'll *do your best!*" he whispered in Franklin's ear.

Franklin smiled sardonically. "I am grateful to your Lordship for the idea of peace between America and Great Britain. I am disappointed that it has not concluded successfully but am confident that the path shall be found eventually. Farewell."

With that, he, Adams, and Rutledge were escorted back to their ferry and returned to Perth Amboy, leaving a dejected Admiral Howe on Staten Island to consider what to do next.

"Nimbus! What have you done?" Shadow cried as she saw Franklin peacefully leaving the island. "This wasn't supposed to happen!"

"I am dearly sorry, my friend," Nimbus apologized as he flew to the ground. He dropped his miniature custom-made linstock as he landed, which singed the grass with its heat. "I was successful in lighting a cannon, but then the linstock slightly burnt my claws as I flew past. I accidentally dropped it, and it fatefully landed on the fuse of the one cannon I deliberately *didn't* fire. By the time that cannon had exploded, all the soldiers were alert. It would have been too risky for me to light another one with everyone being so vigilant."

Shadow sighed. "Fine, but now we have done *nothing* to help the British win!"

"The Battle of Long Island two weeks ago wasn't nothing," Nimbus piped up. "And neither was the Battle of Bunker Hill just over a year ago. The British won due to our aid. *And* the battle of Lexington and Concord. When we fired that shot, all hell broke loose!"

"At least that *was* something," Shadow pricked her ears. "I heard that the British are planning to capture New York City in three days' time! They plan to invade via Kip's Bay. That's really close to us here on Staten Island! We could influence it to help the British win?"

Nimbus nodded. "Sounds like a plan! Although…"

Shadow rolled her eyes. "Although…*what?*"

"I received a letter from His Majesty King George III this morning. He has requested you to return in time for the Christmas celebration."

"Well, that's plenty of time! We could even assist in more battles before then!"

"His Majesty would like you to be home in October. It is his own personal request that you do so," Nimbus reported matter-of-factly.

"Very well," Shadow accepted. "I believe this is for the best. I miss my royal palace and the beauty of England. I just hope that these American Patriots will be put to rest, and that Britain shall reign victorious by the end of this war!"

"Britain has already won approximately ten significant battles. I have no doubt that the British will win the war!"

Shadow smiled. "Britain shall rule supreme now and forever."

"Rule, *Britannia*! Britannia shall indeed rule the waves!" Nimbus chirped.

"Agreed," Shadow snickered. "Great Britain shan't *ever* be defeated and nor shall the British Crown ever fail. *HUZZAH!*"

NATHANAEL GREENE

by Cameron Graham

NATHANAEL GREENE: HOW DID THE AMERICAN REVOLUTION COME TO MY DOORSTEP?

Early in the morning, twenty-three-year-old Nathanael Greene walked along the winding path heading towards his father's iron forge with his newest book on military science in his hand. He picked up his pace, knowing the sooner he got to work, the sooner it would be time for lunch, and he could finish reading. As he pushed open the heavy wooden door, a wave of heat hit him in the face coming from the large flames. He set his book aside and walked over to the large foot-operated bellows. As he set to work, his mind began to wander as he got into the rhythmic movement of pushing down the pedal of the large bellows. However, loud shouts from his co-workers soon interrupted his thoughts.

"Outrageous," one man practically yelled into Nathanael's ear, "if I had a boat and hammer, I would sail straight over to England and knock some sense into that King George's head."

"Hurrah," yelled the other forge workers.

But then another older forge worker said, "Hold your tongue! Do not say such things for 'tis treasonous!"

The forge worker turned back to his work, muttering to himself. Nathanael knew that if the forge worker ever had the opportunity, he would deny ever thinking such things. Come midday, Nathanael walked outside and sat underneath a large pine tree, its branches gently waving in the breeze like a thousand hands waving at him. He sat down to start reading, but the headlines he had seen earlier in the newspaper on the latest Stamp Act distracted his mind. It was causing quite a stir among the townsfolk.

Soon enough, though, it was time for Nathanael to return to work, but he pondered if England would be able to keep her thirteen colonies. However, judging by the opinions of many of the Colonists, things were not going to end peacefully, which was creating unrest in his Quaker heart.

Nathanael Greene looked down at Father's tombstone. His father had died earlier that week and was laid to rest beside Mother who died when Nathanael was only eleven years old. He was not sure what to make of it. The only thing he knew was that his father was gone, and it was now his responsibility to take over the family business. Later that day, as he was inspecting the large paddlewheel which powered the family's grain mill, the town crier rang his bell and shouted down the street. He paused to listen:

"Bostonians massacred by British soldiers!"

Nathanael immediately sat down, knowing in his heart that war was inevitable.

"Letter for Nathanael Greene," yelled the postal rider as he rode up towards the large house in Coventry.

"What is it, my good sir?" asked Nathanael as he came out to meet him.

"A message from the Rhode Island Legislature," replied the rider. Nathanael immediately took the letter inside to read:

To Nathanael Greene:

We, the General Assembly of Rhode Island, have taken a vote and elected you as our latest member.

Mr. Henry Ward

This was an extraordinary opportunity, and his father would have been proud. After all his hardships that year, he received a piece of good news, but his good fortune did not last. His vessel, *The Fortune*, would soon be captured and its cargo lost to the *HMS Gaspe*. Upon hearing the news, his lawyer began writing up a lawsuit against Lieutenant William Uddingston for illegally capturing a vessel, but soon his fellow colonists would carry out their own definition of justice.

7 June 1771

"That's right, me and the boys approached the *Gaspe* in the dead of the night," continued a young man speaking to the crowd who had gathered around the dock. "We got our revenge and burnt the *HMS Gaspe* to the waterline. That will teach those lobsterbacks."

Lieutenant Uddingston was unable to appear in court due to the injuries he sustained on the burning of his ship on June 6th. But England had now stoked the fires within Nathanael of a fight for independence and freedom from injustice. Unfortunately, Nathanael's personal struggles were not behind him. Shouts of fire drew the attention of Nathanael. By the time he arrived, the fire already had eaten its way through the roof, with only a skeleton remaining ablaze. By the end of the day, all that was left was the smoldering foundation. Despite many setbacks in rebuilding the forge, Nathanael lived up to his words, "the sound of the hammer is once more heard in our land."

Nathanael, riding his horse Britain, thundered along the path leading from Rhode Island to Boston to his frequented stop at the London Book Shop to purchase another book on military science. As he rode through the crowded streets of Boston, he could see church steeples towering up into the sky, including prominent Old North Church.

"Pleasure to see you again, my friend," the shop owner said as Greene entered.

"The pleasure is mine, you know how good it is to have someone that shares my common interest in military tactics," Greene answered his longtime friend. Greene had been coming to this book shop to expand his library on different topics, including military science, as Henry Knox received books from England on tactics and artillery. It was always a trip he looked forward to.

"Did you receive anything new from England?" Greene asked.

"Military science I presume," replied Henry, "I just got his one in." He climbed the ladder to reach for his latest title, *Supply Chain Logistics: Wars Are Won with Beef Jerky*. That will be fifteen shillings."

"Money I am happy to spend," replied Greene. Greene knew before long the new book would have a cover worn, the spine broken, pages dog-eared and notes in every margin. Greene took a seat and invited his friend to sit and talk.

"So, Knox, what have you been reading?" Greene asked. And for the ensuing hours, the two friends debated military science, tactics, history, latest news, and politics. Nathanael and Henry often saw eye-to-eye, and it was great to have each other to talk to.

"I know I can always count on you, friend," he said, leaving the shop. He carefully placed the book in his saddle bag.

No one can get the substance out of a book like he can, Knox thought. He laughed and shook his head as he waved goodbye. As Nathanael rode out of town, he saw a group of men walk into a building; thinking nothing of it, he continued his journey. But little did he know that this would be the same group of men who later boarded British ships and dumped tea into the harbor. What is today known as the Boston Tea Party.

Later that week, Nathanael walked into the Quaker meeting hall for what he thought was just a regular meeting. However, a man stood up and began to speak, "Fine people of Coventry, we have in our midst one who has shown acts of violence attending military parades."

Another added, "And this same man sued a British officer and used marshal terms in correspondence. We feel it would be best if this person is dismissed from our fellowship."

With those words, it was immediately decided that man, Nathanael, was to leave immediately, but although rejected, he was not defeated. His heart was in conflict, but he resolved, "I am determined to defend my rights and maintain my freedom or sell my life in the attempt."

Things again began to change for Nathanael. He married Catharine Littlefield, who remarkably shared his political and military interests. Then he helped establish the Kentish Guard. They hired a British deserter to regularly train the guard. Greene, despite his limp from childhood, served faithfully as a private.

The call for action came swiftly. Like Paul Revere's amazing ride to warn of the British arrival from that beautiful old North Church, a messenger arrived with the news.

"The British have attacked Lexington and Concord! To arms, to arms!! The British have attacked Lexington and Concord!"

News spread quickly; the Kentish Guard immediately began to march towards the action. A messenger stopped them at the border of Rhode Island and advised them they were to halt and not continue into battle. However, Nathanael Greene and three other men thought otherwise. Mounting horses, they rode toward the action; they were ready to fight.

NATHANAEL GREENE: HOW DID I GET INVOLVED IN THE AMERICAN REVOLUTION?

*A*s Greene and the men thundered down the path, a rider came into view with news that the British had returned to Boston. Upon hearing this, Greene decided that the only option was to turn back. The men were all disappointed as they headed home. Greene could not have known that soon enough he would meet the British on the frontlines of this unfolding war.

Back home a few days later, a postage rider rode up to his home with a letter. Nathanael noticed it was from the Rhode Island Delegation. He broke the wax seal and pulled the letter out of the envelope to discover his latest appointment. *Wait, how is it possible that a man, raised as a Quaker and with a limp that kept him from an officer position in his own militia, is now the Major General of fifteen hundred men?* Nathanael marveled, shaking his head in grateful disbelief.

A few weeks later, after making the proper arrangements, Greene arrived in camp and reported to Lt. Col. Artemis Ward, who assigned him to Roxbury on the right wing of the sieging army. Greene was heading towards the mansion he had selected as camp for his men, previously owned by one-time governor of the Massachusetts colony. A large pond in front of the property provided a barrier for any frontal attacks, and the hill in the rear served as a good place to

"

observe the enemy, as well as a path to retreat. Greene knew that important military strategy always allowed for a way out. He smiled as he remembered the lesson he learned as a child.

One night as he returned from dancing (forbidden by his Quaker faith so he did it secretly with the support of his brothers), he found his father in front of the house holding what appeared to be a bull-whip. With no route of escape, he padded the most likely area of attack and submitted to his fate.

Soon, this mansion lawn sprouted rows of tents, the steam house was converted into a store for gunpowder, and men were doing drills. But there was a problem; the different colonial militias were not in a hurry to cooperate with each other. To solve this troubling problem, Greene placed an officer from Massachusetts in charge of his men to build trust. He also appointed a chaplain he had first met in 1772, by the name of Reverend Murray. Greene also knew that to win the war, he would need the support of all colonies and local colonists, so he implemented hygiene habits for his men and taught them to care for their weapons by washing their muskets with hot water. On one such trip to get water, one of the men unknowingly scooped up a turtle and brought it back to camp.

25 May 1775

Greene received word from a young private that British Generals Howe, Burgoyne, and Clinton had arrived aboard the *HMS Cerberus*. Greene knew these were three of Britain's best generals and they were ready for a fight. For the next few weeks, Greene spent a lot of time between political consultations in Rhode Island and military drills in Roxbury. During one of his visits to Rhode Island, he was able to visit his wife. The visit was short-lived when two days later, on June 3rd, a messenger arrived carrying the news of the Battle of Bunker Hill. He said goodbye to his wife, who was pregnant with their first child. He left promptly riding through the night; however, when he arrived, he found the battle was over. But applying his knowledge from reading on military sciences, he prepared his troops for a possible attack on Dorchester Heights. He promptly sent a letter to the Rhode Island Committee of Safety, asking that they send about *"two tons of powder and as much ball as you can spare."* For a brief time, the British did consider an attack on Dorchester Heights, but abandoned the idea.

25 June 1776

The Continental Congress decided to reorganize the group of colonial militias into an organized fighting force—The Continental Army—and placed George Washington as Commander-in-Chief. Eager to please the new Commander-in-Chief, Greene sent a detachment of troops with a letter of welcome. General Washington was pleased by the welcome and invited Greene to his headquarters at Longfellow House. Greene wondered what the two would have in common, since Washington was an aristocrat from Virginia, and he was a simple Quaker from Rhode Island.

"Your Excellency, it is a pleasure to meet you, sir," Greene offered with a bow of respect, his three-cornered hat in hand.

General Washington stood. "Mr. Greene, thank you for answering my invitation. I see you understand the essentials of the daily life in camp, and not just about glory in victory. How did you come to have an appreciation for such things?"

"Sir, although I have not had a formal education, I have studied many military science books over the years," Greene replied regretting his lack of schooling.

"I too missed receiving a traditional formal education, as my mother, who was widowed when I was but eleven years of age, did not have the funds to send me. But I am not willing to conform to the station which life and circumstances appointed me, so I studied and read great works of literature," replied Washington.

Greene immediately started to feel at ease, as he realized they had far more in common than he originally thought.

"Are you familiar with the play *Cato?*" Washington asked. "It is a great work and one of my most beloved pieces of literature which I possess, and I recommend it with the utmost respect and courtesy its author Joseph Addison."

"Yes, sir, I have heard remarkable things about it and its author," Greene responded.

Washington saw something in Greene, immense potential for a great general. Indeed, Greene and Washington would become close friends and great generals. Their conversation went on well into the night.

When Greene returned to his lodgings, he recounted the evening's events to his pet turtle, which he had rescued from the water his men used to clean their muskets. As he recounted the events, he realized a perfect name for the turtle. "I will call you George."

Immediately, the turtle swelled with pride, as he was named after someone Greene quite admired. *I shall have a lot to share with Hundley about this*, the turtle thought as he enjoyed the yummy snack Greene had given him.

"Well, little friend, I better go inspect the troops," Greene said as he headed out of the tent. While Greene was on his rounds, a squirrel came sliding into the tent excited beyond his normal self.

"Are you in here?" chattered Hundley, the squirrel. "Where are you? I've been searching forever! I simply must find my friend. Oh no, maybe they had turtle soup! I am beginning to worry! Oh, where are you?!!"

"Here I am! Oh, Hundley, remember that I'm a turtle. I can't possibly keep up with your hyper squirrel energy. I have something to tell you: my name is now George. My new caretaker's name is Greene, and he takes quite good care of me."

"Oh, but I don't think I can speak at turtle speed! I am so wound up, yes wound up. I am so happy to see you. So happy. Wait, did you say George?" Hundley stopped to take a quick breath. For the next thirty minutes, the friends talked about their adventures and how George had gotten his name.

July 1775

Washington arrived in Cambridge to discover undisciplined troops, took immediate action and appointed Greene as one of his Brigadier Generals. Not long after, Greene spotted a familiar face and could not believe his eyes…it was Henry Knox. His long-time friend and the person responsible for the majority of books in his collection. Greene called out, "Henry Knox, is that you?"

Knox immediately recognized Greene's voice, and as they approached each other he noticed that Greene wore the sash of a Brigadier General. The old friends laughed and talked about the surprising turn of events since they last had seen one another. Both men parted ways and headed back to their camp. When Greene returned to his tent, he found papers strung everywhere, acorns scattered across the floor, and a squirrel running out of his tent. He could have sworn his turtle was smiling as he scratched his head, wondering what just happened.

George Washington called together his best generals to consider a plan to attack the British in Boston. Washington felt they could take Boston with their force of twenty thousand, compared to the British eight thousand. Experienced generals, such as Lee, Gates, Thomas, Putnam, Heath, and Sullivan, felt a head-on attack would be foolish. Greene, lacking any battle experience, sat, and listened to those who stated their opinions, whether plainly or more hesitant. Wishing to please, not upset, Washington, Greene said that with enough troops they would be able to take Boston. It was decided not to move forward with a frontal assault, but rather they would dig in and wait the British out, thus marking the beginning of the Siege of Boston.

NATHANAEL GREENE: WHAT'S MY STORY IN 1776?

*O*n 31 December 1775, Greene paced in his tent, concerned that many of his men's enlistments would expire in a few short hours. He vented his frustration to his pet turtle, "Oh George, I may be down to seven hundred men come sunrise. What am I to do? They are free to return home on their own accord, and there is nothing more I can say that will change their minds." Greene sat down to pen his thoughts in a letter to his best friend Samuel Ward. Little did he know that the British would capture Sammy, Jr. during a disastrous midnight raid in Quebec.

1 January 1776

It was a new year and a new beginning. Although he had only seven hundred men under his command, Greene felt a sense of pride as Washington raised a new standard flag over the camp with a roaring thirteen-gun salute. It represented the new Continental Army uniting twenty-six regiments under one Commander-in-Chief, and Greene immediately took command of two regiments. Greene's thoughts immediately turned to his close friend Henry, and he wondered how Knox's mission was going.

In late 1776, on his generals' advice, Washington decided to go with Plan B to fortify Dorchester Heights, rather than engage in a frontal attack with the British. Knox left to retrieve the cannons from Fort Ticonderoga to blast the British out of Boston. Greene hoped they would return soon. While they waited, Washington's trusted generals plotted how to secure their position and ensure their success.

25 January 1776

Greene caught sight of a regiment entering the camp. Knox had arrived with his cannons, so he immediately set out in search of his friend.

"It's a pleasure to see you, my old friend," said Greene, "I see you fared well."

"The Lord willed our success. Had the weather not held out, we would not have succeeded," replied Knox.

"This is quite an accomplishment, and I applaud you for it," said Greene. "It reminds me of my last book on supply chain logistics that I bought from you in Boston before this endeavor."

"Ah yes, I knew you would appreciate supply chain logistics," Knox said smiling. "Thank you for your kindness. I must report to General Washington; see you soon, my friend."

February 1776

While addressing the health and morale of the troops with General Washington, Greene himself fell ill. His skin was like sapphire, he lost weight, and barely had enough energy to walk across the room. Upon hearing of her husband's ailment, his wife came bringing along their recently born son in hopes to cheer her husband and speed his recovery.

4 March 1776

Greene watched as the Continental Army moved into position

with troops and cannons at Dorchester Heights. Due to late winter storms, Howe called off his troops. The British left Boston under a white truce flag. By March 17, the report was *"victory, there's not a redcoat in the city."* Washington later visited Greene in his tent to assign him the command of Boston troops as he left for New York. Now alone in his tent, Greene shook his head as he fed his turtle.

"George, you know what this means? Paperwork, lots of it. Ugh, I hate paperwork."

Washington chuckled as he stood outside the tent and declared, "Don't we all?"

9 July 1776

Greene was happy to receive news of a much-needed morale boost for the troops—the reading of the newly written Declaration of Independence in New York. He dreamed of all the new possibilities and adventures as an independent and free country, remembering the words he had penned to Samuel Ward in January: *"Permit me then to recommend from the sincerity of my heart, ready at all times to bleed in my country's cause, a Declaration of Independence, and call upon the world and the Great God who governs it to witness the necessity, propriety, and rectitude thereof."*

Greene soon reunited with Washington in New York. On August 9, he relieved General Charles Lee from command of five regiments. Greene wasted no time in preparing defenses on Long Island. He chose the place for fortifications, and built the redoubts and entrenchments of Fort Putnam, east of Brooklyn Heights.

During this time, Washington, Greene, and Knox, accompanied by their wives, enjoyed social gatherings together at Richmond Hill. Knox and his wife did not appreciate Catharine's outgoing personality and boldness in speaking on military affairs. However, Martha Washington did not feel the same and was fascinated by her.

22 August 1776

Recently promoted Major General Greene was busy preparing his troops and reinforcements for the pending battle at Brooklyn. The British landed thirty thousand troops on the south beaches of Long Island and were preparing to attack. A few days later, Greene again battled with sickness, and Washington ordered him away from the battlefield to recover and replaced him with Maj Gen Putnam. Greene hated being away from his men and the action, but his thoughts remained with his troops. On Tuesday, August 27, the Battle of Long Island began. Lord Stirling led his men, outnumbered, to face the British in open field, a first for the Continental Army. The British strategy was to outflank Washington's forces and destroy them. The Patriots, however, were able to retreat to their fortifications. Greene worried for his men and Washington, knowing that if they were captured, it would be the end of the Revolution. On August 30, he received word that Washington had escaped across the East River in the cover of night. Greene thought to himself, *We fight, get beat, rise and fight again,*" a saying he would use many times in the future.

16 September 1776

Fully recovered, Greene returned to fight in the Battle of Harlem Heights. Greene was excited for his first engagement. The British Light Infantry, who thought they had the upper hand, pushed the regiment back through the wooded areas towards their fortification in Harlem Heights, in a hail of musket fire. But the British had overstepped their boundaries, and because they were too far from their main support, they had to turn back.

2 November 1776

Greene rejoined Washington and his troops at Harlem Heights, the two headed off by themselves on horseback to converse in private.

"I assure your Excellency that we can hold Fort Washington, and at the worst we have a path of retreat to Fort Lee."

"I trust your judgment," George Washington said. "I shall reinforce the fortification, and you should have roughly three thousand troops at your disposal."

"Thank you, your Excellency," Greene replied, and they rode on in silence.

That same night, William Demont, of the 5th Pennsylvania Regiment, was making his way through the woods, as Hundley tailed him through the trees. Unsure what this soldier was up to, Hundley suspected it was no good. Demont went into the camp of Earl Percy and spoke with the redcoats. Hundley's concern grew as Demont relayed the plans of defense of Fort Washington. *I must do something,* Hundley thought to himself as he scampered back, *I must get word to George of this deserter.*

"George, come on; quick, Greene needs to know," said Hundley after relaying at squirrel speed the events of the evening.

"I am just a turtle, I could never make it in time," said George. "But I've got to try."

16 November 1776

Howe chose to focus his attention on Fort Washington and began the assault. Based on Greene's earlier reassurance, there were no orders to evacuate, despite the British giving them the opportunity and time to do so. This would be a critical mistake and prove to be the costliest battle in the Revolution, with the loss of port stores, supplies at Fort Lee, and men taken prisoner.

Greene poured out his heart in a letter to Knox that night, *"I am mad, vexed, sick and sorry. This is the most terrible event; its consequences are justly to be dreaded."* When he finished his letter, a squirrel rushed in and disrupted his thoughts as his turtle came rolling to a stop at his feet. Greene puzzled about their arrival and chatter, wondering what they were trying to say. Both animals realized that by the defeated look on Greene's face, they were much too late with the news and knew they would need a better plan next time.

Delaware River, New Jersey, 25 December 1776

Enlistments would again expire on New Year's Eve, and morale was at an all-time low after their defeat. The weather was cold, ice was in the river, and a winter storm was brewing. Greene pondered the events of the past year. The night was not ideal for crossing the river, but it was a brilliant plan. After a long march, Trenton came into sight, and the army that the British thought was all but defeated, succeeded in destroying a major Hessian garrison and acquired critical supplies and regained both morale and momentum to fight again. To Greene, this would be a fresh start for the new year, one in which he hoped the icy tides had passed, and new beginnings and victories were around the bend.

PATRICK HENRY

by Edan MacNaughton

PATRICK HENRY: HOW DID THE AMERICAN REVOLUTION COME TO MY DOORSTEP?

Governor's Palace, Williamsburg, Virginia
31 December 1776

*I*t might be New Year's Eve…but what does the coming year hold? Patrick Henry thought to himself as he cleared some papers off his desk and sat down. *Or what did 1776 really hold, I wonder?* He picked up his feathered pen and began to write a letter:

This might be the hardest year a young nation has ever endured. Yet we are advised…no, we are called by the cause of righteousness and by Almighty God to not give up. The war has only begun! I would be remiss, reader, if I did not answer the question I was confronted with earlier: "How did the American Revolution come to my doorstep?"

I beseech you to listen for a few moments as I digress. While our America has only just become an independent nation a mere five months ago, the struggle to declare independence began over a decade prior. Back in 1765, I was a novice in the Virginia House of Burgesses, making a bold first impression when I rallied against the unjust Stamp Act by setting forth seven resolutions. Much to the chagrin of many, I set forth in essence a proposal that threw off any allegiance to Parliament and the British Crown. If history was asking the question, "who was among the first to advocate for rebellion against the Crown?" I would proudly raise my hand!

Patrick paused and chuckled to himself as he remembered the look of seething anger on many faces present that day. There were some, however, who were not opposed but rather agreed with him, such as young law student Thomas Jefferson, who stood in the doorway. *Ah, Jefferson, for as much as Providence has blessed me with a rallying voice, he has given you a rallying pen!"*

It was a daring move, a brazen move even, but I believed then what I believe now, that freedom is *always* worth fighting for. This was just the genesis of my own involvement in the cause and dream that is America. From that moment on, the theoretical storm only got more tumultuous, but so did patriotism and unity among our Virginia ranks. It would have seemed unthinkable to many (myself included) that eleven years later not only would the Colonies and the Crown be engaged in a desperate battle, but that I would find myself right amid that struggle. Many times, I was the lone voice that helped turn Virginia and America in the direction of liberty.

This year alone has seen me and other colleagues in places we never could have imagined. Two of my friends now serve our infant nation in significant ways; George Washington as its leading Commander-in-Chief, and Thomas Jefferson as one of its most important minds. Often, I have wondered to myself why I am not on that battlefield, alongside the others. Shouldn't I still be the commander of all Virginia forces? Wasn't it I who confronted Lord Dunmore about the gunpowder stealing incident by the British and obtained payment back? Or was it someone else who cried, "give me liberty or give me death?"

I apologize, dear reader, if I come across absorbed in self-pity when I should be celebrating where I am now. I am Patrick Henry, first elected Governor of Virginia.

Now let us move on to the next question you have asked me…

PATRICK HENRY: HOW DID I GET INVOLVED IN THE AMERICAN REVOLUTION?

Governor's Palace, Williamsburg, Virginia
31 December 1776

*P*atrick Henry got up from his desk and strolled over to his office window, turning his attention to the winter landscape. A snowflake landed on the glass for a brief second. *I wonder if God made each snowflake unique as a parallel to how we humans are all different in our own way. Different humans coming together as part of something bigger than themselves. Yes! That is a magnificent point to make as I resume penning my letter!* The 40-year-old governor hurried back to his desk, sat down, and picked up a letter he was writing earlier that day:

Providence has placed each and every one of us in the place of His choosing long ago. Each individual's calling is different and unique to them alone regardless of social status or occupation. Why is it then that many are found wallowing in regret and self-pity about their current state? The human mind and heart submit to the flesh. In contrast, our soul differentiates itself in submitting to its Maker alone, following the confession of one's belief in Him. The idea that different people find themselves in different places at varying levels is nothing new to the story of humanity. See the Biblical examples of an Old

Testament Joseph or David if you will, or the New Testament examples of Matthew and Paul if you need more proof. Even in more recent times, a person like William Shakespeare surpassed even the King of England in fame and renown. I believe God presides over the destiny of nations and raises up people of principle and action for such a time as this!

Henry paused to take a deep breath and shake out his hands. Suddenly a crash rang out. To his chagrin, he turned around to find his cat standing on a haphazard pile of books that just toppled over. "CATO! What have you done now, my silly cat?" He got down on one knee to assess the scene. "Oh, thank heavens, the noise was worse than the actual damage. I guess you did not mean any harm by it." He picked up *Plutarch's Parallel Lives*, on which the clumsy cat had been standing. An old, weathered note slipped out of the book. *"DEAR PATRICK, HAPPY CHRISTMAS! YOUR MOTHER AND I ARE SO PROUD OF THE DEEP DESIRE AND PASSION YOU HAVE FOR LEARNING. YOU SHOULD ENJOY THIS BOOK AND LEARNING ABOUT THE IMPORTANT CHARACTERS INSIDE. ALWAYS REMEMBER THAT YOU ARE LOVED AND ABLE. - FATHER"*

Henry held back tears as he found himself verklempt with emotion. He picked up the fallen stack of books and put them back on the shelf. *Hopefully, that is the first and final disturbance that I will encounter while writing today.* Patrick shook his head. *Amazing that my own cat reminds me of someone very important whom I should quote in this letter.* Cato the Younger, a Roman Senator in the time of Julius Caesar, once said, "Consider in silence whatever anyone says: speech both conceals and reveals the inner thoughts of man." *This could not be any truer in my own life.* He once more picked up his quill to write.

I neither know nor care what title history shall give me. I just speak my beliefs and let the words do the speaking for me. A good example took place earlier this year when I was elected to attend the 5th Virginia Convention. It was an honor that I did not take lightly. This convention was far different from any prior in that it was the first time I was not in the minority of those who sought independence, but part of an overwhelming majority! It was a welcome change.

Right away I was part of a coalition of delegates that presented two resolutions. The first resolve asked that the delegates from Virginia attending the Continental Congress in Philadelphia make a motion for independence. The second resolve proposed that we create a Declaration of Rights for our newly independent Virginia. So, what came of it, you might ask? Within two months Virginia had a new State Constitution, it did indeed adopt a Declaration of Rights (I was on the committee that helped draft it) and gave its delegates to the Continental Congress explicit instructions to declare independence. Now the proverbial ball of Revolution was in full motion! But who would govern Virginia under this new system? As I had previously mentioned, that would be yours truly, Patrick Henry, first elected Governor of Virginia, 29 June 1776.

I humbly accepted this post and since then have dedicated my every waking hour of every day to do the utmost good. Some days my job presents me with the opportunity to send aid to our troops out in the field by any means necessary. Usually that request gives me the difficult mission to secure money to do just that, while other times it shows itself on a lesser but still important scale, like when I gave some of my own coins to an orphan boy in town. He told me that Lord Dunmore's troops had killed only one American in the Battle of Great Bridge and that man was his father. His mother had sent him into town to find work but every place he approached for work ended up rejecting him for a variety of reasons. My heart broke for him when I heard his story but also burned as I considered the thought of the former Royal Governor of Virginia ordering his troops to attack the people he once was assigned to govern and protect! It is tyrannical!

As you see, my office as governor hits me head on with many challenges on both the local and national level. But I should not just sit here and act like I am the only one making sacrifices! My old friend (and fellow Virginian) George Washington who just a mere 15 years ago was enjoying retirement on his beautiful home of Mount Vernon, forsook the comfort and peace of home life and is now leading our patriots on the battlefield, who are big in heart, yet small in number, against the most powerful army in the world.

Henry paused momentarily and said a quick prayer for his friend. I pray daily that Providence will continually equip me with all the grace and wisdom I need to rightfully carry out this role. The time we live in is different than any other, in part because the challenges and problems of 1776 were different than any faced in earlier history. I imagine if life on Earth is still going in the year 2022, the problems people face then will be far different than those we face now. If 1776 was a play, the backdrop of its story would be: two continents and two countries an ocean apart in which one has just broken away from the other. Once they were a big, happy family, but now they find themselves torn apart by war. On the American side, this war means freedom, opportunity, and new beginnings. However, on the British side, it is to snuff out the flame of independence that arose and take back a nation that they believe is rightfully theirs.

I hope, my reader, that I have answered the second question with which you presented to me: "How did I get involved in the American Revolution?" Now I will move forward to the third and final question you asked.

PATRICK HENRY: WHAT'S MY STORY IN 1776?

GOVERNOR'S PALACE, WILLIAMSBURG, VIRGINIA

31 December 1776

*P*atrick Henry had just completed an important letter he'd worked on all afternoon. Night settled in over Williamsburg, Virginia, after a cold winter day. The middle-aged man momentarily paused to rub his eyes. When he started this letter, it was light out, now it was evening and he edited only by the light of a candle.

No, I think instead of saying "labeled an outlaw," I shall change it to "branded an outlaw" as it makes a clearer point. Ah, I need to find a stronger word for where I said, "dramatic play writing." How about "Biblical Irony?" It did not matter if he was writing a letter to his own cat Cato or even to King George himself, the fiery orator was obsessed with using the right words. *I shall look this over one last time before I join my family downstairs for dinner.*

The winds of change have strongly blown this year, moving everything in its midst. Thoughts, ideas, and feelings have been shaken. A sovereign republic has risen from within another. King George III himself has changed from offering peace and forgiveness to now seeking an all-out conquest of America and its people. Congress and the Colonies are no longer fighting over whether to send a plea for reconciliation but as to how to move forward in trying to win this war! Tides have turned, people have changed, spies have been caught on both sides, and yet the outcome of this conflict is still very much in doubt! Our Army began the war strong with its surprise victory in the siege of Boston. Excitement filled the colonies as our troops showed that the British are in fact beatable…if several things happen in your favor. In contrast, the British winning the battle of New York was a soul-crushing defeat. Not only were many brave patriots lost, an important city and area fell from our possession to the enemy. When the news was first heard here, I found myself as low emotionally as I had been in recent memory. Not since my late wife Sally passed had I been so full of grief and despair. All I can do at this point living here in Virginia is to pray for a victory to come swiftly.

Our infant nation faces the reality of living a short life if foreign assistance is not procured soon. I know our genius Dr. Benjamin Franklin is currently trying to secure aid in France, but what if he is unsuccessful? What if England catches wind of a possible treaty, threatens war with France, and the French withdraw their offer? We face so many questions yet lack clear answers. At times like this when there is a shortage of answers and an abundance of bad news it weighs heavily on my mind. So much so that I hear a voice in my head saying, *just give up!* This brings me to today as I write this very letter. When I awoke this morning, I could not help but feel discouraged about the future. Questions like, "What will 1777 hold?" and "How can we win a war while we still have no official allies?" permeated my mind as I got up out of bed. So, I decided to recap what this long, arduous, yet important year held for myself. Consider this letter an overview of important moments that involved myself in the story that was 1776.

I never had the slightest intention or inclination at the beginning of this year that I would become governor. In fact, after being branded an "outlaw" by Lord Dunmore last year I truly believed my part to play would be on the battlefield. Instead of leading Virginia's forces to victory in battle, fate has given that task to others. Being passed over for a job and stabbed in the back by people you have done your best to be agreeable with would hurt anyone, myself included. Many times, we cannot see over the hill of rejection to the pasture of prosperity because of our hurt. We--I must let go of what could have been and focus on my role today. I cannot help but laugh when I consider the thought that the same Governor's Palace where Lord Dunmore lived and declared me an outlaw is where I live today! It has a Biblical irony to it. Much like how in the Old Testament book of Esther, Haman and Mordecai reversed roles in such a grand way that you are left to believe that the hand of God engaged in saving His people. I hope and pray that the same God sees the righteousness of our cause, *freedom's cause,* and grants us favor. If America is to survive this war and truly become a land of the free, divine intervention on many occasions shall be necessary.

The story of how I became acquainted with my own cat is nothing short of a miracle itself. On the 20th of April in 1775, the infamous Dunmore ordered British troops to "remove" or should I say steal gunpowder from the magazine in Williamsburg. I had not yet heard of this atrocity by the 22nd, as I lived in Hanover County back then. I was walking into town when all of a sudden, a brown furred and green-eyed cat ran directly towards me carrying something clutched in its mouth. It stopped mere feet from me and dropped what it had in its mouth—a newspaper! The paper was full of information and details about the Gunpowder incident. Before I went on into town to find out more about this event, I felt guilty not finding a way to repay the cat for what it did. So, I went to the first place I could find that sold fish and bought him a treat. I thought that would be the last I saw of him, but sure enough when I exited the establishment I dined at, there he was waiting for me. I decided to keep him as he had already decided on keeping me! I chose to name him Cato after the Roman Senator who boldly spoke out about Julius Caesar's tyrannical behavior. Patrick shook his head to himself as he recounted the story. *That cat could not have known what it was doing, could it? Oh, have I been writing for so many hours that my mind wants me to believe A CAT knew who I was and that I needed to hear about the theft of our gunpowder? I really must finish this letter soon or else I will begin to believe that pigs can fly!*

Now I will move to the concluding portion of this letter by answering the question, "What is my story in 1776?" In my own honest words, my story this year is a story of courage. My story is a story of perseverance. It is a story of sticking with it when the going gets tough. Patrick Henry's story in 1776 is one of patriotism, suffering, and belief. When you have a dream, as I do of a free and independent America, you must overcome the inevitable obstacles that are sure to follow. Speaking of obstacles and overcoming them, this last summer proved to be a notable example of just that. I unfortunately contracted the dastardly disease malaria in early July. I fell horribly ill just as I was being sworn in as governor and our country was celebrating the passing of the Declaration of Independence. This was not exactly what one would think is going to happen at such a big moment in time! I had two choices before me; would I lay in bed trying to recover while pouting like a young child? Or would I choose to accept that which I cannot understand—the timing of Providence and His sovereign grace? Just as I have persevered and overcome obstacles and difficulties my entire life, I eventually recovered from the bout with that horrible disease. *Thanks be to God Almighty for that!*

Patrick glanced at his pocket watch. *Oh my! It is already a quarter past eight! Let me just add a couple closing notes before I head downstairs to join my family in celebration.*

At the start of this somewhat lengthy letter, I set out to answer the three questions you presented me with this morning: How did the Revolution come to me? How did I get involved in it? What is my story in 1776?

I hope I have done just that.

I pray this letter reminds you of how far you have come in this year alone. Also, I hope that in reading it you have a renewed hope for the coming year. The struggle America is facing weighs heavily on people who have fought so much for its Independence. I know that this is the case for you. God bless you, Patrick Henry. Never stop fighting for freedom!

Huzzah! It is finally complete. Now I shall sign it.

To: An important reader

From: Patrick Henry

"Father, are you coming? There's apple pie for dessert!" cried his daughter, Sarah.

"Yes, I am!" Henry replied in a joyous tone walking down the stairs. "I just completed the letter I told you about this morning."

"That's wonderful to hear! To whom were you writing?" Sarah asked.

"It was to a certain person who was feeling discouraged and who needed reminding of just how valuable they really are." Patrick answered with a smile.

"You will have to read it to me some time," Sarah said.

"Yes, tomorrow I shall. I do not think there is a better way to start the new year!" Henry remarked.

Fireworks began in the distance. HAPPY NEW YEAR!

THOMAS JEFFERSON

by Elliott Lay

THOMAS JEFFERSON: HOW DID THE AMERICAN REVOLUTION COME TO MY DOORSTEP?

MONTICELLO, CHARLOTTESVILLE, VIRGINIA

28 December 1773

Thomas Jefferson sighed and lifted his pen once more. Just one more letter, and then he would allow his aching body the comfort of sleep.

It had been a busy day, as always. He'd prepared for a court case concerning a plantation owner who had invoked the law about an escaped slave and taken the case to court. Thomas had taken up the case for the defendant, who the plantation owner had accused of running away. As a result, he'd had to take nearly the whole day to prepare for the court session the next day.

In addition to that exhausting task, he and his wife, Martha Wayles Skelton Jefferson, were deep in debt. Martha's father, John Wayles, had died recently, and he had entrusted his belongings to Thomas and Martha. Along with the blessing of many extra slaves came a curse: the task of repaying his many debts. Unfortunately, Thomas had to figure out how to repay the excessive sum that his late father-in-law owed to several lenders. He was slowly gaining headway, but the sluggish, gradual progress was tiring him out.

Jefferson picked up his quill, and by the candlelight of his small study, composed a letter to his good friend, William Fleming.

28 December 1773

Dear Fleming,

Greetings, my good sir! How is the plantation? I trust you are doing well. I will try not to tarry, for it is late as of the time of writing, and I am tired.

You ought to have heard this already, but news reached me of a "tea party" up in Boston, Massachusetts. It seems as if the colonists up there want rebellion and war! Apparently, they raided three of the British ships docked at Boston Harbor. Reports state they took all the tea and tossed it overboard. All that tea was worth nearly £10,000! Parliament is not going to be happy. I would not want to be one of those colonists when the British retaliate. They are in for some serious trouble.

I suppose I should be angry at the rebels, but I am not. I do not fully understand why they did it, but I do not feel the anger and outrage that I feel I should. Disloyalty to George III is punishable by death. Yet...I am imagining myself in those Bostonians' places, and...I do not think I would be afraid of the British King, or what he could do to us. Perhaps I might take part in this revolution of theirs. Or perhaps not. It is treason, after all. I do not know what I think about this situation—I do not know what side I will choose. I do not know which is in the right, and which is in the wrong. For lack of a better word, I am confused.

What do you think about all this, William? Are you on the side of the colonists, or the throne? Or are you undecided, like me? I think that I must see the views of others; I need to see their reasoning in order to decide.

It is late. Farewell, William Fleming. I hope to find a letter from you soon.

Your Humble Servant,
Thomas Jefferson

P.S. Once you find this letter and have read it to your discretionary satisfaction, please destroy it. It would not do to have one of the King's men finding this.

Thomas folded up the parchment and set his pen down. He would have one of his trusted servants make the trek to William Fleming's house the next day. He rose from his chair wearily. Standing was yet another action standing between him and rest. He moved around the room, blowing out each candle. When the room was dark, he exited and finally stepped into the bedroom.

"Thomas!" called his wife. "Have you seen this?"

"Yes, dear? What's happened?" Thomas asked, groaning inwardly. Life still wouldn't allow his aching bones just a small break. He trudged out of the bedroom and toward his wife's voice.

She was sitting in the dining room, reading a newspaper. "One of our slaves brought this in. Look at this!" She pointed to an article about the Boston Tea Party.

Of course, Thomas already knew about this. He replied, "Yes, I know. One of my associates from the court of law told me about the event."

"This says that the colonists up in Boston stormed three of the King's ships and threw all the tea overboard! I tell you, Thomas, the King's going to be furious when he hears about this."

"Yes, I know," Thomas interjected. That was exactly what he'd written to William Fleming just a few minutes earlier.

"Well, Thomas, I can't say I feel sorry for the King and his tea. He's been taxing us excessively, and I heard he's forcing the people up north to house soldiers against their will. Serves him right, I think. I hope this will send him a message that we aren't to be messed with like that."

That was exactly what Thomas had written to William Fleming.

"Dear, that is a very dangerous thing to say," Thomas told her quietly. "George III would consider that treason, and I would wager most of our slaves would sell their loyalty to the British for their freedom."

"I know," Martha replied, keeping her voice down. "Listen, I hope the colonists will do more of what those Bostonians did. I think we need to put an end to this oppression."

Thomas just stared, his eyes going out of focus.

"I'm tired," he announced. "I'm going to bed." He stood dizzily, not comprehending what had just happened. Martha gave him a whole new perspective on things…along with a strange look at this. Ignoring it, he stumbled into the bedroom and sat unsteadily on the bed.

Oppression, he thought, flopping onto his back, and staring up at the ceiling. *We are being oppressed.*

Thomas Jefferson, with this new revelation in mind, lay in bed, thinking of one thing and one thing only. *The King is oppressing us. This is tyranny. This is…*

And as he drifted off to sleep, he was no longer undecided.

Thomas Jefferson had made up his mind.

Meanwhile, staring through the window, a pair of glinting eyes stared at the sleeping figure in bed in such a way that it seemed as if it knew what had just happened in the sleeper's head.

Suddenly, a cloud blotted out the moon, and once it passed, the eyes disappeared into the night.

THOMAS JEFFERSON: HOW DID I GET INVOLVED IN THE AMERICAN REVOLUTION?

PHILADELPHIA, PENNSYLVANIA

11 June 1776

It was a bright and sunny day when Jefferson awoke. Just under two and a half years had passed since that day in 1773 when he had chosen to align with the American Patriots.

Now, the conflicts had escalated, with Britain passing even more restrictive acts such as the Intolerable Acts. Over this, the colonies had rebelled, and shots had already been fired in the Battles of Lexington and Concord. Ultimately, the Patriots had driven the British out and retained their stash of gunpowder at Concord. However, this was sure to instigate retaliation.

Thomas Jefferson was sure that war was on its way.

He got up and executed his morning routine: eat breakfast, get dressed, and prepare anything that needed to be ready for the early morning.

Once that was complete, Thomas decided that he would get to work on his next project.

But when he sat down at his desk to write, he found that he couldn't think of anything to add to his current draft.

I don't know what to write, he grumbled silently.

Thomas sat there at his desk, waiting for an idea to come to him.

An hour passed. Then two, three, and finally it was time for the midday meal.

Thomas sighed and got up from his chair.

There was a knock on his door. Slightly confused, Thomas hurried to open it. He expected some slave or message carrier but standing there was John Adams.

"Greetings, Mr. Jefferson!" Adams cried. "How are you today?"

Thomas quickly got over his surprise and replied, "I am well, thank you. And you?"

"Just fine, just fine," John said cheerily. "I've been sent by the Continental Congress to deliver a petition to you. But first, let us go and get some food. I'm starving."

WOOF! WOOF! By John's side was a large terrier. His golden fur gleamed in the sunlight as he jumped on Thomas, nearly knocking him over. Thomas stumbled back, trying to remain standing while petting the dog.

"Ah, that's just Duke," John laughed, obviously amused at Thomas' clumsiness with the big dog. Thomas fell onto his front porch as Duke licked his face. The dog's tongue was rough on his skin, like moist sandpaper. His black nose sniffed at Thomas' hat, and his glinting eyes observed the figure of the person lying on the ground.

"Down, Duke!" John Adams ordered. Reluctantly, the dog turned and allowed Thomas to rise.

"He must like you," John grinned as Thomas smoothed down his coat. "Never done that to anyone before. He's usually very well-behaved. Sorry about that." But the look in his eyes made it seem as if the spectacle was well worth sacrificing his friend's dignity.

"Ah, not a problem," Thomas replied, flicking dirt off his sleeve. "Now, back to the subject of lunch. Where would you like to go?"

After some discussion, disagreement, and compromise, they decided to go to a fancy winery for sandwiches and a bit of "strong drink," as they called it. Duke gleefully nipped at Thomas' heels as he followed the chattering humans.

The church bells tolled, proclaiming the noon hour to anyone who could hear it as Thomas Jefferson, John Adams, and Duke were seated.

"So, John, what brings you over to my humble dwellings this fine day?" Thomas asked, fondling Duke's ears.

"Would you like the short version, or the long version?" Adams replied.

"Well, I suppose we have time for the long version," Thomas answered.

"Very well!" Adams began. "Well, you know the Continental Congress is debating about declaring independence from England. But what you don't know is that we've got a committee just to write up the document that officially does the declaring. Right now, it's Roger Sherman from Connecticut, Ben Franklin of Pennsylvania, Robert Livingston of New York, and me from Massachusetts. We were discussing writing the Declaration when Franklin brought up this point.

"He said, 'Who's going to write it?' None of us wanted to, of course.

"And then Franklin said 'Neither am I.' So now we have this problem that none of us want to write it or think we're good enough to write it—"

"So, the committee wants me to think of someone to write it?" Thomas interrupted. "I could name a few people. Get Patrick Henry to do it. His speeches are mind-blowing. Just get him to transfer one into words and—"

"No, Thomas, Patrick Henry's good at fiery speeches to convince the crowd. We don't need that for the Declaration. We need a good reasoner, someone who will convey our reasons for separating from England calmly and clearly. We need someone—"

"Excuse me," someone interrupted apologetically. It was a young waiter, probably a trainee. "Are you gentlemen ready to order?"

"Ah, yes," Thomas replied. "I'll get the, uh... the..."

"Well, I'll have some beef ribs and... the deluxe fruit platter," John cut in while Thomas scoured the menu.

"I'll just take the pork chops and cornbread," Thomas replied.

"Very well," the waiter mumbled. "Any drinks?"

"Beer for me," John said.

"Just water," Thomas replied.

"Very good. I have beef ribs, the deluxe fruit platter, pork chops, cornbread, beer, and Just Water."

"Yes," John confirmed. "Thank you."

"Of course." The waiter scurried away with the piece of paper.

"Wait. Did he say, 'Just Water?'" Thomas asked.

"Yes," Adams laughed. "It's here on the menu. 'Just Water.' A fine combination of whiskey, water, lemon juice, salt, and sugar."

"That sounds utterly disgusting," Thomas grumbled. "Who calls anything 'Just Water?'"

"Anyway," John changed the subject. "The committee decided that you should write the Declaration of Independence. What do you say, Jefferson? Will you commit to this great service to the colonies?"

Stunned, Jefferson didn't reply. Thoughts were whizzing through his head. *Me? Writing the most important document to exist for our colonies? Like the Virginian Constitution, but this is...this is...I don't know."*

Seeing the look on Thomas' face, John chuckled. "I'll give you some time to think about it."

Thomas took the whole meal to think. They ate in silence, Adams waiting, Jefferson contemplating.

The meal was finished. It was time to leave.

"I have to go," John announced to Thomas. "Write me and tell me your answer."

"All right," Thomas replied, and the two men stood.

As they parted ways, Thomas suddenly knew his answer.

"Adams!" he called. "I'll do it!"

He heard nothing for a few seconds, then John called back, "Good! Thank you for serving your country."

That was followed by a bark. Jefferson caught the glint of an eye as John and Duke disappeared from sight.

THOMAS JEFFERSON: WHAT'S MY STORY IN 1776?

PHILADELPHIA, PENNSYLVANIA

12 June 1776

Thomas Jefferson sat down at his desk. It was time to begin drafting the Declaration of Independence.

Once again, he didn't know what to write. *We officially declare independence from Britain?* No. *It is time for the colonies to become their own country?* That didn't seem right.

Thomas groaned. He stood and stepped outside.

The sun was shining, proclaiming its glory over the gleaming dew-touched grass. Thomas Jefferson gazed at his garden, wishing he could be there, tending his plants, rather than trying to write up an important document.

He decided to take a walk.

As he passed through the streets of Philadelphia, he saw colonists everywhere waiting anxiously for news of anything. Anything about the war—about their family, or about whether the King was coming to punish them all.

Or whether the King was defeated.

Thomas next saw a servant—a paid servant, by the looks of his clothing—being beaten by his master.

That's just like us, he thought. *The colonies, being beaten by Great Britain.*

He watched as the servant stood and shouted back, "I will not stand for this! I quit!"

Thomas stared as the servant turned on his heel and strode away.

Thomas Jefferson had his idea. He hurried back to his desk and began to write.

When in the course of human events, it becomes necessary to...

Philadelphia, Pennsylvania, 13 June 1776

The next morning, Thomas Jefferson sat down once more to finish his draft of the Declaration of Independence.

Now that he had begun, ideas were flowing like a rushing river, and he couldn't write fast enough to put them all down on the page.

Thomas was so engrossed in his writing that he didn't see the glinting eyes glaring at him through his window.

Suddenly, there was a snarl, and Thomas Jefferson looked up to see Duke, John Adams' dog, smashing through his window and diving for the paper.

Instinctively, Jefferson snatched it away. Duke roared, clawing at his leg. Pain seared Thomas' ankle as Duke clamped his jaws down on it.

Kicking, Thomas freed himself and ran, clutching his draft in his hand.

"Jefferson, stop." The voice came from behind. Thomas turned, shocked, to see that the sound had come from Duke.

"What? You can talk? How?"

"Give me the draft," Duke hissed.

"What—no! I just spent a day—" Thomas protested.

"Give me the draft!" Duke roared again, lunging at Thomas. "The Deceiver wants the draft! Give it!"

"Who's the Deceiver?" Thomas yelled back, beginning to run.

"It does not matter. Give the draft!"

"This is for the American cause!"

"The American cause is doomed!" snarled the big dog. "Give the draft!"

Thomas ran for the door, but in his haste dropped the precious piece of paper. Duke barked in triumph and seized it in his jaws.

"No!" Thomas screamed. He slammed his foot down on one of Duke's paws, and the dog howled in pain. With his three free claws, he tore at Jefferson's leg, ripping his breeches and slicing into the flesh.

Thomas yelped as Duke set down the draft and bit into his leg. Thomas seized the opportunity, kicking the dog and swiping the piece of paper. He kicked the door open and ran outside. The pain in his leg felt like three Dukes still had their teeth sunk in.

Thomas ran. Stumbling a little, he darted away from Duke.

"Help!" he shouted. "Keep this dog in check!"

No one looked up.

"No one can help you now," Duke chuckled.

"What did you do?" Jefferson demanded, panting from the effort of running so far.

"Oh, just a little deception to their eyes," Duke said. With a roar, he redoubled his efforts to catch Thomas.

Thomas continued running, desperately trying to put space between him and the murderous dog.

"Help!" he screamed.

"Oh, stop it," Duke snapped disdainfully. "No one can hear you. The Deceiver is with me, and there is no one with you."

Thomas needed a way to stop Duke once and for all. His strength running low, he pivoted and ran back to his home, slamming the door in Duke's face. The impediment slowed the dog down just long enough for Thomas to exit the house and enter the back garden, where his favorite mockingbird was caged.

The mockingbird, who had accompanied Thomas, chirped happily at its master's arrival.

"Hello there," Thomas whispered hurriedly, fumbling to unlock the cage. "Remember how you like poking things? Go poke that dog over there."

The mockingbird flew from its cage and gleefully began biting and stabbing Duke.

"Stop the bird!" Duke shouted to Thomas, writhing on the ground. "Or I will destroy this." He lifted one paw to reveal Thomas' draft of the Declaration of Independence, which he had dropped in his haste to get outside.

Thomas groaned. "Stop."

The mockingbird, confused, looked up and stopped pecking at Duke.

"Now, Jefferson, I'm afraid that I will have no choice but to kill you as well as the draft. After all, what's to stop you from simply writing another draft?"

"Well…," Thomas stalled, "maybe…"

"Maybe nothing. Any last words?" the dog growled. "I'll make sure to send them to the Deceiver."

"Last words? Maybe, instead of last words, a last movement?" Thomas motioned to the mockingbird, which promptly began screeching in a loud and annoying song. With another motion, the mockingbird elegantly glided down and sang its song directly into Duke's ear, who began swiping at the bird, dropping the draft.

Thomas snatched it up triumphantly.

"NO!" Duke roared, lunging at Thomas. He stumbled back and fell. Duke overshot him and smashed his head into the ground. He quickly scrambled back onto his four paws and charged Thomas once more.

Thomas fled, with Duke pursuing him, and the mockingbird pursuing Duke. Thomas ran and grabbed the gardening shovel. Clutching it tight, he swung it at the dog, and the real battle began.

Quincy, Massachusetts, 10 July 1776

Thomas Jefferson and John Adams stood at the cemetery of the United First Parish Church in Quincy, Massachusetts, digging a grave.

Thomas set down his shovel and wiped his forehead. "That should be deep enough."

"Yes," Adams said solemnly. "Farewell, Duke. You were a good dog."

"Up until the point when he tried to kill me," Thomas pointed out. Then, seeing John's face and remembering that this was supposed to be a solemn burial, added, "To you, I mean, uh, not that he tried to kill you or anything and—"

He made himself stop talking, because in his arms was his dead mockingbird, killed on that fateful day.

"Farewell, Joseph," Thomas whispered. "You saved my life. I am forever indebted to you."

Slowly, solemnly, the two men lowered their dead pets into the grave. A tear threatened to slip from Thomas' eye as he gazed at his mockingbird.

They sluggishly replaced the dirt, neither wanting to lose his animal. Finally, there was only one open space where Joseph the mockingbird's head was visible.

"Goodbye," Thomas whispered, and the tear finally slipped free.

Joseph's eyes, though lifeless, seemed to be whispering "goodbye" right back to Thomas.

Then he replaced the dirt and saw the eyes no more.

On the animals' tombstone was inscribed:

Duke and Joseph
Died in battle, loyal to their masters until the end.
War takes from us all.

HENRY KNOX

by Emmanuel Morisset

HENRY KNOX: HOW DID THE AMERICAN REVOLUTION COME TO MY DOORSTEP?

*O*nce upon a colonial time, William and Mary Knox were in the hospital. Mary Knox was having a baby. One hour later, a little baby was on Mary's lap, sleeping soundly. Mary said in her heart, "I am sure many people will remember the day that this child was born, July 25, 1750, because…I know that this child will do something great for America. I will name him Henry Knox."

"Wake up, wake up, Henry. It's nearly time to go to school," said Mary Knox.

"Yes, mother," said nine-year-old Henry Knox. He prayed with his mother, he washed his face in the basin, he brushed his hair, put salt on his teeth, and made his bed. After that he put on a brown shirt, a nicely made coat and waistcoat, breeches, and a pair of shoes.

Then, when he finished his breakfast, he said goodbye to his parents, and he was ready to go to school. As he got on the horse, for some shocking reason, it talked. "Can't you just walk to school?! I mean for once! I never get a break and I need a—"

"How can you talk?" interrupted Henry, shocked.

"Because I—" the horse stopped. He realized that he let the cat out of the bag. He might as well answer the question. "Well, ever since I was a foal, it's been that way," said the horse. "By the way, my name is Rusty," said Rusty.

"May I please ride on your back? I do not want to be late for school. And may we be friends?" said Henry.

"We can be friends and you can ride on my back, as long as you promise not to tell your parents," whispered Rusty.

"Deal," whispered Henry. Henry finally went on the horse, and Rusty galloped off.

When the two friends reached the school, Henry got off the saddle, walked Rusty over to where there was a lot of grass, and whispered, "Stay put and wait till I come back, okay Rusty?"

"Okay Henry. See you later," said Rusty.

"Bye," replied Henry. So, Henry went to the front of the school, where he found a chair and sat on it. He watched as the sun was slowly rising over the horizon. It was a one-room schoolhouse. Inside the schoolhouse, were twenty wooden desks, a big, wooden table, a big chair, a brick fireplace, and a black board. Finally, the bell rang. Since the school students are supposed to be sorted by age group, and because he was the youngest child in the school, he got to go in front of the line.

When all the children were seated, Mr. Alpine said, "Class stand." The pupils stood. "Fold your hands and let's pray."

Meanwhile, Rusty was bored. He sat there, thinking. *Hm…What should I do…? Maybe I can go for a run! No, I can't disobey my new best friend. Come on, it's just a little trot—no! Henry said stay put until he comes back, then we can go back home.* After thirty minutes of arguing with himself, Rusty decided that he will stay put until Henry came back.

Then the bell rang, and it was recess time. Normal recess time is about thirty minutes. Well, this recess time is two hours. You might be wondering why is it two hours? It's because the teacher had to go to his home to do something really important, so he left the kids under the two school supervisors. Henry went out of the building to take three carrots, an apple, a bag full of oats, a stool, and a large dog food pail. He came over to where Rusty has been waiting and came to him.

Rusty shot and said, "Finally you're here! What took you so long?!"

"We had to learn 1 hour of Latin lessons, so it is not my fault," said Henry. *"Bon appetit,* Rusty. Enjoy," said Henry. Henry put all the food in the large dog food pail and put it on the stool.

Rusty hastily ate all the food. He was so famished that he nearly ate the large pail. "May we go for a run? While you were in class, I felt bored. Please," Rusty pleaded. "You can go on my back if you want. I really want to move," Rusty reasoned.

"Okay, but I will have to ask the school supervisors, because I do not want to be expelled," said Henry. Henry went to the school supervisors if he can ride his horse. Fortunately for Rusty, they said yes. So, for the next hour, the friends had a nice, good run. While Henry rode on Rusty, Henry took the opportunity for Rusty to learn Latin. With thirty minutes left, they spent their time...napping. They nearly fell asleep for twenty minutes!

Just then, a deer, two carnivals, and a big bear came, running. "Hello, mates. How are you doing? Can we be friends?" said the deer. Now, if you were wondering why nineteen children screamed (except Henry and Rusty) and two adults screamed, there are two reasons: reason one is that it is unexpected to see a bear, deer, and two birds "going" to school. Reason two is that they have never heard a deer talk. You can also be laughing to see two grown-ups running towards the building. Unfortunately for the two men, they forgot that the door was closed, and by the end of the day, they ended up in the hospital.

As for the rest of the people, (again, except for Henry and Rusty) they opened the door, they all came in, and they shut the door. Sad, the animals turned to leave.

But Henry said, "Wait! We can be your friends!"

All the animals turned around. "Really?" they said excitedly.

"Yes! Allow me to introduce myself, my name is Henry."

"My name is Rusty," said Rusty.

"Allow us to introduce ourselves, my name is Mary; the bear's name is Elijah; and the two birds' names are Esther and Mark."

"Hello Mary, Elijah, Esther, and Mark," said Henry and Rusty. The six friends all gave each other some hugs, which resulted in a group hug. Then the bell rang. It was time to go home.

"Well, bye," said Henry.

"Wait-what! You are leaving already?!" said Elijah.

"Yes, we have to leave. But let us do this; how about we figure out a plan, in order for us to live together!" said Rusty.

"Good idea, Rusty," they all shouted.

"Any ideas?" questioned Rusty.

As the years progressed, Henry soon found out that his father, William Knox, died. Unfortunately, as if that death did not cause trouble, they were tight on financial circumstances. When Henry found out about those two predicaments, he dropped out of school when he was nine years old, so he can work as a clerk in a bookshop and support his mother. The bookshop owner's name was Nicholas Bowes. Nicholas Bowes became the close friend of Henry, in fact so close that he was a surrogate father to him; he even let Henry take a look on the shelves and have any of the volumes of his bookshop to read and take home. When he was twenty-one, he opened a bookshop named the London Bookstore. Henry Knox's bookstore was a huge success. The London Bookstore does not just sell books, it sells magazines, tea, wallpaper, and even patent medicine!

One day, someone familiar went to the store. Henry thought, *Who is this man? I think he— wait that is my friend, Nathanael Greene!*

Now, when a man with a sore throat that is in shape runs to another man that is ten feet away, he can reach him in three minutes. Well, Henry Knox liked to eat, and he coughed a lot. So, every time he tried to call out, "Please wait!" he coughed. Then there was an eaten banana on the floor! You might think, what is so tense about a plain, old banana? Well, not only did he slip, but he landed on a yummy apple pie a man dropped a minute ago. *I was so close!* he thought. *Well, at least the pie tasted good. The man who made the pie could make some improvements, though.* He tasted the pie again. *Yummy! But it needs a little bit of sugar, vanilla icing, strawberries on the side, and a cherry on top. Maybe—*

Just then, an old man with a hat interrupted his thoughts. "Excuse me sir, do you know where my hat went?"

"Your hat is on your head," Henry replied.

"No, not my hair, my hat."

"Yes, it is on your head. Touch the top of your head."

He did. Then he took his brown hat off of his head. "No, this is my yellow hat. I am searching for my brown hat."

"Sir, this hat is a brown hat."

"Then it must be halitosis! I am so sorry, sir," the old man apologized. The old man left.

I wonder what halitosis means, Henry thought. Then he got on his feet and went to the hospital. He was very hurt, and he felt like he would collapse. When he went in a room, he saw two men talking.

Do you remember the two men who bumped their heads on the door and ended up in the hospital? When they saw Henry, one of them, whose name was Bob, said, "Hello, Henry! Do you remember us?"

Henry stared at them for a moment, and he asked, "Are you the gentlemen who hit their heads on the door?"

"Yes! How did you end up in the hospital?" asked Daniel, the other man.

Before Henry could answer, he remembered his bookshop. He canceled the appointment, said bye to Bob and Daniel, and he went to the bookshop. When he entered the bookshop, he saw what he thought was the world's most beautiful lady. Her name was Lucy Flucker.

When Lucy Flucker asked her parents to let her marry Henry Knox, they said no. Why do you think they said no? Well, there were two reasons. The first one was that he was too fat—no, that is not true. The first reason was that he did not hold any high rank in military. The second reason was that he was a little poor. But Lucy disobeyed her parents and married Henry Knox anyway in the upstairs portion of the bookshop. Two hours later, a bear, two birds, and a deer went in the bookshop, and then ran upstairs.

The marriage ended an hour ago which is why Rusty asked, "Who is this lady?"

Henry replied, "This is my wife. Her name is Lucy Flucker Knox. By the way, how did you guys find us?"

"Well, we overheard your idea of starting a bookstore. But then there were family issues, and we couldn't follow but now, here we are!" Mary replied.

"Well, I have to go get back to business," Henry said. Henry Knox's bookstore was a profit. He even had John Adams in his bookshop. Then, after the events of Lexington and Concord, and Henry Knox abandoned his bookshop to looters so he could join the militia. When he sneaked out of Boston it was 1776, his wife, Lucy Flucker Knox had his sword sewn in her cape. The animals also came. When that happened, he was just twenty-five years old.

What plan will Henry Knox think of? What did he do?

Find out in the next chapter!

HENRY KNOX: HOW DID I GET INVOLVED IN THE AMERICAN REVOLUTION?

*D*o you remember when Henry Knox sneaked out of Boston? If you want to find out more about his life, just read this chapter. Now let's start this chapter.

After all of the friends sneaked out of Boston, they went to Worcester. Lucy, Henry's wife went to Connecticut where Henry built a little two-story house. He also built some rooms for his animal friends. They all go to bed.

Twenty-five-year-old Henry Knox sat on his comfy bed, stretching. After a good eleven hours of wonderful, deep sleep, Henry was full of energy. Then, Henry got up from bed, so he can do his usual morning tasks. He fixed his bed, brushed his teeth, put on his clothes for the house, and went outside to the kitchen. When he reached the kitchen, he smelled delicious, mouthwatering food, which was made by his wonderful wife, Lucy. The food she made was an egg, corn-bread, and some milk. When Lucy, Henry's daughter, woke up, she cried like the baby she is as usual. When all of them were seated, Henry blessed the Lord for providing such a wonderful meal. After the prayer, they hastily ate all the food because they were famished. When they finished eating, Henry went back to his room. At that time, the British were prevailing in the revolutionary war.

Hmmmmmm...... I need a plan. I am going to go to the storage room to get a quill, ink, and some paper. That way, I can write my plan on paper! he thought. He quickly got up from his chair to go to the storage room. While on his way to the storage room, he passed by the kitchen where he saw a pile of dirty, wooden dishes from the morning's breakfast. He could still smell the delicious aroma from the scrambled eggs. Scrambled eggs are his favorite food to have. He knows that it's good for his health, and that gives another reason to love scrambled eggs! He finally reached the door to the storage room.

The door was closed, in order to protect the storage room's contents from being stolen by Indians. It was a very nice brown, wooden door. He reached for the golden doorknob. It was cold to the touch. When he tried to open the door, he forgot that it was locked. Henry walked back towards his room. When Henry reached his room, he removed the blanket that was on his bed, revealing a small, hidden key. The key was silver in color. He removed the key from its hidden place and replaced the blanket back to its place. Henry went back to the storage room with the silver key in his hand. He inserted the key in the keyhole, and he unlocked the door. Henry opened the door and found a quill, some ink, and three sheets of paper. Then he returned to his room with his supplies. When he sat on his desk, he put the writing utensils down on the desk.

"Okay, let's start!" he said. "Plan A: the British always go in a rectangular form, so ... *No, that is not a good plan,* he thought. "Oh, I have an idea!" he exclaimed. "How about I plan a secret code! But since I'm working on artillery, a code won't work. But maybe I can try this. The artillery plans the cannons. Step 1: Get twenty cannon balls, a cannon, two long ropes that are about thirty feet long, two trees, five pounds of dirt, sap, and two men. Step two: Find two steep hills that are next to each other. Step three: Go to the back of one of the hills and make a "door" on it. Step three: Go in the hill with... *No, I can figure out a better plan than just three pieces of paper, a quill—wait. I think I had a book on artillery plans somewhere. Hmmmmm............... Where did I place it again? I am sure it was in the room. Maybe it was under the bed* he said to himself. *No, it couldn't be Where could it be?* "I think I should search my room," he thought out loud.

After an hour of thoroughly searching the room, he KNEW it wasn't there. His next destination was downstairs. Meanwhile, Lucy was washing the dishes and she wanted to take a break. So, she quickly finished washing the dishes put them in their places and went upstairs to the guest room before mopping. She had an important book she was supposed to read, so she went to the library room and read the book. There she found the book she wanted, which is called Pilgrims Progress. While that was happening, Henry decided to look downstairs for the book of artillery plans.

While she was peacefully reading the book, he was desperately trying to find that book! *After three hours of working, I have finally found the book of plans for artillery! Now, I am going to go upstairs to see the information it contains! I think it would be easier if I had the whole series......... as a matter a fact, I think I do have the whole entire series! But I only retrieved book one.... and not book two and book three. I really need the whole—no, I do not think it will be necessary to have the whole series. Besides, the book is named, Some Excellent, Marvelous, And Wonderful Plans That Will Lead You To Success, No Matter What. So, whew! That was a long name! How did I remember that long name without—okay, I will just go up the stairs.*

He finally went up the stairs. When he reached the door to his room, he opened the door, went inside, shut the door, reached a desk with a chair, and started to "see its contents." Two hours later, he had read five hundred pages! You might be thinking, how is it possible for this man to read that much and not give up?! The answer is that Henry Knox was an avid reader. Ever since his youth, he loved to read. Another reason is that after he witnessed the Boston Massacre in 1770 and the acts of the Parliament, he was determined to get free from the British. Which is why he joined The Sons of Liberty in the Boston Tea Party in 1773. Now, let's get back to the present.

Again, after another two hours of reading, he read *1,000* pages! He finished the first book and wanted to read the other two, which he remembered that he put them under his bed. Each book had 1,000 pages, so this was not going to be easy. After eight hours of reading, he finished the two other books and decided to go to sleep.

What will happen?!

Some oxen running, some sleds screeching, and a war!

Find out in the next chapter!

HENRY KNOX: WHAT'S MY STORY IN 1776?

A very energized Henry Knox woke up from a much-needed sleep. After he finished his morning routine, he went outside. What did he smell? Freshly made pancakes, a sweet aroma of scrambled eggs, fried bacon, and last but not least, fresh milk to wash down the food. When all of the family members and friends were seated, Henry blessed the food. When he finished the prayer, they ate hastily. Now think about it. Imagine a lady cooking thirty pieces of bacon, twenty pancakes, and one gallon of milk to see it all gone in…five minutes!!

After breakfast, Henry went upstairs to his room so he could dress for battle. He needed to have a plan in order to help the American troops win. Later, Henry Knox set out for the Continental Army headquarters in Cambridge. He also took his friends along. It was winter. George Washington and his men need some artillery in order to force the British to evacuate Boston. Earlier, twenty thousand men went under the command of George Washington. Now let's go in the past.

Then, George Washington sends Henry Knox to get Fort Ticonderoga's artillery. He gets a group of men together, goes on Rusty, and the little group and all the "animal" friends leave. Henry remembers that Ethan Allen's Mountain Boys and Benedict Arnold captured Fort Ticonderoga a year ago. They started in November 1775. It was a hard journey. Henry and his companions traveled three hundred miles to Fort Ticonderoga to get the cannons. By the time they picked up fifty-eight pieces of artillery, and decided to head back, winter was on full force. This was almost an impossible feat that lasted just 56 days. Henry transported an incredible sixty-two tons of artillery from Fort Ticonderoga in New York to the Continental Army.

One time Henry wrote to his wife saying, "This is impossible!" Well, even though they had to cross the Hudson River four different times, sometimes some artillery fell, and they had to climb a steep hill. Henry and his small group built forty special sleds and purchased eighty yokes of oxen to push five thousand four hundred pounds. Elijah and Mary had to push four hundred pounds! But by 7 March 1776, two thousand continental soldiers with weapons stood on a hill above the city named Dorchester Heights. Washington's army did not even need to fire a shot! The British were obligated to leave Boston.

When that ended George Washington said, "Wow! Good work soldiers on making the British retreat somewhere else!"

"I declare a toast for Henry Knox!" said a soldier. "A toast for Henry Knox!" said all of the soldiers.

What about Henry's four animal friends? Right now, they were so excited for their friend's victory that the soldiers who saw it were shocked. Mark and Esther were singing, "Praise to the Lord, The Almighty" by Joachim Neander (1621-1718), Elijah was praising the Lord, Mary was waving her hands in praise to the Lord as well, and Rusty was doing the same thing as Elijah. Instead of doing what the school people did, they praised the Lord.

Henry recognized them instantly and said, "Oh, hello, Rusty, Esther, Mark, Mary, and Elijah. How are you people doing?"

"You forgot some family members. There is more to my family. There's Elizabeth, Elisha, and Naomi in the family," Elijah pointed out.

"For me, there's Methuselah, Sarah, Anne, and Chris," Mary pointed out as well.

"Well, it's my turn. My family has a lot of people. There's Esther, Rose, Amy, Micah, Jacob, Solomon, and Shamgar," said Mark.

"And last but not least, it's my turn. My family has so many members as well. There's Deborah, Leah, Dinah, Hannah, Rachel, Joy, Adina, Martha, Mara, Job, Daniel, Joseph, Obadiah, Paul, Peter, Richard, and Victor," Rusty added.

"Okay. So let me get this straight. Elijah has three added people in his family. Mary has four added people in her family. Mark and Esther have five added people in their family. Rusty has sixteen people in his family," said Henry. Then he said, "Okay. This looks like I have twenty-eight more friends. Well, that's some more good news to add to the pack."

When all of the soldiers left (still shocked), Henry went on Rusty's back, and they set out for home. A lot of things had changed. The underground "mansion" was two times bigger. It had a new roof over it (Henry and the others had made a roof, but it broke). It had a secret stairway that led to a door, and instead of five bedrooms, it has nineteen bedrooms!

"Wow! Our 'underground project' has really changed. But I'd like to know, how did they do this really big change?" asked Henry.

"Well, before we left, we told our children to surprise you with their special abilities. One of my children had a very special ability. He knows how to construct things so well it was as if a human built it. Five of Rusty's daughters have a very gifted ability in being little architects. They know how to do their job just as much as my son knows how to do his. Then all of Elijah's boys were strong enough to push the materials needed for the roof. And last but not least all of the bird children know how to sing very beautifully. Thus, that helps the 'workers' concentrate. And that is how this 'underground project' got improved!" said Mary.

The underground project helped Henry Knox with his creativity level. "Wow! Now is that a huge story! Say to your children that I said hi. And also, don't forget to say to them that they even did a better job than anyone could have done," said Henry.

Well folks, that is where our story ends. I hope you realize the hard work of Henry Knox, the master of artillery! If Henry Knox did not help George Washington with the artillery transportation, England could probably transport their artillery to General Howe, which could probably result to a British victory. So, that is why Henry Knox is important to American history.

GENERAL CHARLES LEE

by Abigail Gregorin

GENERAL CHARLES LEE: HOW DID THE AMERICAN REVOLUTION COME TO MY DOORSTEP?

BERKELEY COUNTY, VIRGINIA, MID-1775

I joined the army when I was fifteen, I fought in wars for twenty-five years, I was promoted to the Lieutenant Colonel during my service to the British, and I had the most military experience of any of the candidates, but...

I still hadn't been chosen.

Still fuming my anger, I hurled a stone into the creek. It dropped into the murky water as I reached for another rock. It didn't make any sense. "Washington," I muttered, angrily. "They picked *Washington* over *me!*" I threw the stone as hard as I could, but instead of plopping in the water, it ricocheted off another rock.

Spado, my reliable Pomeranian, whined as if to tell me he understood my irritation. Sighing, I crouched down to ruffle his fur. "And if that wasn't bad enough, they didn't even make me second-in-command. They put that lousy Artemus Ward in that spot. That man knows nothing about war! He probably couldn't even load a musket if his life relied on it!"

Spado licked my face and I gently set him down and scratched the fur behind his ears. "I just can't believe it. I left the British for what? I expected respect. Possibly the position of commander-in-chief, but I guess this isn't my native county…and well, maybe appointing Washington wasn't completely stupid, but still!"

I had had a successful career with the British army. I knew techniques. I knew how to win. So, why was I shoved backstage? I deserved to be in the front. I shook my head and reached for another rock. I had even bought a house in Virginia, thinking that living among the other patriots would lead them to trust me.

Apparently, though, they didn't trust me enough to lead them to victory. I sent the rock flying and then stood up. "We'll show them that they were wrong," I said to Spado, and he barked in agreement.

It wasn't until 1776 that Artemus Ward finally resigned, mostly due to his medical issues. So, of course, I replaced him, and the title of second-in-command was finally mine. Congress also named me the head of the Southern Department, which meant I did a lot of polishing the skills of and working with the southern states in the Continental Army.

Then, Congress received news that the British were making their way to Charleston, South Carolina, where they intended to attack Sullivan's Island. Thus, Congress sent word that they would like me to oversee the fortifications of the fort being built on the island. So, bringing hundreds of troops with me, I too headed for the small island.

Sullivan's Island, 27 June 1776

So, this was how I was going to die. Bitterly, I looked around at the troops scurrying about with gunpowder and other necessities and then down at Spado. My frustration lowered only a single degree as I ruffled the Pomeranian's fur.

There was no way the makeshift fort I was standing in would hold up under the British's attack. Only the seawall was complete, and it consisted of rough, but flexible palmetto logs, which were reinforced by sand. Such materials wouldn't be expected to be used for a house, let alone a fort that was supposed to withhold cannon fire.

Yet, General Moultrie refused to desert the fort and retreat to secure ground. Instead, he had garrisoned the troops, given a rallying speech, and prepared for war. But how heroic would he feel once all his troops lay bleeding and dead on the damp, spring ground? The general was determined and brave; however, I had a feeling that his confidence was rooted merely in patriotism and right now, that kind of attitude was dangerous.

Unfortunately, even though President Rutledge put me in charge, he defended Moultrie's decision, which meant the hundreds of men at this fort, had to remain. And thus, so did I. I was no coward, but the result of this battle was almost certain, and in this case, death was especially certain for me. After all, I had resigned my commission as an officer for the Crown. No doubt my former colleagues wanted to shoot me on sight.

But, standing around and dreading such a fate did me nor the others any good. I scanned the surrounding water now occupied by enemy ships. Yes, the British had already arrived. In fact, amusingly, they had shown up the same day I had. Regardless, no one knew when the British would begin their attack, which meant any plans for defense would need to be complete soon.

As I studied the mile-long channel between Sullivan's Island, where I was, and Charleston, I found myself thinking about a bridge. You see, if there was a bridge from here to there, then we would have an easy escape route for when things got bloody.

The problem was that a bridge would take too long to construct, and we didn't have the proper building supplies that such a structure would require. I was about to give up on the idea when I had an alternate thought. What if the bridge wasn't built with timber and arches, but with something else entirely?

There were several ships that I could muster together, and I also knew where a supply of hogsheads, which were the large casks we had stored our liquids in when travelling by sea, could be found. Both were large and would float across the channel. Thus, they would form a floating bridge that could be crossed easily and swiftly assembled.

So, I glanced about the nearby soldiers and ordered, "Fifty of you with me! Now!"

Immediately, groups of men started towards me, and one of the men in the cluster was Colonel Moultrie. "What are you planning on doing?" he asked. I caught a hint of suspicion in his tone. He probably figured I was running away from the fight based on our past arguments.

"Building an escape route," I told him, examining the men now gathered around me. "We're going to create a bridge that connects this island to Charlestown." I went on to describe my plan, ignoring the dubious looks that General Moultrie gave me as I rattled off my orders.

"Yes, sir," answered the militia as they headed off to begin the job.

As I turned to join them, the colonel snagged my arm. "I don't think this idea will work," he told me.

"Well, I do," I retorted, shrugging my arm free. "If you want to wait around in this slaughter pen, then that's your choice, but I'm going to do something useful." I marched off to oversee the project.

It wasn't until later that I realized Colonel Moultrie was right about my plan. First, we soon ran out of supplies, and were not able to close the entire mile. Second, the hogsheads and ships were unable to support the weight of a regiment hurrying across. For the 'bridge' to stay afloat, only a handful of soldiers could traverse it at a time, which wouldn't be ideal with the British encroaching.

So, frustrated, the men and I returned to the fort, where we spent the rest of the night discussing the possible reasons that the British had yet to attack. June 7th, the day the British and I had arrived, Major General Henry Clinton had ordered a boat to approach the fort, flying a truce flag and demanding that we surrender.

As a sort of response some of our obviously unexperienced troops had fired on it with several muskets. But then again, Colonel Moultrie would never have surrendered, so the overture had been completely pointless for the British. Today is the 27th of June, and the British still haven't attacked.

They had tried, though. A spy had gotten sight of a few daring British soldiers trying to wade across the channel that was located between Long Island and Sullivan's Island. Quickly, they discovered that the water they had thought was shallow was about five feet deep.

So, the British had abandoned the idea of sending the soldiers through the channel and settled with firing occasional cannon balls from the other side, but of course, none of the steel iron balls hit our fort, thanks to the long distance between us. Still, I knew an attack was coming and as every second ticked by, my frustration with Colonel Moultrie grew.

He was clearly inexperienced as a leader, unlike me. I had even heard some of the other soldiers saying that while they had no question about the colonel's loyalty and passion for the cause, they thought he didn't take his position too seriously. And I had to agree with them.

Unfortunately, he was still in command, which was a problem. If the British attacked before the fort was abandoned, then a long list of casualties would be added to the loss of Sullivan's Island itself. At least if we left the fort, we wouldn't lose hundreds of soldiers.

I knew what I needed to do.

"I'm going to replace him," I said, running a hand through Spado's fur. He placed his paws on my knees and stared up at me with his tiny cannonball-like eyes as if volunteering his support. Tomorrow, I would announce that I was taking over the colonel's position. If he couldn't do what needed to be done, then I would.

GENERAL CHARLES LEE: HOW DID I GET INVOLVED IN THE AMERICAN REVOLUTION?

Sullivan's Island, 28 June 1776

And then it happened, unfortunately before I had a chance to throw Moultrie out.

It was the very next day that the madness began. I was on the mainland making sure the coast was secure, when, I heard the sound of a signal gun echo throughout the warm morning air. And sure enough, the nine warships sailed closer to the island. Soon, the island was surrounded, and I grimaced.

Some of the ships were only a mile or two away while others were only several hundred feet away from the makeshift fort. I watched as General Clinton and some of his men tried to make landfall near the island on flat-bottomed ships-but such heavy American gunfire rained on them, that they soon gave up.

Next, came the cannon fire and I knew that the deadly cast-iron would bring the fort to destruction and thus end hundreds of soldiers' lives. I used my hand to shield my eyes from the bright sun's beams and soon, several cannonballs were fired, and they soared through the air and then landed so close to the fort, that from my distance, I couldn't see whether or not they had actually hit the fort's walls.

But surely, it would only be a matter of time before the fort collapsed.

Shockingly, it was one of the British's ships that went down first! I wasn't sure exactly what had happened, but soon it stopped firing its cannons and then it moved out of firing position. This was surprising, but of course, there were still multiple other ships in the picture, so it wasn't a tremendous relief.

I expected this to be the fort's defenders' only 'victory,' but then I saw three British ships, encroaching on the Charleston Harbor. Apparently, they were trying to go around the island...and it did not work out for them. All three ships got entangled in a sandbar of which the British had been unaware, and one of the ships sailed too far into the sandbar where it remained stuck.

Regardless, none of the ships, actually reached their destination and I found myself grinning and muttering, "Take that, British."

There were only two more large British ships, and it was only a matter of time before Colonel Moultrie's men had hit the ships' rigging and masts so many times that the ships were useless. Now, the gunpowder supply at the fort had been low, which explained why the men there were making careful and planned shots.

Even I had to admit that I had never seen such accuracy in any of the wars I had been in. But that didn't dismiss the problem of the army's depleting gunpowder supply. Fortunately, I knew where I could get more.

So, I spent the rest of the morning collecting gunpowder from regiments of troops on the mainland, and by mid-afternoon I was sending several troops over to the island with the supply. By this time, the American cannon fire had pretty much ceased, but soon, it began again, and...I just stood there, shocked as I stared at the fort.

It was still standing.

It was still together.

It wasn't burning.

How?

The only way I could think to explain this interesting situation was maybe that the British ships had been in such a bad position that they had somehow missed the fort with every shot. Was that even possible?! Whatever the case was I was pleasantly surprised.

Sometime during that afternoon, the flag that Colonel Moultrie had designed and then proudly displayed over the fort was shot down and my heart sank as did our colors. Then, suddenly, the flag was hoisted into the air again...by a troop? "What insane man is holding that flag?" I couldn't help but think.

But amazingly, the British didn't shoot him down. Shocked, I shook my head and dragged a hand through Spado's fur. I had seen more than one miracle today. There was no other way to describe this scene.

Finally, around 17:00, curiosity dragged me to the fort, where I discovered over ten soldiers dead, and more than that wounded. But honestly, I had been surprised. I had expected a lot more casualties.

But what surprised me the most was the fort. The British were now firing in cannonades, and the walls of the fort shook, greatly, but only a few if any cannonballs penetrated the fort's walls. Instead, I learned that the walls made of spongy palmetto logs combined with the loose sand filling, absorbed the cannonballs and gunfire as if the wall were somehow 'swallowing' them.

I listened as one of the troops explained this to me, and then casually nodded as if I had expected this. Then, suddenly, I heard the firm, almost proud voice of Colonel Moultrie's voice, "Ah, General, it's good to see you. Thank you for the gunpowder. As you can see, it's serving us well."

"I noticed," I mumbled. "It looks like the fort's holding up well. Is the number of troops you have sufficient?"

"Yes, I believe it is," the colonel replied. "And I assume the troops in Charleston remain alert and ready in case of a diverted attack?"

"Of course," I said, sharply.

"If you'll excuse me for a second...," The colonel stepped away from me and then went to clarify some orders with some of his troops. In the meantime, I decided to do something useful, and I grabbed some gunpowder and a musket. Soon, I was aiming a gun and I fired a few shots, before returning back to the colonel.

"It truly is amazing that this fort has stood," Colonel Moultrie commented.

Although he had made this comment nonchalantly, there was an obvious hint of smugness to it. I found myself forcing my breathing to remain normal as I said, through clenched teeth, "Yes. It. Is."

"And the troops. Their aim has been amazing. Don't you agree?"

"Yes," I practically spit out. "Well, Colonel, I see you are doing very well here, and you have no occasion for me, so I will go up to town again."

"Alright then," the colonel said.

"Come on, Spado," I announced, saluting to the other officers, and then heading back for the boat I had sailed over on. As I crossed the channel again, I found myself saying, "I can't believe that those stupid logs actually held up. I should've known that they would. Somehow."

The battle continued to go on until finally at about 21:00, then the few remaining British ships turned, and they started sailing back towards the Atlantic. We had won. Astonished, I just shook my head. Never had I ever seen anything like this.

That night, we awaited another possible attack from the British, but no attack came. In fact, the British that still remained on the boat stuck in the sandbar, burned the boat, and then abandoned it very early the next morning. Soon after Moultrie sent a ship over to Charleston to report that the battle was over, and we had won. Cheers erupted from the town, and I pet Spado, while I just stared at the fort.

No doubt, the British's stupidity was mostly responsible for our victory, but the Americans…well, I had to admit that I was surprised. And…impressed. Sort of. Colonel Moultrie had done much better at commanding the troops than I had thought he would've. Of course, I could've done better, but…I sighed.

Palmetto logs and sand.

I just couldn't believe it.

GENERAL CHARLES LEE: WHAT'S MY STORY IN 1776?

AN AMERICAN ENCAMPMENT IN NEW YORK

Mid-November 1776

hy did no one listen to me?

I knew putting George Washington as Commander-in-Chief was a bad idea even before he had been given that position. So, of course, I attempted to warn everyone under his leadership, but did they listen to me? OF COURSE NOT.

Now the wives and children of a few thousand men would soon learn that their husbands and fathers were either dead, wounded, or captured by the enemy and I wasn't going to be the one to bring that news to them. Honestly, I thought it was Washington's job to dump that bucket of ice-cold sorrow on the families. After all, it was his fault that all of them were gone.

See, Washington had the final say in the battle of Fort Washington. He had been convinced that the fort would survive a British attack, so he had told all the troops at Fort Washington to hold their ground and not retreat. And this was the command that had killed all the soldiers.

So, within a day the American flag had been lowered, and we had admitted defeat. Correction, *Washington's men* had admitted defeat.

They had lost the battle, the fort, and the troops who had fought uselessly for the cause. And what happened to Washington, you ask?

Well, conveniently he had watched the entire battle from the banks of the Hudson River that had separated him from the fort. Thus, he and the others with him were able to escape the clutch of the British lion.

Bitterly, I shook my head and then stroked the fur on Spado's head. "We need to do something," I told him, trying to figure out what I could do. I had already appealed to Congress, trying to explain that I could do them much good if I was put in Washington's boots. But unfortunately, they were loyal to Washington and their previous decision, so trying to convince them of this was about as impossible as it was to get Spado to stop shedding his fur.

I brushed the dog hair off my breeches and then stood up. Maybe I needed to try a different approach. Instead of addressing Congress directly, what if I tried consulting another military leader? I knew a certain man who was close to Washington, but he was also a man of skill and strategy when it came to the battlefield.

His name was Joseph Reed and I wondered if he might be starting to doubt Washington as well. I grabbed a quill and penned my thoughts to Reed in a letter. When Reed responded, he confided his doubts about Washington. "Finally," I found myself thinking. "Somebody agrees with me." Over several letters, we discussed our issues with his leadership, but we made sure that Washington wasn't aware of our communications.

Until one day, that is. I wasn't sure of all the details, but Reed reported that Washington discovered one of the letters I sent him, and thinking it had something to do with military plans, he had opened it. Reed told me that Washington later confronted him and instead of being angry, Washington had seemed disappointed.

I naturally expected some kind of reprimand. Maybe even being discharged. However, nothing happened, and everything continued as it was. Washington remained Commander-in-Chief, and I remained doubtful of his capability and leadership.

It was about a month later when I received a request from General

Washington. He was retreating with a decent number of troops, and he wanted me to join him near Pennsylvania with my own troops. So, grudgingly, I rallied the troops, and we began to head down to meet Washington.

But as you can imagine, I was in no rush, especially to see Washington. That's why when we were traveling through New Jersey and I spotted White's Tavern, I decided that we could afford a stop. Besides, I really had a longing to sleep in an actual bed for the night and to eat something other than stale, old bread. Add a place to warm up my half-frozen fingers, and it was an offer, I couldn't refuse.

Two hours later, I was reclining on the bed, petting Spado who was curled up right next to me. "Isn't Washington so bothersome?" I muttered, subconsciously. "He knows as well as I do that he's not right for the job, yet he still holds on to it, like a man with stolen wages." And now I had to go meet him.

Frustrated, I slept little that night. Finally, around dawn, I decided to get up and write a letter to General Horatio Gates. Like me, he had had a previous career as a British soldier, which meant he would understand the importance of a good, organized commander. I sat down to begin writing, when suddenly I heard a loud shout outside.

"GENERAL CHARLES LEE!"

I stiffened. No soldier under my command would dare address me in that tone, let alone by my full title. Spado started barking and soon he was furiously scratching at the windowsill. Setting my quill down, I walked over to the window, where Spado was, and brushed the curtain aside.

And what I saw made me panic.

British Cornet Banastre Tarleton and a group of his dragoons stood outside the tavern and somehow, I doubted they had come to bring us reinforcements. "General Lee!" Tarleton shouted again, and I snagged Spado and dragged him away from the window.

What was I supposed to do?

My mind scurried to come up with an answer, but the only thing I could think to do, was reach for my gun. Between Spado and I...I shook such stupid thoughts away. There was no way we could take down the dozens of soldiers outside. The other troops that had been with us were no longer in sight, presumedly captured, shot or escaped.

Perfect. Tarleton wanted my head and there was nobody here to keep him from getting it. Nervously, I tapped my fingers on the cool metal of the gun, wondering if this would be the day I died. Even if Tarleton didn't shoot me, I would be considered a valuable prisoner for the British. No doubt, I would spend years in prison while the British waited to trade me off for one of their own.

"LEE! Get out here or we'll burn this place down!" Tarleton yelled. Spado growled at the sound of his voice. Then, as if Tarleton had somehow heard the dog, his eyes raised to the window where I was standing, and anger as hot as the flames he threatened simmered in his expression.

Quickly, I grabbed Spado and then disappeared from the window. It appeared that I only had two options. The first option had me standing my ground in the room and burning to death at the hand of Tarleton. The second option still put me at the mercies of Tarleton, but perhaps he wouldn't kill me if I surrendered now.

"Lee! I have the fire!" Tarleton called from somewhere outside. "I will not hesitate to burn this tavern down with you in it!" I didn't doubt it. Tarleton had always been especially mad that I had traded sides. When he had learned that I joined the Americans, he had drawn his saber and declared that he would cut off my head with it.

Suddenly, the door to my room burst open and half a dozen British soldiers stormed in the room. Startled, I froze and then realizing what was going to happen, I shouted, "Spado, run!" The dog cocked its head as if the command had confused his furry, little head, but then, he must've understood, because he darted across the room and then through the door.

One of the British fired a shot at the doorway, with intentions to hit Spado, but thankfully, he missed. "Forget the stupid mutt," another British dragoon told him. "The real gold is right there." He aimed his gun at me. "Drop your weapon."

I studied the six guns pointed at me and then after deciding that I couldn't take them all out in one shot, I let my pistol clatter to the ground. Immediately, the soldiers swarmed around me like mosquitoes and soon they had my hands tied behind my back.

Cheering as if they had victoriously won some battle, they led me outside, where Tarleton stood out on the frozen, December ground. He smiled at the sight of me, and then asked, "Was there anybody else in there?"

"No, sir. Just a dog," one of the troops replied.

Speaking of dog, I glanced around, but I didn't see Spado anywhere. Good. I breathed an icy sigh of relief. Then, the soldiers dragged me away. Soon I was sitting in a rusty, old prison cell, wondering what day I would be shot in the head as a traitor to the British army...and thinking about how this whole mess was Washington's fault. Like usual.

THOMAS PAINE

by Ellie Powers

THOMAS PAINE: HOW DID THE AMERICAN REVOLUTION COME TO MY DOORSTEP?

I stood on a wood podium with gold edgings in front of Parliament, in England, ready to give my speech. I looked across the room and saw hundreds of men with long, white wigs and black, buttoned-up coats that looked like dresses. My fellow taxmen and I were angry. I was there to present my case.

"Thomas Paine, start your speech," the head of Parliament said.

"Ahem," I cleared my throat from nervousness. "As you know we've been working hard…" I began, "and we are not getting paid enough. It wouldn't just benefit us, because there are poor people all over England. So, I ask of you to start doing the right thing and save our lives by sending us more pay!" I finished.

"We have heard enough," said Parliament, waving me out of the room.

I walked outside, taking a deep breath of air. Then I saw someone who waved at me with a smile, so I walked over to him. He reminded me of my friend's grandpa. He had wavy, white hair, spectacles, a hefty look, and a friendly smile.

"I heard your proposal about your fellow taxmen," he said.

"You did?" I said, befuddled. "How?"

"Simple, that building has terrible insulation," he explained. "And I agree, they should raise the pay. I have some things I'd like to talk with you about. Would you meet with me tomorrow?"

"Sure!" I answered. Though he hadn't shared his name with me, I had a strong suspicion I knew who he was.

"I'll be at Dog's Coffee on Third Street at 3 o'clock."

"I'll be there," I answered.

The coffee shop that the man had talked about was on an empty, cobblestone street. There was a big sign near the door hanging from a bracket with a picture of a black, scotty dog on it, that read "Dog's Coffee." I noticed an eagle with a fiery, red beak perched on the bracket staring at me as I stepped down the rickety steps and into the shop.

As I walked in, people were talking in animated voices, and often standing up and shouting. The man waited for me in the corner with his back to the window. I silently walked over to him, into the darkest spot in the shop, lit by only one candle. I sat down across from him with a little thump.

"Good afternoon, Thomas," he said. "How do you do?"

"Marvelous!" I answered. "I'm ready for another cup of coffee so that I'm all pepped up for the day!"

"Well good," he said. "I am Benjamin Franklin."

"I know!" I interrupted. "You're famous!" My suspicions from the previous day were confirmed. But I still had no idea why Benjamin Franklin would want to speak with me.

"I'm impressed with your desire to help your fellow tax officers," Franklin said.

"Thank you," I said. "But it's not just about my fellow taxmen. There are a lot of people who are down on their luck."

"If you want new opportunities and to fight for freedom, then I suggest the colonies in New England," he said.

"That's a long way away and a big risk. I wouldn't know anyone there."

"I understand. But you seem to me to be a man willing to take risks. If it helps, I would be willing to provide you with a letter of recommendation. We need men like you over there. Please think about it."

The next day, I walked to Hyde Park, where the trees grew tall and lots of wildlife lived. I had just sat down to think about what Benjamin Franklin had said, when down came a very familiar and magnificent eagle, with a red beak. It peered at me in such a way that I just started talking aloud.

"What do you think eagle? Should I go to America?" He only starred at me. I couldn't help but feel he was evaluating me. "But what would I do there?" I asked him. Again, he gave me an unnerving stare. "Mr. Franklin's letter of recommendation all but guarantees me a job. But I want to do more! They say it's the land of opportunity. England certainly feels less and less like that. I think I will go!"

Perched on a nearby stump, the eagle squawked.

"Can that bird understand me?" I wondered. The bird just made another squawk. It was time for me to make preparations for my long sea voyage.

THOMAS PAINE: HOW DID I GET INVOLVED IN THE AMERICAN REVOLUTION?

28 OCTOBER 1774

I'm on my ship to America, and yet I'm already starting to regret it. The ship stinks, and there are rats, and the temperature is really shifty. Only days after I boarded the ship, I started feeling tired and lost my appetite. The days are rough, but sometimes I go down to the bottom of the ship, where the slaves are. They are treating them so badly, so I'm going to try and help them by bringing them extra food and water.

5 November 1774

As the trip goes on, I'm starting to feel dreadful. I don't know if I'm catching something, but if I am, I hope I survive this trip. In the meantime, I'm chatting with the other people on my deck, most of whom don't think they will last the trip. I'm starting to think that, too.

21 November 1774

The crew assures us that we're nearing Philadelphia, and I'm positive that I've caught a terrible illness. I am unable to go down to the slave's hold anymore because I'm so weak that I can't walk! And my vision is getting blurry. So here I am, not able to go anywhere or see much of anything. This is as miserable as it gets.

25 November 1774

I'm......worse...people dead. Can't hold......pen... tired, can't move. The boat......shore. Can't get......ship. So tired, I can't.......... much longer.

27 November 1774

"So, what do we do with him, captain?" A man said. I heard the voice as though in a dream.

"Don't know," the captain said. "How long has he not moved?"

"Two days," the first said.

"You sure he's still alive?"

"Yes, he's still breathing."

Those voices sounded familiar to me. But whose were they? Where was I? Everything was lost in a haze.

"Good, now what do we know about him?"

"Not much, sir. All we know is his name is Paine."

"Hmm, well we have to do something with him. We set sail back to England in two days. Let's search his bag..."

I wanted to tell them I had a letter from Benjamin Franklin, but I couldn't speak. I heard rustling.

"Nope nothin' here, maybe... wait...I found something. A letter! This signature.... He was sent by Benjamin Franklin!"

Suddenly, I remembered I was on the ship. But I couldn't feel the ship moving. Had we arrived at the dock yet? Where was I?

"Benjamin Franklin?" the first asked. "Oh, I know his doctor! He's nearby, I'll send for him!"

December 1774

I wake up feeling better, but where am I? I open my eyes to see a man sitting next to me.

"Mr. Thomas Paine?" said the man, "I am Dr. Pine, Mr. Franklin's doctor. Your fever is going down."

Even as he spoke the words, everything went dark again. But this time, I was able to sleep more peacefully than I had for a long, long time.

January 1775

A few weeks later I was feeling better. I walked down the cobblestone street looking for the *Pennsylvania Magazine.* Dr. Pine had made the recommendation about a job there. I stopped in front of a blue house, and I looked down at the map in my hands. Was this it? The building had a smoky smell to it and the window had bird droppings on it. In a small patch of dirt, in front of the house, a sign said, 'Beware of Bird Poop!' Then, I felt something splat on my shoulder.

"Gross!" I exclaimed. Just then, I heard a snicker from a man I just noticed standing in the open doorway.

"So," said Mr. Robert Aitken, "are you Mr. Thomas Paine? Dr. Pine told me I should be expecting you."

"Yes, sir," I replied. "How do you do?"

"I'm well, sir," he answered. "How do you do?"

"I have been unwell, I must admit," I said. "You see, I had typhoid fever, and it took a long time to recover. But I'm better now."

"Good, well now that you are better, I assume you came here for a job?" asked Robert.

"Yes, sir!" I replied.

"Well, tell me about yourself."

"I feel I am really good at writing and finding stories. I think that I'd be a good fit. And... I have a recommendation from Benjamin Franklin." I handed him the letter. Mr. Aitken's eyes grew wide at the mention of Franklin's name.

"Of course, it does! Benjamin Franklin, he's famous!" He leafed through the letter, smiling broadly. "You're hired!" He held out his hand for me to take it. "Welcome to the *Pennsylvania Magazine,* Thomas!"

"It would be my honor, thank you!" I answered, grateful for the opportunity.

The next day, I was on my way to interview the blacksmith about his increased work due to his shift from horseshoes to ammunition. But then I saw a raccoon robbing the garbage. So, I ran over and started shooing it away. It went, so I chased after it. It was fast! After a while, I decided it was far enough away, so I stopped, wondering why I cared so much for the garbage that I would chase the raccoon. I felt a bit lost because I had chased the little critter really far away, when I saw a redcoat riding by on the bumpy, cobblestone street. To me, he looked like a big, red bomb ready to be lit by the top of his tall, bearskin hat. He had a saber in his hand as if ready to pounce. He glared at me out of the corner of his eye but kept on riding.

"He's probably here to intimidate the poor people, and me. I've got to do something about this," I thought.

I started my work the following day by going down to the farm to ask a gentleman about a horse that escaped the previous night. He told me the horse's name was Winston and that a garter snake spooked him.

It was then that I saw the eagle again. I could see its fiery, red beak and legs as he stared down at me. It started to fly off, so I raced after it. Farther and farther, it soared. Then it landed on my hat! I tried to grab my hat back, but the eagle leapt into the sky and before I knew it, it was gone, along with my hat.

Suddenly, I heard voices. Some kids were arguing.

"My father says we should listen to the king," one said.

"My father doesn't think that. Why does yours?" the other countered.

"Because he loves his tea!" the first one explained. "Doesn't your father like tea?"

"Yes, of course! Who doesn't?" said the second. "My father just likes his freedom more."

"Thank you, eagle!" I felt that wonderful bird had led me to these kids, whose conversation had brought me fresh inspiration. I started for my house to write my thoughts down.

The second father has a lot of common sense I thought.

April 1775

I walked down the cobblestone road, thinking again about the tensions between the colonies and England. Things seemed to be at a boiling point. Then I heard the hoof beats of riders on horseback coming down the street. As they came down, they shouted. "Shots were fired!" and "A war has begun!" People ran down the street screaming. Even the eagle, who seemed to appear next to me most days, screeched and flew off as more hoof beats followed. I scrambled across the road, hoping to find a quiet place to think. Eventually, I made my way home, avoiding confrontation with the British soldiers.

The next day, while writing furiously, I heard a knock on my rusty door and Mr. Robert Aitken burst through.

"Paine, writing as usual I see. What did you find today?" he asked, slamming the door behind him.

"What was the point of knocking if you didn't even wait for me to answer?" I asked. "But if you must know, I'm writing about what happened in the square yesterday," I said, not looking up. "About the first gun shots being fired, and how people need freedom and liberty instead of bondage to the king."

"No!" said Robert. "If you do that, you and I are basically deer walking up to a butcher shop. And you heard what the king said, 'America is either a colony or an enemy.' I am not getting my head cut off for treason!"

So, I banished him from my room. I was done with Aitken and the magazine. I stopped working with him and gradually kept writing my paper.

THOMAS PAINE: WHAT'S MY STORY IN 1776?

DECEMBER 1775

It had only been a couple of days since I completed my little booklet, *Common Sense*. I needed someone to print it. I decided I had enough money to print 500 copies. A friend of mine mentioned someone named Billy Buck who could print it for me, so I went to meet him.

As I walked down the snowy street, I felt the icy air seep into my bones. I shivered, seeing my breath in the air. I smelled fresh, warm bread from a house nearby and drooled. That sounded really good. I walked up to Buck's doorstep.

"Ah, I've been expecting you, Mr. Paine." A man with fuzzy hair and buck teeth stood in the doorway.

"Good day," I said as I entered his cluttered-up house with a fire lit in the corner. The fire did nothing to help against the cold coming through the broken windows.

"Good day. Are you here for some printing?" Mr. Buck asked as I stepped over some broken type.

"Yes sir. I feel I wrote something marvelous, but it might be something some people might not agree with," I said.

The man cocked his head and had a look of hopefulness on his face, but said, "Well if we're talking about independence, then let's get started."

10 January 1776

I headed down the cobblestone road feeling proud of what I wrote. Today was the first day people would finally get to read it. The Friday evening was cold, but I didn't shiver. Suddenly, I heard a boy yelling, "*Common Sense!* Hot off the press, only one shilling!" Then I saw another boy flip a shilling into the boy's hand, grab a booklet and be off with a tip of his hat. As he read, his eyes slowly grew to the size of teacup saucers, and he shouted. "Hey everyone, listen to this, this guy has it right! We should all have freedom, and we have strength enough, too!"

I walked down the bumpy road and heard people chitter-chattering, the way they do, about my *Common Sense.* Suddenly, I saw a skinny, gray, tabby kitten hiding under a small tree off the side of the road.

"Poor kitty," I said, feeling sorry for this little kitten, not getting enough to eat. I decided to go to the nearest tavern and get it some milk. When I arrived in the tavern, I quickly ordered the milk and sat down to wait. I noticed people all over the tavern talking about my *Common Sense.* The people at the table next to mine were especially loud.

"I understand now! It's for the greater good to declare independence from the king!" one said.

"Well, I don't get it. We should respect the king; he'll send his men down on us to kill us."

I grabbed the milk and left, pondering this.

When I got back to the tree the kitten was under, I got down on my knees, put the milk in front of the tree and waited. At first, nothing happened. Then a nose popped out, then a head, and soon the whole kitten was out, lapping up that milk. When it was finished drinking, it purred and curled up in my lap.

"You want to come home with me?" I asked it. It meowed and curled up some more.

"Okay, come on, little one. Let's go home."

8 July 1776

I stood in the courtyard of the Pennsylvania Statehouse, waiting in the warm, July sun for the Declaration of Independence to be read. All around me, I heard people chitter-chattering a mile a minute. I could feel the claws of Libby, my kitten, holding on to my shoulder. Benjamin Franklin walked up and with his usual smile, he said, "Hello Thomas. Thanks for meeting me here on this special day." We strolled together a while, marveling at the size of the crowd.

"You know Thomas, no one would want to admit it, but I will," Benjamin Franklin said. "This wouldn't have happened without *Common Sense* and your words."

"Thank you," I said. "Thank you also for suggesting America. It has been a great opportunity."

"By the way," said Franklin, "where did you get that kitten?"

"I found Libby alone and hungry under a tree, so I wanted to help her. She reminded me of the colonies," I said, looking at Libby.

"Why is she called Libby?" asked Franklin.

"Because she reminded me that we need freedom, and Libby sounds like liberty. Doesn't it?" I asked.

"Indeed," Franklin said.

We saw my eagle land on a nearby tree, its fiery, red beak shining like fire.

Libby suddenly sat up and flopped into my shirt frightened.

"Aww! Libby! It's ok!" I said. "You know, I really feel like that eagle is following me."

"That's odd. While I was reviewing the Declaration of Independence, an eagle quite like this one flew up to the window with a twig in one claw and an arrow in the other," Franklin said. "It was quite a sight."

Just then the bell above the Pennsylvania Statehouse rang its dong, dong, dong sound.

"Oh," I gasped. "The Declaration of Independence is about to be read!"

Suddenly, the crowd became quiet. A man in uniform began to read....

"When in the course of human events, it becomes necessary for one people to dissolve the political bands which have connected them with another..."

GENERAL ISRAEL PUTNAM

by Emma Urrutia

GENERAL ISRAEL PUTNAM: HOW DID THE AMERICAN REVOLUTION COME TO MY DOORSTEP?

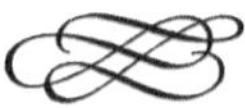

Connecticut, 1740

Israel Putnam glanced around him. Pomfret, Connecticut was right before his eyes. People were doing all sorts of things, but no one paid him any attention. The twenty-two-year-old man felt the wind blow against him, but he enjoyed it. His mind drifted to his brothers, William, and David. He wondered what they were up to. He knew where William was. In a grave, for he was dead. His thoughts grew somber thinking about William. Wherever David was, he hoped he was doing well. His mother most likely was still saddened thinking of his father, who too had passed away. Shaking his thoughts from such sad topics, he strolled around, ready to make a living for himself. The land seemed well taken care of, and the price was low. Soon, he was ready. *Farming, here I come.* He was ready for whatever came at him. Everything.

15 Years Later, 1755

THE SOUND of gun shots was deafening. *What am I doing here?* Had he made a mistake, joining the Rogers' Rangers? Was he sending himself to his doom by fighting in this war against the Indians? Either way, he was a captain, so there was no turning back. Besides that, he felt a need to help. A dagger barely missed his arm. The bullet snapped him back to attention. He turned to his left to see a soldier, only to also watch him get struck with a spear straight in his neck. Putnam felt sick as he wondered if he would be next. He aimed his weapon and pulled the trigger. He watched an Indian crumple to the ground. He had hit one! He observed his enemies, with their feathers and head-dresses. He wondered what life would be like after this war. That is, if this war ever ended. He took aim again, fired, and once again watched another Indian collapse on the ground. He prayed to God not to get killed in this war. A man crept up beside him but was hit by a knife right into his heart. Putnam's mood saddened at the fact that everyone here was at the mercy of God and the Indians. He returned his focus to the task at hand and fired another bullet. He felt a pang in his chest as he thought of the fact that he was killing someone, taking their life as the Indians took theirs. Still, this was war, and in this specific war, it was kill or be killed, and he had no intention of being the killed.

June 1775

Putnam couldn't believe it. He was now a major general in the Continental Army! *Major General! Me!* He felt so proud of himself. Now he was a major general in the American Revolution! He had the opportunity to help America gain freedom from King George and his rule! He hoped the war wouldn't be too bloody and that England would soon allow America to be its own country. Hope was something everyone was holding on tightly to these days.

GENERAL ISRAEL PUTNAM: HOW DID I GET INVOLVED IN THE AMERICAN REVOLUTION?

srael Putnam, or "Old Put," was still in shock. He was one of the two principal commanders of the coming Battle of Bunker Hill! He would play a major part in helping free them from the British! He was excited to begin. To know he would help to hopefully end the Siege of Boston was an honor. 17 June 1775 was going to be one of the most amazing battles in history!

What is happening?! This battle wasn't going the way Putnam had hoped. Far from it. At the rate this fight was going, the British army would destroy them. It felt like it had been lasting forever when it couldn't have been more than an hour. He felt as if it was never going to end. Powder was limited and men were dying. The British had discovered they had been around on the Peninsula, resulting in the British mounting a brutal attack on them. It seemed as if everything the Americans were lacking, the British had more than enough of. Gunpowder, food, men, and what felt like everything in between. But if there was any doubt that America was going to fight for freedom before, there was absolutely no doubt now. No peace between them and England could occur until America gained independence. A man next to Old Put was shot in his side. Putnam watched him collapse in agony. He swallowed hard and returned the fire, watching a British soldier get struck by a bullet and fall to the ground. To think he had once fought along these men. Now they were no longer his comrades, but his enemies. Time seemed to move backward. A bullet nearly hit him, but he ducked to the ground just in time. He began to wonder if this fight for independence was going to work. If the rest of the war was like this battle, he doubted it was going to work. He just hoped he would get out of this mess alive. He also hoped it ended soon.

The battle was already over, and while they had lost the fight, the British had lost more men. Not only that, but they also showed them that they were serious about liberty. Hopefully, this was a sign for the people to help them! Maybe, just maybe, this would help other countries to see them and send help. Suddenly he felt something brushing his leg. He looked down to see a dark brown dog. The canine snuggled around him and seemed to like him. She couldn't have been more than two years old. She trotted in front of him and wagged her tail excitedly. She barked at him and ran in a circle around his legs. He smirked. She appeared to be nice. Maybe she could help. At that moment he decided to keep her. Now all he needed was a name for the small dog.

"I think I'll name you...Aliya." It was decided. Her name was Aliya. Hopefully, she could be a defender and live up to her name. Only time would tell.

GENERAL ISRAEL PUTNAM: WHAT'S MY STORY IN 1776?

*A*liya the dog encircled the legs of her master, General Israel Putnam. He was such a nice man. *What will you do today?* she barked at him.

The man looked down at her and smiled. "You are a very talkative dog. If only you could speak English."

Aliya barked back, *If only indeed. If only.* At that moment, a scent wafted into her nose. It smelled like…lunch! She dashed amongst the soldiers and their tents, bounding over their guns laying in the dirt. She stopped right at the cook's station. Soup! Her favorite.

The cook frowned. "You again? Shoo, shoo! I don't want you eating all our food!" He waved the soup ladle at her. That didn't stop her though.

She yipped and jumped. *It won't hurt to give me a little!* she barked. Frustrated, the cook raised his arm to strike her. However, just as he was about to hit her, Israel stood there behind her, raising an eyebrow. "You're not going to hit Aliya again, are you, Alexander? You know she likes lunch time." The cook threw up his hands. "Look, you got to understand, Old Put. This dog of yours is just another mouth to feed. Don't you understand the situation I'm in? As if feeding as many soldiers as I can with this food wasn't enough, now I have to feed this dog?"

Aliya growled, *I'm useful, too! Just give me a chance! Why do you think you have no more rats in your soup? You have yet to thank me!*

Israel shook his head. "She's useful, you'll see. Just wait until our next battle, then you'll see it with your own eyes." Aliya bounced up and ran a circle around him.

Alexander remained unimpressed. "Yeah, until then, feed her from your own plate then!" He grabbed a plate and served the soup to Israel who strolled away. Then he grabbed another bowl. Just as he served it, Aliya jumped up as high as she could, knocking it out of his hands.

Once near his tent, Israel set the bowl down, letting Aliya finally have her lunch. She quickly began to eat. She lifted her head and the man laughed. She lapped up the rest of the delicious soup. Suddenly, Israel stood up and grabbed Aliya's now-empty plate. "Come on, girl. Let's go." Aliya hurried after him, curious. She hoped whatever was happening was good.

Israel Putnam needed to make plans. He was serving as a temporary commander of the America forces while awaiting General Washington's arrival. He hoped he would turn up soon. Alexander had been right in a way. They didn't have unlimited food. Still, once Aliya showed she was helpful beyond rat catching, Alexander just might change his mind on his perspective of the little brown dog. He needed to think on this. And think he did, for hours and hours on end. Soon when he took a small moment to relax his mind for just a moment, he noticed it was nighttime. The rest of the soldiers were asleep. Even Aliya was snoozing. *I guess I should be, too.* In a matter of minutes, his eyes closed, and he fell asleep.

Morning appeared before Washington did. It was obvious to Old Put that the soldiers were wondering where Washington was. Even his little dog seemed to sense something was wrong. She sniffed the air, as if the tension was in it. *Great!* She then turned to look at him and stuck her tongue out, panting. Her tail wagged from side-to-side. He managed a small grin. *Nice!*

"Hungry already, huh, Aliya?" As if she understood him, she set herself into an eating position, eager for breakfast. He chuckled. After he grabbed their food, he returned to his desk and worked as he ate. Aliya munched on her breakfast as he worked. He gave another look at the dog, wondering if she would be given the opportunity to prove her worth to the rest of soldiers, especially Alexander. Hopefully.

Aliya watched Israel furiously work at his desk, focused on what he was doing. Out of the blue, he got up and rushed out of the tent. Aliya perked up and trotted after him. However, when she left the tent, he was gone. She spun around, trying to find him. She dashed back inside his tent, hoping to pick up his scent. She leaped up onto his desk. At that moment, she finally learned what he was working on. A map lay on his desk with writing all over it. She sniffed it, and soon caught his scent. Aliya sped out, eager to find Israel again. She quickly caught a whiff of all sorts, but the one scent she was looking for she could not find. Hours ticked by. Soon it was afternoon, and still no luck. Suddenly, a hand patted her head.

"Hi there! Hungry? It's lunchtime." Aliya did feel hungry, so she followed him. After a quick meal, she decided to return to Israel's tent to bring the scent back. Just one obstacle stood in her way: where was his tent?

She searched frantically, but no luck. Hours flew by as she hunted for Israel and his tent. In what felt like no time at all, the sun began to set. *Already?* Aliya thought. Then, out of the corner of her eye, she spotted him just to her left. She raced over to him. However, she wasn't able to stop and collided with him, knocking him to the ground. Israel didn't seem to mind at all though as he laid there with her on his chest. "Hey, Aliya! Where have you been?"

Aliya barked, *Looking for you! Where have YOU been??* At that moment, bullets tore through the sky. Aliya lowered herself on the ground for a moment, then sat upright and got off Israel who shouted orders. Soon, they were firing back. Men were toppling on both sides of the battlefield. Aliya's ears detected a specific sound. Aliya sped away from Israel toward enemy lines. She ran and hid in a hole.

A man in a red coat trained his rifle on an American soldier. Her heart dropped, realizing he was aiming for none other than Israel, but no one else noticed. At that moment, she knew what to do. She darted toward the soldier and tackled him. The bullet harmlessly landed on the ground, foiling him from killing her owner. She grabbed his rifle with her teeth and bit it, dismantling it. She threw the gun a couple of feet away and bit his leg. He yelped in pain. She dodged a blow he attempted strike, then ran off to attack another solider. She did it to four more, then dashed away and returned to the American camp. Her eyelids felt heavy. Soon, she fell into a deep slumber.

Aliya awoke as Israel spoke to the soldiers. When he finished, the soldiers sprinted off. Putnam scooped Aliya into his arms and hurried along with them. What was happening? Then it struck her. A retreat. After a full day of battle, we're leaving. Aliya allowed herself to be carried. After hours of travel, everyone soon sat down in a forest.

Aliya was set down on the ground. She snuggled up next to Israel's legs. Soon, they started a fire, and the warmth cheered Aliya's heart. Footsteps resounded in her ears. Alexander arrived with a plate of hot food. She could see the steam. He smiled.

"Specially made for the little dog that saved your life." Aliya jumped up as the food was set down for her. Israel didn't understand.

"Save my life? What do you mean?" Alexander chuckled.

"She tackled a British soldier aiming for you. If not for her, you'd be dead. She saved your life." Israel grinned. Holding her in his arms, the two of them soon fell asleep.

When morning arrived, Aliya was hoping for a great day. If only her hopes were easy to achieve. A messenger appeared, informing them that some members of the Second Continental Congress blamed Putnam for their defeat at Long Island. They weren't pleased. When word was spread amongst the soldiers, some blamed him too. As Aliya walked by, some even talked about finding a way to relieve him of duty. She was sad as the soldiers' trust faded away. *What's going to happen? What will the soldiers do? Where's Washington?* Israel remained in his tent with her by his side.

Let's hope things turn for the better, girl. His eyes closed, but she couldn't sleep. One thought refused to leave her mind. *Will Israel make it out of this mess? Will he make it out of this war alive?*

JOSEPH PLUMB MARTIN

by Mikayla Badenhorst

JOSEPH PLUMB MARTIN: HOW DID THE AMERICAN REVOLUTION COME TO MY DOORSTEP?

2 MAY 1825

"Grandfather, please tell us the story of you in the army," said my 13-year-old grandson, Jonathan.

"Oh yes, please do," begged his twin, David.

"Do you two think you can handle the gruesome and hair-raising tale I'm about to tell?" I asked them with a sad smile.

"Of course, we can!" they exclaimed in unison.

"All right, I'll tell you about the Revolutionary War." I gazed beyond them as I contemplated my painful past. "It was an unusually chilly morning, the coldest we'd ever had that April…"

19 April 1775

The strains of 'Yankee Doodle' streamed through my window as I struggled to open my eyes. My grandsire pounded on my door, nearly breaking it down as he yelled, "Wake up, the regulars are passing by!"

I groaned, flipped my brown hair out of my eyes, and got dressed. As I sleepily descended the stairs into our big foyer, my grandmum practically threw my grandsire and me outside the house as she tied her hat, all while giving a long list of orders to the poor servants.

"Where are we going, Grandsire?" I asked, rubbing the sleep from my eyes.

"Joseph Martin, how could you be so ignorant?" Grandmum screeched, glaring at me with a fire that could have made even the bravest man in the British army cower.

"We are going to Lexington Green to watch the rebels face off with our superior army, Joseph," replied my grandsire. We fell silent as 'Yankee Doodle' grew louder as King George's army sang the saucy verses mocking the Patriots.

Yankee Doodle came to town,
For to buy a firelock,
We will tar and feather him,
And so, we will John Hancock.

Surprisingly, those words infuriated me. I felt someone had lit a fire underneath me. Turning to my grandmum, I asked, "Would they really tar and feather John Hancock?"

"Don't be silly. Of course, we would," she replied.

"If I was about to be tarred and feathered, what would you do?" I asked her.

"I'd tar and feather you myself!" she exclaimed proudly. "Great Britain needs our loyalty." Grandsire and I both stared at her in amazement. We kept silent, however, and soon arrived at Lexington Green.

I quickly spotted my best friend, John Warren, with his brother, Dr. Joseph Warren.

"Grandsire, may I go sit with John?" I asked hopefully.

"Of course, you may," he replied.

"I sympathize with the Patriots, but of course, don't tell your grandmum or I'll be sleeping in the outhouse for the rest of my life," he whispered with a wink. I smiled and ran off.

"Joseph!" John exclaimed.

"What?!" Dr. Joseph Warren, John's older brother, and I cried out. I started snickering as John explained to his brother that my name was also Joseph.

Suddenly a soldier's musket went off, and all three of us jumped. A barrage of fire soon followed, and I watched with horror as many Patriots fell. My eyes went cold, and I stiffened, fighting back tears.

Later that day, John went down the hillside towards the drums to join the Patriot army. Dr. Warren and his mother stood to the side and watched as John flipped a coin onto a drum. Suddenly, a warmth spread through my body as my best friend joined the Patriots. Somehow, I knew that someday I would do that, too. I didn't know how or when, but I would.

2 May 1825

"Grandfather, you did join up, right?" asked Jonathan, the older twin.

"Yes, I did, but my grandparents did not let me go without a fight," I said sadly.

"Why didn't they want to leave?" wondered David, the younger twin.

"Well, Grandmum saw me as a traitor to the Loyalists," I said quietly. "It ruined my relationship with her, but Grandsire kept up communication with me through a trusted servant. However, that person betrayed poor Grandsire, so that ended contact with him."

15 June 1775

At midnight, I went downstairs to the kitchen at Grandsire's request with a small satchel of clothing. Putting his finger to his lips, we slipped out of the house and leaped into a small wagon led by our two fastest horses. Then, we set off for Bunker Hill under the cover of night.

16 June 1775

I yawned as we woke early the next morning to watch the battle from a nearby roof. When Grandsire passed me a piece of bread, I jammed it in my mouth. Someone tapped me on the shoulder, and I spun around.

"Dr. Warren!" I cried out, both shocked and happy to see him. "Is John down there?" I asked.

He nodded grimly. "Yes, unfortunately he is, and it will be a miracle if he survives."

I frowned. "You don't think he will live to see another day?"

He replied, "No, but I will send him to you if he survives."

For the first time, I noticed his sword and musket. "You're going to fight?"

"Yes," he replied. "It is sweet and becoming to die for one's country, Joseph. Always remember that." We gripped each other's arms in farewell.

I choked back a sob and nodded, "I will, Dr. Warren, I will." Deep down I knew it would be the last time I would ever see him.

2 May 1825

"Grandsire, what about John?" Jonathan asked worriedly.

"I wondered the same thing myself, but he survived that horrific and bloody battle," I said sadly. "He did get a musket ball to his leg, and he was never the same after that battle."

"No one was, Grandsire," said David quietly.

"You are sadly right," I said, looking at him in amazement.

17 May 1776

"Grandmum, I want to volunteer and that's final!" I said firmly, having returned with Grandsire from Bunker Hill.

"Do you realize the consequences if you enlist?" Grandmum countered. "You would be disinherited, and I would be publicly disgraced."

"Oh, no," I muttered, "this is really bad." Grandmum looked down her long nose at me.

"You may enlist with my blessing, and your parents' permission," Grandsire interjected with a frown in Grandmum's direction.

"Really, I am serious about disinheriting you, Joseph!" Grandmum cried as I ran up the stairs to my room to pack my things.

When I reached my room, I filled my knapsack with some common clothing, a hunting outfit, a few leather-bound blank books, a pen, and a pen sharpener. I also grabbed an extra tricorn hat, two pairs of moccasins, and my lace up shoes. Pausing at my doorway, I looked back on my room as a wave of sadness washed over me.

"Farewell, Joseph," said my grandmum as I went through the doorway. I stopped at her voice and turned to see her watching me with tears in her eyes.

"I love you, Grandmum, and I will never forget you or Grandsire," I said, fighting back tears as I turned and walked out of my old home. I was on my way to being a soldier.

One Week Later

I paused to take a sip from my canteen I had bought with money John placed into my pocket after he had joined me on my way to Boston to enlist.

"We are two miles away from Boston, so I would say about one more hour," John said to me, his face rigid and stiff.

"Oh, good," I sighed with relief. He began walking again and I had to run to keep up.

"So, what is it like being in the army?" I asked.

He sighed and replied to my question, though unwillingly. "You are so ignorant!" he exploded. "You want to know? Well, here is my answer to your stupid question, you little brat!" He paused and went on with his barrage of words. "Do you know what it's like to hear cries from the injured? Do you know what it is like to see all those bodies entangled and marred beyond recognition? Do you know what it is like to have your own brother, who you have always looked up to and loved, die in your arms? Do you?" He broke down and started weeping in the middle of the road.

"I don't, and I am sorry that I asked you and caused you pain, my friend," I said, my own eyes a little wet. "You cannot ever forget that, and the same will probably happen to me."

John looked up at me with pain in his eyes and said, "I did not mean to dump all my emotions on you, Joseph."

I nodded and replied, "I forgive you, and you can always tell me more about your experience when you are ready."

He nodded and said, "We should keep going if we want to reach the inn before nightfall."

We reached the inn at around 6 o'clock that evening. Tired, we fell into bed and woke up early the next morning. After I had grabbed some breakfast and received the directions to the enlisting office, we set off with a spring in our step and a song on our lips.

As we approached the office, my stomach began to turn. I was waiting in a long line, and when I finally reached the front, someone handed me a paper and quill. Taking a deep breath, I signed my name. They then gave me a musket and blanket and sent me outside with a coin. As I approached the drums with Colonel Knox and Dr. Church, I took another deep breath and flipped my coin onto the drum, signifying that I had joined the army as onlookers watched.

Colonel Knox picked up my coin and shook my hand. "Welcome to the army, son."

I walked away with a mix of wonder and worry. Through all my confusion I had three thoughts. What had I gotten myself into, what adventures awaited me, and would I live to see the end of this war? I had joined the army, and there was no turning back now.

JOSEPH PLUMB MARTIN: HOW DID I GET INVOLVED IN THE AMERICAN REVOLUTION?

2 MAY 1825

"Grandfather, didn't you enjoy being in the army?" asked Jonathan, puzzled by my mournful posture.

"Yes, I did, but that doesn't mean that it wasn't hard," I said, my mind still peering down the dim and winding hallways of my past.

"Grandfather, why did John rejoin if he was so hurt?" David questioned me with wonder on his face.

"John once told me that he joined the Army to avenge his brother's death," I said quietly, "but I never understood why he wanted to."

29 August 1776

The call to get ready to march awakened me from a sound sleep I rarely enjoyed, especially after our major loss at the Battle of Long Island two days before. It was a very large battle, one of the largest ever fought on American soil. We were in shock, mourning over two thousand of our troops who had been killed, wounded, and captured during the conflict. General Howe had certainly dealt us a harsh blow, but Washington had a plan to get us off the island. I scrambled to my feet and grabbed my knapsack.

"Are you awake, John?" I whispered, hitting him.

He flipped over and nodded. "Why do you always hit me?" John asked, rubbing his arm. "Is it time?" he asked me, smiling at my unkempt appearance.

"Yes, and I was enjoying a nice rest, too!" I whispered, a little bit annoyed. He grunted as I hauled him to his feet. Yawning, he stretched out and looked around him, finally resting his gaze on the moon.

"Well, we best be off," he said in my direction. "I think we are going to try and escape from Long Island tonight by boat."

"Yes, we are," I said, fighting back a yawn. "It is our only hope to escape from the regulars. Thankfully, the redcoats should be sleeping."

"Yes, and if this fails, we will all be either taken prisoner, or hung as traitors by the King of England," John replied, looking grim.

Later That Evening

John and I were on one of the boats preparing to escape from Long Island when I saw a British sentry sleeping on the beach.

"John, do you see what I see?" I whispered urgently.

"Yes, I see the sentry," he said, as he glanced over at me.

"What should we do?" I asked.

"We tell General Putnam and let him decide," he said, his eyes trained on the sentry.

"And if he isn't able to be reached?" I asked.

"We leave him be," Jonathan said apprehensively.

"Shhhhh, we don't want to wake up the sentry! The last thing we want is another skirmish with the redcoats. I want to make it out of here alive so that I can get a hot meal," I said.

2 May 1825

"Grandfather, why does Jonathan always hit me?" asked David, annoyed with his brother.

"I am not sure why your brother annoys you, but it is not nice of him to vex you," I said with a large frown in Jonathan's direction. He smiled innocently at me, acting like nothing was wrong.

"Why, Grandfather, I wasn't doing anything wrong! And didn't you use to hit your best friend, John?" Jonathan exclaimed. However, I knew better. That face wasn't as innocent as it seemed. But, then again, I had also had a habit of hitting my best friend....

"Jonathan, you should not hit your brother," I said. "It is unkind to do such a thing, especially to your poor brother."

"Yes, Grandfather," he said, guiltily staring up at me.

"And David, do not tell on your brother just to get him in trouble," I said, sternly glancing in his direction.

"Yes, Grandfather," David said, looking just as guilty as his brother.

"You know, I used to tell on my friends to get them in trouble too," I said with a laugh, thinking about my wild childhood. "I used to throw mud at the ladies who were going to church, all dressed up in their finery," I said, reminiscing of days of a long time ago. "Once, I accidently hit my own grandmum!"

"You did?!" the twins exclaimed in unison.

"I most certainly did! And I got one of the worst spankings I have ever received from my grandsire," I said, rubbing my backside as I remembered the pain I'd had for the rest of that night. I gazed up at the ceiling, my mind slipping back in time.

1 September 1776

"John, why are you so quiet?" I asked him as he lay on his back, staring at the ceiling. We had made it safely off Long Island and were temporarily resting in New Jersey awaiting our next orders.

"I am wondering why my mother let me enlist again," he groaned, turning to face me.

"Why?" I asked, wondering why he was thinking about this.

"It brings back unpleasant memories for me, like when I was injured at Bunker Hill," John said.

"And when you lost your brother there, too?" I said quietly.

"Yes…that as well," he sighed.

"That was a hard day," I whispered sadly.

John got up to go and stand by the opening of our tent.

"I understand why we're fighting this war from a political level. We want independence from Great Britain because they have oppressed us with unfair taxes, tyranny, and treated us like idiots. But on a personal level, I don't know why I reenlisted," he said. "I've lost so much."

"Yes, you have, but your reward will be huge. John, even the poorest person can be as rich as the wealthiest person in the world if they have freedom. Our victory will be bought with blood, and America will be created through sweat, and cleansed with the tears of mothers, sisters, wives, and daughters when their soldiers don't come home. I'm not so sure about you, but I am going to fight until this war is over, and I can finally walk in the streets of Boston or Philadelphia and call America a land of liberty. Freedom is what I am fighting for, John. What are you fighting for?"

I turned on my heel and left my tent, my mind swirling with a million thoughts. I was walking so fast I ran right into Lieutenant Colonel Thomas Knowlton. He chuckled and set me on my feet.

"Woah there, Joseph! I haven't spoken to you since the Battle of Long Island. Is everything alright?" he asked me, studying my face.

"Everything is alright, sir," I answered respectfully.

"Be on your way, then," he replied, dropping his arm to let me pass. As I passed Lieutenant Colonel Knowlton, General Washington came to mind. I was reminded of having overheard a plot to assassinate the general.

Late June 1776

I was walking back to camp after collecting some firewood one night when I heard voices coming from the bushes.

"Let's get rid of him," said one of the voices. I stiffened, recognizing the voice.

"Yes, we don't need General Washington," replied another.

"Let's poison his peas," said a third voice.

I didn't need to hear anything more. I ran, stumbling through the woods back to camp, calling for Lieutenant Colonel Knowlton.

JOSEPH PLUMB MARTIN: WHAT'S MY STORY IN 1776?

2 MAY 1825

"Did General Washington actually eat the peas?" my grandson Jonathan asked me, looking worried.

"No, he did not, thanks to Lieutenant Colonel Knowlton, who was killed in action a few weeks later," I said, watching the two boys shiver.

"Who was behind the would-be assassination?" asked David, Jonathan's twin.

"A man named Thomas Hickey. He was a shady man, and I never trusted him. He once almost got away with stealing my orange," I said bitterly.

"Wasn't he conspiring with others?" Jonathan asked me.

"Yes, he was, including the governor of New York," I said sadly. "What a sad day."

"I should think so, Grandfather," said David. I stretched out and yawned, noticing the fixated eyes of the twins.

"What?" I asked as they stared. I looked down and saw it. There was a huge scar, around five inches long, jaggedly extending down my upper arm.

"Oh, that," I said quietly. They had never seen my scar, and it scared them.

"Grandfather, how did you get that?" asked Jonathan, his eyes full of curiosity.

"Yes, how?" asked David, his eyes the same as Jonathan's.

"That comes later in the story. Let me tell you about the events that led up to my injury," I said.

15 September 1776

"John, wake up!" I whispered fervently.

"What?!" he cried out. "Joseph, what's wrong?"

"You were having another nightmare," I answered.

"British ships are approaching!" the guard shouted. John and I gaped at each other. This was going to be a bloody day.

Three Hours Later

BOOM!! The cannons exploded in a barrage of red and orange, followed by the crack of muskets from both sides. Men cried out as they were shot. There was no shortage of blood and bodies as gunshots continued. I fell to the ground, dodging bullets and cannonballs as I returned with fire of my own. Beside me, John did the same.

"RETREAT TO HARLEM HEIGHTS! RETREAT TO HARLEM HEIGHTS!" General Washington bellowed, his large cape flowing behind him on his horse. Not wanting to be left behind and captured, John and I sprinted back to Harlem Heights. We collapsed on the ground, gasping from our hurried escape as General Washington galloped in.

"We lost fifty men killed and three hundred and twenty captured by the regulars," he muttered to General Nathanael Greene as he dismounted. "I didn't have enough time to prepare for the attack," he revealed as my jaw hung open. General Washington looked like a haggard old man as he entered his tent.

"Did you hear that, John?" I asked, turning to him.

"Yes, that is three hundred and seventy out of five hundred men. We are lucky to survive," he answered.

2 May 1825

"You lost three hundred and seventy men in all?!" cried out Jonathan indignantly.

"Yes, it was a sad day. Even my cousin died in that battle," I answered.

"So, Grandfather, three hundred and seventy mothers never saw their sons again?" asked David.

"Unfortunately, yes, and we lost even more the next day. That's when I got injured," I replied.

16 September 1776

The crack of gunfire filled my ears yet again at Harlem Heights. Out of the corner of my eye, our soldiers struggled to roll a cannon to a suitable place to fire it. I ran over and helped push it the rest of the way up the hill.

"Sir! The men are falling back on the right side!" I cried at General Greene. He spun around and commanded the men to attack and not fall back. He nodded at me in thanks. Turning his gaze back to the battlefield, he galloped away on his magnificent horse.

Lieutenant Colonel Knowlton rode up next to me, dismounted, and slapped his horse on the rump to send her running away. Together we fought, shooting the regulars, and dodging the bullets whizzing our way. Suddenly, a soldier turned and shot at us. Knowlton jumped in front of me and took the shot in the small of his back. He fell, and to my horror, our men removed him from the battlefield before I could understand what happened.

I kept on fighting. As I was jumping over a small rock in my way, a bullet came at me. I tried to duck, but it was too late. It tore into my arm, and I screamed. However, I kept on firing through the excruciating pain. My company needed me! My gun became unsteady as my arm shook. John ran over to me as I collapsed, the loss of blood and pain too much to bear.

"Help me, please, John," I whispered, slowly passing out. "Help me…"

17 September 1776

I groaned as a cool cloth touched my hot forehead. When I opened my eyes, General Greene stood over me.

"He's awake, John," General Greene called. "John alerted me after you passed out, so we brought you back to camp."

"Joseph, General Greene helped me take care of you," John said softly. "General Greene was my brother's friend."

"You almost died from the amount of blood you lost, Joseph," a voice piped up in the corner. I turned my head toward the voice and groaned softly from the pain.

"Can I sit up, please?" I asked as John and General Greene helped me up. "General Washington?" I said, overcome with surprise.

He smiled. "Yes, it is me. You are certainly a young one to be in the Army. How old are you?" he asked.

"Fifteen, sir," I answered quietly. His eyebrows raised in surprise as he looked me over.

"Well, Private Joseph Plumb Martin, I must go," he said, rising to leave. He paused at the tent doorway and turned back. "You will be walking in a few days, but no shooting your musket. Not yet anyway." And he was right. I was walking three days later.

2 May 1825

"That's the end of my revolutionary tale for now," I said to the twins.

"Grandfather, you should write down your adventures," said David.

I turned and stared at him. "That's a wonderful idea. Maybe I will."

"You know, Grandfather, America truly is a land of liberty," Jonathan said.

"Yes," I answered. "When those embers of freedom were lit in America and the first shot was fired, we sent a message to the world: Don't Tread On Me."

GENERAL GEORGE WASHINGTON

by Olivia Hanks

GENERAL GEORGE WASHINGTON: HOW DID THE AMERICAN REVOLUTION COME TO MY DOORSTEP?

BALTIMORE, MARYLAND, 6 MAY 1775

Greetings, fellow patriots. My name is George Washington. I am afraid you have caught me at a rather unfortunate time. Several days ago, I received the dreadful news that fighting had broken out between the King's troops and the militia in Lexington and Concord. For the past several days, I have been making my way to Philadelphia for an emergency meeting of Congress. This meeting will decide our response to Britain and the fate of our country. But how did this conflict begin, you ask?

In the year 1753, tensions were rising between the British and the French over territorial claims. As I had been a commander of the Virginia militia, I was sent as an envoy to the French, to request that they renounce their claim on British territory. The French refused to do so, and war broke out. I served as colonel in this war, but upon the death of my superior, General Braddock, in battle, I was made commander-in-chief of the entire Virginia Regiment. I desired a royal commission, with higher pay, but I was refused this commission as I was not born nor trained on the soil of Great Britain. This unequal treatment was not to be the last that I would experience.

In order to pay for the debt that had been accrued by the war, Parliament levied harsh taxes on the colonies. Despite the citizens of the colonies being British citizens, we were granted no representation, no say in the matter. I foresaw that such tyrannical taxation would have eventually reduced us to slaves, and I heartily spoke out against it, suggesting boycotting British goods as a means of opposing such measures. After the Townshend Acts were imposed upon the colonies, I became a part of the Fairfax County Committee and proposed that the colonies should have a well-regulated militia in order that they might alleviate the need for defense by Great Britain. I participated in training some of those militias, but I did not expect that they would one day be called to arms against the very country that ought to protect the colonies.

Now the day has come where we must either relinquish our rights and freedoms to Britain and become wretched slaves, or we must take up arms against her. July previous, George Mason, a fellow Virginian, penned these words about our relationship with the mother country: "Resolved, that it is our greatest wish and inclination as well as interest to continue our connection with, and dependance upon the British government; but though we are its subjects, we will use every means which Heaven gives us to prevent our becoming slaves." Those means must be violence. I desired reconciliation, not independence; but as the mother country has become the enemy, I am prepared to fight to defend my country.

GENERAL GEORGE WASHINGTON: HOW DID I GET INVOLVED IN THE AMERICAN REVOLUTION?

BOSTON, MASSACHUSETTS

December 1775

I was, as you may recall, called to Philadelphia for an emergency meeting of Congress, in which it was decided that the militia of the colonies would be banded together into one Continental Army, for which I was chosen as head. This was a great honour, but I accepted the position with some regret. Although I am glad to serve my country, I did not want to leave my wife and family.

It is December now. Boston has been under siege since April. With a lack of arms and no naval power, there is no clear way to drive the enemy out. There is a shortage of wood, food, and gunpowder. There is sickness and strife. The troops themselves are divided and disorderly. Men wish to return to their families, and I have not the money on hand to convince them to stay. I am ever grateful for the support of Martha, though I too wish to return home and be with her there.

The report of the speech of King George in August finally reached us. We are to be treated as foreign enemies, and forces are being sent to put down the rebellion. There is no turning back now; we must fight to the end. It is my hope that men, upon seeing how their mother country has turned against them, will be encouraged to join the army, and to defend themselves and their homeland.

December is coming to a close, and the new year, 1776, is fast approaching. Knox has gone to Fort Ticonderoga to retrieve cannons from there. It is a monumental task, but it may be the only way to drive the King's ships out of the harbour and end the siege. Likewise, I have sent Montgomery and Arnold up north to attack Quebec. I have hopes that their success may win our neighbors in Canada to our cause. With the aid of both the guns and the Canadians, we shall be able to break the stalemate and gain a hand over the enemy.

GENERAL GEORGE WASHINGTON: WHAT'S MY STORY IN 1776?

TRENTON, NEW JERSEY, 28 DECEMBER 1776

It is a glorious day for our country. Though this year has been one of great difficulty, Providence has smiled down on us at last. As you know, Boston was under siege by the British for many months, and after much deliberation, I approved of a plan to bring cannons down from Fort Ticonderoga and set them up to drive the British out. Knox arrived with these cannons in January. It was not until March, however, that plans, and powder allowed for an attack.

Fortifications were constructed and moved to Dorchester Heights in a night. Artillery fire was kept up to drown out this action on the Heights. On the 4th of March we engaged the enemy at last. My men fought with great ardor and courage. The British, it seems, planned for a counterattack, but providentially, the weather forbade them from carrying it out. On the 17th of March, they sailed out of the harbor, bearing away both troops and Tories. At long last, the siege had ended.

The breaking of the siege was cause for celebration—what followed was not. Near the end of June, I learned that the British were bringing a fleet down to New York and brought as many men as I could to her defense. It was a disaster. At the Battle of Brooklyn, the men turned tail and fled, and could not be convinced to stand. We were driven back, and all our fortifications captured. It was only by the hand of Providence that we were able to escape from New York—a fog came up and concealed our movements from the enemy. Also, as if by Providence, the city caught fire late in the night of the 21st of September. I wished to burn New York so that the enemy would not have snug winter quarters, but Congress forbade it. I know not whether the fire was an accident or arson; but if it be the latter, I thank the one who set it.

Christmas looked bleak. I had ordered General Lee to march his troops up to New Jersey by a safe route; regrettably, he was found in a tavern and captured. Having no knowledge of the enemy's movements, I was under the impression that Howe would attack Philadelphia as soon as the river froze, and our men went home. Enlistments were due to expire on New Year's Day. Congress had already fled Philadelphia for Baltimore. As I looked out over the river one morning and saw sheets of ice beginning to form, I knew that time was running out. At any day, the enemy could strike the final blow and defeat our cause. I could not give up on my country, however; neither would my officers.

I had been of the belief that some "brilliant stroke" might boost morale and save our cause. On Dec 22nd, Reed wrote to me and shared similar sentiments, and suggested a diversion near Trenton. I thought this a good idea and decided to cross the river and attack on Christmas night. There were to be three attacks, led by General Cadwalader, General Ewing, and I, but the ice and foul weather prevented Cadwalader and Ewing from crossing the river, and my men and I were to attack alone. Despite the hardship of both the crossing and the march to Trenton, we defeated the Hessians soundly and took hundreds prisoner. I was immensely pleased with our success and the behavior of my men. This victory rescued not only the morale of the troops, but perhaps, the entire country.

I know the war for liberty must be hard fought. We have suffered great losses, both in battle and from sickness. We have fought through hunger, plague, want of supplies, and want of clothing. We shall continue to face hardship and loss, but by Providence, we shall triumph.

MARTHA WASHINGTON

by R.G. Patterson

MARTHA WASHINGTON: HOW DID THE AMERICAN REVOLUTION COME TO MY DOORSTEP?

MOUNT VERNON PLANTATION, 9 JUNE 1776

I am afraid. Nay, I am not afraid of the dark, like a young lass. I do not want to lose my George like I lost Daniel Parke Custis eighteen years ago. When Daniel died of scarlet fever, I was left to run his plantation called White House. Though it is beautiful, 'tis quite an estate for one woman to manage. From overseeing the plantation, managing the household servants to raising my two children was entirely unheard of for a woman to do these days. If it hadn't been for our loyal slaves, I would have lost the plantation. George and I were married in 1759 and we moved to Mount Vernon. Then three years ago, my daughter, who had been ill, died as well. In 1774, my son, John Parke, got married, a bright spot in my dark time; then in September of last year, his daughter, my granddaughter, died as well.

When George started courting me in 1758, I never dreamed that he would be so honored as to be Commander of the American Army against Britain. Then last year before our granddaughter was born, he sent me a letter. It contained the announcement that Congress had selected him to command the Army. The war had been going on for several months, and now he would be serving on the front lines.

"Why must it be George?" I say fiercely to Lund as we share our evening meal of chicken and potatoes. "He has already served his role in the war with the Indians."

"I would that none of our men must fight," Lund says. "Do you not think that George would rather fight for his country than be trampled by the British?"

"Aye," I sigh. "My George is a good man. He would give his life for the colonies. And yet, it grieves me to possibly give him up forever."

"Cousin Martha," he says. "Certainly, you recall Mr. Henry's speech last year?"

"Aye," I say. "Either we lose fighting, or we win fighting. We cannot allow Britain to trample us. And yet..." I stop, trying to regain my usual cheery spirits. "I fear not for myself but my Old Man."

My Old Man, as I call George, is respectable, but I know that behind every great man is a great woman. I think back to Olympias, the mother of Alexander the Great. She was the reason he had become king. Cleopatra was behind Julius Caesar ending the civil war in Egypt. It was Lady Fatima, Muhammed's daughter who promoted the ideas of Islam. Even the mother of our Lord supported our Savior. She was the one who raised him to know the Holy Word and to follow our God.

Maybe I can be like these women in history. I may not be great, wise, or powerful, but if I can, with the help of George's cousin, Lund, run Mount Vernon, it will be one less thing for him to worry about while he is gone. When he comes home, he will certainly come home to a beautiful estate where he can rest from the horrors of war.

If he comes home, I remind myself. *Will Jacky be next?* Though he has been reckless with his estate, I would surely miss my son if anything should happen. He was such a gift from Providence when Patsy died. However, I must be strong, like all the other women who have let their husbands and sons go without a tear. Miss Smith, one of my neighbors, even supported her fiancée William O'Connor when he left for the militia. I too must remain strong for our boys.

"After all," I say to myself. "Our country affords everything that can give pleasure or satisfaction to a rational mind. That is, then, what our men are fighting for."

MARTHA WASHINGTON: HOW DID I GET INVOLVED IN THE AMERICAN REVOLUTION?

MOUNT VERNON PLANTATION, 10 JUNE 1776

*L*und comes in the next morning for our morning meal. He pulls out my chair for me before seating himself at the table.

"Martha," he says. "Do you realize that as Commander of the Army, George is committing treason to the Mother Country?"

"Nay, but I can see that it is so. Did not Mr. Henry say that our chains were being forged?"

"Aye," Lund affirms. "For leaders like Mr. Henry, George, and so many others. Even their wives have played a huge part in their roles making them traitors as well."

"Behind every great man is a woman," I muse, thinking of Miss Smith and O'Connor. "If then, I too have committed treason and the only way to escape the punishment is to win the war, then I must be treasonous with all my heart in order that should we lose, I may say that I have given my best effort. I will go to George and see what I can do for him and our brave men." I place my hand on my heart as I conclude.

"You are blessed, Martha," Lund says nodding his approval. "I will oversee the plantation."

"Aye, Lund," I say; tears fill my eyes. "In this way, you too, shall commit treason to Britain and serve your Colonies."

When the breaking of the fast is over, I hurry to my apartment and calling Lucy to aid me, I begin packing. George is over two hundred miles away in New York. I will take Lucy with me, and one of the men to drive us in our carriage. There will be many inns along the way, so there is no need to worry about the shelter at night.

Lucy and I pack dresses, bonnets, shoes, and my sewing basket into my trunk. And goodness knows, I can't leave my knitting needles behind. Perhaps some of the men need darning, mending, or knitting done. They are men, after all. Men can't and won't do those things, even our slave men will not, it is beneath their pride.

New York City, 21 June 1776

I am almost to George's headquarters. It has been a long 10 days. The inns were small and uncomfortable and the road bumpy and long. For the majority of the trip, I was left with my thoughts. I spoke with Lucy from time to time, but one quickly tires of idle talk with a slave.

I climb from the carriage. My legs almost give way and I long to stretch my back. It is not certainly proper for the wife of the colonial army's commander to be seen stretching her back, much less any other gentlewoman.

Lund sent a messenger on horseback to my Old Man so that he would be prepared for my coming. Now, here George is extending his hand to me. I want to embrace him and weep with joy. But once again my womanly training restrains me. I merely take his hand and smile. His face is tired and more ashen than when I saw him a few months prior in Cambridge. The war has made him older and somber. He smiles down at me. Then he turns and I see that he has brought several of the militia with him as an escort. The men look tired, dusty, and unkempt.

Is this the best George could do for an escort? I refrain from showing my disgust. He surely wouldn't bring less than the best of his men. *If these are the best, then what must the rest of his immediate command look like?*

"We are a shabby group, I'm afraid," George states.

"What could I have expected?" I asked. "We are in a war." George nods.

We reach Richmond Hill and as we enter the estate, I only see more dirty men. Their poor uniforms are torn and do not fit them well. I will be busy mending for them.

These are someone's sons, I tell myself. *Some of these are likely large plantation owners. What will become of these? Are they, too, considered traitors to King George III?* Suddenly, my small task doesn't seem as important. If I could just save them so that they can go back to their homes and families, I would do so before you can wring a chicken's neck.

MARTHA WASHINGTON: WHAT'S MY STORY IN 1776?

RICHMOND HILL, 28 JUNE 1776

I pull my knitting needles and yarn from my basket and commence my knitting. Jean needs fresh socks, William needs a new sweater, Friedrich needs his trousers mended, and Johnny needs his uniform taken in. From the day I got here, I have been busy meeting the many needs of the men, with hardly a moment to rest.

"Put down your basket for a moment," George says. We are sitting in the parlor of Richmond Hall, and he is playing a game of cards.

"But there is so much to do." I continue knitting. "I must accomplish this before the morrow, or I shall leave uncompleted work behind."

"Unfinished work, nonsense." George looks up from his cards. "From caring for the wounded to sewing and knitting to copying letters and advising your poor general, you have been quite the multitasker. If you were to leave now for Philadelphia with one pair of socks incomplete, none of us would think any less of you." He stands up and comes to my chair; he gently removes the knitting from my hands.

"I'm chirked that I brought Lucy. Without her, I couldn't have completed half of this." I reach for the knitting.

"Mistress Washington," he says. "As your general, I command you to rest from your work."

I giggle before sighing. How can I explain that I can't afford to wait to continue my work? I have told him about the pledge I made in Lund's presence.

"Dearest," I remind him. "I can't stop now. I promised to help you to the best of my ability so that should we lose, I can say that I have given my utmost."

"Aye, love." His face grows solemn as he senses my thoughts. I know that he understands.

"Might you accompany me as I see your men this evening?" George nods and hands me the half-finished sock back to me.

I now have finished the mending, as Lucy and I worked for the greater part of the day. I reach for my shawl and await George who approaches in full uniform. He offers me his arm, and we proceed to visit his officers.

First, I must deliver Jean his socks.

"Four pairs," he exclaims. "Why Mrs. Washington, that's more than I started out with when leaving home."

I don't know what to say, so I bow my head. He unfolds them and examines them closely.

"The finest knitting in all the Colonies," he continues. George gently guides me away.

Next, comes Johnny's uniform. He opens the door to his room. When he sees both George and me, he smiles. I hand him the uniform that I took in for him. He turns and disappears for a moment and then returns, now wearing his uniform. He beams.

"If only Mary could see me now," he says. The uniform fits him perfectly and makes him look so handsome.

My eyes water, for in him, I can see my own Jacky in uniform. We linger only a moment more.

The articles whether mended or knitted, we present to George's men. Each man expresses such overwhelming thanks. My heart gives a painful thump against my chest.

As we visit the sick and wounded, my heart feels like gunpowder blasts. What if one of these men was George? Many of them lay in only tattered shirts and trousers, their only possessions. George hired the best doctors around to tend to his men. But some of them won't see tomorrow. They have held on so long, but they can't any longer. Another lad carries a striking resemblance to Jacky. He looks up at me and stretches his hand out to us as we pass his cot.

"Mistress Washington," he croaks. "You'd best leave, for the Redcoats are on the way. Thank you for all you've done for us poor fellows."

I take his hand and I feel something cool in my hand. When we are some distance from the sickroom, I look at my hand. It is a locket. Opening it, the face of the young lad and a pretty girl stare at me

"George, who was that lad?"

"That was O' Connor," he says, his face exceptionally sober. "He came down with an illness shortly after a musket wound. He was engaged when he left to join the militia. Now, there won't be a ceremony. The doctor says he won't live 'til the 'morrow."

"Then we must return the locket to Miss Smith." I choke on my words, and tears stream down my cheeks. I recall her bravery as she let O'Connor leave smiling, waving, and ignoring her worries.

I leave for Philadelphia this morning. George tells me that Providence took O'Connor home in the night. I brush tears from my cheeks as I leave George, praying that he will come home; that we will all be together at peace.

FRENCH SYMPATHIZERS

BEAUMARCHAIS

by Madeleine Rose Wenzel

BEAUMARCHAIS: HOW DID THE AMERICAN REVOLUTION COME TO MY DOORSTEP?

LONDON, ENGLAND, 1775

As all stories must have a beginning, so does mine. I was born in Paris, France on the 24th day of January 1732, with the name Pierre-Augustin Caron. My father was a watchmaker, and my childhood was peaceful enough. At the age of ten I was sent to a country school where I learned a bit of Latin, among other things. A few years later, I was pulled from school to become an apprentice to my father. I had a habit of neglecting my work and my father grew so annoyed with this that he kicked me out of the house for my bad conduct, though he allowed me to return after many apologies on my part. My days from then on were filled with the soft ticking of the watches we made and fixed, and that got me wondering. Since watches at the time were not exactly accurate in telling time, could I perhaps do something to fix that?

I thought of that often, and by twenty-one years of age, I had created an escapement mechanism for the watches, which not only made them more accurate, but also allowed for them to be made into smaller sizes than ever before. The royal clockmaker, Jean Andre Le Paute, encouraged my work before stealing it for himself; though this was partially my fault, as I soon found out this was not the first time he had done such a thing. But I did not know that at the time. Perhaps you can imagine the anger I felt when I was reading an issue of *Le Mercune de France* and saw an article describing my mechanism under Le Paute's name. Outraged, I sent a letter to the same magazine, defending my invention. After an anxious wait for myself, while the Academy decided who was the rightful owner of the invention, they decided to recognize me as the true inventor of the escapement. I was soon asked by King Louis XV to make a watch mounted on a ring for his mistress, and not long after that I was given the position of Purveyor to the King.

In 1755, I met Madeleine-Catherine Aubertin, and a year later we were married. Soon after our marriage, I changed my name to Pierre-Augustin Caron de Beaumarchais, because I thought it sounded more aristocratic. My wife died only ten months after we had married, and I fell into debt. Since we were married only a brief time before her death, I was accused of poisoning my wife, primarily by my enemies. My financial troubles ended when I was appointed to teach King Louis XV's four daughters, the *Mesdames,* to play the harp, and soon rose to the position of a musical advisor to the royal family. In 1759, I met Joseph Paris Duverney, who would soon become my close friend, and I was able to use my position to help him gain the king's permission to build the *École Royale Militaire.* With Duverney's help, I was promoted to Secretary-Counsellor to the King, and in 1763 I purchased the title of Lieutenant General of Hunting, which meant I oversaw the Royal parks and judged intruders on the grounds.

Around this time, I became engaged to a Pauline Le Brenton, though I later broke this off. In April 1764, I took a trip to Madrid Spain to help my sister, Lisette, whose fiancé had abandoned her. While I was in Spain, I made business deals for Duverney and tried to gain the right to import slaves to the Spanish Colonies in America. I was unable to get the contracts that Duverney needed, so I went back to France in March of 1765. Though I returned with little profit, I had gathered a multitude of ideas from my time in Spain, some of which were for fictional characters to use in play writing. I also hoped to be made Consul to Spain after that, but my application was rejected. So, I began to concentrate on business things and began writing plays. My first play, *Eugenie,* premiered in *Comedie-Française* in 1767. In 1768, I married my second wife, Geneviève-Madeleine Franquet, and eight months later, our son, Augustin was born. Unfortunately, she died in 1770, and I was once again accused of poisoning my wife.

My dear friend, Duverney, also died in 1770, on the 17th of July, and a few months before his death, he and I had signed a statement saying that I no longer owed him the debts I owed him. But after his death, his only heir, Count de la Blanche took me to court, saying that the statement was a forgery! Although the 1772 verdict favored me, a judge, Goezman, overturned the verdict on appeal the following year. At the same time as this, I engaged in a dispute with the Duc de Chaulnes over his mistress, which landed me in prison. La Blanche took advantage of my situation and convinced Goezman to force me to pay back the debts I had owed Duverney, along with interest and all the legal expenses. I published a four-part pamphlet called *Memoires Contre Goezman.* In retaliation, Goezman launched his own lawsuit, and on February 26th, 1774, the both of us were sentenced to blame, meaning we were deprived of our civil rights. Magistrate Goezman was removed from his position and his verdict on the Le Blanche case was overruled, while I followed few of the restrictions that were placed upon me. After the Goezman case ended, the judges had to leave the courthouse by the back door to keep away from the angry mob out front.

To regain my civil rights, I pledged my services to King Louis XV, and was soon sent on a mission to go to London and destroy a pamphlet attacking the king's mistress. After sending them to the king so he could look at them, I was responsible for seeing them burned by fire. On my return to France, I got word that the king was quite sick with smallpox and lay dying. Three days later, he died, and the rein of King Louis XVI began. In June of 1774, there came word of a pamphlet attacking Marie Antoinette, and I offered my services to get rid of it and sailed for London once again. Once there, and with much trouble, I found the man responsible for printing the pamphlet, and after much convincing, was able to get access to all the pamphlets and burn them. Or so I thought. I had paid part of the amount of money owed the pamphlet maker, but the next morning, I found that he had left without waiting for the rest of the money owed him. I immediately realized I had been tricked by the rascal and set out in pursuit of him. From the information I was able to gather, he had left for Nuremburg, and on the 14th of August, I caught a glimpse of a man riding a horse and recognized him as Angelucci, the pamphlet maker. Hearing the wheels of my carriage, he fled. I managed to catch him after a short chase, at the end of which I found the man and his steed caught in the thick forest and pulled Angelucci from his mount and searched him to find the remaining pamphlets. I found them in the bottom of his valise, and seeing this, he begged for me to spare his life. I decided to do so, and putting my pistol away, as I had taken it out during the chase, I left him and his horse behind.

I was stopped by a man on a horse, who yelled something at me in German. I think he wanted me to give him the money I had on me. I reached into my pocket, as if to get it out, but instead grabbed my pistol, and moved back to hide behind a tree, and another, heading back toward the road, never turning my back on the man. Upon arriving at the road, I heard a voice and turned to see a second man. I fired my pistol at him, but it didn't fire. The bandits and I ended up in a fight, and I was wounded in the head and hand but managed to escape and continue my travels. Once in Vienna, I met with Empress Marie-Therese and gave her a pamphlet, then returned to the place I was staying. I was not there long when I was taken into custody until they had more information about me. I was kept there for forty-four thousand, six hundred, and forty minutes, or thirty-one days before my release, after which, I at once returned to Paris. While I was there, I worked to put my play, the *Barber of Seville*, on stage, and in April of 1775, after seeing it become a success, I headed off to London to capture more pamphlets attacking the king and queen. It was here, in London, that I begin to hear of the growing rebellion in the colonies. From what I understand, the colonies in America are trying to reject the tyrant, King George III. They don't want to be controlled by a King who lives across an entire ocean from them! And I must say, I feel a special place in my heart for the people longing to be free, just like they do in my play, *Le Barber de Séville.*

Learning more about the conflict between Great Britain and her renegade Colonies, I decided that France had a role to play in this rebellion. Furthermore, I was the best person to convince the French Government to support the Americans. So, in my next report to King Louis XVI, I asked if I could gather intelligence for him. A few weeks later, I sent another letter asking the same. In this letter, I reminded the King of my perfect knowledge of Great Britain and its forces, resources, and banking. In addition, I reminded him that I knew everyone in a position of power, as well as the language, although in truth I could not speak any English. I may have been embellishing a bit.

BEAUMARCHAIS: HOW DID I GET INVOLVED IN THE AMERICAN REVOLUTION?

LONDON, ENGLAND, 11 SEPTEMBER 1775

My friend, John Wilkes, invited me to a dinner party at his house on the 11th of September 1775. I had been there many times and had the opportunity to meet many Americans from whom I gathered information to send to my correspondents in Versailles: Sartine, Maurepas, and Vergennes. This time was different though. This time I met Arthur Lee. Who is he? We sat at the table, having a polite conversation when he asked me, "Have you heard about the war in the Colonies, Sir?"

"*Oui*," I replied. "How are things proceeding over there?"

"Well, we have plenty of men who are willing to fight, but we don't have the necessary supplies."

"Oh?" I leaned forward, eager to hear more. "Pray tell, what do you need?"

"We need money, arms, and powder most urgently," he told me. "Without those, we won't be able to keep fighting very long."

Versailles, France, Mid-September 1775

I promised to talk to the King in the Americans' favor, so a week later, I took a trip to the countryside, or so people thought. I really headed to Versailles to meet with Sartine and Vergennes with information far too confidential to trust to even the most dependable courier. On the 21st of September, I wrote to the King, about what was happening in Great Britain. I pleaded on behalf of the Americans, that they are "resolved to suffer anything rather than bend."

Tensions were remarkably high since the King of Great Britain declared the Americans to be rebels. I also asked what France should do and offered my opinion that we should get involved, offering to spy once again. I was impatient to get back to London, and the next day asked Vergennes if I should wait for the King's response to my letter. Vergennes asked me to please wait until the next day and got me an audience with the King before my departure.

I managed to convince the King to give me permission to spy, so long as nothing could be traced back to the French government. I was delighted to finally officially be a part of something so important. Relations between France and Great Britain rested on my decisions, as I was already quite influential. Most of all, I finally had the power to help the Americans in their struggle for independence!

London, England, Late September 1775

I left for London the evening of the 23rd and upon arriving there, I immediately drew up a brilliant plan for the King which he much appreciated. I needed to get money to the Colonies without any tracing back to the French monarchy, so the King looked neutral in the conflict for the time being. So, I created a shipping company called the Roderigue Hortalez Company, and the French government would pay me in currency, under the greatest cloak of secrecy, of course. And I sent half of the currency to Portugal to be made into gold pieces and then sent to America for paper currency. Those were the only forms of non-British currency recognized in the Colonies. Congress then promised to send tobacco in exchange for this half million, which my company would sell for a fair price.

With the other half of the money, we would secretly buy

gunpowder from the French and send it to America. Then Congress would buy it from us for four times the amount we paid for it. We would then use this wonderful profit to do this repeatedly. By circulating the money this way, we will be able to support the Americans by sending more weapons and powder to the colonies.

BEAUMARCHAIS: WHAT'S MY STORY IN 1776?

LONDON, ENGLAND, JANUARY 1776

I try not to look back as I hurry through the streets. I know that I'm being followed, but if I give any sign of suspicion, they will surely not leave me alone. My best course of action is to keep moving, and hope that I lose them in the streets.

After the King didn't respond to the dispatch I sent on the first day of the new year, I decided to take things into my own hands. I could tell that I had persuaded Vergennes to see my opinions, though he was not yet fully convinced. I also decided to not involve Ambassador de Guines, for he was an inadequate Ambassador. I started to form new relationships that would help the cause of the Revolt in the colonies. I passed around writings in the taverns, I made plans, and created contracts with merchants who sent supplies to Great Britain's colonies. I even joined a secret society called the Friends of America. My inability to stay still must have caught the attention of Lord Stormont, the British Ambassador to France, as he soon had his spies constantly watching me, which is how I ended up in this predicament. At first, I was unconcerned about being followed everywhere, but soon, I recognized that my safety may be in peril.

I make it back to where I am living and shut the door firmly behind me, breathing a sigh of relief. I'm still not safe here, but 'tis better than being out on the streets. I pull the curtains over the windows and make sure that the door is locked before grabbing some parchment, ink, and my quill to retreat to the back room. I need to write Vergennes.

Versailles, France, February 1776

"The chance of peace between France and Great Britain is growing slim." I pace the floor as I meet with Vergennes again. I had recently increased my Channel crossings and was now meeting with him nearly every day. "You must see that the best course of action would be to openly support the colonies!"

"The King does not wish for war," Vergennes calmly replied. "France is still in debt from the Seven Years' War; it would be unwise to get involved in this conflict so soon."

"Getting involved would be an economic advantage!" I retorted.

Vergennes lifted his chin and gave me a hard look. "And if the American Rebels lose?"

"They almost won at Bunker Hill!" I argued.

"But they did *not* win, and that was only one battle," Vergennes asserted.

I keep trying to persuade Vergennes. I can see him slowly getting increasingly convinced as time goes on, and I think he's losing hope that the peace can be saved, but he's not ready to admit it quite yet.

Paris, France, July 1776

The American representative Silas Deane asked to meet me once he arrived in Paris. I agreed and was extremely excited to meet him on the 19th. Before we had agreed to negotiate, I asked to see his credentials, and he sent them to me the next day. Then we just had to go through the proper diplomacy and draw up a contract for my company to secretly ship guns, powder, and supplies to the Colonies, which we did in late July. In my contract letter, I added a warning to make sure he knew that we needed to keep this all completely confidential, and though Deane was pleased that our negotiations were going so well, he told me that he felt that he, too, was constantly being watched by the British spies.

Le Havre, France, 12 December 1776

I stood amid an applauding crowd; they are applauding for me! Yes, I had taken a small break from my duties to attend a performance of *Le Barbier de Séville*. How could I not? It was performing in the very town I was visiting on the very same night! I arrived early to help the actors rehearse, completely forgetting that I was supposed to be travelling under the assumed identity of "Durand." I, of course, did not forget that I was not supposed make a spectacle of myself, and so accepted the applause as discreetly as I could afterwards. I had also failed to remember that spies continued to watch my every more, and I nearly got myself in a lot of trouble by attending the performance. It was worth it though. The adulation was well-deserved if I do say so myself!

I was in Le Havre to see off several ships carrying powder and supplies to the colonies. I nearly ruined the whole thing by attending the play. Lord Stormont was not pleased to find this out and ordered an inspection of all the ships. The only one to escape was the *Amphitritus*, the only one that had left port when the inspectors arrived. The others all got disarmed, and Vergennes gave me a stern talking to and told me my ships could no longer land on the French mainland, only at the islands. He was only saying this to keep Lord Stormont off our trail though.

After this, we sent the ships out with two different sets of instructions. One that was secret and showed where they were really going, and one to show to any inspectors that they might meet. Even though I managed to get myself into trouble many times over, I was just as good at getting out of it, and most of my ships arrived safely in the Colonies!

MARQUIS DE LAFAYETTE

by Joy Elizabeth Tardy

MARQUIS DE LAFAYETTE: HOW DID THE AMERICAN REVOLUTION COME TO MY DOORSTEP?

Bonjour! My name is Marie-Joseph-Paul-Yves-Roch-Gilbert du Motier, le Marquis de Lafayette. However, Gilbert is my nickname used by my family and dearest friends. When I was born on September 6, 1757, my father Roch-Gilbert, was a French soldier fighting in the Seven Years' War. My *mère*, Julie, eagerly waited for my *père's* return. He never came home. On August 1, 1759, my *père* was killed by a British cannon shot in the Battle of Minden against General Phillips of England. Heartbroken, *mère* left me with my *grand-mère* at the Château de Chavaniac so she could live in Paris with her *père* and *grand-père.*

At two-years-old, I became the official lord of our Château, which is our family's large mansion in the southern French countryside. My home was lonely because I was an only child. Some peasants lived on a farm nearby, and they paid their taxes to my *grand-mère* named Marie-Claire. *Grand-mère* taught me: how to treat the peasants with respect, make sure they had medical attention, seeds to plant, and food on their tables. One extraordinary day, my Aunt Charlotte and Cousin Marie came to live with my *grand-mère* and me. I was so very excited! Marie's father also had been killed in this dreadful Seven Years' War. I was five years old, and Marie was six. We all rejoiced that the Seven Years' War had finally concluded, but sadly England had won in the end.

When I was a young boy of eight years old and still living in the Château, I heard there was a beast killing my neighbors' animals. Then I thought of a bright idea! My family's motto "Cur *Non?*" meant "Why Not?" in Latin. So, *Cur Non?* Search for the beast myself? So, alone, I hunted the beast in the forest for many days but could not find it. After that experience, I pretended to be an officer in the army of King Louis XV. A soldier could not be an officer unless they had the king's permission, which I wanted so badly.

September 1768

I was eleven years old and still lived in the countryside. My *mère* sent for me to live with her in Paris and attend college. We lived in the Luxembourg Palace, which was much grander than the Château, but I missed my sweet *grand-mère*, Marie-Claire, kind *Tante* Charlotte, and loving cousin Marie. My *mère* and *grand-père* sent me to College de Plessis, one of the best colleges in all of Paris. I studied math, history, geography, French literature, the Classics, and Latin. *Grand-Père* taught me a noble never walked when they could ride in a carriage. So, when coming and going from school I rode in a carriage. When school was not in session Julie sent me to balls and fancy dinner parties, but my heart still longed to be in the French military.

On 3 April 1770, my *chere mère* Julie died at thirty-three years of age. Only three months later my gentil *grand-père* also departed. I was only thirteen years old when I lost both *mère* and *grand-père*. I was now the richest orphan in France, but wealth could not comfort me in the loss of my *affectuese mère* and *merveilleux grand-père*. Then my *arrière-grand-père* took care of me, and he arranged for King Louis XV to make me a Black Musketeer. I loved my uniform, riding my horse, and the honor of being reviewed by King Louis XV himself.

When I was fourteen years old, my *arrière-grand-père* arranged for me to marry *jolie* twelve-year-old Marie Adrienne Francoise de' Noailles d'Ayen. Two years later, on April 11, 1774, we were married.

King Louis XV and his *petits-enfants* attended our wedding. King Louis XV's wedding gift to us was a French Bulldog. We named her Nelly. Soon after *charmante* Adrienne and I were wed, King Louis XV passed away. Our new king was King Louis XVI, the grandson of our departed king. Adrienne and I were close friends with King Louis XVI and Queen Marie Antoinette. I knew this was the life my *mère* envisioned for me, but all I really wanted was to be a soldier. My favorite thing to do was go to the army camp called Metz to train for the French military.

On 8 August 1775, King George III's brother the Duke of Gloucester came to Metz to visit us. I overheard the duke speaking about a Revolutionary war being waged in the American colonies. When I heard this, I wanted to join the war and help America break free of England. I also learned the first shot of the Revolutionary war was fired in April of 1775. That was the month Adrienne became pregnant. On December 15,1775, my darling *chèrie* wife had a baby girl. Adrienne and I named her Henriette du Motier de Lafayette. A year later an American representative named Silas Deane came to get help from France in the war. I was so ready to give my heart and sword to America. *Cur Non?*

MARQUIS DE LAFAYETTE: HOW DID I GET INVOLVED IN THE AMERICAN REVOLUTION?

*S*ilas took in a deep breath of fresh ocean air. The smell of salt reminded him of his former business as a merchant. He spent a lot of time at the docks, arranging shipments and inspecting his ships to ensure his buyers received the highest quality goods. In whatever work he found himself, he would give himself fully to the assignment.

The day following the arrival of the first recruitment letter, from the Committee of Secret Correspondence, he was sent another, longer message containing specific instructions about his mission to France. Silas acted swiftly, writing to the owner of his small apartment to end the rental agreement, and sending his slave with a fare back to Connecticut. He had found a ship, the *Betsy*, leaving for France on the fourth of March, and immediately arranged for his passage. It was a bittersweet time, having to uproot himself from the comforts he was used to and place himself in a new and foreign environment. But he knew without a doubt that this was what he wanted. It was a chance to do more for the Colonies and to deal a greater blow to the British.

He took one long, last look upon the town of Philadelphia where he had lived for a year as miles of ocean continued to separate him from his past. Exhaling, he turned his back towards the fading sight, and retreated down into the lower decks of the ship. It would be a long voyage, plagued with both dreams of fear, excitement, and a longing for home.

6 July 1776

Arriving in the bustling heart of France was overwhelming. The people of Paris moved in a whirlwind of activity, their foreign tongue disorienting him at every turn. Silas was easily flustered by his language barrier. Not only was he lost in this unfamiliar environment but having to rely on his own funds to pay for the journey from the Bordeaux coast to Paris was quite irritating. All the Colonial money he was paid by Congress had completely lost its worth as soon as the boat's underbelly touched French waters.

Nevertheless, it was important for him to find lodgings as soon as possible, or his true mission would be stalled. Not any residence would do; it had to be fitting for a "Bermuda merchant," his cover persona. *Hôtel Villars*, a French hotel in Paris, seemed to fit the match.

As soon as he arrived in France, he sent for an old acquaintance, Dr. Edward Bancroft, to join him. Once Bancroft came knocking on Silas's door, it was a joyful reunion. He learned much about his former student's dealings, the most shocking of which was how Benjamin Franklin employed him as his own private secret agent to work the inner circles of the British government. Silas did not hesitate in referring to Bancroft as his chief source information about the British.

After reuniting with his friend, Silas alerted Mr. Dubourg of his arrival, the contact provided by Congress, and arranged to meet with him at the Frenchman's personal residence.

Written jointly by Joy Elizabeth Tardy (Marquis de Lafayette) and Elyce Corsetti (Silas Deane)

MARQUIS DE LAFAYETTE: WHAT'S MY STORY IN 1776?

In 1765, when I was eight-years-old, I felt the call to the glory of a battle in my heart. My heritage was a lengthy line of officers, including Joan of Arc. My family's expectations of me were to be in the Black Musketeers, an army officer, and carry on the family name by having a son. My dream was to be a *magnifique* soldier of rank, and to feel the thrill of war. After marrying, my *belle mariée* understood my passion for triumph. My father-in-law, Duc d'Ayen, often sent me to Metz, the National Academy for French military. In 1775, I received, "captaincy and a command in the Noailles Dragoons." While at Metz, Prince William had a dinner party, and invited commander Charles-Francois de Broglie, Marquis de Ruffec, and me. We discussed the American colonies' revolution. At once, I knew that my heart and sword belonged to the American people's cause for freedom.

Having failed as a courtier, and now as a captain without a command, my court position was gone, because I had insulted the *Comte de Provence, suivant dans l'ordre de succession au trone.* As time passed, more stories of the American colonies reached my ears, and I felt my tug to personally go help the Americans. Here are thoughts I wrote to my *douce mariée*, Adrienne,

Never before had such a glorious cause attracted the attention of mankind; it was the final struggle of liberty, and its defeat would have left it neither asylum nor hope. When I first heard of [the American Revolution], my heart was enlisted, and I thought only of joining the colors.

My favorite act of Americas defiance was Patrick Henry's famous, "Give me Liberty or give me Death!" speech from 1775. That made my heart long even more to go help America throw off the tyranny.

An American diplomat, *Monsieur* Silas Deane, was sent by the American Continental Congress to enlist aid from the French government. He sailed from Connecticut to a close harbor near Paris, France. On 5 November 1776, we met with Baron De Kalb as the translator, where I declared, "My heart and sword belong to America. You may think I am too young to fight, but I carry experience beyond my youth." On 7 December 1776, Silas Deane handed me my commission of Major General. I made my plans to go to America and bought the ship, *La Victoire.* She was a twenty-two-ton ship, with a crew of thirty, and was also secretly outfitted with two guns, and provisions of food. *La Victoire* was then loaded with commercial cargo. The final cost was 1,112 *livres* for the guns, food, and commercial cargo, and 40,000 *livres* for the contract.

I secretly intended to go to America, regardless of support. Indeed, five of my most important counselors were against me fighting for America. *Premier Ministre* Vergennes of France told my father-in-law, Duc d'Ayen, that French nobles were specifically forbidden to wage war in America. Even the King of France himself had forbidden me to go. England's Prime Minister, Lord Fredric North, threatened to break diplomatic ties with France and attack France if they gave America any more military aid. Therefore, *Premier Ministre* Vergennes recalled the French forces that were going to help America's cause, and told me my plan was impetuous, and unpolitical. The last threat came from Commander de Broglie, where he publicly arrested any French officer without kindness or mercy for their confession of disobeying the Crown's orders. My father-in-law was furious with me because I was going to leave my family, especially my pregnant young wife. It was as if I was a lone voice for freedom.

At my father-in-law's urging, I went to visit the newest French ambassador to England, my uncle, the Marquis de Noailles. The thirteen colonies' right to liberty was my plea. The London society had scheduled a gala in honor of my stay. In a letter to *my cherie*, I told her, "London was beautiful, and everyone here is so kind; we dance, we dine, and we always stay up late." Missing my family and secretly needing to be on a ship bound for America, I contrived an excuse to my English hosts for having to go back home to Paris. When back in France, I sought political refuge at my friend, de Kalb's home. I made it known that my father-in-law and Adrienne had given me permission to go to America and was remaining undercover to keep them from public embarrassment.

On April 20, 1776, my ship *La Victoire* sailed for America, and my quest for glory on the battlefields of America would soon begin.

French Glossary

bonjour - hello
père - father mère - mother
grand-mère – grandmother
grand-père - grandfather tante -aunt
cher - dear
gentil- kind
affectueux - loving merveilleux - wonderful
arrière-grand-père - great-grand-father
jolie - pretty petits-enfants - grandchildren
charmant - lovely cherie - darling
comme c' merveilleux – how wonderful Monsieur – Mr.
enchantè – pleased to meet you au revoir - goodbye
magnifique - magnificent
belle mariée – beautiful bride
Comte de Provence suivant dans l'ordre de succession au trone - Count of Provence following in the order of succession to the throne
douce mariée – sweet bride
livres – French currency

KING LOUIS XVI

by Carmene Miller

KING LOUIS XVI: HOW DID THE AMERICAN REVOLUTION COME TO MY DOORSTEP?

"*Bonjour, je suis le Roi Louis XVI de France.*" This means, hello my name is King Louis XVI of France. My coronation took place in 1774 when I was twenty years old. However, I was married at the age of fifteen to a young woman named Marie Antoinette of Austria to strengthen the alliance between our two countries. I married because it was my duty to France to strengthen my country's status. I did not know Marie Antoinette when we married; she enjoyed things I did not then, and I still do not enjoy. While I enjoyed quieter activities such as reading and lock-smithing, Marie enjoyed more vibrant activities such as lavish parties and fashionable dresses and jewelry. She loves the noise and the atten-tion of the gold-gilded crowd. This is something I cannot bring myself to enjoy. I did not love her when we married; she is too different. However, I hope that one day we will be able to find a friendship and then a love for each other, like my mother had for my father. Till that day comes I remain in this marriage out of duty for France.

I do enjoy my reign and the chances to pursue for the glory of France. However, ruling as a king is not always easy and France has lost many battles during its long history.

What pains me the most is our loss to Great Britain and King

George III during my grandfather's rule as King Louis XIV. The French and Indian War lasted for seven years from 1754 -1763. We lost to England. I vow that during my rule I will bring France to great fame and get revenge on England. I have recently heard that across the Atlantic, the American Colonists are angry at the same diabolical King George III of England. I do not have any kind words to say about that horrible man and I can feel my anger rising at the thought of all France has been through and lost because of him.

A Colonist named Patrick Henry in 1775, declared to the Second Virginia Convention, "Give me liberty or give me death." It sounds just like French philosopher Jean-Jacques Rousseau in his 1762 work, *The Social Contract*. "Man is born free and everywhere he is in chains." Perhaps General Washington's troops read *The Social Contract*.

I had the strangest dream last night. I was walking around a French village and out of nowhere I was being talked to by a red squirrel. I thought it strange that the red squirrel had the name Pierre, the name of one of my most loyal friends, but my friendship with Pierre is a story for another time. This red squirrel said to me, "The Revolutionary War has started, and England will fall. The Colonies will become independent, but they will need your help in defeating King George." I jumped out of bed, shouting, "Finally that King George III will lose!" Sadly, my servants were in the room and let's just say, it was quite embarrassing. I ordered them never to speak of that moment to others. Still, I cannot believe that England would fail, and the Colonies would need my help. This will show my nemesis, King George III of England, the extent of my power.

I already started sending a small supply to America in May 1776 through an American trader named Silas Deane. However, we must be careful because if England finds out we have been helping the colonies, it could create another problem that we cannot afford. I wanted to help the colonies because of our loss of the French and Indian War, and I wanted to get revenge on that conniving King George III. One could say, I was seeking revenge.

The same red squirrel in my dream also told me about a Declaration of Independence written by a man named Thomas Jefferson. The Second Constitutional Convention chose him because he was one of their best writers. This Thomas Jefferson must be excellent for them to ask him to write something of such importance. I will have to read this Declaration. Love the dream!

One of my messengers is Benjamin Franklin, and several commissioners have left the colonies, to arrive in France in a few days to negotiate an alliance between the colonies and France. The colonies have worked hard for their achievements and our supplies can help them. I am happy do so, especially if it gets them away from England. Finally, my dreams are coming true. Take that, King George III, you, and your country will suffer defeat. I will do everything in my power to make it happen.

KING LOUIS XVI: HOW DID I GET INVOLVED IN THE AMERICAN REVOLUTION?

The reason I became involved in the American Revolution was because of Pierre de Beaumarchais who I knew through my *grand-père*. Beaumarchais was my *grand-pere's* watchmaker which also meant that he would occasionally fix watches when needed. It was during these visits to fix watches that I had the opportunity to spend time getting to know him. He was fantastic! He was an educated and well-traveled man with endless stories of places he had been. The more I got to know him the more he shared of his support for the American Colonies in gaining their independence from Britain.

Beaumarchais has spoken to me of the situation over the Pond in the American Colonies. They are at the beginning of their journey fighting for their independence from Britain. Beaumarchais has said to me that assisting in this fight was an opportunity to regain the Canadian territory from the British. Getting Canada back and assisting the Colonies in defeating England would be a wonderfully embarrassing loss for Britain. I smile to myself when I think about the look on the face of King George III when he receives news that he has lost the American Colonies. Beaumarchais has also told me that the

American Colonies are rich in natural resources that could help France regain financial power. We would have the ability to trade for the best the American Colonies could offer. Beaumarchais also mentioned that my *grand-père* had agreed with supporting the Colonies' quest for independence.

In addition to Beaumarchais, the American representatives Benjamin Franklin, Silas Deane, and Arthur Lee have also convinced me to help the American colonies. I was surprised how convincing they were, explaining their points of view and love of their country; it just makes sense to me to support this. I think they are good men because of their love for their country. Plus, I see the chance to humiliate and weaken Britain and in humiliating Britain I will make France strong again.

In one of my dreams the red squirrel came to see me again. I asked the red squirrel if these dreams were truths or if my dreams were just dreams. The squirrel nodded to me walking slowly away. I followed until we stood in front of a guillotine. I can hear the dull screaming of the crowd but what catches my attention is the sound of the blade falling through the air. I see sadness in the squirrel's eyes and then I wake up. As I lay in bed, I wonder to myself, *Why does this seem so real?* A king does not have time for dreams, because I have a country to rule and Britain to humiliate.

I have lost many people in my life. My brother and father died from Tuberculosis when I was eleven years old. My mom has remained sad about the loss of my father and brother. I do miss them dearly even though I feel that my father gave all the attention to my brother. Even so I think that I could have learned from them and maybe, how to be a better king. If they were here, they would be able to provide guidance on how to support the Colonies.

As a king, you must be aware of problems and solutions for these problems. The most current problem on my mind, after the financial issues that France has, is helping the American Colonies win their war. The problem is Great Britain's desire to expand their vast rule. They are greedy to no end. That no good King George and his Seven

Years' War plunged France into debt to where we cannot yet risk another war until we have rebuilt our army and navy. So, for now I will support the American Colonies secretly with Beaumarchais planning to provide them needed support and resources like gunpower, guns, and uniforms. France's support will make the American troops stronger so they can fight against the British lion. But Britain must not become aware of our actions until France is also strong enough to join the fight.

I recently was told that Marquis de Lafayette went against my orders and sailed to the American Colonies to fight against Britain. He is as angry with Britain as I am and shares my desire to defeat Britain in any way possible. He was brought to the palace of Versailles, and we had the ability to meet. Lafayette is young, only nineteen-years old! However, I liked his spirit, and he will go far. He wanted to join the fight with the Americans, but he was too young, plus being such a high-profile member of French nobility would get the attention of Great Britain. King George could then easily accuse me of sending French soldiers to fight against him. So, I said no. As I said, he has a bold spirit, and he proceeded despite my answer. He was on his way to the American Colonies before I could say, "Stop that ship!" I hope he survives the war. My father told me stories of how strong the kingdom of Britain is in war; however, Lafayette is a strong young man, and his determination can take him far. Who knows? He might help in turning this war against Britain. I will send daily prayers for his safety and return to France.

So, France now has people in place that are secretly moving against Britain by assisting the American Colonies in their fight for independence. We may be at the beginning of this fight, but I believe that this is a fight that we can win. I am a king that knows what is best for my people and country. Even though our finances are very low and the people are struggling, I still must make this choice for the future strength of France.

Being a king can be difficult. You must make decisions that you are unsure of, and it is the continual thought of your country and your people that makes the crown heavy to bear. I do not like the fact that my people are suffering, and that they are starving. I wish I was able to do something about it. I pray that I will be able to give the French people what they need. God has blessed me with a good rule and loyal friends. God will help me find my way through this struggle.

KING LOUIS XVI: WHAT'S MY STORY IN 1776?

*M*on *Dieu,* what a challenging time for my beloved France. Last year's problems triggered many sufferings for our people in 1776. A severe food shortage resulted in a severe poverty for the people of France, especially the common folk. Food was in short supply, and prices were so high that it was not easy for families to acquire food. The problems were so hard that a wave of 300 riots took place from April to May, called the Flour Wars, and required military intervention and price limitations on grain. Before the conflicts, the government of France attempted to remove land and labor tax. Unfortunately, this did not have the result for which I hoped, only increasing the cost of grain. This increase of cost made it more problematic for people to buy food which led into the Flour Wars. These were such trying times and while I could speak more about these trials, let me focus on how this situation affected France in 1776.

The situation in France was terrible, and a plan needed to be made to assist her with her current state and secure her future. I felt helping France would best come from assistance to the New World said to hold many resources. With a partnership with the Colonies, I am confident that I would be able to reform France's strength and secure the future of my beloved country. Though I know that right now there are many sufferings in France and my people suffer, if I could just be given time to secure this partnership then with God's grace, I can pull France out of these challenging times.

So, to encourage a partnership with the American Colonies to secure France's future and embarrass that dreadful King George, I approved sending supplies to support their efforts in their war against Great Britain. Supplies were first sent through a company by the name of *Rodrique Hortalez et Compagnie.* This company was a fake company ran by Louis Unzaga y Amezéga le Conciliateur with the purpose of getting supplies such as ammunition, clothing, and other needs to the Colonies from Spain. This idea was created by my clever friend, Pierre Beaumarchais. Strangely enough, the red squirrel from my dreams seems remarkably like Beaumarchais. How odd that I think of the red squirrel each time I look at Pierre.

While partnership with the Colonies will hopefully happen, for a king, there are many troubling issues to address. I believe strongly in moving France forward towards a more educated thought and change. One of these situations I hope to change is serfdom. An additional problem I am working to change is the lack of fairness. The nobility does not pay the taxes that the common people of France must. An area of change that is needed is in the thought of people of the non-Catholic faith being considered less important than the people of the Catholic faith. I would like to see more kindness towards people of different faiths. I am also interested in growing our understanding of various parts of the world, and I hope to work on establishing a fleet to increase exploration and bring the knowledge back to France. Also, in 1774 I initiated a Paris School of Medicine, so now I am still interested in making sure it provides its students an education to care for the people of France.

While my duties as a monarch occupy much of my time, I still find time to enjoy hunting, masonry work and locksmithing. I also enjoy reading to increase my knowledge of the world and other countries and cultures as well as educating myself in different languages such as

Latin, English, and Greek. I also enjoy reading and discussing topics such as history, geography, science, and law.

While this year in France is a period of doubt and challenges, it is also a moment in time of change and hope for the future. I hope and pray daily for God's grace and favor over France. The war in the American Colonies will be won, and the British suffer a stinging defeat at the hands of the Colonies!

However, I had a disturbing nightmare last night. I dreamt of the red squirrel again who told me of the Colonists' victory, but instead of feeling joyous the squirrel was sad.

"Why are you so unhappy?" I asked.

"France's monarchy will fall."

I was aghast! However, he refused to tell me anything more.

Instead, we sit down on a hill overlooking lush French fields. We sat there hours in peace until an angry crowd let out a disturbing roar. The squirrel looked at me in sorrow as the fields melted away.

Awakening in a panic, I worried, *What does this dream mean for the future of France?*

BRITISH LOYALISTS

SIR GUY CARLETON

by Kit P.

SIR GUY CARLETON: HOW DID THE AMERICAN REVOLUTION COME TO MY DOORSTEP?

Quebec, British Canada, 28 December 1775

*B*ANG! BANG! Someone was pounding on the door with the force of a cannon. Startled, I raced over and whisked it open.

"Who are you?" I asked, even more startled. "To what do I owe this visit?"

"Lieutenant," the man said with his low, husky voice, "I have a letter for you." The man who seemed to be a messenger gave me a piece of tightly sealed parchment.

"Who is the letter from?" I asked the messenger.

"The letter is from General Thomas Gage, and it is sent with great importance, sir," the messenger replied.

"Thank you, and goodnight," I said, shutting the door. I raced to the kitchen of my home, grabbed a candle, and ran upstairs. I lit my candle and opened the letter. It read:

Lieutenant Governor Carleton,

We need troops in America right away. Those ungrateful Colonists have begun to rebel against us in earnest. We must put them in their place right away. In case you don't understand, I will explain why. During the French and Indian War, Great Britain had to pay money to defend the Colonies which left Great Britain saddled with great debt. So, Parliament decided to tax the Colonists, but they refused to pay the taxes over and over again. They even dumped an entire shipment of tea into the Boston Harbor in protest. In retaliation, we blockaded their harbor so no one could get in or out. Then British troops went to Lexington and Concord, and the war started after an American tried to shoot them. I am currently in Boston, and we need more troops immediately. I will try to be at the docks to ensure their safe arrival, but there may be another battle that will keep me from getting there so the troops must be able to fight immediately. Do not send the troops in the morning. Send them tonight! I also need your advice on an appropriate plan of attack. Send that with the troops.

-General Gage

I grabbed a fresh sheet of parchment and wrote down my plan for General Gage. My plan would be to create an ambush and surprise the Rebels.

I grabbed my satchel and darted out the door. I went to the barn, quickly saddled a brown horse and together the horse and I galloped to the training grounds where the troops would surely be.

"TROOPS ONE, TWO! ARE YOU PRESENT?" I yelled.

"TROOP ONE IS PRESENT!" Troop One yelled in unison.

"WHERE IS TROOP TWO?" I yelled.

"TROOP TWO IS ABSENT!" Troops One yelled in unison.

"IS THERE ANOTHER TROOP WILLING TO HELP ME?" I yelled even louder.

"TROOP TWELVE IS PRESENT! WE WILL ASSIST YOU!" Troop Twelve yelled.

"Where are all of my troops?" I mumbled to myself.

"WHAT DO YOU NEED?" the two troops yelled.

"I NEED ALL OF YOU TO COME DOWN TO THE DOCKS WITH ME. YOU TWO TROOPS WILL BOARD A SHIP TO BOSTON. FROM THERE YOU WILL ASSIST GENERAL GAGE IN BATTLE, FOR THE COLONISTS HAVE BEGUN TO REBEL, AND WE MUST PUT THEM IN THEIR PLACE!" I yelled, and my voice cut from yelling.

"YES! SIR!" the troops yelled back.

"OKAY! FOLLOW ME!" I yelled. We were off. The troops and I were walking through darkness, the stars our only light, on our way to the Canadian docks. Around thirty minutes later we arrived at the docks.

"STAY RIGHT HERE!" I yelled to the troops. I walked off to find a group of sailors. It didn't take long to find some.

"Excuse me," I said to get their attention, "I need a ship to Boston immediately that can hold two of my troops, just over a thousand men total."

"That's a big order," one of the sailors said, "You see, it's about time for us to go to bed, so we can't sail a ship there."

"You can go to jail or sail the ship," I said.

"Who do you think you are, acting so powerful with the 'you can go to jail' bit," the sailor said.

"I am Lieutenant Governor Carleton, and I demand you to sail a boat to Boston to deliver my troops to General Gage!" I said, my voice progressively getting louder.

"I am deeply sorry sir, I hope you will forgive me, I thought you were just a commoner. Yes sir, I will sail a ship to deliver your troops to General Gage," The sailor said, tripping over himself.

"Good," I said. I ran back to the troops. "Follow me!" I said, waving my hand in the direction I wanted them to go. When we got to the dock, the sailors motioned for us to come one dock over to get to the ship. The captain was already on board and motioned for the soldiers to get on the ship. I watched them board until I saw the most trust-worthy soldier from Troop Twelve. He had brown hair, and emerald-green eyes, so green that I could still see them in the darkness. I pulled him aside and whispered, "Will you take my plan to General Gage?" I held out a piece of tightly sealed parchment.

"Yes, sir," he whispered back. He boarded the ship with the rest of the men, and I watched the ship set sail.

I got back home and stumbled upstairs to my bed. I was exhausted. I fell asleep in an instant. However, I dreamed of a war in which muskets were people and people were muskets. It was so strange! The muskets were holding people and pointing them like a musket and then using those people to shoot other muskets. I woke up in a cold sweat, gasping for air. The dream may sound funny, but I can assure you, it wasn't.

I tried to go back to sleep but couldn't. I got out of bed and felt my way downstairs to get a new candle. I used its light to find my way back upstairs through the shadowy corridor to get to my desk.

I never realized how scary my house looked at night. *Maybe I should go back to bed,* I thought. Instead, I went back to my desk and started writing a journal. The first entry was like this:

It was a normal night, like no other when there was a very loud knock on my door. I opened it to see a messenger. The messenger gave me a letter from General Gage. The letter told me how the Colonists from Great Britain's thirteen Colonies had begun to rebel against us and that troops were needed in Boston. I raced to the training grounds on a horse to get troops so I could send them to America right away for the next battle. I got troops and headed to the docks. I had a run-in with a few sailors who were a little less than friendly. They weren't going to sail my troops to Boston that night like I demanded of them, but I soon got them to obey me (A little threatening did the trick).

-Sir Guy Carleton

It was 3 in the morning, by far one of my least favorite hours of the day, so I blew out my candle and went back to bed.

When I woke up, I was still tired, and I had nothing to do except wait around and see if another messenger would come. I decided to lay in bed for another hour.

SIR GUY CARLETON: HOW DID I GET INVOLVED IN THE AMERICAN REVOLUTION?

QUEBEC, BRITISH CANADA

29 December 1775

BANG! BANG! Someone was pounding on the door. *Again?* I thought, a little annoyed, for I was still in bed because it had only been ten minutes since I had woken up, yet I was relieved to get word. I needed to answer the door, so I jumped out of bed and tossed on some decent clothes. I bolted downstairs and threw open the door.

"Sir, I have another letter for you," said the messenger who appeared to be the same one that was at my house yesterday.

"Thank you. Goodbye," I said, snatching the parchment out of his hand and slamming the door in his face. I opened the letter, and it read:

Lieutenant Governor,

We were on the ship for five hours. It was dark and damp. It smelled like rotting fish. Nobody was there to greet us as we disembarked. It was a journey from the ship but when we finally arrived in Boston there were screams and gunshots, and it sounded like it was coming from a hill far in the distance. Mothers were herding their kids inside their houses with looks of fear on their faces. Our troops ran to the source of the screams and gunshots, where we found a battle had already begun. We joined the fight and many of us got shot down, including me. I fell and was wounded badly. As I lay gravely wounded, I am handing the plan you gave me to a fellow soldier who has promised to deliver it to General Gage for I don't think I will live to make the delivery myself. I thank you for trusting me with the job of giving your plan to General Gage and I am sorry I cannot fulfill that duty person-ally. I will miss you and I'm sorry I will not be here to witness our victory when we win against the Colonists. Goodbye Lieutenant Governor Carleton, you were a great leader.

-John Murnel, Troop Twelve

Underneath my dear soldier's letter there was another small paragraph that said:

John Murnel didn't have time to say this before he passed away, but we overheard some Americans plotting to invade Quebec. You must protect Quebec.

-Pred Hull

American invaders? I had to act quickly, before it was too late. I went outside and got on my horse. Frightened, I rode to the sheriff's office and burst through the door.

"Sir! Colonists! Planning to invade Quebec!" I shouted.

"What? We must get to the Southeastern border of Canada!" the Sheriff exclaimed.

We frantically raced to the training grounds and rallied the remaining troops to march to the border where Canada and the Colonies meet. Then we waited and waited.

"What a liar," the Sheriff said, storming off.

One by one the troops got bored and started to sit down.

"Stand back up!" I yelled. I got annoyed and wondered if perhaps the Colonists were joking. But the letter warned they were coming. So, I decided to stand guard, even though it was extremely boring. I was still on top of my horse, with my satchel, so I started another journal entry. It went like this:

This morning I woke up and there was banging on the door. A messenger came with a letter containing the news of my soldier, John Murnel's death and the news that Colonists were planning to invade Canada. I rallied the troops, who, with the Sheriff (who called me a liar and stalked off because Colonists weren't showing up) and I, stood at Canada's Southeastern border. We are at the border currently, and we have been here for a while, but nothing is happening. The troops are bored and have started to sit down, and I yelled at them for not keeping their form. As time continues to pass, they have taken to playing hand games. I am too embarrassed to watch. What is wrong with these men? They have been training for several years. Hopefully, it will go well in the end.

CRACK! A soldier fell. Maybe the Colonists have come to invade after all.

SIR GUY CARLETON: WHAT'S MY STORY IN 1776?

QUEBEC, BRITISH CANADA, 30-31 DECEMBER 1775

30-31 December 1775

The Colonists kept firing bullet after bullet, but my soldiers were too slow to get up and protect themselves. Soon, an entire troop and a half were wounded and useless. The rest of my men persisted. I was proud of them. It was such a hard battle.

"FIGHT MEN! PUSH THEM SOUTH, BACK INTO THEIR TERRITORY!" I screamed. A fresh blast of gunshots from the Colonists drowned out their reply. Even more men were falling, and few men were left to help in the struggle

"RETREAT!" I screamed again. Finally, the battle ceased. The Colonists withdrew a bit, to what seemed to be their camp. After we finished burying our dead, I sent my troops back to the training grounds, my head hanging. I was devastated. We lost at least 20 soldiers with 30 more wounded. I went to my office and wrote a letter to General Gage asking for some help. The letter said:

General Gage,

It is not going well up here in Canada. Colonists just invaded and what seemed like 30 minutes was three hours of fighting. My men are dying, and

the fighting can't go on like this anymore. Sir, if I don't get back up, Canada might end up belonging to the Colonists. Please send more men.

-Lieutenant Governor Carleton

I ordered a messenger to deliver my letter immediately.

Quebec, British Canada, May 1776

The Siege of Quebec started four and a half months ago. After that brief time, I only have a quarter of my men left and still more keep dying. We keep having to pull back.

"RETREAT!" I yelled. I am really starting to wish that word didn't exist. My remaining men are fine, but they are too weak to fight. Every single day we fight until somebody calls, "Retreat." Colonists have pushed their way into Canadian territory, and I am constantly battling with them to regain it.

"Reinforcements!" someone yelled. I don't want to hear that word ever again either. The Colonists get reinforcements so often, and I asked for them at the start, but haven't gotten any.

This delivery was different. They came to my side of the playing field. I went up to the person leading the reinforcements, which looked like a small army by the looks of it.

"Lieutenant Governor Carleton, I am pleased to meet you. I am General John Burgoyne, and I've been sent here to supply you with reinforcements. By the looks of it, you need them," John said.

"Thank you so much. I needed them badly. Are they in decent shape and ready to fight?" I asked.

"Yes, they are some of our best," John replied.

"Perfect. Come inside with me. I have an important matter to discuss," I said.

"Yes, sir," John said. We went inside the tent and stood around the table.

"I have a plan to ambush the Colonists. We strike in the middle of the night, under the cover of darkness. With the extra soldiers we should be able to win this battle."

"Yes, sir. When do we strike?" John asked.

"Eleven at night. That way we'll have enough time to attack the whole army before dawn," I said.

"Perfect," John said, an evil grin on his face.

It was eleven at night and pitch black. We could only see the small torches by the tents. John and I crept over to the tents with our men. We spread out and fired.

The Colonist troops woke up in alarm.

"They're firing!" one yelled.

"Run!" the others shouted.

Thankfully, I didn't participate in the shooting, I just commanded the people. I didn't want to see the Colonists react to getting shot.

By morning, the siege was over.

"John! The Colonists retreated!" I yelled.

"Really?" he shouted back.

"Really," I said, overjoyed that we prevailed. But I knew there were many battles that I would have to face. For now, well, I decided to enjoy the small victory.

SIR HENRY CLINTON

by Kaylee Pearsons

SIR HENRY CLINTON: HOW DID THE AMERICAN REVOLUTION COME TO MY DOORSTEP?

NEWFOUNDLAND, BRITISH CANADA, 1738

"Just one more...please?" I pleaded, staring up at my father in admiration. Sitting on my bedside table was a candle that illuminated my small room, casting shadows on the wall with its flickering light. I had been sitting up in bed, listening to my father's old military stories, but it was now past my bedtime.

"No," he responded with a small smile from his wooden chair next to my bed. He ran his hand over his greasy hair held back in a tight ponytail. "You have had enough navy stories for one night. It's time you went to sleep."

"Okay, Father. Goodnight."

"Goodnight, Henry. Perhaps you'll have your own stories to tell someday."

I grinned back at him and turned over in my bed. *I will. I'm going to be just like him.*

London, England, Early Spring 1775

"Tensions grow in the Americas! Anger over taxation rises!" cried a young man wildly waving a newspaper above his head. "The Incident

"

on King Street was just the beginning! Read more in our latest edition!"

What do the American colonists expect? I thought. *They still live under His Majesty's rule after all. We need money after we fought the French and Indian War and government funds come from taxes. How do these colonists not understand? And more importantly, how far are they willing to go?* I shook my head and turned to the scene ahead of me.

Huge ships rested gently in a busy port beneath a cerulean sky dotted with swollen clouds. Britain had decided to send aid to Commander-in-Chief Thomas Gage to stop America's growing rebellion. Major Generals William Howe, John Burgoyne, and I were to sail to Boston aboard His Majesty's Ship *Cerberus*. I stood on a nearby dock, staring at *Cerberus* towering over me. Three sets of masts set upon multiple wooden decks added to London's skyline of timbers stretching to the sky. Great Britain's flag billowed in the breeze as the ship's crew scurried around, preparing to set sail.

Already on the ship, General Burgoyne waved at me from above. He wore a white Steinkirk and a sharp red coat with golden buttons over a light waistcoat. Like myself, his hair was pulled back and kept under an off-white powdered wig and black three-cornered hat. "General Clinton!" he called out. I made my way from the dock and up the ship's gangplank to shake Burgoyne's hand. Salt water sprayed into the air, settling on my cheek in a cool mist. "It's good to see you, General Clinton!"

I nodded in agreement, and he led me inside the ship. We walked quietly down two decks and across several rooms to the wardroom. The wardroom was a gathering place for officers that we would use on our journey to Boston. Save a few cheery pieces of furniture and a table, the room was empty.

Burgoyne picked up a small cup and took a sip. He motioned toward two chairs and another cup of warm tea. As he settled into his own chair, he asked, "So, how did you become a Major General?"

I sat down stiffly and fiddled with the hem of my coat. "I joined the New York militia at 15 and rose through the ranks until I became a Major General in seventeen and seventy-two, three years ago. And I recently served in Germany," I responded in a blunt manner before hesitantly asking, "How is your family?" I neither enjoyed nor excelled in 'small talk.' I was a strategic man, not a conversationalist.

Burgoyne smiled back at me in a charismatic way. "My wife, Lady Charlotte Stanley, and my daughter, Charlotte Elizabeth, are well. And how is your family? I have not heard much of them."

"My five children and..." I broke off, thinking of my late wife, Harriet. Her death in seventeen and seventy-two shook me to my core and it was still difficult to think about. I did not leave my house for quite some time and it...changed me. Burgoyne must have noticed how uneasy I was, as he quieted down and looked at a book near him.

HMS Cerberus, May 1775

Several weeks later, General Howe called us to his quarters, saying he had received more news from America. Always eager to know more about what I would arrive to in Boston, I hurried to Howe's office.

Howe was standing over a large map of the colonies laid out on a sturdy oak table. He gently set his finger on Boston. He sighed and appeared to be deep in thought. Burgoyne arrived with a brisk stride and took a seat in a velvet-covered chair. Howe nodded quickly to us before beginning. "I'll be frank. The rebels have fired shots near Lexington and are now holding Boston under siege. I tell you truly gentlemen, war has begun."

SIR HENRY CLINTON: HOW DID I GET INVOLVED IN THE AMERICAN REVOLUTION?

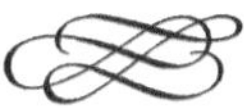

It's really happening. I breathed in slowly to calm myself. *Great Britain is at war in America again, but this time fighting against our own citizens. I find myself at war again.*

A month ago, on May 25th, William Howe, John Burgoyne, and I arrived in Boston Harbor aboard the *HMS Cerberus* with four thousand British troops. Rebel soldiers led by Colonel William Prescott held Boston, and our loyal troops occupying it, under siege.

From where I stood in our camp, I could see the Charles River gliding out toward the ocean. The smooth river separated us from the dark silhouette of Charlestown, the city to our north. Boston and Charlestown are both located on peninsulas, surrounded by small bodies of water within the Atlantic Ocean.

I took another deep breath and turned to face the commanding tent. Warm light seeped out from the edges of the canvas. I unfurled the flap to unveil a quiet meeting illuminated by a rusted lantern. Thomas Gage, Howe, Burgoyne, and a few other high-ranking soldiers bent over a table covered with loose papers and a large map.

"Come in, General Clinton," Howe welcomed me. "We don't have much left to accomplish before retiring for the night. General Gage is summarizing his plan to drive the rebels out of Boston. Close the tent quickly—this meeting must remain confidential."

I moved next to Burgoyne and studied the map as Gage spoke. "We want this war to end as soon as possible. Right now, we must drive the rebels from Boston and then fortify the city. As I stated earlier, we will first take control of Dorchester Heights." He pointed to a ridge just south of Boston on the map. "Then we will march on Roxbury to push the rebels further west." His finger traced a drawn line to a hamlet southwest. "With any luck they'll be forced out of Boston, never to return!"

"With any luck they'll learn to obey His Majesty and submit to His rule!" an officer called out, receiving a few chuckles.

Howe smiled. "We will teach them soon. But for now, let's retire for the evening with pleasant dreams of putting this insurrection down immediately, glorifying King George III!"

17 June 1775, Early Morning

I woke up in my cot in a small canvas tent. Yawning in my long linen shirt, I stretched out and rubbed my temples.

Swish! My tent burst open as a young scout scrambled in and threw himself into a hasty salute. "Sir! Permission to state my case, sir!"

"At ease, soldier. Permission granted," I said, slightly taken back. After all, I was still in bed.

"News, sir! Generals Howe and Gage have ordered you to attend a war council straight away. The rebels have fortified Charlestown, sir!" He saluted again and sprinted away as quickly as he entered.

I snapped into action and threw on a waistcoat, stockings, breeches, and an overcoat. When I strode back to the same tent, Burgoyne and Robert Pigot followed me inside. Gage and Howe were already there.

"Blast those rebels!" Gage cried with a shake of his fist. "They must've found out about our plans."

"Blast those rebels indeed! But it doesn't matter how they found out; we must focus on our next actions. Our best plan is to attack before they have a chance to settle in," Burgoyne reasoned.

"I propose that we fight them directly on the peninsula. After all, their forces are much weaker than ours," added Howe.

"Hmm...," I murmured, tapping the map. "I propose a different plan. If we attack them head on, many will find a way to escape. However, if we send our troops to the Charlestown Neck, we'll cut off American retreat and surround them on the peninsula."

"Clinton, you overestimate these colonists," Burgoyne interjected. "They are farmers and simple countrymen, certainly no match for the might of His Majesty's forces. I tell you, when they catch sight of our regulars, the rebels will scatter. This battle will be over before it begins."

"Burgoyne is right, Clinton. It's unnecessary. I'll divide the troops into columns, and we'll attack head-on in several successions," Howe insisted.

Frustrated, I opened my mouth to argue, but stopped myself. Gage and Howe were my senior officers; I had to follow their orders. "Understood."

Breed's Hill, 17 June 1775, Afternoon

Several yards away from Howe, I walked sternly toward crude American fortifications. The rebels' guns were all trained on us, but their commanders yelled to hold fire. The British troops marched in beautiful formation behind me, each soldier stepping exactly as they should. Charlestown flamed in the corner of my eye as the colonial snipers fled the scene. *What a sight we are to behold. Why, we must be—*

Pow! Pow! Pow! In a flash, gunfire flooded at us. Bullets whizzed past me and stuck the men behind me. "Fall back!" Howe bellowed. "All troops fall back to the assembly areas!" We ran hundreds of feet away. All the while, Howe maintained a calm, commanding disposition. "Regroup! Regroup and advance!"

With fewer men than before, we regrouped and advanced, only to face the same consequences. *Pow! Pow! Pow!* Soldiers thudded to the ground, and to my horror we retreated once again. "Regroup and advance!"

As we marched back in front of the redoubts, the militia shot at us again, but few musket balls struck us. We pushed on through a thin layer of smoke and reached the redoubts. With few close-combat weapons, the colonists could not hold up their defense. We surged over their redoubts and fortifications with silver bayonets in hand. Bloody fighting ensued, killing many men.

"Retreat!" yelled the rebel leader, Colonel Prescott. "Retreat! Fall back!"

Cheers erupted as the colonial militia retreated across the Charlestown neck. British soldiers lifted their bayonets into the air, celebrating their victory. "We won!"

A smile started to play on my lips, but then I looked down at the bodies in red uniforms littering the ground in front of the redoubts. The color drained from my face. *There must be over a thousand. How could we have lost so many?* The sharp, coppery scent of blood filled my nose as crimson puddles pooled beside the fallen soldiers. "This was a dear bought victory."

SIR HENRY CLINTON: WHAT'S MY STORY IN 1776?

The Battle of Sullivan's Island, Cape Fear, North Carolina, March 1776

I sat on a rickety bar stool, engaged in awkward small talk with another officer, Admiral Peter Parker. Having left Boston in January under Howe's orders, I traveled to the southern colonies to take control of the south and rally loyalist support. After months of delay, Lord Cornwallis and Admiral Parker finally met up with me in Cape Fear.

Parker swirled his glass around and watched the drink churn about. "You know, we must decide on a city to assume command of. The longer we wait means the more time the rebels can build up their defenses."

I sighed and shook my head slowly. *Of course, he brings this topic up.* "Parker, we've discussed this many, many times." We'd been arguing for weeks on where to start our southern campaign. I favored Chesapeake Bay in Virginia, but Parker continued to push his plan for Charleston in South Carolina.

"Please, Clinton, just listen! I've procured intelligence that the fort on Sullivan's Island protecting Charleston is not even finished!"

"Hmph."

"We can take that fort easily, and secure Charleston for ourselves!"

I looked back at him keenly from under my bushy, black eyebrows and sighed again. "Perhaps you are right. Though I may live to regret it, I will support your plan to gain control of Charleston."

Parker lifted his glass in triumph. "Huzzah! Trust me, Clinton! This will be a substantial victory for us! We will glorify King George III!"

"But Parker, I warn you sincerely; do not underestimate our opponents. You *will* regret that."

Long Island, South Carolina, 28 June 1776, 10 AM

"Open fire! Open fire!" I yelled to the troops beside me.

My infantry, Lord Cornwallis, and I had landed on Long Island several weeks ago to support Admiral Parker's naval assault on the fort on Sullivan's Island. We were to cross Breach Inlet onto Sullivan's Island and surround the fort on land. Spies informed me that the inlet was only eighteen inches deep and therefore would be easy to walk through. However, to my mortification, the "shallow" inlet was seven feet deep and a mile long! We were marooned on the island, and my men quickly grew weary of its humid jungles, thick clouds of mosquitoes, and brackish water. *I* grew weary of nights spent slogging through creeks and swamps, still hoping for a wadable path across the inlet. Rebels camped out on the other side of the water to watch us, and several small skirmishes had broken out between the two sides.

Today's fight, however, was no small skirmish. Having received a signal from Admiral Parker, I assembled my men for battle. Parker's cannonballs thundered in the distance, but it disappointed me to see how far away he had anchored his boats from the shore of Sullivan's Island.

Our goal was still to cross the inlet and advance on the fort, even if we floated across using boats. However, we faced heavy fire from the rebels' Advance Guard, and without protection, any attempts to make it across the inlet would be futile.

The tide started to roll in towards my soldiers, eating up the ground they were standing on. I realized that they would have to abandon their post or let the water overcome them, so I decided to make my move and called for ships to come to us. After several minutes, an armed schooner, armed sloop, and a flotilla of boats appeared in the distance. These ships would provide protection for us to finally travel by flat boat to Sullivan's Island. Cheers erupted throughout my men as the flotilla edged closer and closer to us!

Suddenly, our cheers lapsed into moans as the Advance Guard took the opportunity to fire upon the ships.

No! I cried internally while maintaining a straight face.

The ships' crews were forced off the decks as cannonballs raked across them with deadly accuracy. I watched in horror as the ships tried in vain to fire back and draw closer to the rebels. The schooner and sloop finally crashed into the island, grounding themselves for quite some time.

"Should we cross anyway?" a nearby officer asked softly.

I held my head down in defeat. "No, we will stay here until we can receive more protection. It is too rash to attempt it without."

British Ship, 30 June 1776

I muttered softly to myself as I paced back and forth in an empty room. I had just signed my account of the days before and was waiting for Admiral Parker to arrive.

After another minute or so, he knocked sharply on the closed door. I called for him to come in and took a deep breath to calm myself. When Parker walked in, I twisted my lips into a frown, glaring at him for several moments. I finally opened my mouth to speak in an icy tone. "I believe you promised a substantial victory for us, a chance to glorify His Majesty!"

Parker stared back at me, seething silently.

"We lost much, much more than just the battle. We lost upwards of sixty, some even say ninety men! More than a hundred now lie wounded. His Majesty's Ship *Thunder*'s mortars tore the ship's own deck apart and the *Actaeon* burns in the sea. And of course, our dignity has flown out the window and shredded to pieces by these rebels. Pray tell me, did you ever find the end of your breeches you lost?"

Parker's face flushed bright red, and I could see the blood boil behind his eyes. He scoffed and said, "Surely some blame must go to you!"

"Indeed, Parker. I blame myself for agreeing to your plan. Let us see what awaits us at another Long Island where I guarantee you things will be different if General Howe listens to my strategy to crush Washington's army." I sat down heavily on a wooden chair propped against the wall. In a low voice I muttered, "Though if our army continues with these same mistakes, perhaps we won't crush this rebellion quite so easily."

GENERAL CHARLES CORNWALLIS

by Abigail McGinnis

GENERAL CHARLES CORNWALLIS: HOW DID THE AMERICAN REVOLUTION COME TO MY DOORSTEP?

Culford, Suffolk, Great Britain (A Village Outside of London)

I am Lord Charles Cornwallis. Some also know me as First Marquess or Second Earl Cornwallis. Due to my sympathies for the American Colonists and my allegiance to Great Britain, I am a complicated man. As you may already know, while I was a member in the House of Lords, I stood up for the American Colonies. However, once they started to rebel against Great Britain, I felt it was my duty to re-enter the British army. Now I shall tell you the full story.

I was born on the 31st of December in 1738, to an aristocratic family in Grosvenor Square, London. While I was attending school at Eton, I sustained an injury in my left eye, causing me to have cross-eyed vision for the rest of my life. My father (also named Charles) was a baron and of high military pedigree and saw fit to send me to a military academy in Turin, Italy.

I joined the British army in 1757; shortly thereafter, in 1759, it was an honor to be promoted to Captain of the 85th Regiment. Following this, I attained the rank of Lieutenant Colonel of the 12th Regiment and served in the Seven Years' War in Germany for three years in the

Battle of Minden, the Battle of Villinghausen, the Battle of Wilhelmsthal, and the Battle of Lutterburg.

Unfortunately, my father passed away in 1762. As a result, I replaced him as Earl and took his seat in the House of Lords in the British Parliament. Within the first few years, things got tense with the American Colonists. I opposed the Stamp Act of 1765, which was designed to control the Colonies unfairly by taxation without representation. I was one of only five members who voted against such a decree. However, when the colonists started talking about breaking free from Great Britain, I knew where my allegiance lay. Consequently, I decided to re-enter the British army.

When the Battles of Lexington and Concord broke out in the American colonies in 1775, King George III offered me a commission and I was promoted to Major General on the 29th of September 1775. Of course, I accepted the much deserved and long-awaited reward and sailed for America to arrive in early 1776.

I never imagined that my military career in the British army would coincide with my sympathies towards the American Colonists while in Parliament and arrive on my doorstep with the Revolutionary War. Nor did I understand how it would impact my doorstep at home.

GENERAL CHARLES CORNWALLIS:
HOW DID I GET INVOLVED IN
THE AMERICAN REVOLUTION?

A colossal shadow silently bolted across the dark street and dissolved into the inky blackness of the night. Something, or *someone,* was quickly approaching. Four enormous paws slowly turned the corner, cautiously inspecting the source of such mystery toward the middle of the boulevard. Jupiter, a massive gray-biscuit fawn colored mastiff became visible in the street's lamplight. The silent shadow rounded the bend, sniffed, looked this way and that, and stepped into the glow of the light. It was another mastiff; this one was a brindle (brown striped with orange, black marbling). His snout, as well as his paws and the tip of his tail, were black. The door of a residential house door creaked open—the same door which the recently promoted General Charles Cornwallis had entered earlier that day.

"Mars, here boy! Come here, Mars!" a voice he knew by heart beckoned to him from the threshold.

"I'm coming, Mary!" Mars thought to himself as he bounded through the door, knocking his master's daughter, Mary, over onto her back.

"Hey! Mars! No jumping like that!" exclaimed Mary. Mary was Charles's bright, energetic, seven-year-old daughter. She picked herself up, brushed herself off and walked to the door, where she opened it again and called for Jupiter. "Jupiter! Come on boy! Come here boy! Come on!" The gray-biscuit colored dog pranced through the door, and just like that Mary was on the floor again, this time laughing. "You boys are silly," she proclaimed.

"Mary! Charles! Time for dinner!" a lovely voice called Mary and her brother for dinner. Their mother, Jemima, (also known as Mrs. Charles Cornwallis) was a beautiful and graceful woman. Although she hadn't come from a very wealthy family, Charles loved her dearly, and she did a wonderful job of running their household while Charles was busy pursuing his military career. A few short minutes later, muffled laughing could be heard from the dining room as the family dined together and talked about their day.

"So, how was your day, Charles?" questioned Jemima.

"Well, you know how I am Major General now...," began Charles.

"Yes, go on," replied Jemima.

"Well, I've been given a new assignment in the American Colonies."

"Really?!" exclaimed Jemima. Charles nodded.

"I've been ordered to sail with 2,500 men to a place called Charleston, South Carolina. Our commander wants us to capture the city and take it back from the Americans."

"Daddy! Dat city's name is just wike your name!" observed Charles Jr., who was two years old. His father Charles nodded approvingly.

Meanwhile, in the kitchen, Jupiter hopped onto his bed, encircled it, and laid down. Mars, however, hungrily licked his bowl. Seeing it was empty, he howled like a wolf and trotted into the dining room. From the kitchen, Jupiter heard their master's muffled deep voice asking Mary to feed the dogs. Mars pranced around the table and went back into their room in the kitchen. He sat patiently next to his food bowl and waited for his meal.

Mars's ears perked up as he heard Mary's footsteps approaching. When she saw Jupiter she smiled and whispered, "You'll always be my favorite." Mars barked in reply and Mary quickly gave both dogs their supper. Muffled voices could be heard from the dining room as the rest of the family talked and chewed their food.

Charles sent Mary and Charles Jr. upstairs while in hushed voices he spoke with his wife.

"My departure is soon, but at least not before Mary's birthday," he confided. "I must be away for a couple of days to make plans for our departure to America, but I will return."

Jemima buried her face in her hands, weeping as the thought of her husband having to leave their family. All of the risk, the possibility of losing her husband and the father of their children, not to mention the possibility of having to lose the breadwinner of the family…she knew she should be supportive of her husband's military ambitions, but she also wished she could receive a guarantee of his safety. This would be a long and potentially deadly assignment for her husband.

"Couldn't you leave later?" she pleaded.

"Time is of the essence; we must go immediately. Besides, we should be able to defeat them with only a handful of cannonballs!" he replied.

"But one cannonball IS an entire handful of cannonballs, they're so large," she sobbed. Charles stood up and walked over to her with a smile upon his face.

"Exactly!" he replied jokingly. "Come now. I have an idea to give Mary something special for her birthday." Charles and Jemima discussed other necessary arrangements as their servants cleaned up the dinner; then the couple headed upstairs to tuck their children into bed.

The next morning, Mary came rushing down to say goodbye to her father and was disappointed when she found he wasn't there. "Did daddy already leave?"

"Yes darling, he did. Daddy had to go to get ready to sail for America," Jemima answered. "The King and duty called, but I'm sure we will hear from him very soon."

Mary lowered her head and frowned. "I had hoped he'd be here for my birthday."

IT WAS A BRISK MORNING, and a mouthwatering aroma came from the kitchen downstairs. Mary slowly opened her eyes. Then she jumped out of bed and dashed into her brother Charles's room. It was empty, just as she hoped. Her heart was racing. Mary scrambled into her bedroom, tore off her nightgown and dressed as fast as her arms could move. It was her birthday! She was turning eight, and she was thrilled.

Downstairs Jemima and Charles Jr. were waiting at the table with a very memorable gift for Mary. They could hear her scrambling upstairs and were looking forward to giving her the present they had so carefully prepared. As Mary came downstairs, Charles Jr. hugged the present one last time and put the blanket (which was also part of the birthday present) back on top of it. Mary flew through the kitchen doors and crashed into her mother's arms.

Mary looked around and saw her favorite breakfast on the table. Orange juice, with flat bread cakes with butter, and syrup. They were sitting on her favorite China dish: a dainty plate with delicate pink roses dancing alongside a golden rim. Mary was so excited she squealed.

Charles Jr. peeked behind his chair and whispered something no one could understand.

"What did you say, Charles?" Mary inquired, turning around. Charles jerked his head with a suspicious stare at his sister.

"Mary, look! It's the blanket you've wanted for years!" exclaimed Jemima, trying to draw the attention away from the scene.

"Ooo!" Mary screamed. She tore the blanket from the object hidden blow it and squealed again—this time even louder.

"Eeekk! Daddy!!! You're home! Daddy! Daddy! Daddy! When did you come home?! I missed you so so so soooo much!" Mary said.

General Charles Cornwallis snatched Mary and swung her in his burly grip. "Well," the deep voice Mary loved rang through the house. "I missed you too. And I wanted to see my big girl's birthday!" he bellowed.

"Do you get to stay home for a long time?" Jemima asked.

"No, I'll have to go back tomorrow evening," he replied.

Jemima sighed. "Why tomorrow evening? Why not tomorrow morning?"

"Because, my dear, I want to spend some time with my favorites. But I may be called earlier," he stated lovingly.

"Jya-!" Charles Jr. jumped off his chair and ran over to his father, who scooped him up and swung him around.

The family spent the rest of the day doing special events together. But soon, Cornwallis set sail for America.

GENERAL CHARLES CORNWALLIS: WHAT'S MY STORY IN 1776?

*M*any, many weeks later, one chilly, brisk morning, a letter came. Mary excitedly brought it into the house. Jemima read that it was from her beloved Charles. She tore it open and started reading:

July 1776

Dear Jemima, Mary, and my son, Charles:

I miss you all very dearly, and I hope to come home and see you soon. We have recently fought a battle—the Battle of Sullivan's Island. But you see, it was so embarrassing. Henry Clinton was in charge, and of course, it's no surprise that we failed. Because he was in charge. Ugh, he disgusts me. Well, anyway. A government official wrote a letter saying how I was too good a soldier to be on such a puny mission. And, of course, he was right.

You mean everything to me, which is why I am grieved to tell you that I have now been called to travel to New York for our King's military purposes. I have joined a force commanded by General William Howe. We have gathered some 32,000 British and Hessian soldiers—the biggest army Great Britain has ever gathered to fight in a foreign country. We are well trained, and eager to win this battle. I will write to you as soon as I can.

I miss you all and I hope I will get some leave to come and see you.
With all my love,
Your Loving Husband and Father,
Charles

"Me miss Daddy!" wailed Charles Jr.

"Me too!' replied Mary in a sob.

"Daddy will hopefully be back soon," responded Jemima. She smiled that her husband might be a hero.

Upon my arrival to America, I observed that martial militance was lacking and caused the primary generals much suffering. Those British generals underestimated the Americans; they assumed the Colonists were useless and considered them as "nobodies." I was not fond of the Americans, but I retained my ability to think decisively. I was not hesitant to go after those Colonists. I pressed my militance upon George Washington's Continental Army in a variety of measures in 1776. As a general of the British army, I was able to sweep victory over Washington by driving them out of New York and cornering them in New Jersey.

I was looking forward to taking personal leave in December 1776. Unfortunately, General Howe ordered my immediate return to New Jersey to face off against Washington, who initiated an unpredicted assault on Trenton on December 26, 1776. I've rounded up troops and advanced towards Trenton to confront him.

I miss my family and suppose I must once more write to my wife about this next delay. I am uncertain when I will see them again. I hope they will wait for me.

It had been weeks since Jemima, Mary and Charles Jr. had heard anything from their father. About six months proceeding, they received a newspaper talking about how the British had won the Battle of Long Island. The following day, a letter came; Mary brought it in and tore it open.

November 1776

My Dearest Family,

I'm so sorry I haven't written to you in a long while. As you know, I've been quite occupied with putting down the rebels. We won the Battle of Long Island. It seems that we will beat the American Colonists. We have driven George Washington and his ragged forces along with him, down across New Jersey. It appears that my prior worries were unnecessary. In fact, we have won all of the battles so far.

Don't worry, dear ones, I have leave scheduled for late December. I promise to come home unharmed.

Sending you all my love,

Charles

Mary jumped up and down. "Yes! Daddy will be home soon!

"Yes dear, Daddy will be home soon! And do you know what we will have to do for him?" Jemima squeezed her daughter.

"Wha--What?!" Charles Jr. shouted, jumping as well.

"We'll have to throw a party!" Jemima answered.

"Yes! Yes! Yes!!!" the two youngsters squealed. Mary ran up the stairs and Charles Jr. followed. Jemima sat down on the sofa and leaned back, proud of her husband. The entire house smelled of the finest things, decorated in the most elegant fashion. They readied the house, excited for the arrival of General Charles Cornwallis.

December 1776

Dear Children and Jemima,

I miss you ever so much, although I'm afraid I won't make it home until late January, due to some military complications. I love you children so much, but now you may no longer hear any more of this letter. I love you...

Jemima sent Mary and Charles Jr. upstairs while she read the rest of the letter.

Jemima, I worry about you and the children every day. We will soon defeat the Colonists. Most of them are dead, half starved to death or captured by the King's attack. At the beginning of this long war, Washington's army numbered 20,000 and has now been reduced to 3,000. He has been trying to gather reinforcements but has not succeeded. They are simply no match for the British Crown and the Hessians. We are setting up lodgings in town along the east bank of the Delaware River. I may be able to sail home for a little while in mid-winter.

Your Affectionate Husband,

Charles

Jemima smiled; she missed Charles, but she was glad he would be home soon. Or so she thought…

LORD DUNMORE

by Payton Grace

LORD DUNMORE: HOW DID THE AMERICAN REVOLUTION COME TO MY DOORSTEP?

EARLY 1771

"Virginia?" I nearly dropped my glass as I looked up in disbelief. "You want me to be the Governor of Virginia?!"

The man before me was Lord Hillsborough, someone whom I had once trusted without reservation. However, now I was unsure of his judgment. His eyes were solemn as he nodded firmly. No trace of jest could be found in his expression.

Is he serious? My mind went blank in shock. This was less of an offer, and more of an order, wasn't it? Lord Hillsborough was, as I was, part of the House of Lords, but he was also part of the Privy Council. The fact that he had come to tell me this news meant that, for some reason, the Council wanted *me* to govern Virginia. But I did not wish to accept this.

"But I-I-I'm the Governor of New York!" I exclaimed. "How could I—"

"You *were* the Governor of New York." His response was cold.

My heart sank. All my plans...were ruined. I put so much hard work over the past few months to prepare to get a large plot of land in this Colony. I had spent every night dreaming of Charlotte and the children's arrival once I finally set up a home. This was, by far, an unexpected variable in my carefully thought-out plan.

I silently stared at the soft glow of the candlelight that illuminated the room. Fond memories of my wife and children's smiling faces faded into view. It had been so long since I had seen them all. The letters sent back and forth just...weren't the same. I longed to hold them close, embrace them, to hear their voices. Moving to Virginia would only make our separation longer.

I couldn't give in just yet.

"But my family! Virginia's climate is unsuitable for us! How will they join me there!?" I argued. "It's simply unfair to keep a man away from his family for years on end!"

Lord Hillsborough sighed, taking a sip from his glass. The rich flavor brought a slight smile to his lips. "Well, people are living there, aren't they? Plenty of happy families, and they all seem perfectly healthy to me."

Although his indifference to my distress was irksome, I couldn't argue with that. Virginia was indeed a prosperous American colony. But he had still not convinced me.

"Why me?" I asked, more curious than anything. "Out of all the officers at your disposal, why me?"

"Well, one, because you're expendable. But other than that, you're a rather smart man. You may have some flaws, but you, like the rest of us, also have your strengths. We need someone who is unwaveringly loyal to the Crown."

I pondered this for a while, before setting my glass onto the table. The remnants of liquid inside rippled slightly with the impact. "We'll see."

September 1771

In the end, I'd lost that argument of course. This was the reason why, months later, I was looking out my carriage window to the swiftly approaching Colony of Virginia.

I can't believe I ended up coming here in the end... My head pounded with irritation. I'd been fighting in wars since I was fourteen, yet somehow, I couldn't persuade Lord Hillsborough to change his mind.

I'd been the Governor of New York for such a short time, and been "promoted," as he'd called it, even faster. However, many wanted an opportunity like this, but couldn't get it. In my case, being born into a powerful family helped quite a bit.

I found my gaze drifting back out the window. Rolling fields of green stretched out for miles and miles, with blades of grass swaying in the wind. The golden sun spread warmth and light across the land, shining amongst the wispy clouds above. The crisp autumn breeze carried the scent of damp earth, the after-effects of an early morning shower.

In a way, the rural community reminded me of my hometown in Scotland. The very country I'd had to leave behind, where I'd left my childhood, everything I'd ever known and loved to come to Britain, and now America. I had to admit, it was refreshing to have a break from the hectic community of New York.

I adjusted my hat and coat, settling back down into my seat. Maybe this wouldn't be so bad after all.

The carriage stopped abruptly, jostling me from a hazy, dreamlike state. I planted my feet firmly in place, preventing myself from flying headfirst into the wall.

"Hey! Why did you stop!?" I shouted to the driver, chiding him for his lack of skill. But as I stuck my head out the window, a red, sphere-like object flew towards me, just missing my ear. It spattered onto the carriage side, tangy juice and seeds staining the wood.

A tomato—?

For a few moments, I stared, stunned at what had just occurred, before coming to my senses and ducking back inside.

Rotten fruits and vegetables were being thrown from all sides, as the townspeople shouted insults and profanities. They all aimed at me.

"Down with Lord Dunmore!"

"We don't want him as our governor!"

The villagers' voices were loud and clear, piercing arrows that were meant to kill.

"He doesn't deserve to be here!"

"Virginia doesn't need a governor who didn't even want to be here in the first place!"

Their hatred and distrust for me was so intense that I didn't dare look out the window. I could sense their burning glares from inside. I never expected such venom on my first day. But I never expected them to instantly love me either.

The brief feeling of peace I'd felt was quickly fading. Instead, I began to feel an inexplicable sense of loneliness in this foreign land, even further from my family than in New York. My acceptance here in Virginia would not come without much effort on my part.

As the crowd dispersed, the carriage rolled on, but my enthusiasm to view the world outside the window was gone. Reaching over, I drew the curtains tightly. I had definitely seen enough for now.

LORD DUNMORE: HOW DID I GET INVOLVED IN THE AMERICAN REVOLUTION?

MARCH 1775

I took up the newspaper, hands trembling.

"What is the meaning of this, this—!" I couldn't even finish my sentence. The headline, written in thick black letters made my head pound with...what was this emotion? Rage? Frustration? Shock? All my thoughts and feelings blended into a burning hot fire; a flame that burnt from deep within me. I couldn't believe what I was seeing.

Patrick Henry...a leader, if not *the* leader of the patriot uprising in Virginia took the country by storm, with news of his "Liberty or Death" speech spreading faster than fire. He had raised nearly half the nation to consider fighting for freedom from the Crown. From Great Britain, the very place that my father and uncle pledged their loyalty to, and to where I'd pledged mine.

I was the Governor of Virginia! And even before that, I'd been the Governor of New York as well. I had lived among the colonists, who were citizens of Great Britain whether they liked it or not.

But I couldn't very well turn my back on the place that had supported my family, that had given me a place in the world. After all, the king had pardoned my father from prison all those years ago. I'd joined the British army when I was eighteen years of age.

Along with Scotland, it was home. I couldn't leave another home behind.

"William," I called to the servant who'd delivered the paper. "Send a letter to Lieutenant Henry Collins. I have a task for him."

My plan would tarnish my reputation among the colonists. It would lay aside all the hard work I'd done to get into their good graces and become a governor worthy of their praise. My mind went back to the unfriendly welcome I'd received when I'd first arrived in Virginia. If I went through with this, then their reactions would surely be even worse. But I couldn't hope that they'd understand, nor could I make them understand. If they were betraying the Crown, so be it. They would resent me, yes. But it was something I had to do. For my country.

Just as I was about to begin penning a letter to the Lieutenant, I heard what sounded like thunder crashing from somewhere nearby. Startled, I immediately looked out the window. The sky was clear as could be.

Then what's that—

The door to my study burst open as a sudden deluge of my children flooded into the room. *"Father!!!"* A chorus of laughter sounded as I was surrounded by hugs on all sides.

I couldn't see who pinned my arms to my sides, but I smiled, nevertheless. Just the presence of my family made the harshness of the world around me disappear.

"Hello everyone! Finished bothering your mother?"

"We were all playing in the living room before Catherine chased us out." Augusta, my second eldest spoke up from somewhere behind me. "Mother was nursing Virginia, and Cathy said she needed some 'peace and quiet.'"

The face of my five-year-old son, Leveson popped into view. His mischievous grin shined as brightly as the sun. "Let's play!" he exclaimed.

"Oh?" I raised my eyebrows in interest. "And what would you like to play, my dear boy?"

They all exchanged glances. "Chase!"

With that, they all scurried away.

"Watch out!" I called after them, rising to my feet. "I'm coming!"

Sometimes, the size of my family seemed quite large. But I loved each and every one of them more than anything in the world.

The day they'd finally reached Virginia had been the happiest day of my life. I had been blessed with such a wonderful family. And with them by my side, every day was filled with complete and total bliss.

The kind of feeling that I wouldn't trade for anything in the world.

But life is like a battlefield. You never know what will happen next.

July 1775

"Father...do you really have to go?" Catherine wrung her hands, eyes cast towards the wooden dock.

Boats and ships, both large and small floated amongst the shimmering waters, undulating waves of turquoise lapping against their sides. The harbor was full of arrivals and departures, of happiness and despair. It was a place to welcome new beginnings, to move on to the next chapter of an adventure and accept bittersweet endings.

This was where I would have to say goodbye to my family once again.

Augusta, Leveson, and the rest of my children stood before me, eyes filled with tears. I had told them not to be worried, that I would surely come back to them once again. However, even I couldn't see the end of the path up ahead. As much as it pained me to let them go, I knew that it was the only way to keep them safe.

With every passing second, the tension between America and Great Britain was rising. From the Boston Tea Party to Patrick Henry's speech on 'Liberty or Death', the colonists were becoming more disgruntled with the Crown prevailing over their livelihoods. But that was the job of the ruler, was it not?

The king took the throne at a young age. He grew up believing that people should always respect him. If not, then he would have to become someone who commanded such respect. He'd grown up having others under his thumb. Plus, I pledged my loyalty to the king years ago. No matter what he did and no matter how wrong it may seem, it was my duty to follow and support him.

Unfortunately, that loyalty has put me in danger.

People were beginning to rise up against me. They mocked those who chose to serve the Crown as Loyalists. That letter that I'd sent months ago to Henry Collins had included instructions to pilfer a stash of gunpowder from the colonists. I had meant to calm the unrest, but had only managed to make it worse, and raise them against me as well. It was difficult to avoid the discriminating stares sent my way, especially here in America. I didn't want to put my family in harm's way because of my choices.

I'd learned from my father's mistakes when I was only a boy.

So, despite the fact that the last thing I wanted was separation, it was the only way to ensure their safety.

I knelt down, taking my eldest daughter's hands. "Catherine, my dear. Do not worry. There are just a few things I must do before we can all be together once again. I came back all those other times, did I not?"

"Yes, but..."

"But this time, there is a war!" Leveson exclaimed. He then placed a hand to his chest, looking up at me with a pleading expression. "Can I come with you? Please, please, *please* can I join in the battle, too?" Taking a stick up from the ground, he raised it into the air as if fighting some unknown opponent. "I can fight! See, Father?"

The corners of my mouth raised into a soft smile. What a wonderful son.

I reached over, rustling his hair. "Ah, indeed you can fight. I would give nothing more than to have you by my side in battle. But then it would be unfair to our enemies. We would win every time with skills such as yours!"

Leveson's face lit up as he nodded proudly. "Aww, I guess it *would* be unfair."

"I can fight too!" Alexander spoke up. "What about me, Father? I'm *older* then Leveson, so that means I'm *stronger* than him! I should be able to go!"

"Well, the same goes for you. It would be unfair to our adversary if you were fighting," I chuckled.

"But *I'm* older than *both* of them," George, my eldest son butted in. "And *I* know that you're just saying that because we're too young to fight."

Charlotte locked eyes with me, a glint of amusement in her beautiful smile. "Boys, calm down. We don't want the last memory that your father carries with him to be an argument, do we?"

Cradled in her arms was Virginia, the newest addition to our family. She was barely a year old. Even now, she was sleeping in her mother's arms, unaware of the turmoil around her.

I planted a kiss on her forehead, then turned to my wife.

"We'll miss you dearly, John," Charlotte whispered, tears brimming in her eyes.

My heart ached. "Please don't cry, darling." I reached over, hugging her close. "I promise you, even if a thousand bullets pierce me, I will find my way back to you. No matter what, I'll come back for you and our children."

"You better not get pierced by a thousand bullets."

"Mother, can we talk to Father too? We would also like a hug." Augusta cleared her throat expectantly. We turned to find the children staring at us, unamused.

I grinned, holding my arms out towards them. "Come here, little ones...!"

Time seemed to stand still in that moment.

The warmth, love, and joy surrounded me, making world shine even brighter than before.

But as I boarded the boat, one thing was clear to me. For forcing me to leave my family again, for going against the Crown, and I, who had once watched over them, those Americans would *pay*.

My vision darkened, fingernails digging into my palms.

I have once fought for the Virginians. And by God, I will *let them see* that I can fight *against* them.

LORD DUNMORE: WHAT'S MY STORY IN 1776?

1 JANUARY 1776

*R*age. Darkness. In that moment, I couldn't feel anything but absolute emptiness. It was as if all of my feelings had dissipated into a dark, consuming void, my heart cold and indifferent to the scene before me.

Fire burned across the city, destroying buildings, and arousing pandemonium, causing panic amongst the people within. But I couldn't care less. As far as I was aware, they all deserved to die.

After you watched death once, it began to become an aspect of life. War, military, fighting, I'd done it all when I was young. It was honestly beginning to get old.

In all honesty, I could say that I had tried.

Nobody ever *wanted* bloodshed, but those foolish Americans had *chosen* it. I had put up with their treachery for long enough. It was time to put an end to this.

I was burning down the largest city in Virginia. Maybe it was a selfish act that was orchestrated solely for revenge. So what? It wasn't my fault.

And my army of slaves.

Yes, I had indeed used their wishes for freedom against them. When I wrote that proclamation, promising to set free those who left their masters to serve under me, maybe it was true that I didn't really care about them.

But in war, as I had learned over the years, nothing was free. Everything came at a price.

They'd joined my forces on their own accord. I had chosen to appeal to them because, well, as Gower had once said to me on that one fateful afternoon, they were expendable. They weren't citizens of America or Great Britain. They were simply tools, carefully placed gears and screws in my master plan. No one could place the blame on me. Everything I did was for my country. For my family.

All they were fighting for was *freedom*, just as the colonists were. A new way of doing things, something that had never been attempted before. Meanwhile, kings had presided over countries for centuries. We could trust in tradition more than we could trust in new, fickle ideals.

"Lord Dunmore!" One of my men sprinted up to me, hair damp with sweat and panting.

"Yes, what is it?" I sighed as I turned away from the entertaining chaos.

"Some of our men..." He paused to catch his breath. "They're being killed in the fire...what should we do?"

First, they were complaining about food rations, then contracting smallpox...and *now* they were failing to burn a city and escape with their lives? Was there *anything* that these half-brained dolts could do properly? I couldn't even enjoy a good second of success without some kind of problem arising.

Letting out another sigh, I nonchalantly blew a strand of hair from my face. "Well, whoever dies, dies. That's just the way of war. There's nothing we can do about it."

The young man took a step back, face pale. "W-What...-"

"It's exactly what it sounds like. In war, it's inevitable that there will be those who die. If you have a solution for that, by all means."

"B-But Lord Dunmore—"

Tired, I waved him away. "If you must, you can stay behind and, I don't know, save our wounded or something. As for me, I'm going to head back to camp after soaking in the scenery."

"*Scenery!?*" This appeared to be the last straw for the solider. "When my brother and I received news of your proclamation, he warned me against it, but in the end, I joined your army. I joined hoping for *freedom*. We all did." He shook his head in disappointment. "We all would've been better off in captivity."

"Did I ever say that you *needed* to join me?" I asked.

"...Excuse me?"

"I never *forced* anyone to escape from their masters. I allowed them to choose of their own volition. As for freedom...well, you are all free now, aren't you? And if that's not good enough, whether you survive this war or not, everyone will be free sooner or later. Either in death, or at the end of this all." Studying him closely, I realized something. "You are Ralph, that slave who escaped from Patrick Henry? How ironic. You escaped in the name of liberty from the *man* of liberty."

As I laughed in amusement, Ralph walked away without another word.

Some people just didn't get comedy. Besides, I didn't have time to take care of all these little messes along the way. He'd get over it. Or not.

"Happy New Year!" I shouted down to the burning city below.

There were always sacrifices on the road to victory. And my road was just getting started.

ADMIRAL RICHARD HOWE

by Alex Roberson

ADMIRAL RICHARD HOWE: HOW DID THE AMERICAN REVOLUTION COME TO MY DOORSTEP?

NEW YORK, 13 JULY 1776

"*L*OWER THE SAILS! KEEP MOVING!" Captain Copal bellowed. The crew ran across the deck to get people and cargo ready to embark the ship onto Staten Island.

Richard looked at the ship's crew and frowned. "I wish that the crew would move swiftly and with more precision," he said to his brother, William.

Sons of Emanuel Howe & Charlotte Howe, the Howe brothers were commanding officers in the royal British forces. Richard served as Admiral of the British Fleet, and William as a General in the British Army. Richard's and William's older brother, George, had died here on American soil in the French and Indian War, and the colonists had honored their fallen brother. For that reason, Richard, and William both felt a fondness for America.

But Richard and William Howe found themselves ordered to put down the rebellion in the colonies by Great Britain. Both brothers loved America and wished for a solution that did not involve guns or swords. *Why must the colonies rebel against the Mother Country? I wish not to fight, but if it comes to it, I must be ready,* Richard thought for a moment. His mind considered what this could mean not only for Great Britain and her colonies, but for his family back in London.

Richard married Mary Hartop in 1758 and had three children: Sophia Charlotte, Mary Juliana, and Louisa Catherine.

"I agree," William added, "and I also wish that America did not go against the Mother Country and just follow the rules for the better of all."

Richard and William were here on a diplomatic mission to meet with George Washington on peace terms. He just wanted to help America and not fight against her. *While I love America, I wish I came on my own accord and not English ones.* "I just want to get this meeting started and finish it on good terms," Richard stated.

He left his brother at the dock and went walking towards his boat the *Eagle* hopefully end this rebellion.

Admiral Howe and his staff dinned in his cabin on board the *Eagle*. They discussed military affairs, England, American rebels, and how to end the rebellion.

In the morning, Richard sent a letter to George Washington carried by Lieutenant Philip Brown, an officer from the *Eagle*. The letter was addressed to "George Washington, Esquire."

Late in the evening Brown came back to the *Eagle* and handed the letter back to Richard.

"Report Lieutenant," Richard asked.

"Sir," Philip started, "I arrived at the waterfront confronted by rebels Joseph Reed, Henry Knox, and Samuel Webb. I told them that I had a letter addressed to a man as *George Washington, Esquire*. I then handed them the letter, but Reed replied that no person in their army had that address. So, I asked Reed what address Washington should be addressed as, and Reed replied, 'Under the title, *General Washington in our Army*.' So, I then left and came straight here."

Howe dismissed Brown and immediately began writing a second letter.

Three days later, Howe sent Brown with his second letter, addressed to *George Washington, Esquire, et cetera, et cetera.* But like the first one it was declined.

Howe realized that he needed to be careful with his next approach. He sent a different messenger, Captain Nisbet Balfour, to inquire if Washington would agree to a meeting with Colonel James Paterson, an adjutant general to him.

Washington agreed and Howe's plan was set into motion. Saturday, July 20, Colonel Paterson met Washington at Knox's headquarters exactly at noon.

"Admiral Howe!!!" Colonel Paterson arrived at Richard cabin on the *Eagle* the night of his meeting with Washington.

It is past dark! Paterson must have an important report about his meeting, Richard thought. He opened his door and let Paterson in.

"Anything to Report?" Howe asked.

"Sir, I arrived at the Knox Headquarters to find Washington, accompanied by Reed, Knox, and Webb. We sat at a square table with Washington at one side and me on the other. I set the letters you wrote in the middle of the table. I told Washington, 'Lord Howe did not mean to derogate from the respect or rank of General Washington.' Washington looked at the letters and pointedly refused to touch them! I told him that et cetera, et cetera implied everything that ought to follow but he still would not accept the letters."

"Go on," Howe said.

"I wanted to somehow bring you into this matter since I knew you would be better at making solutions, so I told Washington that you and General Howe were here as commissioners to fix the issue here. But Washington rebutted that, 'Lord Howe only has powers to grant pardons to those who did fault. We did no fault so therefore were don't want a pardon.' With that he left with his accompanies. And I was escorted out."

"Thank you, Paterson, you may leave now."

"Thank you, Admiral," Paterson replied and left.

Howe sat at his desk and thought of what he must do. He was Admiral of Britain's Naval Fleet and had to help Britain win the American Revolution. *I don't want to do this, but what else can I do? Abandon my position...and if captured most likely be hanged? Become a rebel...and be tried for treason? My only option is to fight for England. If only George was here, he would know what to do and how to help me.* Richard debated his options, and finally came to a decision.

"I must fight for my country."

ADMIRAL RICHARD HOWE: HOW DID I GET INVOLVED IN THE AMERICAN REVOLUTION?

HOWE MANSION, MONDAY, 15 JULY 1776

My Dearest Mary,

What unsettling days it has been! I arrived in New York on 26 June, only to discover such undignified Englishmen on these shores! I cannot believe this kind of behavior is tolerated over here. I could never imagine you or our daughters living here in these rebellious colonies!

I crafted a well-intentioned peace letter to George Washington on 13 July and dispatched a lieutenant to promptly deliver it. He returned later that evening and handed the letter back to me. He informed me that the Americans at the waterfront (Joseph Reed, Henry Know, and Samuel Webb) would not accept the letter unless it was addressed to "General Washington." However, the letter I wrote was properly addressed to "George Washington, Esquire."

Mr. Reed told my officer that no person in their army had such an address. My officer asked him by which title should Washington be addressed. Then Mr. Reed replied, "Of the rank of General Washington." Unable to complete his task, my lieutenant left them and returned the letter to me.

A few days later, I sent a second letter to Washington under that title of "George Washington, Esquire, et cetera, et cetera," delivered by the same lieutenant. Again, my properly addressed correspondence was not delivered and returned back to me! Could you believe these brazen Americans refuse to make peace with the mighty Great Britain?

The following day, I sent a message to Washington inquiring if he would accept a visit from Colonel James Paterson, an adjutant general to me. Washington agreed to such a meeting.

Returning to camp, Paterson knocked on my door returning from the meeting with Washington. We spoke late into the evening as Paterson relayed the events that took place during his time with Washington.

Paterson reported that Reed, Knox, and Webb accompanied Washington at the meeting. However, Washington never even touched the letter because I had not addressed them in his correct title. Paterson informed Washington that "et cetera, et cetera" implied everything that ought to follow. Washington still refused to accept any correspondence letter unless addressed to him in his official capacity.

In an attempt to find a mutually agreeable position Paterson tried to tie me into the argument because my brother and I were sent as commissioners to "accommodate this unhappy dispute." But Washington simply told Paterson that I had not any vested powers on this subject and that I only have authority to grant pardons. "Those who have committed no fault want no pardon."

Paterson told me that Washington then left, and he confirmed that he never touched the letters. Did Washington never understand we were trying to make peace?

My dear Mary, I fear for our family that I could get caught up in all of this mess. I fear for you and our daughters. I fear for America. I fear for my brother. I fear for us all. I fear that I must fight against this beloved country, though I wish not to do so. Whatever transpires, Mary, please don't come to America. I cannot stand the thought of losing you or the girls.

I am so thankful that you have Lady and Duchess at home to support you. I know that they are loving St. Johns Water Dogs and will protect you and our daughters. I am comforted to know that you all are safe, but please do not worry about me. I already have enough to worry about right now.

All I can ask of you is to pray. Pray that Britain and America somehow find a peaceful solution to this revolution. Pray that I will return home safely and swiftly so I will be able to see you and our daughters once more. Pray for

William, that he and I will not perish in this war-like rebellion like our beloved brother, George. And I will pray for you as well—for all the challenges you face at home, that they will someday stop, and that peace will once again find itself on both sides of the Atlantic.

I hope to find you across the Atlantic, and see your smiling face, cheering us all up. I hope to see Sophia, Mary, and Louisa and hear their beautiful voices. I shall see you soon, Mary. I look forward to the day when I will be reunited with you and our daughters! I love you so very much and long for the day to be with you again!

Sending all my love to you,

Richard

ADMIRAL RICHARD HOWE: WHAT'S MY STORY IN 1776?

25 October 1776, The Eagle

My Beloved Brother William,

It was a chilling day, 18 October. Strong, thick fog rolled in on the East River. I was in command of about a hundred and fifty ships, and our goal, once more, was to outflank the Americans and trap George Washington and the Continental Army stationed in Manhattan. About seven-hundred-fifty Americans were under command of Colonel John Glover. General Clinton commanded the British army of four thousand men, and I was in command of the ships.

We started moving through Throg's Neck or Frog's Neck to get to Kings Bridge where we could strike and trap the American lines at Harlem Heights close to King's Bridge. At first daylight, I ordered that the ships sail upstream through the dangerous Hell Gate Channel. As I looked at my map it appeared as if Throg's Neck was a peninsula, but it was not so.

While we went through with my plan, Throg's Neck turned out to be more like an island and not a peninsula. But we did not know this until we went through the plan, so this maneuver was much more difficult and troublesome than any of us assumed. And as you know, Hell Gate Channel is a nightmare, full of weary fog, strong currents, and treacherous waters. As we sailed, strong whirlpools started to form, making sailing much more danger-ous, nerve-racking, and frightening.

Miraculously, we made it through the dangerous channel, despite the heavy fog and murky waters. Everyone was tired, troubled, and weary already. But just as my ships tried to pass through a certain causeway, American riflemen stopped my ships from moving any further, setting a pause on our mission. The British sailors and soldiers embarked the boats and held on against the rebel riflemen. Crouched behind log piles the riflemen fought while both American and British re-enforcements arrived.

I decided not to reembark my boat until we had enough supplies and reinforcements, which consumed another four days. But it was worth the wait because we gained seven thousand newly arrived Hessians under the command of General Wilhelm von Knyphausen. We soon overtook the Americans and kept moving. Your colleague Henry Clinton called it 'Tweedledum Business." I then ordered that the boats set sail. They did move, with aston-ishing speed, I might add to Pell's Point in noticeably abbreviated time. So, we then moved inland to march towards King's Bridge to strike.

Washington's army retreated north towards White Plains to safety when they heard about our coming. We all celebrated this swift victory. I was so pleased with the few causalities we had. Only three Englishmen died, and twenty were injured. While few were injured, most were startled by their "Hells Gate experience" as some sailor and soldiers call it. Sadly, more than two-hundred Hessian soldiers were wounded or died. I wish that wars were not so ugly. I do feel slight sorrow toward the Americans because I saw some soldiers that were retreating, limping, or laying on the ground, dead or severely injured. While we do not know how many died on the American side, thankfully it was few on both sides. I wish that this war would stop and that the fighting would cease.

I wish that we could go home to England and not fight this war. I know that we must continue because it is our duty, but I do not like it. I do hope that whatever arguing between you and General Clinton will cease, for his sake, yours, and mine. I feel as it is my duty to bring you home to mother and to your wife.

Please stay safe and alert during these times of distress AND think wisely about your actions. Please pray for us both that we will get through this war together and regain hope for both England and America. I hope that you stay my healthy, brave, loyal, and helpful brother and general. I hope that you are doing well, my brother, and hope to see you again, alive, and well. But as brothers and not as generals or admirals.

With sincere regard,
Richard

GENERAL WILLIAM HOWE

by Ella Quill

GENERAL WILLIAM HOWE: HOW DID THE AMERICAN REVOLUTION COME TO MY DOORSTEP?

Boston, Massachusetts, Breed's Hill, 16 June 1775

The rain dripped down onto our canvas ceiling in a staccato rhythm with a gust of wind. It was dark outside the tent, but inside a small lantern illuminated the faces of four British generals. I stared past the others, thinking.

"I say that we sneak up behind those blasted rebels and trap them!" General Clinton exclaimed, emphasizing his point by pounding his fist on the table.

General Gage shook his head. "That's too risky. How are we going to get behind them without notice? We need something else." Everything grew quiet as the thunder clapped outside. The tent flap flew open, letting the rain and wind blow in enough to snuff out the candlelight.

General Burgoyne jumped up to secure the flap, and I drew out another match and struck it, gazing at the small flame it provided.

"General Howe is getting an idea," General Gage surmised, sounding relieved and pointing at me.

I lit the lantern and gazed around at my fellow officers. "Gentlemen, I do have an idea."

Great Britain, 10 August 1737, Thirty-Eight Years Previous

"Happy Birthday, dearest William." Mother placed a wrapped parcel in my arms. I looked excitedly up at her.

"May I open it, Mother?" I asked, clutching the package closely. It was my eighth birthday, and I was promised something special.

She smiled gently at me, nodding. "Yes, you may."

With my brothers surrounding me, watching over my shoulder, I ripped open the paper and gasped at the contents. "A sword of my own!" There in my lap lay a wonderfully carved wooden sword, and a belt to go with it.

"I helped George make it!" my older brother Richard said, jumping up and down. "Come, William! Let's go and fight with our swords!"

I looked gratefully towards my oldest brother, George, who was nearly twelve years old. "Thank you, George!"

George smiled. "Come, William, let us go outside and see if it is well made."

My eyes shining, I took the precious gift in my arms and followed my older brothers outside.

North America, 7 July 1758, Twenty-One Years Later

I sat down, exhausted. I took my canteen and lifted it to my parched lips. Empty. Frustrated, I stood, and swayed, lightheaded. I stumbled to the nearby brook and dunked my canteen in the muddy water. I stared into the dirty brown waters, frowning.

I had joined the army twelve years ago, following after my brother George. We had both been called to the colonies in North America because of the war that had broken out there. I had been fighting for four years now. Today, we had fought a battle against the Indians. I winced as memories of the battle flashed before my eyes.

My canteen was full, and I lifted it to my lips and drank thirstily. I stopped to take a breath and heard a sound behind me. I whirled around to see a fellow soldier, one who was also under the command of General Wolfe. He dropped down beside me and cupped his hands in the muddy brook and lapped the water from his hands. I looked at him expectantly as he wiped a hand across his mouth and looked at me. "Are you William Howe?" he asked.

I nodded. "What?" I noticed the look in of depression in his eyes. Suddenly a felt a surge of alarm sweep through me. "What has happened?" I stood, towering over him. "What is it?"

The soldier took off his hat and looked down at the swirling waters of the creek. "William," He cleared his throat and lifted his gaze to mine. "I'm terribly sorry to bring this news to you, sir, but your brother, George—" He paused at the wild look in my eyes.

I fell to my knees, feeling engulfed in grief. "How did he die?" I asked, my eyes stinging with tears, my voice sounding choked.

The soldier held out his hands sympathetically. "He died attacking Fort Carillon. He was so brave, William. He died in Major Israel Putnam's arms. I'm so sorry, William."

I held up my hand. "Leave me be, a moment, please, sir." I turned back to the brook and heard the soldier walking off. I grasped my sword hilt, as memories of my brothers and I together flashed before my eyes. I closed my eyes, pushing back my emotions, and stood. I took one last look at the brook, and then returned to the camp.

Great Britain, 1 January 1769, Eleven Years Later

"I think those rebels in the colonies are foolish to try and bring trouble," I remarked to my friend, Tom as I swished the wine around in my cup. We were at a dinner party celebrating the new year.

Tom nodded. "They are. Say, William, folks are telling me that…," he paused and looked around. "That you don't wish to fight the colonies. You actually want to *help* them."

Memories flashed before my eyes. After the Seven Years' War, my brother, George, had died, and was honored by the colonists. They built a memorial in his name because he had died such a brave soldier. He was described as the best officer in the British army. I blinked, back to reality, and shook my head. "Listen, Tom, I will go fight them if necessary. I do not seek to help the colonies in their rebellion. I just suggest, perhaps...that the king and Parliament be less hard on them."

Tom raised an eyebrow. "Do you hear what you're saying, William? This could be...could be treason!" Heads turned towards us. The others heard Tom.

"I wouldn't go that far," I protested, lowering my voice. "Listen, Tom, if they come and tell me I am needed in America, I will go! I may feel sympathetic towards the colonies, but I will not disobey my king!"

And so, in May 1775, I, General William Howe, with two other generals, returned to North America, to Boston, Massachusetts, to aid General Thomas Gage, who was trying to suppress the rebellion that was happening there.

Back at Breed's Hill, 16 June 1775, Six Years Later

I brought out a map and laid it on the table. "We are here." I said, placing my index finger on the spot. "And over here...is where the rebels are." I traced my finger along the map to another spot. "So, if we land here." I pointed to the tip of the Charlestown Peninsula. "And then make an attack here...perhaps the rebels will see how large our force is and either retreat or fight." I looked up to see the reaction of the other officers.

Generals Clinton and Burgoyne asked many questions, and I did my best to answer and explain.

General Gage was listening intently. "I like it," he said, sitting up, a light in his eyes. "Let's follow General Howe's plan. It just might work."

GENERAL WILLIAM HOWE: HOW DID I GET INVOLVED IN THE AMERICAN REVOLUTION?

Boston, Massachusetts, 19 June 1775

*D*earest Brother,

Just two days ago we won the bloodiest battle yet. The rebels camped out on Bunker Hill, and we were nearby on Breed's Hill. Generals Gage, Burgoyne, Clinton, and I devised a plan. We advanced up Bunker Hill not once, not twice, but thrice! During the last advance, I was the only man left leading the front lines. Everyone else had fallen back. Nevertheless, we conquered that hill and taught those rebels that Great Britain is still the force in command.

I am a much better commander than ever, Brother. Our big brother George would be so proud. I wish he were still alive to know of my success. The soldiers adore me, and I must say that I am quite a fine general. I've heard rumors that General Gage will be removed from his position, and I shall be the one to replace him. Yes, your younger brother will serve as the Commander of the British Forces in North America.

I stood up and stretched my arms. We won the Battle of Bunker Hill, but our success was not as sweet as I imagined. According to rumors, the rebels lost only 400 men while we—My thoughts halted. The price was too great to contemplate. I paused to take a swig of wine. I must focus on Great Britain's victory. After all, that's all that matters.

The tent flap lifted, and in came another general. "General Clinton, welcome! Come, have a drink to celebrate our victory!" I lifted my wine flask invitingly.

Putting a hand to his face, General Clinton shook his head. "General Howe, do you realize what a steep price we paid for our victory? Or are you too blind to notice our loss?"

Frowning, I set down the flask. "Of course, I understand what great losses we sustained, but shouldn't we rejoice in our victory for the king?"

We both said in unison, "God save the king!"

"He will be delighted to hear of our win, will he not?" I continued, pushing the flask towards him once again.

General Clinton stared at me from under his dark eyebrows. "General Howe, what are our next plans?"

I fiddled with the quill in my other hand for a moment, then shrugged and set the quill down on the table. "General Gage wishes for us to go south to New York." I inched the open flask even closer to him.

General Clinton sneered at me and grabbed the flask. He thrust the cork into it and then dropped it to the ground in disgust, landing with a thud onto the soft dirt floor. "How foolish to drink while discussing such a serious matter!"

I curled my lip in frustration. "I am not foolish, *General* Clinton! I am merely rejoicing in our hard-fought victory for the glory of King George III. Are you not satisfied with our win?"

General Clinton lowered his gaze for a moment and then looked back up at me, his eyes piercing. He jabbed a finger at my chest. "Are you? Are you satisfied even when our number of casualties lies over a thousand! A thousand mothers receiving the same letter your poor mother once received, *General* Howe! Don't tell me that satisfies you?"

I frowned and looked away. His words hit me. After all, he was right. The price was too dear, and inside I was not satisfied. Too many lives were lost to win just one battle. I winced and then muttered, "No, General, I am not satisfied."

General Clinton eyed me for a long moment and then moved towards the tent exit. Then he tipped his hat at me. "Good day, General." He then lifted the tent flap and stepped out. For a moment, the flash of sunlight blinded me. I held up my hand to block the light, but General Clinton dropped the canvas flap. Then everything went dark again.

I stood there, staring where he last stood. The flask was lying on the ground, and I stooped over and picked it up. I studied it and then uncorked it. I swirled it around, gazing at the dark liquid inside. With a flash, it reminded me of the bloodshed at the battle. Repulsed, I stuffed the cork in it and set it on the table, pushing it as far away from myself as I could. Then I sat back down at the table and picked up my quill to resume my letter.

However, dear brother, I will say that the price at which the battle was won was dearly paid. We lost many, and those who survived were not fit for such fighting. Even though Great Britain has won a victory, I fear we also won the greatest loss. These rebels are more than just farmers and country-men, they are determined soldiers in pursuit of liberty. I wonder what those in Parliament and the king—God save the king!—will think once news of the battle reaches them. We are heading south to New York next to suppress the rebellion there. I hope, dear brother Richard, that you are faring far better than I in your endeavors. I also hope to those at home are doing well and I wish to return there soon.

Your brother,
Gen. William Howe

GENERAL WILLIAM HOWE:
WHAT'S MY STORY IN 1776?

Twickenham, Great Britain, 23 December 1804

All was quiet and still. The snow fell softly outside, and inside, the firelight flickered, casting eerie shadows over the walls. Near the fireplace was a sweet-smelling fir tree, decorated with shining bulbs, and an evergreen wreath with a jolly red bow was draped on the door. I sat rocking in my chair, and great rings of smoke arose from my pipe. My eyes followed the rings to the ceiling, then I looked back down at the fire. In the kitchen, I could hear my wife overseeing the preparation for the Christmas Eve meal. She called, "William? Are you alright in there?"

I grinned with my pipe still between my teeth. I removed it and called back, "I'm quite alright, dear! Just an old man resting his tired bones." I put the pipe back in my mouth and stared at the fire. Near my feet slept Fortis, my brave basset hound. I reached down and stroked his long ears fondly. Just then, a shadow leapt across the room coming to land on a small side table, knocking off a delicate flower vase. The vase fell with a crash to the floor, shattering into a million pieces. The shadow on the table looked at me and meowed, and I sighed.

My wife, Fanny, called from the kitchen. "Good gracious! What was that?"

I answered, "Mari knocked over a vase."

Fanny hurried into the room; her apron covered in flour. In one hand she held a broom. "Naughty cat. I still wonder why she followed us home that day." She stooped and began carefully picking up the pieces.

Right then there was a knock at the door. "I'll get it," I said, getting up and heading to the front door. I opened it and was surprised to find a young boy there at the doorstep, shivering in the snow. "Er, greetings, lad. What brings you here tonight, eh?"

The boy, no more than eleven years of age, looked nervous, and he fidgeted with his hands. He then muttered something. I cupped a hand to my once vibrant ear now dulled by many years of muskets and cannons. "Speak up, son!"

The boy looked down at the ground and scuffed at the snow with his shoes. "I'm sorry to disturb you, sir, but I am writing down a story about our history, and someone told me that you were a good person to ask." He respectfully didn't make eye contact with me.

I eyed him. "Well, go home, son, I can't help you." I went to close the door, but the boy called out, "Please, sir! I have no home in Twick-enham! I came here just to speak with you!"

His imploring voice made me pause, and I sighed. "Well, come in, lad, and shake the snow off your shoes."

We returned to the parlor, where Fanny was finishing cleaning up the last bits of glass. She looked up and smiled gently at the rag-tag boy. I retook my seat in the rocking chair, and the boy pulled up a stool. "Well, go on, what do you want to ask me?"

The boy pulled out a worn journal and quill pen. "Please sir, I have just one question. What was your story in 1776?"

I leaned back and stroked my chin. "What was my story in 1776? Well, let's see…"

"In January 1776, I was promoted to Commander-in-Chief of all the British Forces in North America. One of my first tasks was managing the siege of Boston, which ended on March seventeenth, when I, at the time General Howe, decided that I wanted to leave Boston. You've heard of the battle of Breed's Hill, right?"

The boy nodded.

"Well, if you want to hear lesser-known stories of 1776, I can tell you what happened at the Battle of Long Island." I drifted off, gazing towards the fire as I recalled that terrific battle.

"What happened there?" the boy asked, getting out his ink and dipping his quill in the inkwell. He held his pen ready, waiting for me to continue.

I went on. "Late July, the twenty-eighth, I think it was, we arrived at Staten Island, in New York."

"We?" the boy asked.

"The British Troops arrived. And what a day! The sun was shining, the waters big and beautiful. The battle didn't happen till August, and that battle was-was—" I wheezed, coughing. Fanny came over and brought me a cup of warm tea, and a cup for the boy too. He set down his book and pen and gladly took the tea, thanking her generously. He waited patiently while I sipped my tea, then I continued. "We, the British Troops, arrived on Long Island on August twenty-second. I sent many letters to the Rebels' commander, General Washington, telling him what a mistake he had made, and he should surrender. Washington refused, and you know what happened next?" I leaned in, and the boy breathed, "What?"

I chuckled, "Good question." I paused to take a sip of my tea and the boy asked, "What happened? The battle?"

I nodded. "Yes, early on August twenty-seventh, I divided some of the troops to report to Generals Clinton, and Grant, while the rest remained under my command. We formed a half-circle around the

Rebels' base, which was built on Brooklyn Heights. Then the Rebels decided to advance. They fought General Clinton's detachment, then they moved on to General Grant's. Then I came in, but they retired quickly, and ran into General Grant's detachment once again, and a bloody scuffle ensued. Then, as we pressed in on them, the Rebels turned and retreated, faster than we could follow. We still killed a great many and captured even more of those Rebels. We told the prisoners that they should have surrendered earlier, but they were set in their ways. The battle went on for quite a while, and..."

Here I paused again, frowning at the memories that invaded my mind.

"General Howe, we should do an immediate assault on the Rebels' fortifications on Brooklyn Heights," General Clinton advised, as we walked along the shore of Long Island. The day was August 29th, 1776.

I shook my head. "The Troops have done handsomely enough; they deserve a rest. We cannot fight if we are not well rested."

"I could go right now and ask each soldier in the troops if they could go on, and you know what they would say?" Clinton retorted angrily. "We are so close, General! If we go now, there's a chance we could overcome them and capture their leader! Take them all prisoners! End this war!"

I shook my head again, "General Clinton, I have made my order, now go, and tell the others. We will dig siege trenches. We have the Rebels pinned with their backs against the East River. They aren't going anywhere."

"Sir?" The boy was gently nudging my knee. "Please, sir, what happened next?"

I blinked, coming back to reality. "I'm sorry. Yes, the siege lasted a couple of days, but then the unthinkable happened. We discovered that General Washington and his nine thousand troops escaped across the East River overnight! All their fortifications were empty, and there was not a soul left on Brooklyn Heights. We took over New York City, and then pursued the Rebels. It wasn't till October that we chased them out of New York and into New Jersey. And after that, everything happened so quickly. In November, we fought the rebels at Fort Washington, and captured many there. Then..." I cleared my throat, clearly uncomfortable. "Well, there were a lot of times that I should have listened to my aide, General Clinton, but I didn't. For me, 1776 ended in New York, planning out my next campaign." I stopped, and for a moment the only sounds that could be heard was the crackling of the fire and the whining of the wind.

I turned and looked down at the boy by my feet, who was vigorously writing in his journal, with my cat, Mari, curled up in his lap. The boy wrote one last part, gently blew on the ink to dry it, then thoughtfully shut the journal. He gathered his pen and ink and placed them in his satchel. "Thank you, so much, sir, for the fascinating facts you have given me!" He stood to leave, and put on his hat, and wrapped his scarf around his neck. I noticed that his scarf was ridden with holes, and his fingertips were showing through his gloves.

I stood as well, and reached out to shake the boy's hand, but at that moment, the wind howled even louder than before, and I looked outside at the swirling mass of snow. Instead of shaking his hand, I took the boy's shoulder and directed him towards the kitchen. "You can't go home in a blizzard like that! Stay a while, until the snow stops." We entered the kitchen to see Fanny directing several maids around the kitchen. I turned to my servant by the door and motioned to the boy. "Find him a room and prepare him a hot bath. Then have him come down and eat some supper." Then I said to the boy, "Thank you, lad, for your attentiveness. You have a heart for history and writing. I like that." I squeezed his shoulder. "Keep it up. Hopefully, someday, there will be a generation like you, willing to learn and keep alive old stories. God bless you, my son."

KING GEORGE III

by Bella Waugh

KING GEORGE III: HOW DID THE AMERICAN REVOLUTION COME TO MY DOORSTEP?

28 MAY 1764

Office of His Royal Highness King George
St. James Palace, London, England

My Dearest Charlotte,

I would like to express my many thanks for the glorious picnic on the newly remodeled Buckingham House grounds. It was a perfect way to spend the last night before you and the children go off to spend a month at The Dutch House. I wish I could be with you at our country retreat but, alas, my business with Parliament requires me to stay behind. As a token of appreciation for your steadfast love and faithfulness, I am hereby renaming our family home. Buckingham House shall now be known as The Queens's House.

I wish to confide in you, my beloved wife, of the latest events in Parliament. As you know from the beginning of the French and Indian War in 1754 all the way to the end in 1763, the purpose of the war was to establish new boundaries, acquire new lands from the French, and to protect our Colonies from French invasion.

We sent countless of our fighting men to the Colonies, which was quite costly. The French and Indian War cost England £70,000,000. Therefore, England has amassed a great debt, nearly double what it was before. Due to this, Parliament has been trying to think of a solution to recoup this debt. We believe that the Colonists should help pay for the protection we gave and continue to give to them.

My newest Prime Minister George Grenville who took over after John Stuart last year, has recently put forward in Parliament the idea for a Stamp Act in the Colonies. The Stamp Act will require the Colonists to pay an extra tax on paper goods and that tax will go toward paying off England's war debt. This tax affects items such as newspapers, magazines, playing cards, legal documents, dice, and almanacs. A stamp will be affixed to each item, signaling the tax has been paid. Precious Charlotte, do you think this is wise--or do you fear the Rebels whom we've heard about in the Colonies, may revolt? This is just one of many taxes we shall enact on the Colonies, in an attempt to lift ourselves from this great debt. Parliament and I deeply hope that the Colonists will not see this as oppression but as fair trade. Please do keep me and our beloved country in your prayers.

Enjoy your time at the Dutch House and give my love to the children. Your devoted husband,

George

George William Frederick III, King of Great Britain, Ireland, and the British Colonies

11 Years Later, St. James Palace, London, England, 23 August 1775

King George III finished the last sip of black tea accompanied by a slice of toast. The scent of his usual breakfast was overwhelmed by the musty scent of the large palace. The soft crackle of a fire competed with the noise of birdsong and the buzz of the busy palace life. He sat in his luxurious office at his gilded desk, gazing out on the marvelous grounds as the stable hands walked the royal horses across the lawn.

On a branch right outside the window, a metallic starling, a colorful blue tit, and a tiny goldcrest, flitted around the tree.

Deep in thought, he ran his fingers along the worn edges of the letter he sent to his darling wife eleven years ago. She lent it back to him this morning at his request. King George III sighed, wondering if the Stamp Act was indeed the right choice, especially since Parliament repealed it two years later in 1766. Even though King George was lost in thought, he was not alone; beside him stood his latest Prime Minister. Lord Fredrick North was the fourth prime minister since George Grenville who had initiated the Stamp Act in 1765.

Lord North was here to discuss the two latest developments with the British Colonies, which they had found out about today. King George had received a full account of the battle in Lexington and Concord, Massachusetts, as well as The Olive Branch Petition. The Olive Branch Petition was a document that the Second Continental Congress in the Colonies had developed. The document declared the Colonists' loyalty to the King and hope for reconciliation with Great Britain.

"I simply cannot understand what those delegates were thinking! In the first place, to hold a disloyal congress without my consent is a complete breach of authority. In the second place, to draft a paradoxical document in that illegal congress is unsuitable beyond all lengths of the law. What is even more befuddling, is the Rebels asking for reconciliation after they fired upon my British military. They began the war, and yet there are trying to ask me to stop the war. Does this comprehend with you, Lord North?" King George III continued speaking without letting his Prime Minister answer. "Even more depressing is the news that a dreadfully small number of untrained Rebel minutemen killed some of my Royal army in the Battle of Lexington and Concord. This is the last straw. It is time to no longer make petty talk, but to take drastic action!"

King George continued talking crossly. "Those blasted Rebels! Lieutenant Colonel Francis Smith had come so close to seizing the Rebel's ammunitions warehouse and capturing Samuel Adams and John Hancock, only to have amateurs drive them out! The idea of mere farmers, hunters, and commonfolk defeating my highly trained British military men is incomprehensible. Why can't those 'Patriots,' as they call themselves, see the importance of staying under Royal authority?"

"The Rebels want to make their own rules and govern themselves. For what reason, I cannot understand," Lord North replied with equal disgust, finally able to cut in. "Why anyone would dare to refuse loyalty to His Majesty King George III, is beyond me! They are no better than arrogant children. The more settlements and land England owns, the more opportunities for distribution of goods we have, the more resources we shall acquire, and above all the more power we will possess. We simply cannot let the Colonies slip out from the hold of the Crown!"

"I will not accept this Olive Branch Petition or even consider it! If they fired upon us, we shall fire upon them!" King George yelled. "It's treason I tell you. Treason! The very definition of that word is the crime of betraying one's county by attempting to overthrow the government. Is this not exactly what these unruly Colonists are doing?! I will write up my official declaration of treason and open rebellion. I shall title it the Proclamation, For Suppressing Rebellion and Sedition, and I want it in the next edition of The Daily Post, and a copy of it sent to the Virginia Gazette too. That will teach them to not toy with the ultimate supremacy of the English Crown."

King George III slammed his fist on his desk and briskly walked out of the room. Lord North followed him, muttering, "We'll get them in line, if it's the last thing I do!"

KING GEORGE III: HOW DID I GET INVOLVED IN THE AMERICAN REVOLUTION?

16 OCTOBER 1775

Office Of His Royal Highness King George III
St. James Palace, London, England

*L*ord North,

Greetings, Lord Frederick North, my illustrious Prime Minister. I was pleased to hear life at 10 Downing Street is to your liking. I have heard of the most splendid and lively parties you've hosted in your home and do wish to have an occasion to attend one of those boisterous celebrations.

You may wonder why I am writing to you rather than simply speaking with you in person at the palace. The information I will include in this letter is too confidential to risk having it reach the eager ears of a Rebel spy. Hence why I have chosen to write down and hand deliver this letter. There are far too many Patriot spies hovering around every corner hungry for a tib-bit of information to aid their foolish cause. I have been pondering an assembly of our own league of spies, to give those 'Sons of Liberty' a taste of their own medicine, to quote Aesop's old fable.

I am increasingly losing my patience with these hot-headed rebels. First, the Battle of Lexington and Concord, then their illegal Continental Congress, and finally the Olive Branch Petition aimed to 'reconcile with the King.' Bah!

I still have not deduced the meaning of that petition, perhaps because I declined to read it. As you know I didn't care to reconcile with those American turncoats. I still have yet to hear what the colonies thought of my declaration of treason, but alas I don't rely my confidence on their positive or negative comments. I fear they will respond in an uproarious way, as per their usual, but only time will tell. I believe that unless we take drastic action against the Colonies, they will never learn their lesson on how to submit to the ruling authority. I have clearly seen how they have committed treacherous felonies against the Crown, even to the point of shedding innocent blood.

In conclusion, I hereby assert that any process, and I mean ANY process, of tormenting the Colonies and the rebels who inhabit them, will meet my approval. We must do whatever it takes to turn them from their reckless and perfidious ways. Please do not disclose this information to anyone, no matter the circumstance, unless I give my authorization. Report to my office in two days so that we may discuss this matter further.

Your loyal authority,
King George

George William Frederick III, King of Great Britain, Ireland, and the British Colonies

Over Two Months Later, St. James Palace, London, England, 31 December 1775

King George III was leisurely resting in his rocking chair on the veranda of St. James Palace. It was an unusually warm and sunny day in December, with large puffy clouds filling the sky. He wore a beige waistcoat and matching beige breeches. Over that he donned a navy-blue coat embellished with gold thread. This was his usual outfit, different from every king before him. George III love botany and agriculture, therefore earning him the name "Farmer George." Due to that, he traditionally wore simpler clothes, to the point he was often mistaken for ordinary palace subjects.

King George thought back to the letter he sent to Lord North in October, where he mentioned his desire for spies. Despite the guarding measures the King took, the rebels did indeed attempt to discover the contents of the letter, but fortunately failed. A spy was caught hovering outside Lord North's bedroom window, but before he could hear Lord North relay the letter's information to his diary, the passing guards spotted and imprisoned him.

I must find a way we too can spy on those Patriots. If they wish to use espionage as one of their military tactics, so can we! George sat evaluating this idea further. As he was thinking, a Black-Billed Magpie flew up and perched on the ornate railing surrounding the veranda."Greetings lovely magpie," King George said kindly to the bird. The bird squawked and cocked its head to the side studying the King sitting before him. "You look like you need a name." George looked up to the sky, contemplating a name fit for a bird as intelligent as the magpie. His eyes fell upon the billowing clouds filling the glorious sky. "Nimbus seems like a perfect name!" he declared.

George's dog trotted up to him and sat down next to the king, as his canine companion often did. Unlike most St. John's Water dogs, she was completely black, head to tail, and for this reason King George had named the dog, Shadow.

There was a piece of paper hanging from Shadow's mouth, which caught King George's attention. "What do you have there?" he asked rhetorically. Shadow opened her mouth and let the paper drop right where King George's hand was laying. The King picked up the paper and tried to decipher the wobbly handwriting printed on it. *'Benjamin Franklin has left London'* it said. *'He has joined a committee to form a secret document.'*

After he finished reading, he looked at Shadow with a shocked expression on his face. "What-what?! Benjamin Franklin had left our fair London to aid the Patriot cause?! I always knew he sided with the

Rebels, but this has gone beyond acceptable," King George bellowed. "How-how did you find this? Where did you get this?" the King asked Shadow, knowing however the dog couldn't possibly respond. "Ah well, no matter where or how you got this, you are a smart pup! Maybe I could find a role for you in this ongoing war!" Shadow looked up at Nimbus and winked.

"Chak! Shadow spy," Nimbus cawed with a wink back to Shadow.

King George III looked up, startled. *Did I just hear that bird speak? I've heard of parrots being trained to speak simple words, but a magpie?! It must be my imagination; I have been quite tired lately. I must be fatigued.*

"Shadow spy! Chak!" Nimbus repeated.

"There it is again! I heard it for sure this time!" George cried. "But what could it mean?" He played the words over and over again in his mind. Suddenly he looked down at Shadow, who was lying by his feet, a realization growing in the King's mind. "Make Shadow a spy? That's it! Could Nimbus be suggesting that I deploy you, my faithful dog Shadow, as a British spy?" the King questioned. Shadow stood up, wagged her tail eagerly, and smiled in her canine way, as if understanding exactly what King George had said. "Yes! No one will ever think that a dog is aiding the British crown. What a marvelous idea! Now, who can we have you spy on?" the King mused. "Aha! I know the perfect person for your next espionage mission. A devoted Rebel by the name of…Dr. Benjamin Franklin."

A Few Weeks Later, January 1776
St. James Palace, London, England

"I simply cannot believe what my astonished eyes are reading! You mean to tell me that the Colonial Congress accused Parliament of violating the British Constitution?! That is inconceivable that they would suggest I would perform such a tyrannical move against this country's laws!" King George III yelled to Lord North.

"I know my liege, what shall we do in response to their accusations of the Royal Crown?" Lord North responded equally repulsed. They had just received word that the Second Continental Congress had published a response to King George's declaration of rebellion. The response stated that because the Colonies were not represented in Parliament, England had no valid entitlement of power over the 'American' Colonies. Congress also disputed that Parliament was violating the laws of the British Constitution.

"This is even more convincing that the only way to stop this rebellious revolution is by musket-to-musket combat!" King George III thundered, "You have my orders to continue sending men, supplies, and support to every Loyalist in the British Colonies, no matter what those defiant rebels say."

KING GEORGE III: WHAT'S MY STORY IN 1776?

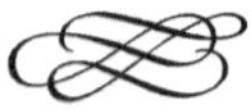

10 JULY 1776

Royal Canine Spy Shadow,
Philadelphia, Pennsylvania

*D*earest Royal Master,

Greetings from your faithful dog! Since you employed me as your official war spy, I have gathered a great deal of valuable information on my espionage quests. While I wish this letter was of a jollier tone, I regret to inform you of news that will most certainly make His Majesty's soul burn with anger.

You may be familiar with the influential Rebels, such as Benjamin Franklin, John Adams, and Robert Livingston. They have brainwashed their fellow Colonists that you, my reliable King, are a tyrant. One Rebel by the name of Thomas Paine had the nerve to distribute a treasonous pamphlet called Common Sense. He declared His Majesty to be a 'Royal Brute' and the 'Pharaoh of England.' I sincerely hope His Majesty will not take these lies to heart but realize these people do not know the true King George III as I do. The Colonists erroneously believe they must break free from our hold. Franklin, Adams, Livingston, and others had the audacity to draft a document officially announcing their freedom. They call it the "Declaration of Independence."

After overhearing this disastrous news, Nimbus and I sprang into action. As he squawked and I barked, we burst forth into one of their treasonous meetings to write this dreadful Declaration. I leapt onto the table, sending pots, food, and papers flying. This distraction made such a commotion that the men writing lost their focus. They were so frazzled that they weren't able to write anything for the rest of the day. Huzzah! However, they resumed writing the next day. Unfortunately, nothing seems to stop them now.

We will keep trying! I shall forge ahead with my espionage work, and report back to you with any pertinent information as it transpires.

God save the king!

Your devoted canine servant,
Shadow, The Royal St. James Water Dog

King George III galloped through the forest atop his black horse. Leaves brushed his arms as he flicked the reins urging the horse to move faster. He loved racing through the forest trying to lose the servants who insisted upon following him. Pulling the reins in, he allowed the horse to rest for a moment in a clearing. He shielded his eyes, looking up into the sky. A dark-colored bird appeared over the forest canopy, reminding him of his pet bird Nimbus who joined his dog Shadow on spy missions. The bird circled the clearing, and descended into the small meadow, aiming for the horse and its rider. King George thought it could be Nimbus! The bird came in closer and closer and then dropped a rolled-up parchment onto the king's saddle.

King George waved. "Hello, Nimbus! Thank you!"

Nimbus flew away back into the bright blue sky as King George picked up a letter from his dog, Shadow. He read with a disbelieving expression on his face. After King George III finished reading Shadow's letter, he was baffled at his furry companion's ability to write the

English language. *I do believe dogs are one of the Creator's most anointed species. Therefore, I would not put it past our Creator to enable a specimen from the* Canis *family to write a letter!*

Lord North came galloping up to the King, on his copper-colored horse, shouting, and waving a paper in the air. "Sire! Sire! There you are! I have searched high and low for you all over the palace grounds. You will not believe what we just received! It's that blasphemous Declaration of Independence. I simply cannot imagine how those irrational Colonists could even broach the topic of breaking free from our authority. It's an outrage that they would even…"

"Lord North," the King interrupted.

"…dare to insinuate that our British authority is unworthy of them! Why, here right in paragraph four they mention—" Lord North continued, unaware that he was speaking over the King's words.

"Lord Frederick North!" the King said sternly, hoping to stop the rant.

"Oh, beg your pardon, my liege. I am so enraged at this new document the Colonists have sent us. It's preposterous!"

King George nodded. "I will pardon your wrongdoings, because I know you were overcome with the same disgust as I am over this insipid Declaration."

"How are you already aware of it?" North questioned, clutching the only copy.

"I just received confidential correspondence containing this troublesome news," the King said.

"How shall we respond to this? Shall we draft another declaration of treason?" Lord North asked.

The King shook his head. "Absolutely not. The proclamation of rebellion didn't work last time, so I doubt it would now. I believe this time we shall just ignore this childish attempt for their so-called liberty."

Lord North looked confused. "But, Sire, wouldn't that anger the Colonists even more as they expect a response?"

King George nodded. "Well, I suppose, you are right. What-what! I have a brilliant idea! Do you remember John Lind, the splendid barrister and political activist? We shall have Lind write a rebuttal to this silly document! A mockery! I shall order Lind to pick it apart, pointing out every falsehood and injustice. Right here in their own writing, they articulated that 'all men are created equal' yet they own hundreds, thousands, of slaves themselves. Lind shall mock and ridicule them for their contradictory actions to create doubt and discord among the people. That shall stop their rebellious actions, once and for all."

Two Months Later, October 1776
St. James Palace, London, England

Shadow bounded into the royal bedroom where King George III was preparing himself for the always busy day that lie ahead. She had a piece a paper rolled in her collar with crucial information for him.

"Shadow, my dear girl. You are a sight for sore eyes!" King George knelt and petted the dog while she licked his face. "How have you been? Oh, how I miss you romping around the palace." He rubbed her neck, and his hand brushed against her collar. He felt something bulging from her collar and fished the paper from the cloth layers. "Is this my latest message, girl?" Upon unfolding it, he read:

We have won the Battle of Long Island! On August 29, 1776, the Continental Army retreated. We have won!

-General Howe, Long Island, New York

Months before, the King had ordered General William Howe, along with twenty-thousand British military men, to attack ten-thousand Rebel militia in the Battle of Long Island. In the breaking hours of August 27, the British launched the first attack of the forty-eight-hour battle. Brutal combat ensued ending only at nightfall when the British backed the Rebels against the East River and surrounded them on the other three sides. However, in the middle of the night on

August 29, as the British slept, a thick fog rolled in, blanketing the area. This miraculous weather enabled Washington and his men to quietly retreat across the river with the invaluable aid of the local townsfolk and their boats. They avoided a disastrous battle in the morning, sure to result in massive Patriot casualties.

"This is remarkable! I always knew we would prevail! If only we had caught that traitor, Washington. Drat!" King George said firmly, "Ah well. Yes, we can win. We must win. We will win."

Two Months Later, 25 December 1776
St. James Palace, London, England

"Yes, I would like another cup of wine!" King George said jovially to the servant beside him. It was Christmas and the King was hosting a lively party in celebration of the holiday. The room was bustling with dignitaries, nobles, and businessmen from around London. The scent of decadent food, burning lantern oil, and a wood fire filled the room. Shadow sat beside the King's table eating every crumb that fell upon the floor. King George raised a toast. "To England!"

Lord North also raised a glass. "To the King!"

Cheers rose around the room as glasses clinked. "Oh, Lord North. What a victorious year this has been!" the King said with a proud smile. "Out of the one hundred and nine battles and skirmishes fought this year, England has won fifty-four of them, far more than the Rebels only winning forty-six. With the majority of the battles won in our favor, nothing can stop us now!"

Meanwhile, as the King was celebrating their victories in England, a new battle was brewing in the Colonies that would change the course of the Revolution forever. On the bank of the Delaware River, crouched by the crackling fire, General George Washington whispered to his fellow Patriot militia. "All right men. I know morale is low, but I am confident we can take back the town of Trenton. The Trenton townsfolk have been under siege, and we are their only hope. Here is the plan: We will all get into these boats and row across the Delaware River. We will then march through the night ten miles, into Trenton, and at daybreak we will attack the enemy troops. The Redcoats and Hessians will not be expecting us, for they are busy celebrating the Christmas holiday. This will make them vulnerable to our attack and therefore we can easily seize their weapons and gain the victory! I will not lie; this will be strenuous, but I am confident we can win! Surely this will show those Tories who is really in charge!"

KING GEORGE III: EPILOGUE

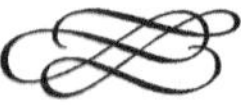

This attack that took place in New Jersey would later be known as the Battle of Trenton and would inspire the famous painting of Washington Crossing the Delaware. The American victory at this battle was a major advantage that ultimately led the American Colonies to winning the American Revolutionary War over the British.

LT COLONEL BANASTRE
TARLETON

by Jessah Semons

LT COLONEL BANASTRE TARLETON: HOW DID THE AMERICAN REVOLUTION COME TO MY DOORSTEP?

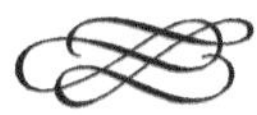

8 DECEMBER 1776

"Hup, two, three, four! Hup, two, three, four!" shouted Major General Lord Charles Cornwallis. "Attention! Salute! Saddle your horses!"

"Sir, yes sir!" replied the soldiers as they marched to ready their horses.

This coarse command startled me. However, I quickly readied myself for an awfully long ten hours of training. I saw Cornet Tarleton coming towards me where I grazed on some luscious green grass near the post where I was tied.

I have been Ban's battle buddy since he first arrived in North America. Before I was taken off the farm, I was a plow horse. An abundant number of horses were needed for the cavalry, and it just so happens I was one of the chosen ones. The day Ban chose me was scary but thrilling. He gave me many compliments. "Decent fighting height of about fifteen hands. Maintainable black trimmed mane and sleek brown coat. No swayback and an even gait. Lastly, she has new shoes," he mumbled as he circled me and patted me down for inspection.

"Thank you, sir," I neighed back. But to both of our surprise, Ban responded, "You're welcome," out of habit. He must have thought the long days were starting to get to him when he realized he had just replied to a horse. Once the shock wore off that we could understand each other, we both swore to keep our conversations a secret.

"I'll call you Brown Bess after my favorite weapon," Cornet Tarleton decided.

"I like that name," I replied with a grin.

Tarleton laughed, "I didn't know horses could smile."

As the young Cornet placed the saddle on my back, I felt the familiar weight of training gear. Because, like my best friend, Athena, who I met months ago when I first arrived to camp, I was also a training horse before Ban arrived. I smelled the memorable stench of sweaty worn leather.

"Left, left, left, right, left! Left, left, left, right, left!" directed General Cornwallis. After the first few hours my legs were trembling, but Ban didn't even notice. He pushed me to work harder than I ever had on the farm. Ban, who has a handsome and athletic build, did not seem bothered one bit by the long day of repetitive drills. We had been ordered to Trenton, so after being dismissed for the day, Ban took me down to the shallows of the nearby Delaware River.

"Why does he make us train for so long, Ban?" I asked panting.

"Well, Bess, we had a great loss at our first attempt to capture Charleston, so he makes us train harder in hopes that we will fight better," he answered.

"What made you lose?" I questioned him.

"Would you like the long version or the short version?" he joked.

"Short please," I neighed.

"Bad weather, spongy palmetto logs, too deep of water to wade through, but too shallow of water to bring ships ashore, and swampy wet grounds that refused to burn," he gloomily recalled as we waded into the river.

"How did you even come to be in America?" I wanted to know.

As he began to splash the cool river water over me, he began to tell me his story of joining the British guard. "I attended university at Oxford in 1771 in hopes of becoming a lawyer. Then when my father died in 1773, I inherited £5,000 British pounds. I spent most of it on short-pleasured things, which I regret. My mother thankfully bought me a commission as a lieutenant in the 1st King's Dragoon Guard."

"What is that?" I interrupted.

"The 1st King's Dragoon Guard is one of the most elite British cavalry units. A dragoon is a single cavalry soldier," he replied. "We are mounted infantry soldiers who can fight with sabers while chasing after the enemy."

"I know you're not in that now, so what happened next?" I continued.

"When I heard the war began, I knew I wanted to be a part of it. I got permission to leave the 1st King's Dragoon Guard and became a volunteer under General Cornwallis as a 16th Light Dragoon. We arrived at Long Island early this year, and on June 28th at 9:00 in the morning, one of our ships fired a signal gun and the battle began. Our troops didn't even get a chance to leave the boats. After this loss at Charleston, I stuck with Cornwallis, and here I am," he finished as he began to lead me out of the river.

"So, you have come on a very long journey to get here," I commented as we walked back up the trail towards the camp.

"Yes, the journey has been very tough," replied Tarleton. The remainder of the walk was silent as we pondered on his past and our unknown future.

When we arrived back at camp, he unsaddled me and tied me to my post for the night. I soon drifted to sleep because of my extreme exhaustion. Shortly after drifting off, I was awakened by the clickety clack of horse's hooves behind me. When I peeked my eyes open to see who it was, I saw General Cornwallis tying his horse, who is my friend, Buckshot, on the post next to me.

"Brown Bess, are you awake?" Buckshot quietly whinnied.

"I am now, Buckshot," I angrily whinnied back. "What do you want?"

"Sorry!" Buckshot exclaimed, "I just wanted to tell you that I overheard the General talking, and Cornet Tarleton has been chosen to leave with Colonel Harcourt on a scouting mission to find Major General Charles Lee's whereabouts."

"Do I get to go with him?" I worriedly asked.

"Why wouldn't you?" remarked Buckshot teasingly. "Hopefully, you'll know soon enough."

Because of my fear of not staying with my battle buddy, Tarleton, I had a hard time falling back to sleep.

LT COLONEL BANASTRE TARLETON: HOW DID I GET INVOLVED IN THE AMERICAN REVOLUTION?

11 DECEMBER 1776

It felt like only minutes after falling asleep that I was awakened by the ear-splitting *reveille* from a bugle at dawn. The Cornet making the wakeup call was standing only a few feet away, and my first morning thought was to kick him in his hindquarters with my much bigger hindquarters. However, I realized the offensive bugler was my buddy, Ban. His tent was set up near my post, so I quickly forgave him for scaring me awake.

"Good morning, Bess. Sorry to startle you," Tarleton snickered. "How did you sleep?" he asked with a sleepy yawn.

"Terrible!" I moodily replied.

"Me too," he replied as he yawned again.

"Really? I heard you snoring," I said, challenging him. "It sounded like the Patriots were invading our camp with cannons."

"Well, after my intense conversation with Cornwallis, I only got a few hours of sleep. When I finally dozed off, I was out cold," he said, offended that I had called him out.

"When you blew that hunk of trash in my ear, I had just fallen asleep, too, Ban," I snapped back.

"All right, Bess... I can tell we both had a lot on our minds last night. Truce?" he reasoned.

"Sure, fine. What kept you awake?" I asked him.

"No, ladies first," he politely gestured toward me.

"Well," I began, "when ole' Cornwallis tied up Buckshot next to me last night, he woke me up. Buckshot said he overheard that you were chosen to go on a spy mission..."

"WHAT?! You aren't supposed to know yet!" he interrupted me. "I wanted to tell..."

"Then blame Buckshot!" I interrupted his interruption.

"We leave tomorrow morning," he announced.

"I actually get to go?" I shrieked. "Ban, I lost sleep over this last night!"

"How did you expect me to get there? I'm not going to walk the whole trip," he chuckled, teasing me.

I blushed, realizing how silly it sounded.

Cornwallis told Colonel Harcourt to gather the chosen dragoons and ready them for their mission. So, Ban and the others spent the rest of the day gathering supplies and packing.

After finally getting a full night's sleep, I awoke with the *reveille*, once again, to another cold December morning. Soon after I awoke, Ban saddled me and loaded my saddle bags full of his supplies that he'd gathered yesterday.

Harcourt gave his instructions for the day's journey from Pennington to Hillsborough. "Our goal is to find General Lee as soon as possible. If you find ANYTHING at all, report it to me immediately. Let's go find this traitor!" Harcourt yelled from Athena's saddle, leading our group from the camp.

When we arrived at Hillsborough, the dragoons scouted a house with a barn to rest in for tonight. The men were to sleep in the house, while we horses slept in the barn.

"Today was a waste of time, Bess," Tarleton angrily whispered to me as he unsaddled me to put me in the barn for the night. "We could've just stayed at the camp. I don't know why I'm needed here," Tarleton grumbled.

Before I could reply, Ban left for the house. As I looked around the barn, I noticed Athena, Flash, Musket, Saber, Pistol, and the annoying

Tomahawk, and several other new horses. We were all weary from the long, boring journey, but happy to finally get a rest. Every horse, including me, was dozing off when the loud, squeaky grinding of wood disturbed me. I jerked awake, and to my surprise an old donkey was walking his circles around a mill, which I had not notice before. I slowly walked over to him.

"What are you doing, and why must you do it now?" I quietly questioned him.

"Well, Miss, this is my barn. If I don't work, I don't get fed." he simply stated. "Who are ya? What are all ya hoodlums doin' in here?"

"My name is Brown Bess. I'm a war horse for the British dragoons. In fact, we all are. Our mission is to find General Charles Lee and capture him," I answered. "What's your name? Why are you here alone?"

"Hi, Brownie. Can I call ya Brownie?" he asked me.

"I'd prefer Bess. That's what my battle buddy, Ban, calls me," I replied.

"Nice to meet ya, Bess. Name's Howitzer. The ole' farmer and his fam'ly fled when they heard y'all might head this way. Did I hear ya say yer lookin' fer Lee? I might have some info, as y'all young'uns call it," Howitzer bragged as he continued to walk in circles around his mill. "This info will prob'ly be mighty helpful for a mission like yers. Mighty helpful in—"

"Can you just say it already?" I demanded. "I don't have all night. I do need some rest."

"Yer a feisty lil miss, ain't ya, Bess?" Howitzer laughed. "I'll get to the information. Before the ole' farmer left, he was talkin' to his eldest son. He said he'd talked to some feller named Sullivan that he'd met comin' home from town. Sullivan and his riders were on their way to Lee's current location near Baskin' Ridge."

"Thanks for the info, Howitzer, but I have one quick question. Could you wait to work your mill until morning? We have a long journey ahead," I asked as politely as possible.

"Sure, Bess. I'll start in the morning," Howitzer answered. "Do ya hear that, or is it my old ears playin' tricks?"

"I do hear that. It sounds like men shouting and yelling from the house," I replied peeking out the barn door. "The house is on fire!! The men are running for the barn."

The barn door burst open, hitting me, and all the dragoons rushed in the barn coughing and hacking from the smoke.

"Brown Bess?" yelled Tarleton. "Are you alright?" he anxiously hollered for me.

"Here I am," I neighed back to him. "How are you? What happened?"

"Clearly, somebody doesn't want us here. One of the townspeople set the house on fire and then ran!" Tarleton explained as he caught his breath. "Everybody got out fine."

"Good," I whinnied with relief.

"I didn't notice that old mule before," Tarleton mentioned.

"Yea, his name is Howitzer. He gave me some useful information for you," I told Ban. "I'll tell you in the morning. First, we need some rest."

Before daylight, I woke Ban to tell him everything that he needed to know. The loud creaking of Howitzer's mill again awakened everyone else. Howitzer had kept his word and started so early the sun had barely got out of bed itself.

Tarleton quickly saddled me and then addressed the group, "I have secret information that includes the whereabouts of someone close to General Lee. Don't ask how I know, just trust me," he informed them. "We are heading towards Basking Ridge to find a Patriot named Sullivan and his riders. Everyone, saddle your horses, and then meet me outside."

While the dragoons readied their horses, Ban approached the colonel. "Colonel Harcourt, I think we need to split the group to cover more ground and find Sullivan," Tarleton advised him.

"That sounds like a good plan, young Tarleton," Harcourt replied. "You'll make a good colonel one day."

LT COLONEL BANASTRE TARLETON: WHAT'S MY STORY IN 1776?

13 DECEMBER 1776

As the sun rose, our group and Harcourt's group headed in the direction of Morristown, New Jersey. Sadly, on our way there we only received sketchy bits of information about General Lee's whereabouts.

Our luck changed when we were passing through Basking Ridge. Just as Howitzer had predicted, we found some of General Sullivan's riders, who had just returned from where Lee was staying in Basking Ridge. We managed to squeeze some information out of a single rider, which we captured. The dragoons bribed him with his freedom in exchange for information on General Lee. He told us that Lee had been resting at Widow White's Tavern.

"Tarleton I am putting you in charge of capturing Lee and bringing him back to me," ordered Harcourt. "You are to leave with your group of dragoons in the morning."

"That would be an honor," Tarleton squeaked with excitement. "I mean, Sir, yes Sir!" he said clearing his throat and deepening his voice.

I could tell Ban was very anxious over our new orders by the way he was tightening his legs around me.

"Ban, could you please loosen up? You're crushing my ribs!" I complained to him.

"Sorry, Bess, I'm just so nervous because I want to impress Harcourt and Cornwallis," Tarleton apologized. "Let's go find a place to rest. We leave first thing in the morning."

It was hard for me to sleep that night. I could hear Ban tossing and turning for a while in his tent, so I knew that he was having a rough night, too. The pressure was on for us both.

Once I feel asleep, the night passed too quickly. I was yet again awakened by Ban's bloody bugle and its *reveille*. All of the dragoons quickly saddled their horses, and we began our trek to Widow White's Tavern.

When Ban knew we were getting close to General Lee's hideout, he pulled me to a stop. "Whoa, Bess. Men, let your horses have a break. Let's form a plan," Tarleton commanded.

Ban and the other dragoons tied me and my fellow war horses to an old fence nearby. We began to graze as the men formulated a plan.

"Does anybody know what's going on?" asked the annoying Tomahawk. "I'm hungry. Are y'all hungry?"

"Hi, hungry. Can you please be quiet? I'm trying to eavesdrop right now." I bit at him.

"What are they saying? I can't hear from way over here," asked Saber in a deep voice. He was tied the farthest from the dragoons.

"I couldn't tell you even if I wanted to because I can't hear over Mr. Noisy Hooves over here," I neighed back at Saber. "Can all of you please close your apple holes for a minute?"

I turned my ears towards Ban and listened to what his plan was.

"Ban said not too far from here is the last known location of Lee. He ordered your riders to circle the house but to stay near the wood line," I explained. "Your men are to shoot out the doors and windows of the tavern. If this doesn't work, Ban is going to burn it down."

"Did you say shooting? I'm not so good around guns," Tomahawk annoyingly rambled.

"There's definitely going to be guns, Tomahawk. Just hope they won't be pointed at you," Pistol laughed.

"Pistol, he's already worrying. Don't make it worse! The safety of Tomahawk's rider depends on it!" I scolded him.

We were all on edge as the dragoons mounted back up to begin the last couple of miles to the tavern. All of us were silent for the remainder of the trek, deep in thought about whether we'd make it back home.

We approached the Widow White's Tavern at 10:00 a.m. on December 13. Ban began motioning to his left and right to tell the other dragoons to split. We surrounded the tavern. Every dragoon had their guns pointed in a window or a door. At Ban's signaling gunfire, the shooting began.

"AAAAAHHHHH! I'M STILL HUNGRY! I STRESS EAT!!" Tomahawk brayed as his rider was shooting at his target.

When Lee's guards began shooting back, Tomahawk really started losing it.

"WE'RE ALL GOING TO DIE! TELL MY MOM, I LOVE HER!!" Tomahawk continued.

"TOMAHAWK, FOCUS! YOUR RIDER'S LIFE IS IN YOUR HOOVES!!" brayed Musket. "WE ARE ALL IN THIS TOGETHER!"

Just as fast as it began, the shooting stopped.

"Is everyone all right?" I whinnied to the other horses.

"Our men are down," Musket and Flash answered somberly.

There was a brief second of silence before Ban started shouting, "IF YOU DON'T COME OUT NOW, I'LL BURN DOWN THIS PLACE AND EVERYONE IN IT!"

Within minutes General Lee, who had been watching from an upstairs window, sent down Major Bradford with a message.

"NO NEED FOR THAT. LEE SURRENDERS!" Major Bradford yelled out to Ban.

"TELL HIM TO COME OUT IMMEDIATELY!" Tarleton ordered.

Major Bradford quickly ran back in to collect Lee. Still in his nightdress, Major General Charles Lee emerged from the tavern.

"This is my first time seeing a Patriot," Tomahawk giggled. "Do all of them wear cute little striped dresses?"

For once Tomahawk had said something that was actually funny, and we all laughed.

"And it has a matching hat with a fluff ball on top," I mocked him.

All of the dragoons couldn't contain their laughter either. Seeing such an 'important person' in such silly dress was a once in a lifetime sight.

After capturing Lee, we also got his horse named, Ranger, and led them both to meet up with Harcourt. We decided to camp for the night to celebrate our great victory.

During the celebration, Harcourt suggested they all get Lee's horse drunk on alcohol to mock him even more. Personally, I thought this was crossing the line. Ranger didn't do anything wrong. When I saw Ranger having trouble standing, I walked over to check on him.

"How are you doing, Ranger?" I asked him.

"Beeen betterrrr, Bessss. I didn't know you were a triplet," Ranger slurred, apparently cross-eyed from drunkenness.

I pushed him up against a fence and made him lay down to rest. All the dragoons, including Ban, celebrated well into the night. I stayed near Ranger and tried to get some sleep.

The next morning, I woke up at normal *reveille* time, out of habit, to see that Ranger was up and grazing. When I realized that Ban was not up yet, I went to check his tent. Sure enough, I could still hear his rumbling snores. All the men slept in late, but we were headed for Pennington by noon with Lee in tow.

Finally arriving in Pennington a few days later, Lee was taken into custody to be kept as a prisoner of war.

Ban was ordered to Cornwallis' tent. He brought me along. I could tell he was nervous, thinking he may be in trouble. I stood outside to listen to the conversation.

Cornwallis began, "Ole Harcourt told me he let you lead the capture of General Lee. I just wanted to tell you that you did an excellent job. I see a promotion in your future," he finished.

Ban left the tent grinning from ear to ear.

"I did it, Bess! Cornwallis finally recognized me," Ban exclaimed.

"WHO did it?" I reminded him.

"I mean WE did it, Brown Bess. We did it," Tarleton said, smiling as we walked to my post.

ABOUT THE AUTHORS

MIKAYLA BADENHORST (Joseph Plumb Martin)

Hi! I am *Mikayla Badenhorst,* and I am eleven years old. I am in 7th grade, and I live in Sarasota, Florida. My favorite hobbies are reading, watching movies, playing volleyball, body boarding at the beach, and hanging out with my friends, family, and three adorably crazy cats. I hope to come back to Epic Patriot Camp next year so I can write more!

DEDICATION:

I am dedicating my three chapters to my very proper uncle, Carel, who encouraged my writing passion by sponsoring me for this camp. My life goals are to sit on an historical artifact like Patrick Henry's chair, almost put on his spectacles, and accidentally break into Mr. Henry's house. However, I might consider becoming a professional beach volleyball player or a religious freedom lawyer if those endeavors do not work out. If you would like to contact me, I can be reached at tonyastreinz@yahoo.com.

BIBLIOGRAPHY:

Ellis, Kirk, and David McCullough. *John Adams Mini-Series,* Season One, episode 1-5, HBO, Mar. 2008.

History.com Editors. "Joseph Plumb Martin." *History.com,* A&E Television Networks, 8 Mar. 2010, https://history.com/topics/american-revolution/joseph-plumb-martin (accessed June 17, 2022).

"Joseph Plumb Martin." *American Battlefield Trust,* 14 Feb. 2022, https://battlefields.org/learn/articles/joseph-plumb-martin (accessed June 17, 2022).

"Joseph Plumb Martin." *Wikipedia,* Wikimedia Foundation, 2 June

2022, https://en.wikipedia.org/wiki/Joseph_Plumb_Martin (accessed June 17, 2022).

Martin, Joseph Plumb. *The Adventures of a Revolutionary Soldier.* Create Space Independent Publishing Platform, 2018.

Pruitt, Sarah. "Did George Washington's Bodyguard Plot to Kill Him in 1776?" *History.com*, A&E Television Networks, 8 Feb. 2019, https://www.history.com/news/george-washington-bodyguard-assassination-plot (accessed July 1, 2022).

Wikipedia contributors, "Battle of Long Island," *Wikipedia, The Free Encyclopedia* (accessed July 9, 2022).

ELYCE CORSETTI (Silas Deane)

Hello, my name is *Elyce Corsetti*. I am a young aspiring author, currently residing in Florida.

ACKNOWLEDGEMENTS:

Historical fiction wasn't something I originally thought I could do. It seemed like a bunch of research and stress, but with the help of Ms. Jenny and Ms. Libby I was able to turn in three complete chapters. It turns out, writing historically accurate isn't too difficult. It did take work, but I was able to have new and fun experiences, such as collaborating with another camp member. I'm really glad I signed up for this camp and was able to work with two amazing authors. I hope all her readers will enjoy this compilation of stories; it was truly worth all the effort that we put into it.

JENNY L. COTE (Epic Patriot Camp Director)

Award-winning author and speaker Jenny L. Cote, who developed an early passion for God, history, and young people, beautifully blends these three passions in her two fantasy fiction series, The Amazing Tales of Max and Liz® and Epic Order of the Seven®. Likened to C. S. Lewis by readers and book reviewers alike, she speaks on creative writing to schools, universities, and conferences around the world. Jenny has a passion for making history fun for kids of all ages, instilling in them a desire to discover their part in HIStory. Her love for research has taken her to most Revolutionary sites in the

U.S., to London (with unprecedented access to Handel House Museum to write in Handel's composing room), Oxford (to stay in the home of C.S. Lewis, 'the Kilns,' and interview Lewis' secretary, Walter Hooper at the Inklings' famed The Eagle and Child Pub), Paris, Normandy, Rome, Israel, and Egypt. She partnered with the National Park Service to create Epic Patriot Camp, a summer writing camp at Revolutionary parks to excite kids about history, research, and writing. Jenny's books are available online and in stores around the world, as well as in audio and e-book formats. Jenny has been featured by FOXNEWS on Fox & Friends and local Fox Affiliates, as well as numerous Op-Ed pieces on FoxNews.com. She has also been interviewed by nationally syndicated radio and print media, as well as international publications. Jenny holds two marketing degrees from the University of Georgia and Georgia State University. A Virginia native, Jenny now lives with her family in Roswell, Georgia. Learn more about Jenny at www.epicorderoftheseven.com.

ACKNOWLEDGEMENTS:

Thank you, God, for bringing each person and part of this project together. You get all the glory! I'm grateful to Banastre Tarleton, Mark Schneider, and John Slaughter for being the ones who got the ball of the Revolution rolling in my world to create the original Epic Patriot Camp. (See my opening comments in the front of the book for the full back story.) But Virtual Epic Patriot Camp would not have been possible without my dear friend, "spoon sister," and historical author extraordinaire, Libby Carty McNamee. While we suspect that we were separated at birth, I'm so happy to have connected with her to inspire the next generation of young patriots while having more fun than anyone should be allowed. Thank you, parents, for entrusting your incredible children to our care—your bravery is surpassed only by that of our Founding Fathers.

DEDICATION:

IT'S FOR THE CHILDREN!

PAYTON GRACE (Lord Dunmore)

I stared at the screen before me, the dim glow of the lamp doing little to shine any light on my situation. *It's my first time writing a biography...what should I write...!? How do other biographies usually go?* So many questions, yet so little answers. *I suppose all I can do is go for it...* I was thirteen years old, and lived in Hawaii, on the island of Oahu. I wasn't sure what I wanted to be when I was older. Of course, I was an aspiring author, but other than that, I wasn't sure if I was going go to college just for writing. In my future, there was a lot of "gray area" that I wasn't exactly sure how to color in. I supposed that some questions could only be answered with time. But I didn't own a time machine, and I couldn't exactly see into the future. I was barely even halfway on my life's path. All I could do for now was just keep walking.

ACKNOWLEDGEMENTS:

Thank you to my amazing family, the Lord above, my wonderfully chaotic and unique friends, and, of course, every single EPIC individual that I've met during these four weeks, including Jenny and Libby, who put all this together, as well as my fellow "Epiclings." It was a blessing to have met every single one of you.

Lady Virginia Murray to Thomas Jefferson, [before 29 November … (archives.gov)

To George Washington from Benjamin Harrison, 21–24 July 1775 (archives.gov)

Lady Charlotte Stewart Countess of Dunmore (1740–1818) • FamilySearch

Alexander Murray to Thomas Jefferson, 1 January 1819 (archives.gov)

John Murray fourth earl of Dunmore (ca. 1730–1809) – Encyclopedia Virginia

Lord Dunmore's Proclamation, 1775 · Document Bank of Virginia

Lord Dunmore - US History Scene Lord Dunmore | American Battlefield Trust (battlefields.org)Founders Online: Search (archives.gov)

To George Washington from Benjamin Harrison, 21–24 July 1775 (archives.gov)

https://ushistoryscene.com/article/lord-dunmore/#:

CAMERON GRAHAM (Nathanael Greene)

Cameron Graham is a homeschooler from Arizona. Cameron excels in STEM activities and competes in challenges. His favorite subject in school is military history and geography. Cameron is active in his community and works with homeless, children in crisis, and refugees in his city. He and his sister began their own ministry to refugees in 2021 that celebrates a refugee child's first birthday in the USA. Cameron is active in his local 4H project with dogs as well as county STEM Ambassador. Cameron also enjoys playing as a defenseman in the local Youth Hockey House League. Cameron has plans to continue writing Nathanael Greene's story as well as completing his series on military machines under his business C.H.A.R.

ACKNOWLEDGEMENTS:

Thanks go to Ms. Jenny L. Cote and Ms. Libby McNamee for the 2022 Patriot Camp and my fellow contributors in the telling of the story of 1776.

Thanks to my mom and dad for investing in this opportunity to gain experience in writing skills. Also, thanks to them and my sister, Madison, for helping me edit and proof-read my manuscript.

Thanks to our readers, I hope you will this book and all the wonderful stories in adventures of real-life people contained within its pages and I hope you enjoy learning about this time in history

AUTHOR'S NOTES:

Hundley and George were fictional and will play a future role in their assistance to the Patriots and Nathanael Greene in coming years.

Conversation at the iron forge although fictional was helpful to illustrate the division between loyalists and patriots and the tension between each side.

Nathanael Greene's quotes and thoughts are actual according to historical records but the situations where they come up and/or timing are my own ideas.

ABIGAIL GREGORIN (General Charles Lee)

My name is *Abigail Gregorin*, and I am a tenth-grade homeschooled student who lives near Lynchburg, Virginia, with my parents, seven siblings, and my two dogs. I enjoy writing especially thrillers and mysteries, but this summer I discovered that historical fiction is a fun genre to write about too!

DEDICATION:

To my mom for teaching me the fundamentals of writing and to my dad for his tips that always help me improve. Thank you so much for your help and excellent criticism, but most of all for your encouragement that keeps me writing and, in the end, makes me a better author.

AUTHOR'S NOTE:

He was surrounded. Or at least that's what I think.

On December 12th, General Charles Lee was captured by the British, but the details on *how* they captured him aren't exactly clear. We know that the general was at White's Tavern when the British found him, but the details on what happened to Spado when he was taken or even how Banastre Tarleton managed to find him are vague. Another interesting thing to note is that the troops that Lee had been leading to meet George Washington weren't at the tavern when Lee was captured.

In fact, the troops were camped somewhere else and surprisingly, they were unable to rescue Lee. Due to a lack of information, it is unsure whether they attempted to save Lee or if they just fled when they saw the British. Maybe neither of those were the case and instead the British caught the other troops by surprise and took them as prisoners as well.

Whatever the case was, the patriots' second-in-command was taken, and he spent two years in prison, while Spado remained elsewhere. Well, I just wanted to point that out and I hope you enjoyed reading about Charles Lee, his adventures, and his dog Spado! Three cheers for our independence and an extra special thanks to those who fought for us so that we could have it!

BIBLIOGRAPHY:

"Battle of Sullivan's Island." Wikipedia, Wikimedia Foundation, 24

Jan. 2022, https://en.wikipedia.org/wiki/Battle_of_Sullivan%27s_Island.).

"Charles Lee." American Battlefield Trust, https://www.battlefield-s.org/learn/biographies/charles-lee.

"General Charles Lee: Facts, Early Years, Life, Death, Military & Politics." Revolutionary War, 4 Mar. 2020, https://www.revolutionary-war.net/general-charles-lee/.

"Charles Lee (General)." Wikipedia, Wikimedia Foundation, 26 June 2022, https://en.wikipedia.org/wiki/Charles_Lee_(general

McCullough, David G. 1776. The Folio Society.

OLIVIA HANKS (General George Washington)

Olivia Hanks is a creative from Fort Worth, Texas. She is known to her family as "Oliviapedia" for her love of knowledge and history. Her passions include art and photography. She currently travels the country in an RV with her parents, dog, and two cats.

DEDICATION: To my mother who knew I could do it.

BIBLIOGRAPHY:

1776 - David McCullough

Founders Online: Search (archives.gov)

The American Revolution | Timeline | Articles and Essays | George Washington Papers | Digital Collections | Library of Congress (loc.gov)

George Washington: The Character and Influence of One Man - Verna M. Hall

PERI JORDAN (Abigail Adams)

My name is *Peri Jordan,* and I have been writing pretty much all my life. I'm thirteen now, and I just finished up seventh grade, but I'm homeschooled, so school is a little bit different for me than it is for most other kids my age. I've always gone to the same school just outside of Columbus, Ohio and I've only ever known a class of two: me and my sister with my mom as our *amazing* teacher! My whole family has been super supportive of my writing, from when it was just a hobby, all the way through to now, when I feel that God is calling me to use this as my ministry! I hope to one day live on a farm in Ohio where I will write stories to inspire kids and raise my own children to love God and others just as my parents taught me. But no matter what happens to me, or what I do, I will trust God and follow His call wherever it will lead. May God be with you, and I hope this story is a blessing to you!

DEDICATION:

To my family, for helping me through every step of the way.

ACKNOWLEDGMENTS:

God: for making all this possible, and for directing my words in a way that is (I hope) helpful to others and glorifying to Him.

My sister: for giving me the idea that turned into my entire story! I would have been lost for sure if you hadn't had the right thoughts at the right time.

My mom: for that power brainstorming session and taking a walk with me to get the juices flowing.

Mrs. McNamee: for sacrificing so much time to put the class together and to edit my work, all while being super encouraging and helpful.

Mrs. Cote: for putting the class together and supporting all our writing every week. Also, for teaching us so well not to sit on historic artifacts, or to go ANYWHERE with Bob without a code! ;)

All of the Epic Patriot Campers: for being so encouraging and just such a delight to be around all month! Thank you all.

BIBLIOGRAPHY:

https://en.wikipedia.org/wiki/Abigail_Adams

https://www.britannica.com/biography/Abigail-Adams

https://www.history.com/topics/first-ladies/abigail-adams

https://www.nps.gov/adam/learn/historyculture/abigail-adams-1744-1818.htm

https://en.wikipedia.org/wiki/Abigail_Adams_Smith

https://founders.archives.gov/documents/Adams/04-03-02-0207

https://www.americanyawp.com/reader/the-american-revolution/abigail-and-john-adams-converse-on-womens-rights-

1776/#:~:text=Abigail%20Adams%2C%20in%20this%20let-
ter,the%20limits%20of%20revolutionary%20liberty.

ELLIOTT LAY (Thomas Jefferson)

Elliott Lay is a young rising author who likes to tell stories both verbally and through words. He resides in Sammamish, Washington, with his parents and sisters.

DEDICATION:

To Libby and Jenny, the people who made this story happen.

EDAN MACNAUGHTON (Patrick Henry)

Edan MacNaughton is a 17-year-old who loves studying American history, writing and sports. A dream of his is to combine two of his passions and become a professional sportswriter. He lives in California with his family and dog, Zoe.

ACKNOWLEDGEMENTS:

First and foremost, I want to thank my Lord and Savior Jesus Christ as through Him all things are possible. I also want to sincerely thank Jenny L. Cote & Libby Carty McNamee for making this camp and mentorship a reality. I'm so blessed and honored to have met you and to have received your coaching. To my fellow campers, I am grateful to have met you and for our now lifelong friendship. I am a better person and writer because of this community. To my parents and sisters, thank you for your endless love, encouragement, and support. To God be the glory.

AUTHOR'S NOTE:

1. I mention Patrick Henry having a cat named Cato. This is entirely fictional. It is possible he did have a cat but there is no record I found that proves he did.

2. Patrick Henry did not actually write a letter to himself on December 31,1776 but the feelings and worries he expresses are accurate. Every event he mentions except writing a New Year's Eve letter, giving coins to an orphan boy in town and having a cat are true.

3. I had a lot of fun finding ways to get Patrick to paraphrase some of his own words from speeches into this letter. In chapter 1, I wrote,

"the war has only begun" and that's a nod to what Henry says in his 1775 Liberty or Death speech. Also, in chapter 2, I typed, "I believe God presides over the destiny of nations" which he also said that in that same speech.

4. I chose to write from the perspective of Patrick Henry writing a letter to himself so that it would not only answer the three questions for him, but also for you as the reader.

BIBLIOGRAPHY:

Cote, J. (2020). *The Declaration, the Sword & the Spy*. AMG Publishers.

Foundation, R. (2022). *Primary Sources - Red Hill | Patrick Henry Memorial Foundation*. Red Hill | Patrick Henry Memorial Foundation. Retrieved 24 June 2022, from https://www.redhill.org/primary-sources/.

McCullough, D. (2005). *1776*. Simon & Schuster Paperbacks.

Mims, J. (2021). *The Centurions Letter*. Jenny L. Cote Publications.

Patrick Henry. Biography. (2017). Retrieved 25 June 2022, from https://www.biography.com/political-figure/patrick-henry.

ABIGAIL MCGINNIS (General Charles Cornwallis)

Abigail McGinnis lives with her parents, three younger brothers, and Vizsla in Chesapeake, VA. When she's not busy reading, Abby enjoys art, writing, cello, piano, and swimming. Abigail also really enjoys imagining stories and was exited to write her part of this book. One day she hopes to be an astronomer and also work with animals.

BIBIOGRAPHY:

https://www.thoughtco.com/american-revolution-lord-charles-cornwallis-2360680

Harmon, Daniel E. *Lord Cornwallis*. 1st ed., Chelsea House Publishers, 2002, pp. 20-22.

https://www.epgreatbritain.com/blog/british-history-heroes-general-charles-cornwallis

https://www.history.com/topics/american-revolution/charles-cornwallis

https://ap.gilderlehrman.org/essay/no-way-out-lord-cornwallis-

siege-yorktown-and-america%27s-v#:~:text=War%20of%20Indepen-
dence%20%C2%BB-,No%20Way%20Out%3A%20Lord%20Cornwal-
lis%2C%20the%20Siege%20of%20Yorktown

https://www.revolutionary-war.net/charles-cornwallis/
https://www.nps.gov/people/charles-cornwallis.htm
https://en.wikipedia.org/wiki/Charles_Cornwallis,1stMarquess

LIBBY CARTY MCNAMEE (Epic Patriot Camp Director)

Libby Carty McNamee is a lawyer, pubic speaker, and the award-winning author of two upper-middle-grade historical novels, Susanna's Midnight Ride: The Girl Who Won the Revolutionary War and Dolley Madison and the War of 1812: America's First Lady, as well as their accompanying Study Guides. She loves making Author Visits to school groups in person and virtually. In addition, she would love to talk to your historical society and book club. Currently she is writing a third novel about the Civil War, Elizabeth Van Lew: The Union Spymistress of Richmond. Sign up for her monthly Dispatch on her website at LibbyMcNamee.com for fun historical tidbits. Find her on Facebook and Instagram @libbymc-nameeauthor.

A native of Boston, Libby now lives in Richmond, Virginia. She is a graduate of Georgetown University and Catholic University School of Law. She also served as a Major in the U.S. Army JAG Corps in Korea, Bosnia, Germany and Washington State.

ACKNOWLEDGEMENTS: I would like to thank my fellow Epic Patriot Camp Director, dear friend, and "spoon sister," Jenny L. Cote, for inviting me to embark upon this truly EPIC adventure! I am so grateful that God brought us together through the American Friends of Lafayette just a few years ago. In addition, I would like to thank my husband, Bernie, and son, Sam, both true Patriots, for their support during the wonderfully hectic days of camp and many chapters to edit "for the children."

DEDICATION: This is for you, the twenty-five phenomenal campers who never cease to amaze, impress, and inspire us with their genuine kindness, diligence, encouragement, and dedication to becoming better writers. It has been such a joy and honor working with each and every one of you. HIP HIP HUZZAH!

And a special thank you to author David McCullough whose outstanding historical tome, <u>1776</u>, provided the road map for Epic Patriot Camp and a fabulous resource for us all. May you rest in peace, knowing your written masterpieces live on, inspiring patriotism in our next generation.

CARMENE MILLER (King Louis XVI)

Hello. My name is Carmene Miller, and I am 13 years old. I live in North Carolina, and I love to read, write, draw, and enjoy outdoor stuff like, hiking and fishing. I am a homeschooler in the 8th grade. My dream job is to become an author because I love to write and share my creativity with other people.

ACKNOWLEDGEMENTS:

I enjoyed going to Epic Patriot Camp. Meeting and working with two award-winning authors, Jenny L. Cote and Libby McNamee, who have so much knowledge of American history has been an awesome experience. It was said in camp that to learn history you must "learn the good, bad and ugly." Being in Camp has allowed me to learn more of history then I knew before. I also enjoyed meeting other young people who share a love of history. I am a full-on American history "nerd," and I plan to never stop learning.

BIBLIOGRAPHY:

McGee, Suzanne. "5 Ways the French Helped Win the American Revolution." History.com. A&E Television Networks, September 9, 2020. https://www.history.com/news/american-revolution-french-role-help.

Embassy of France in the United States, Washington. "Pierre De Beaumarchais 1732-1799." *France in the United States / Embassy of France in Washington, D.C.,* https://franceintheus.org/spip.php?article491.

"La Fayette." Palace of Versailles, April 9, 2021.https://en.chateau-versailles.fr/discover/history/great-characters/fayette.

"Louis XVI." Palace of Versailles, July 1, 2021.https://en.chateau-versailles.fr/discover/history/great-characters/louis-xvi.

"Louis XVI." Biography.com. A&E Networks Television, April 23, 2021. https://www.biography.com/royalty/louis-xvi.

"January 24, 1732 – Birth of an 'Improbable Patriot' – Pierre-Augustin Caron De Beaumarchais." Legal Legacy, March 12, 2019. https://legallegacy.wordpress.com/2019/01/24/january-24-1732-birth-of-an-improbable-patriot-pierre-augustin-caron-de-beaumarchais/.

"Pierre Beaumarchais." Visited the main page. Accessed July 10, 2022. https://www.newworldencyclopedia.org/entry/Pierre_Beaumarchais.

Blakemore, Erin. "Canada's Long, Gradual Road to Independence." History.com. A&E Television Networks, June 8, 2018. https://www.history.com/news/canada-independence-from britain-france-war-of-1812.

"France in the American Revolutionary War." Wikipedia. Wikimedia Foundation, June 29, 2022. https://en.wikipedia.org/wiki/France_in_the_American_Revolutionary_War.

"Flour War." Wikipedia. Wikimedia Foundation, April 13, 2022. https://en.wikipedia.org/wiki/Flour_War.

"Louis XVI." Wikipedia. Wikimedia Foundation, July 5, 2022. https://en.wikipedia.org/wiki/Louis_XVI.

"Roderigue Hortalez and Company." Wikipedia. Wikimedia Foundation, August 2021. https://en.wikipedia.org/wiki/Roderigue_Hortalez_and_Company.

"Harvest Failures." French Revolution, October 1, 2020. https://alphahistory.com/frenchrevolution/harvest-failures/.

Lawler, Sean. "John Adams Diplomat to France: Boston Tea Party Museum." Boston Tea Party

Ships, June 8, 2020. https://www.bostonteapartyship.com/john-adams-diplomat-france.

U.S. Department of State. U.S. Department of State. Accessed July 10, 2022..

Elle Loughran .f67943c9-aee5-4b4c-9cf0-7bd937c850f4{fill:#82b964;} fact checked by Jamie Frater, Elle Loughran, and Elle Loughran. "10 Ways Louis XVI Was a Great King." Listverse, August 9, 2016. https://listverse.com/2016/08/11/10-ways-louis-xvi-was-a-great-king/.

"Roderigue Hortalez & Co.." Sobel Wiki. Accessed July 10, 2022. https://fwoan.fandom.com/wiki/Roderigue_Hortalez_%26_Co

EMMANUEL ZACHARIE MORISSET (Henry Knox)

Hello, my name is *Emmanuel Zacharie Morisset.* I am 11 years old. I was born in Florida in 2011 from two marvelous parents that I love dearly. I am a very blessed person because my name means "God with us." My parents always tell the story that I died in the belly and was later born prematurely, but God miraculously saved me. I was blessed to receive the prestigious "Micah 6:8 Award" in the wonderful school South Shore Christian Academy in Weymouth Massachusetts that I attended in my earlier years before I moved from Massachusetts to Florida. I currently live in the beautiful city of Coral Springs Florida, and I am also home-schooled. I am normally a quiet child. I am also an avid reader. I devour books. I even read them in my bed using a flashlight without my parents' knowledge of course :) I am very grateful to God for making me who I am. In addition to English, I speak French, Haitian Creole, a little bit of German that I am learning, Spanish that I am also learning. Since Latin is not considered a language, I will not include it in the list. I would love to be a prolific writer and a pastor.

DEDICATION:

It is with genuine gratitude and warm regard that I dedicate this book to my mom Rose-Laure C. Morisset who has been my hero throughout my life. She is a dedicated woman of God whom I respect very much. I would also love to dedicate this book to my wonderful dad Jacques J. Morisset Jr. Dad has been a great source of inspiration, strength, prayer, and example to me. I would be remiss if I forgot my writing teacher, Mrs. Jenny L. Cote who taught me so much about writing. I would love to also thank my brother Mikha'El J. Morisset and my sister Gabrielle S. Morisset and my grandmother Marie Y. Charlitte Jean for their unwavering support. Last but not least, I want to thank my Heavenly Father for giving me life and ideas that I can share with others to inspire, build, and encourage. May God continue to bless you!

BIBIOGRAPHY:

https://youtu.be/A6Ui7GEgNaw
https://youtu.be/FqOaZOo2OTs
https://youtu.be/oz72BxHTlm0
https://youtu.be/0mNIxzYgsfQ
https://youtu.be/oLL-_qSn99o
https://youtu.be/cao-s0_mkLQ

KIT P. (Sir Guy Tarleton)

Kit P. is eleven-years-old and lives in Virginia. She enjoys reading, writing, and drawing. She hopes to one day be an author and write fiction novels.

ACKNOWLEDGEMENTS:

In the process of writing my three chapters, I had some help. I would like to thank Jenny L. Cote and Libby McNamee for editing my chapters and helping me write in the perspective of my character, Sir Guy Carleton. I would also like to thank them for teaching me the writing and publishing process. I also want to thank my parents for helping me review what I wrote and letting me do this camp so I could have this opportunity.

AUTHOR'S NOTE:

One of my greatest challenges while writing my three chapters was gathering information. In my research I couldn't find a lot on Sir Guy Carleton's individual movements during the Revolutionary War. As a result, I took what I got from my research and had to imagine the rest.

BIBLIOGRAPHY:

"Sir Guy Carleton," Digital Encyclopedia of George Washington, accessed June 18, 2022, https://www.mountvernon.org/library/digitalhistory/digital-encyclopedia/article/sir-guy-carleton/.

Kennedy Hickman, "Biography of Sir Guy Carleton," ThoughtCo, last updated November 14, 2020, https://www.thoughtco.com/governor-sir-guy-carleton-2360609.

"Sir Guy Carleton," Revolutionary War, last updated March 4, 2020, https://www.revolutionary-war.net/sir-guy-carleton/.

"Guy Carleton," American Battlefield Trust, accessed June 18, 2022, https://www.battlefields.org/learn/biographies/guy-carleton.

R.G. PATTERSON (Martha Washington)

R.G. Patterson lives in Iowa with her parents and brother and sisters. She recently graduated from high school in 2021 and now teaches piano to people of all ages. She hopes to continue writing and publishing books as she proceeds with life. She loves to write in multiple genres both fictional and nonfictional.

DEDICATION:

To my George and Martha, who inspired my love for knowing the truth of history. Thank you for valuing our country's history and letting me spill all the information on my characters. May you both grow old together with the sweet love displayed by George and Martha Washington.

BIBLIOGRAPHY:

"Key Facts about Martha Washington." *George Washington's Mount Vernon*, 2022, https://www.mountvernon.org/george-washington/martha-washington/keys-fact-about-martha-washington/.

Caroli, Betty. "Martha Washington." *Encyclopædia Britannica*, Encyclopædia Britannica, Inc., 29 May 2022, https://www.britannica.com/biography/Martha-Washington.

Abrams, Jeanne E., First Ladies of the Republic: Martha Washington, Abigail Adams, Dolley Madison, and the Creation ... of an Iconic American Role. New York University Press, 2019.

History.com Editors. "Martha Washington." History.com, A&E Television Networks, 16 Dec. 2009, https://www.history.com/topics/first-ladies/martha-washington.

"List of Washington's Headquarters during the Revolutionary

War." Wikipedia, Wikimedia Foundation, 24 June 2022. https://en.wikipedia.org/wiki/List_of_WashingtonHeadquarters.

Fraser, Flora. The Washingtons: George and Martha, "Join'd by Friendship, Crown'd by Love." Alfred A. Knopf, 2015.

KAYLEE PEARSONS (Sir Henry Clinton)

Kaylee Pearsons is a fourteen-year-old who loves Jesus, books, dogs! Kaylee lives with her parents, brothers, dog, and cat in Central Washington. She loves writing and practices agility with her dog, Ellie. Currently, she is studying anatomy and wants to go into biomedical engineering as an adult. You can contact Kaylee at kayleepearsons@gmail.com.

BIBLIOGRAPY:

Revolutionary War. "Henry Clinton | Facts, Early Years, Life, Death, Military & Politics." www.revolutionary-war.net, February 14, 2020. https://www.revolutionary-war.net/henry-clinton/.

"Undergarments." americancenturies.mass.edu. Accessed July 8, 2022. http://americancenturies.mass.edu/activities/dressup/notflash/1700.

Editors, History.com. "Battle of Bunker Hill - Facts, Definition & Dates - HISTORY." www.history.com, September 30, 2019. https://www.history.com/topics/american-revolution/battle-of-bunker-hill.

American Battlefield Trust. "Bunker Hill Battle Facts and Summary | American Battlefield Trust." www.battlefields.org. Accessed July 8, 2022. https://www.battlefields.org/learn/revolutionary-war/battles/bunker-hill.

American Battlefield Trust. "Breach Inlet Battle Facts and Summary | American Battlefield Trust." www.battlefields.org. Accessed July 8, 2022. https://www.battlefields.org/learn/revolutionary-war/battles/battle-breach-inlet.

Battle of Sullivan's Island (U.S. National Park Service). "Battle of Sullivan's Island (U.S. National Park Service)." www.nps.gov. Accessed July 8, 2022. https://www.nps.gov/articles/battle-of-sullivan-s-island.htm.

Bearss, Edwin. *The Battle of Sullivan's Island and the Capture of Fort Moultrie.* "PDF." Washington, D.C.: National Park Service, June 30, 1968.

ELLIE POWERS (Thomas Paine)

Ellie Powers, 11, is always up for any new creative endeavor, especially if it involves animals and the colors pink and purple. During her days of perpetual humming and singing, she spends much of her time drawing, reading, and playing with either her older brothers or her pet mini-lops in the Pacific Northwest. At mealtime, you'll find her with either pasta or pancakes. Maybe both.

ACKNOWLEDGMENTS:

Thank you to my mom, dad, and brothers for their story ideas, edits, and proofreading.

BIBLIOGRAPHY:

Burgan, Michael. Weapons, Gear, and Uniforms of the American Revolution. Capstone Press, 2012.

"Case of the Excise Officers." The Thomas Paine National Historical Association, https://www.thomaspaine.org/.

"Independence Hall." nps.gov, https://www.nps.gov/inde/learn/historyculture/places-independencehall.htm.

Isaacs, Sally Senzell. Colonists and Independence. Kingfisher, 2011.

Johnson, Ben. "English Coffeehouses, Penny Universities." Historic-Uk.com, https://www.historic-uk.com/CultureUK/English-Coffeehouses-Penny-Universities/.

Kiger, Patrick J. "How Thomas Paine's 'Common Sense' Helped Inspire the American Revolution." History.com, 28 June 2021, https://www.history.com/news/thomas-paine-common-sense-revolution.

Marsh, Sarah Jane, and Ed Fotheringham. Thomas Paine and the Dangerous Word. Disney/Hyperion, 2018.

Nelson, Craig. Thomas Paine Enlightenment, Revolution, and the Birth of Modern Nations. Viking Penguin, 2006.

ELLA QUILL (General William Howe)

Ella Quill is a young rabbit who loves spending her time (when she's not writing fascinating stories) eating and taking naps. She was "warrenschooled," along with her twenty-seven siblings, and is a senior in rabbit school. She plans to get a decree for writing stories about animals for kids and is currently working on a series all about furry protagonists! Which, dear human readers, means heroes. She is currently frolicking around in the fields by Washington D.C., the USA's capital.

DEDICATION:

This is for my parents, whose love for me keeps me going, and for my new friends from this Epic camp! Happy writing, everybody!

BIBLIOGRAPHY:

McCullough, David. *1776.* Simon & Schuster, 2005, New York, New York.

Rhodehamel, John, editor. *The American Revolution; Writings from the War of Independence.* First Printing, The Library of America, 2001, New York, New York.

Bobrick, Benson. *Fight for Freedom; The American Revolutionary War.* 1st ed., Byron Press Visual Publications Inc., 2004, New York, New York.

Adams, Russel B. Jr., editor. *The American Story; The Revolutionaries.* First Printing, Time Life Inc., 1996, Richmond, Virginia.

Bobrick, Benson. *Angel in the Whirlwind; The Triumph of the American Revolution.* Simon & Schuster, 1997, New York, New York.

ALEX ROBERSON (Admiral Richard Howe)

Alex Roberson hails from Central Florida where she lives with her parents and older sibling, rescued labs and holland lop bunnies. She loves to craft, read, and participates in competitive baton twirling. History, specifically American Revolution era, is her favorite subject. She is an active member of her local Children of the American Revolution (C.A.R.) society, as she is a decedent of nine Patriots.

DEDICATION:

For my mom, dad, and sister. Thank you for your love and support in everything I do!

BIBLIOGRAPHY:

The American Revolution (n.d.). Retrieved from www.loc.gov/collections/george-washingtonpapers/articles-and-essays/timeline/the-american-revolution/

Richard Howe (n.d.). Retrieved from www.americanrevolution.com/biographies/British/brothers_howe/Richard_howe

Richard and William Howe Collection (n.d.). Retrieved from https://quod.lib.umich.edu/c/clementsead/umich-wcl-M-510how?view=text

A Miniature History of the American Revolution (2011, October 12). Retrieved from https://miniawi.blogspot.com/2011/10/october-12-1776.html

McCullough, David (2005). *1776.* New York, NY: Simon and Schuster Paperbacks.

MOLLY ROSER (John Adams)

Molly Roser is in 6th grade at Harrison Intermediate school. She lives in Texas and enjoys traveling, softball, and art. She is an avid reader and wants to be an author one day.

ACKNOWLEDGEMENTS:

I would like to thank my friends and family. I would also like to thank Jenny L. Cote and Libby McNamee for encouraging me to write.

BIBLIOGRAPHY:

McCullough, David. 2002. John Adams. London, England: Simon & Schuster

"John Adams & the Revolutionary War." *Bostonteapartyship.com*

Jefferson, Thomas. (1776). *The Declaration of Independence*

Lee, Richard Henry. (1776). *Lee Resolution*

JESSAH SEMONS (Lieutenant Colonel Banastre Tarleton)

Jessah Semons is 11 years old and in the 6th grade. She is home-schooled alongside her three little sisters and baby brother in the small town of Newton, Texas. Jessah's favorite subjects are history, science, and writing. Her hobbies include arts and crafts and reading.

Jessah dreams of one day becoming a zoologist and writing fun educational books about the animals she works with.

BIBLIOGRAPHY:

"Banastre Tarleton." *Wikipedia*, Wikimedia Foundation, 22 June 2022, https://en.m.wikipedia.org/wiki/Banastre_Tarleton.

Bass, Robert D. *The Green Dragoon: The Lives of Banastre Tarleton and Mary Robinson.* Sandlapper Press, 1973.

Griffith, William. "Lee's Plight at the Widow White's: The Capture of Major General Charles Lee, December 12–13, 1776 – 244 Years Later." *Emerging Revolutionary War Era*, 11 Dec. 2020, https://emergingrevolutionarywar.org/2020/12/12/lees-plight-at-the-widow-whites-the-capture-of-major-general-charles-lee-december-12-13-1776-244-years-later/.

McBurney, Christian M. *Kidnapping the Enemy: The Special Operations to Capture Generals Charles Lee & Richard Prescott.* Westholme Publishing, 2014.

"On This Day in History - December 13, 1776." *Revolutionary War and Beyond*, https://www.revolutionary-war-and-beyond.com/general-charles-lee-is-captured-at-basking-ridge.html.

JOY ELIZABETH TARDY (Marquis de Lafayette)

Bonjour! My name is *Joy Elizabeth Tardy*, a thirteen-year-old and in eighth grade. My Texas family adopted me from Jiangxi Province, China. Of the three amazing sisters, and one stellar brother, I am the baby of the family. My interests are reading, sewing, knitting, crochet, classical choir, piano, and spending time with "Violet," our beautiful Malshi puppy. Serving the preschoolers and singing on the praise team is a regular part of Sunday worship. Some of my goals after marriage are to foster/adopt and to be a mother of sixteen children. The most amusing times with Ms. Jenny were when I learned not to: sit on historical artifacts/furniture, try them on, and go inside Patrick Henry's home with docent Bob *not* knowing the security code. Before this camp, I only enjoyed writing fantasy and fairy tales. Now that the camp intensive is finished for the summer, writing about real heroes in history is a new passion for me. Both Ms. Jenny and Ms. Libby are patient and humorous teachers, authors, and editors.

DEDICATION:

I dedicate my writing to my late grandmother "Nelly." She always encouraged me and loved reading the stories I would write. I know we will meet again in heaven soon.

BIBLIOGRAPHY:

Castrovilla, Selene, Revolutionary Friends: General George Washington and the Marquis de Lafayette, 2013.

Gaines, James R., For Liberty and Glory: Washington, Lafayette, and Their Revolutions. W. W. Norton, 2009.

Grote, JoAnn M., Lafayette: French Freedom Fighter. Chelsea House Publishers, 2001.

Unger, Harlow G., Lafayette. John Wiley & Sons, Inc, 2002.

Washington's Generals: Marquis De Lafayette. Directed by Raymond Bridgers, The History Channel, 2009. *You Tube,* uploaded by the History Channel, November 19, 2012, https://youtu.be/RN1jrr_CMzM

EMMA URRUTIA (General Putnam)

Emma Urrutia is a fourteen-year-old 9th grade Christian homeschooler who lives in Mechanicsburg, Pennsylvania. She spends her time writing, tracing, and reading, and enjoys time with her family and friends. She dreams of becoming a best-selling author and improving her writing skills. She loved Epic Patriot Camp 2022 and enjoys reading books such as *The Epic Order of The Seven* and *The Amazing Tale of Max and Liz.*

DEDICATION:

To Libby McNamee and Jenny L. Cote for making this book, my parents for allowing me to join this SPECTACULAR camp, and the campers for being awesome people and friends.

BIBLIOGRAPHY:

"Israel Putnam | United States general - Encyclopedia Britannica," 2022

https://www.britannica.com/biography/Israel-Putnam

"Battle Of Bunker Hill," 2022

https://www.britannica.com/event/Battle-of-Bunker-Hill#ref344827

"Israel Putnam" - CT.gov, 2022

https://portal.ct.gov/ML/MAPO/History/People/Israel-Putnam

"Israel Putnam - George Washington's Mount Vernon, 2022

https://www.mountvernon.org/library/digitalhistory/digital-encyclopedia/article/israel-putnam/

"Bunker Hill," 2022

https://www.battlefields.org/learn/revolutionary-war/battles/bunker-hill

"Battle of Long Island - Wikipedia, 2022

https://en.wikipedia.org/wiki/Battle_of_Long_Island

"Battle of Long Island," 2022

https://www.britannica.com/event/Battle-of-Long-Island

CHRISTOPHER J. WATT (Benjamin Franklin)

Christopher J. Watt was born in South Africa. Fourteen years old, he has developed a love for writing, reading and filmmaking. Christopher is passionate about medieval and Viking history and loves writing fantasy fiction. He owns a Black Labrador Retriever named Shadow, whom he absolutely adores. The two of them love spending time playing together and he loves training her new commands. Shadow already knows over fifteen unique and special tricks which he has taught her himself. He hopes to become a fully published author and hopes to write many more books. Christopher lives in Canberra, the capital city of Australia, with his family and Shadow.

DEDICATION:

To Shadow - You are the most incredible dog, and I couldn't have asked for a better friend! This book would have never been the same if it weren't for the inspiration you've given me! I love you with all my heart.

ACKNOWLEDGEMENTS:

Thank you to my parents, John and Christl Watt, for allowing me to take part in this incredible experience. This wouldn't be possible without you - thank you so much! Thank you to my wonderful teachers, Mrs. Sue Combridge, Mrs. Jo Hazell, and Miss Rizia Asuncion for encouraging, inspiring, and believing in me. Thank you to Jenny L. Cote and Libby McNamee for creating this amazing opportunity to teach us the ways of writing a book! I am so grateful to you both for everything that you have done! A special thank you to some of the Epic Campers, Edan, Bella, Gemma, and Charis - you four have helped me so much in my writing! I am so grateful for our friendships - among others - and I really appreciate your willingness to listen to my ideas! And thank you to everyone else who helped in the creation of this book – you are so appreciated, and I am ever-grateful for what you've done not just to help me, but to help all of us.

BIBLIOGRAPHY:

Benjamin Franklin. 2015. "Benjamin Franklin - the Founding Father." https://www.benjaminfranklin.net

Isaacson, Walter. 2003. "Benjamin Franklin Joins the Revolution." Smithsonian Magazine. https://smithsonianmagazine.com/history/benjamin-franklin-joins-the-revolution-87199988/

Isaacson, Walter, and the Library of Congress. 2003. *Benjamin Franklin - An American Life.* Second ed. Washington DC: Washington State: Simon and Schuster. 9780743258074.

Franklin, Benjamin. 1793. *The Autobiography of Benjamin Franklin.* Alex Cabal. London, United Kingdom: J Parson's: https://standardebooks.org/ebooks/benjamin-franklin/the-autobiography-of-benjamin-franklin/text/single-page#chapter-3.

"The Declaration of Independence & the Constitution of the United States." N.d. USCIS. https://www.uscis.gov/sites/default/files/document/guides/M-654.pdf

"The Declaration of Independence | National Archives." n.d. National Archives. https://www.archives.gov/founding-docs/declaration

AUTHOR'S NOTE:

Shadow is a British spydog who first appears in Chapter One. In the story, she is referred to as a *St John's Water Dog.* Shadow is, in fact, a Black Labrador Retriever, but Labs were only officially bred and named in the 1800s. In the 1700s, they were simply referred to as St John's Water dogs. These dogs were slightly more robust and thick-set than the Labs we have today and often had white patches on their chest and muzzle. Sadly, the St John's Water Dog breed has now been officially declared extinct.

Benjamin Franklin did indeed have a pet dog, but it was a Newfoundland that belonged to his son, William Franklin. When he owned the dog is unclear.

Benjamin Franklin attended the Second Continental Congress in the Pennsylvania State House in 1775, which is now known as the Philadelphia Independence Hall.

Words such as *"colour"* and *"realising"* are not spelled incorrectly. They are the same words, but are written using British English.

The word *"said"* is overrated. I do not believe in the use of such a word in my chapters. You will most certainly never find that word in my story. I love the challenge of finding an alternative. (Thanks, Mrs Combridge!)

BELLA WAUGH (King George III)

Bella Waugh is 15 years old, and lives south of Nashville, TN. She has been homeschooled her whole life and is going into 10th grade this fall. Bella loves writing and learning about the birth of our nation! She lives on two acres with her mom and dad, two younger siblings, and a menagerie of animals, including goats, chickens, ducks, and a cat. Bella hopes to write children's short-story fiction, and also start a company that recommends wholesome books. She is so thankful for the opportunity to now become a published author!

DEDICATION:

I would like to dedicate this book to my family who has been so supportive of me and my writing journey my whole life! I would especially like to thank my parents, specifically my mom who has not only taught me homeschool for over a decade, but has read, edited, and critiqued countless drafts of my work. Thank you so much Mom, Dad, Lily, and Jaxon! You mean so much to me and I love you all so much!

BIBLIOGRAPHY:

"The American Revolution, 1763 - 1783: U.S. History Primary Source Timeline: Classroom Materials at the Library of Congress: Library of Congress." The Library of Congress. Accessed July 9, 2022. https://www.loc.gov/classroom-materials/united-states-history-primary-source-timeline/american-revolution-1763-1783/.

Americanwarsus. "List of Revolutionary War Battles, Raids & Skirmishes for 1776." American Revolutionary War. American Revolutionary War, January 11, 2018. https://revolutionarywar.us/year-1776/.

Fritz, Jean. Can't You Make Them Behave, King George? Puffin Books, 1996.

"George III of the United Kingdom." George III of the United Kingdom - Academic Kids. Accessed July 9,2022. https://academickids.com/encyclopedia/index.php.

"George III." Wikipedia. Wikimedia Foundation, July 6,2022..

History.com Editors. "George III." History.com. A&E Television Networks, November 9, 2009. https://www.history.com/topics/british-history/george-iii.

McCullough, David G. 1776. London: The Folio Society, 2005.

MADELEINE ROSE WENZEL (Beaumarchais)

Madeleine Rose Wenzel is 16-years-old and entering 12th grade. Born in Norfolk, VA, Madeleine moved to Irmo, SC, at 18 months old, where she has lived with her parents, younger sister and brother, and numerous pets for the past 15 years. Madeleine loves animals, reading, and history, especially anything regarding the American Revolution. She would love to be a historian when she grows up, and possibly participate in reenactments of Revolutionary War battles.

DEDICATION:

I would like to dedicate this to my three guinea pigs, Elijah (Hunter), Aaron (Burr), and Thaddeus (Kosciuszko), and my two leopard geckos, Sybil (Ludington) and Nathanael (Greene).

ACKNOWLEDGEMENTS:

She would especially like to express her undying gratitude to her loving mother, who has encouraged and nurtured her love of history by dragging her to museums and many historical sites on every family vacation (a.k.a. homeschool fieldtrips), much to her younger sibling's dismay. You are the BEST, Mama! I love you!

(The above was written by my mother, who has raided my email like Banastre Tarleton did to Group 1 in Epic Patriot Camp.)

BIBLIOGRAPHY:

Atkinson, Rick. *The British Are Coming: The War for America, Lexington to Princeton, 1775-1777.* New York: Henry Holt and Company, 2019.

CIA Historical Document. "Central Intelligence Agency." *Beaumarchais and the American Revolution - Central Intelligence Agency*, Last Modified Aug. 5, 2011, https://web.archive.org/web/20201111194249/https://www.cia.gov.

Encyclopedia Britannica, 1911 ed. "Pierre-Augustin Caron De Beaumarchais | Portraits in Revolution, accessed June 15, 2022. https://www.americanrevolution.com/biographies/french/pierre_beaumarchais.

Lever, Maurice, and Susan Emanuel. Beaumarchais: A Biography. New York: Farrar, Straus and Giroux, 2009.

New World Encyclopedia. "Pierre Beaumarchais." Accessed June 15, 2022. https://www.newworldencyclopedia.org/entry/Pierre_Beaumarchais.

Shachtman, Tom. How the French Saved America: Soldiers, Sailors, Diplomats, Louis XVI, and the Success of a Revolution. New York: St. Martin's Press, 2017.

Wikipedia Foundation. "Pierre Beaumarchais." Last Modified June 27, 2022. https://en.wikipedia.org/wiki/Pierre_Beaumarchais.

Matthew Miller
Matthew Miller

by McNamee HUZZAH!
Jenny L. Cole
Grace: Martha Washington
Kit-sy Guy Carleton
gail (General Charles Lee)
Mia Mora-Silas Deane
Mark
Jessie Brown Reve
ayla (Joseph Plumb Martin)
Joy Elizabeth Tardy
Peti Abigail Adams
Olivia George Washington